CHILDREN OF THE WOLF

ALFRED DUGGAN

Children of the Wolf

Coward-McCann, Inc.
New York

F
D

12900

CONTENTS

★

CHILDREN OF THE WOLF

Chapter I

THE BEGINNING

✶

It was just the place for a stronghold, a steep flat-topped hill on the eastern side of the river which marked the boundary of the Etruscans. Nearby rose other hills, some with slopes too gentle to be defensible, others too acutely pointed for comfort. To the south-east stretched level beech-forest, the tree-tops seen from above making a level floor to the horizon, rarely interrupted by the clearings of other settlements. There was good ploughland to be won from the beech-forest, though the task of clearing it was laborious; if the worst came to the worst, and the foreigners over the river proved to be too warlike and well-armed to be robbed, the men in the stronghold might grow their own barley.

All the same, it seemed a pity that the twins had decided to mark out the boundaries of the new camp with all the elaborate ritual that went to the founding of a city. If the place happened to be unlucky the knowledge that it had been consecrated would lead to endless delay before the newcomers cut their losses and abandoned it. As he stood among the throng on the hilltop, waiting for the ploughing to begin, Marcus ventured to grumble about this to the man standing beside him.

He was answered, as he might have expected, by a reference to the wonderful omens which had encouraged the twins. Even to suggest that the new settlement might be unsuccessful seemed to his neighbour to be blasphemy. "You ought not to utter such words out loud," he exclaimed angrily. "A god might hear you, and make it come true. But if silly young men don't deliberately bring down bad luck on the place it *can't* fail. Aren't we led by the sons of Mars, sucklings of the war-god's she-wolf? How long is it since you saw a vulture? They are getting rare in these parts. This morning the twins saw eighteen vultures between them. What do you think of that? And have you heard what they found on that knoll over there, where the working-party are digging the ditch for our outlying fort?"

"No, I haven't heard. They began digging only two hours ago, and I kept away for fear they might put a mattock in my hand. Did they find a crock of gold, or one of those great stones in which a god dwells?"

"Nothing so obvious, but an omen even more powerful. They were digging in undisturbed soil, when suddenly they turned up a human head. Freshly severed it was, and still bleeding. Do you know what that means? It means that our stronghold will one day rule all the land roundabout. The twins have already decreed that the hill shall be called the Capitol, so that the portent will never be forgotten."

"Whose head was it, and where's the rest of him?" asked Marcus blandly. He knew that such a question must annoy any devout servant of the gods; but as a poor and insignificant spearman he disliked the suspicion that the leaders might be surreptitiously practising human sacrifice. One day they might choose him as the victim.

"It was nobody's head, you fool. It was put there by the gods, to show us how lucky we shall be. Aren't you one of us? Aren't you glad to be a sharer in all this good luck?"

"I come from nowhere, and that's where I am going. When my father threw me out I decided to follow the lord Remus. I have a shield and a spear, and when we fight I shall kill a rich foe and take his sword. I am worth my place in the ranks and my share of the booty. But, since I follow Remus, this isn't really my stronghold."

"It is. Remus has accepted the omens, and his followers will live where Romulus has decreed. Besides, you mustn't call it a stronghold. It is a city. Look, they are just going to make it a city. Here comes the leader, with the plough. Silence, every-body, so that the gods can hear his prayer."

Marcus was glad to end the conversation. He was in a bad temper, and his neighbour was just the kind of prosperous, pious giver of good advice whom he disliked; such a well-fed, god-fearing farmer had no business to join a band of desperate emi-grants, warriors prepared to live by the sword until they died young or died rich. If the argument continued there would be a quarrel, and if they came to blows Marcus knew very well which of the pair would be expelled from the band. A leader always sides with the rich against the poor, and he had no kin to back him on this frontier hilltop.

Marcus was nearly seventeen, slender and dark and still gawky with youth. He wore nothing but a ragged tunic and patched sandals; but he had cut his hair short and combed it, and his body was clean. On his forearm, just below the elbow, could be seen the calloused mark made by his shield-grip; that was the emblem of manhood, and he looked at it often.

Now he stood in sulky silence, listening to the prayers. All this ritual meant nothing to him; he had not left home to hear it. Not that he had exactly *left* home, if that meant that he had gone of his own free will. His elderly father had been rash to take a young wife, and Marcus had never reached the point of doing anything unlawful with his stepmother; but that would have come if they had continued to share the same hut. His father had been within his rights in telling him to go. In fact his father had been merciful. He might have waited until he had caught the pair in adultery, and then tortured them to death with the approval of his neighbours; instead of sending his rowdy younger son off to seek his fortune before anything serious had occurred. All the same, his father's second marriage had brought Marcus bad luck.

It was by chance that he had joined the band led by Remus, another example of the bad luck which seemed to be his fate. After all, the leaders were twins, weren't they? Both children of Mars, both fosterlings of the she-wolf, both exceptionally en-dowed with the favour of the gods. How could anyone have foreseen, a month ago, that Romulus would consistently outshine and outwit his brother, who in Alba had the name of being the more daring bandit of the pair?

Marcus meditated in silence on that tricky business of the omens. There could be no doubt that Romulus had lied and cheated, and yet he had been signally favoured by the gods. It had happened only this morning, at sunrise, and all sorts of rumours were still flying through the band. But Marcus had been standing close to Remus, on duty as one of his bodyguard; and he had heard everything with his own ears. Each brother had gone to his chosen hilltop, marked out the sacred templum with his curved rod, and settled down to watch for omens. After quite a short wait Remus had seen six vultures flying together on the good side. That was a remarkable prodigy; for the vulture, which never hunts and yet lives on the fat of the land, is notoriously the luckiest bird in Italy. It was a rare bird, also, and no one on the hill had ever before seen as many as six at the same time. Naturally Remus had sent a message to his twin, bidding him come and hear about this remarkable demonstration of divine favour.

Romulus had replied by telling his brother to come to the other hill, for he had seen an even greater prodigy. That was where they had made their mistake, Marcus realized as he thought the matter over. Remus should have stayed where he was, and asked for details of his brother's omen. Instead he had weakly obeyed the summons, merely because it was rumoured that Romulus was the elder by a few minutes; as though between twins there could be any question of the authority of an elder brother over a younger! And when he had got to the foot of this silly, slab-sided hill where they were standing now, he had been impudently told that as yet Romulus had seen no portent, but that he was sure he was going to see a good one!

Romulus was exposed as a liar and a cheat, who would not recognize a clear message from the gods if it supported his wretched, put-upon brother. That ought to have been the end of his pretensions as leader. But there is no arguing with favourites of the gods, and the gods often favour the most brazen scoundrels. While the common spearmen disputed hotly, and the well-born nobles attempted to keep the peace, Romulus climbed back to his consecrated templum on top of the hill. He had barely reached it when a clamour of excitement overcame the quarrelling below. Flying slowly and purposefully from the right, the side of good omen, came a whole flock of vultures, no less than twelve of them. There was no deception; Remus himself saw the birds, and so did his followers. Those hills must be a great place for vultures. But birds of good omen were what they had come out to see, in accordance with the rules laid down by the ancestors when a site was to be chosen for a new stronghold. The matter was decided beyond dispute; the hill chosen by Romulus would be their future dwelling-place.

Now Romulus alone was marking out the boundary of an enduring city, and that was more than they had expected when they agreed to fortify a camp just on the Latin side of the river. The Etruscans on the other bank might prove too strong for them, for it was already known that they were rich enough to be worth raiding. A camp that was too dangerous might be deserted; but it would be shameful to flee from a newly founded city. Both bands were committed, though the followers of Remus had not even been consulted.

Besides, Romulus was performing the ceremony alone, as though he were not merely the senior partner in a dual leadership. Now he had finished his prayers, and was guiding the holy bronze Plough round the outline of what would one day be the defences. A crowd of helpers kept the plough-team steady, for a bull and a cow never work well together; even when they are special beasts, snow-white, dedicated, already garlanded for sacrifice. But alone Romulus wrestled with the blunt bronze ploughshare, that relic of the ways of the ancestors, used nowadays only in religious ritual. Marcus thought, with an inward sneer at all superstition, that if the chief wanted to be really old-fashioned and lucky he ought to mark out his furrow with one of those fire-hardened digging-sticks which were still used by the savages of the south.

Until this morning Marcus would have boasted that he did

not fear, or even believe in, the gods. But those vultures took some explaining away, and now he had an open mind. Stories of the miraculous birth and childhood of the twins had weighed very little with him when he chose Remus for his leader. Remus was taking out a band of emigrants; he, Marcus, had urgent reasons for getting well away from his father and his stepmother. There was no more in it than that.

From time to time some priestess who had dedicated her virginity to the gods scandalized the faithful by producing a child; though perhaps lusty male twins was overdoing it. If Rhea Silvia could persuade the elders that her virtue was unblemished and that it was all the fault of some incontinent god, well, good luck to her; though in future a prudent man would not believe her unsupported assertions. It was just possible that the twins were the children of Mars, but the excuse had really come out most conveniently when their mother was in a tight place.

As for the other story, about them being suckled by a she-wolf, Marcus believed some of it. He had heard it at first hand from Faustulus, the shepherd who had found them in their abandoned cradle. Faustulus had joined in this new venture, and he was now watching the ceremony; a sensible, level-headed man, who would never invent such a surprising tale. But the original story, as told by Faustulus, was not very hard to believe. There was nothing in it about the children being reared in a wolf's den, or living as members of a family of wolves. Faustulus himself had seen the cradle placed at the margin of the flooded river by the minions of the wicked King Amulius. He had crept away, meaning to come back and rescue the children as soon as the coast was clear. When he returned he was horrified to see a wolf standing over the babies; but they took no harm, for it was a she-wolf heavy with milk, who would permit any soft baby-mouth to suck at her swollen teats. The whole affair, though exceedingly ominous, had lasted only a few minutes. Marcus, who had seen a bereaved farm bitch suckling a young rat, did not doubt that a mother wolf might be guided by the same instinct, for a short time.

All the same, whether the twins were the sons of Mars or not, whether they were the foster-children of the wolf or not, they were equal partners in this venture. Remus should have been helping his brother to guide the bronze plough instead of standing idle with the other spectators on the hilltop.

One angle of the sacred enclosure had been marked by the furrow when Romulus lifted the ploughshare to indicate the site of a gate. At last Remus took action. Carefully avoiding the newly turned furrow he strolled down the steep hillside and halted on the slope. As soon as they saw that their chief did not wish to be walled in by his brother's foundation his band streamed after him; they made up nearly half the company, and soon more than a thousand young warriors clustered on the slope, looking up at the new city as though they were already besieging it. That was not so dangerous as it seemed, for of course they had all left their weapons with the baggage at the bottom of the hill; no one would come armed to the foundation of a city.

Presently Romulus completed the circuit and veiled his head in his cloak as he prayed to the gods, while attendants pole-axed the bull and the cow to honour the guardians of the new city. When all was finished Remus strolled back up the hill and halted just outside the new furrow, gazing at it quizzically with his hands on his hips. Marcus was only two paces behind him, for it amused him to hear the twins quarrel; and Remus would not have breasted the slope unless he intended to utter one of his unkind and unanswerable sarcasms.

Across the scratch in the ground the young leaders confronted one another; each twenty-seven years old, each tall, ruddy and strong, each a true child of Mars, a proven warrior at the head of a band of eager warriors, each as utterly sure of himself as a man can be only when he has survived numberless perils and knows that he can rely on supernatural assistance. Remus looked intelligent and witty as well as strong; Romulus was so busy looking devout that there was no room for intelligence on his blank, regular countenance.

"So there's your city," Remus began. "Isn't it time for

another of your punctual omens? Perhaps the gods are late again. Last time, you remember, you had to lie about your vultures before they remembered to put in an appearance."

"This morning I told you that I had been favoured by portents stronger than yours," Romulus answered. "Perhaps it wasn't true when I said it; but the gods made it true before you could gainsay me. My omens appear when I want them, and just now I don't need another; so there will be no more. Are you looking at my wall? It has been filled with my luck, so that no enemy can cross it. If you want to come inside you must go round by the gate."

"Filled with your luck, is it, brother?" said Remus. "That's very strong luck, I know. May I remind you that I also have a little luck of my own? I too am a son of Mars, a fosterling of the she-wolf. This morning you saw more vultures than I did, but we are still joint leaders of this expedition. It might be interesting to see whether my luck will get me over your wall."

Marcus, standing close, could feel the quiver of excitement that ran through his leader; the excitement that comes to the bravest man when he is about to test the protection that the gods granted him at birth. Romulus understood that his twin was about to do something desperate; he motioned quietly to his *celeres*, the gang of devoted henchmen who kept order in his rowdy band. A celer who had been piling the loose earth of the lucky wall moved up to stand behind his leader, mattock on shoulder.

"Gently, brother," Remus continued. "We don't want your new city to lose its luck because of a quarrel on the very day of its foundation. All the same, I really must test this famous luck of yours. Here goes. Will some god turn me back? Your wall won't. An enemy could cross it as easily as I do." He took a pace forward, and leapt over the furrow.

He landed, smiling easily, beside the celer. The bully shuddered at the desecration, and his hands tightened on his mattock. "As for enemies, this is how we deal with them," he shouted.

There was a sharp crack as the mattock came down; Remus collapsed in a heap, his skull splintered.

THE BEGINNING

Marcus stared, his mouth open and his hands hanging idle by his sides. Things were happening too fast for his mind to follow; and anyway Remus, the leader he had chosen only a few days ago, did not mean much to him. But in the crowd were warriors who had followed their dead lord for eight years, ever since he revealed himself to his grandfather. "Remus is dead. Get the man who killed him," shouted someone in the front rank. The whole group of unarmed but vigorous young men surged forward against the holy furrow.

For a moment Marcus thought of running down the hill to fetch his shield and spear. That seemed the most sensible thing to do, but it might look to his comrades as though he were running away from his first fight. He pushed forward in the mob, feeling at his girdle for his little eating-knife.

Within the furrow the celer who had done the murder could no longer be seen. (He fled to the Etruscans, and never again appeared on the Latin side of the river.) But the other followers of Romulus gathered to defend their wall. Some of them had spades or picks, and they outnumbered the opposing band; as the attackers hesitated there was a momentary stillness.

A peacemaker seized his opportunity. Faustulus, foster-father of the twins, the only middle-aged man on the hilltop, could be easily recognized by his grizzled hair. "Boys," he called, "what's done is done. You can't bring Remus to life again. We don't want any more murders."

"Murder it was, and we'll avenge it," shouted someone from the back of the crowd. A stone as big as a fist flew through the air. It was sped by a young shepherd who had just remembered the sling looped round his brow to keep the hair out of his eyes, the lethal sling which was more deadly to marauding wolves even than savage sheepdogs.

The stone whizzed straight at Romulus, who could not dodge it because of the dense throng at his back. It seemed that the expedition was about to lose both its leaders. But Faustulus could not bear to see both his foster-sons dead at his feet. As he jumped forward to guard his leader the stone caught him in the throat. Again there was a sharp crack, as when the skull of

17

Remus had been crushed; with his neck broken Faustulus was dead before he hit the ground.

The calamity brought peace, as nothing else could have brought it. Faustulus was by a full generation the oldest man in the expedition, and among the veteran followers of the twins he had been reverenced as a father. Someone raised the wail of mourning, and in a moment it was taken up by the whole company. At the first lull, as the mourners paused for breath, Romulus jumped on a hillock to address them.

"Spearmen," he shouted, and the formality of the address made them all feel calm and responsible. "Spearmen, we came here to found a city, on a site that has been filled to overflowing with the luck of Jupiter, with the luck of my father Mars—your father Mars. The city has been founded, filled with luck, blessed by omens more favourable than the greatest prophet could foretell. It is ready for us to dwell in. Let us dwell in it, peaceably, as good comrades. It is true that I have incurred the pollution of fratricide. I take the whole of that to myself, and not a particle of it will infect you. The luck bequeathed to me by my divine father is strong enough to overcome it. The man who struck the deadly blow has fled, and he will never return within these holy walls. When we have built our huts and marked out an open square for a templum I shall fetch from Lanuvium certain holy things, things which once belonged to grandfather Aeneas who brought the sacred line of Venus to Italy. You will see them, before I put them in a safe place where human eye shall never look on them again, for so long as this sacred city shall stand. I say again: the luck of this city, my city of Rome, can overcome all misfortunes. But we who live in it must live united. Let any leave who wish to do so. They go with my good will. But to those who stay I shall be the chieftain, the King, King of Rome. Will you obey me?"

Marcus looked at the chief, ten years older than himself and so in his eyes a mature man in the prime of wisdom. It was less than a month since he had agreed to follow Remus. That had been nothing but a pointless episode; there was no need that he should vow vengeance for a leader he had hardly known. The greatest asset of Remus had been his luck, and now it had been proved that the luck of his twin brother was the stronger. He decided to serve faithfully the new chief whom Fate had put over him.

As far as could be seen, not one of the followers of Remus abandoned the expedition; though a few may have slipped off unobserved. Marcus followed in the crowd which went carefully through the unploughed gateway and lined up with the adherents of Romulus. When the new King understood that the threatened battle had been averted he once more addressed his followers, now all standing within the city.

"Our enterprise has begun with a fatality. This evening we shall burn my unfortunate brother on a splendid pyre, with all the rites needed for the welfare of his spirit. The pollution of his death I take entirely on myself. Luckily, as you can see, no blood has been shed; and unless blood lies on the ground the Old Women cannot track down the guilty. Nevertheless, a few minutes ago our hearts were filled with hatred. Before the city springs to life that hatred must be purged from us. Let us all gather brushwood for a great fire. When the wood has been heaped up I shall kindle it with my sacred flint, repeating as I do so a prayer taught to me by my father Mars. While the fire blazes we shall all jump through it. Thus shall we leave in the flames all feelings of enmity which are unfitting for the citizens of one city."

So it was done; and the common effort of gathering brushwood and carrying it to the hilltop brought the first stirrings of a sense of community to the assembled warriors.

When the ritual had been accomplished Romulus set his men to building shelters for themselves, and to bringing up the baggage from the valley. That night they slept in the new city. But when they awoke on the morning of the 22nd of March, 753 years before the Incarnation, there was still much to be done.

During that first spring, while they planted the barley which must keep them through their first winter, King Romulus found time for a private talk with every one of his new subjects. Marcus was one of the last to be interviewed, for a clanless exile without even a sword was among the least important members of the new community. But Romulus spared no pains, and took as much trouble to inquire into the private life of this insignificant spearman as if he had been the head of a powerful family.

In the raw unpainted wooden hut that was the King's house they talked together, squatting on billets of wood beside a pan of charcoal. First Marcus must explain how he came to be so utterly alone in the world. "Chief—I mean King," he said nervously, blurting out the whole truth lest he be accused of concealing the worst, "my father drove me from my village, and my name has been removed from the muster of my clan. But I was not accused of a crime for which the clan-elders might punish me. It was rather that my father feared I would commit a crime if I remained in his hut."

"How was that? I don't understand."

"My lord, I had a young stepmother."

"I see. But as yet you had done nothing wrong? Then why did your father send you into exile without even the protection of your clan? Surely it would have been enough to arrange for you to leave?"

"Yes, my lord. That was how it started. But later we had words, and I answered until my father swore that I might not stay a moment longer. It had been planned that I should leave with the Sacred Spring, which was due to set off in two years. Do you have the custom in Alba? All the children born in one year must emigrate when they grow up, and they take with them the increase of the flocks born in the same year. I wasn't born in the sacred year, but they would have taken me. Then we had this quarrel, and my father chased me with a stick. So I had to leave. I am too old to be beaten, but I could not strike my father. In my village we don't do that."

"I should hope not," said the King. "No one does. But did your father really want you to go? What about carrying on his line?"

"I have an elder brother. Perhaps I should say I had one;

20

now I have no kin. I possess nothing but a spear and a shield, and I have those only because they were a gift from my mother's brother, and my father could not touch them. But at the next battle I shall get a sword."

"Yes, you need a sword, and a helmet, if you are to take your rightful place in the levy. It's right that you should win them for yourself. Now what else do you need, that I, or my city of Rome, can offer you?"

"Not much, my lord. But then I have nothing. A patch of ground to grow my barley, a corner where I can store my plunder, a roof where I can sleep safe from my enemies, comrades to avenge me when I am slain."

"I can give you those, though I cannot give you more. You need kinsmen to take an interest in you, to tend you if you are sick and to buy your freedom if you are enslaved. You can't expect three thousand citizens to look after you as though you were cousin to all of them. So tomorrow you must join a kindred. I am dividing the whole body of citizens into thirty kindreds; choose one of them, and stick to it. That will give you a clan-name as well; I won't ask your old one, for it has been taken from you and it might be unlucky to pronounce it. Is there anything else?"

"No, my lord. Or rather, only one thing. You have mentioned luck, and I know that you are one of the luckiest men in the world. Is there anything you can do to help me to regain the favour of the gods? I must now be suffering under their displeasure, since I am so lonely and friendless and poor."

Marcus was surprised to hear his own voice uttering these words. He used to think of himself as an enlightened scoffer, and suspect that all this business about the favour of the gods was just another invention of the old to keep the young in order. Now, without friends or advocates in the other world, he felt lonely and isolated.

"You will share in the luck of my city," Romulus answered. "That is all I can do for you, but in the end you will find it sufficient. If you fear the enmity of your father you won't want to share my personal luck. I have offended pretty heavily against the gods of the kindred; though what I did was righteous, and I shall give my answer when I am accused."

"Very well, my lord. I shall have kindred to avenge me, and a wall to shelter me. That is a great deal. With the gods I must make my own terms."

"Even there the city can help you. There may be death on my hands, but my ancestors were endowed with holy things of great power. Soon I shall bring them here to Rome; and there are rituals that we must perform, all together. The men of Rome will know how to serve the gods and to please them. Wait until the barley is sown, and you shall see."

On the next day Marcus chose his kindred, from among the thirty groups into which Romulus planned to divide the whole body of citizens. It seemed odd to call a young man of twenty-one his father; but there was no other way of joining a kindred, for in the new city there were no elderly men. Aemilius was a noble from Alba, who had been driven to emigration by the poverty of his house and the number of his elder brothers. He was an affable young nobleman, very pleased to increase the number of his followers. He told Marcus that he might use Aemilius as his second name, and reckon himself personally a full member of the Aemilian clan. But he added that only men of the genuine descent by blood might offer sacrifice on behalf of the kindred; as soon as they got hold of someone who could write (for there was not a single scribe in the new city) they must make a supplementary list of the new members of the clan, whose descendants could never succeed to the chieftaincy or rank themselves as equal with those born of the true blood. That seemed fair enough, and very much better than having no clan at all. Marcus Aemilius willingly agreed to these conditions.

When the barley had been sown and might be left to do its own growing until harvest Romulus did not lead out his army to raid the Etruscans, as had been expected. He announced that before his men did any fighting they must increase their luck by appropriate service to the gods. To begin with he brought his own ancestral Guardians from the sacred Latin city of Lanuvium. These Guardians already had a long history. It was said that grandfather Aeneas, the first recorded ancestor of King Numitor, had brought them to Italy from the fallen city of Troy; that had been long ago, at the time when all the divine cities were sacked by the Peoples of the Sea. But their origin was even more ancient. Before Troy had been founded they had been lodged in the magic island of Samothrace; before that, in the very beginning of the world, a goddess had given them as the dowry of her daughter who married a mortal man. Romulus himself was descended from this goddess; but then most men, if you went back far enough, had some supernatural being in their genealogies. It was not the divine descent that impressed Marcus as he saw the holy things carried in procession to their new home, but their amazing antiquity.

In appearance they were not impressive. There was a large earthenware jar, of the kind used to hold the ashes of a corpse; it was certainly old, but it might have been empty. Everyone who saw it was disappointed, until Romulus explained that within it was a very ancient wooden image of the Maiden, the gift of his divine grandmother to her mortal son-in-law. He had wished to display the image to the people, but soothsayers had advised against it; for the wood was filled with divine power, which must not be dissipated by spreading it through a multitude. The soothsayers had prophesied that while this image remained safe in its lodging the new city could not be captured by an enemy.

Behind the mysterious jar were borne on a second litter the remaining holy things: an old green spearhead that was the emblem, perhaps the material body, of the speargod Quirinus, and two staffs of bronze, wreathed with bronze serpents. That looked more like strong magic, and the onlookers were impressed; nobody knew what power they embodied, for they were not objects associated with the Maiden, or with the Mother, or with Skyfather. But snakes are uncanny things, and snakes of bronze must be very potent indeed. The arrival of these supernatural protectors encouraged every citizen of the new foundation.

Romulus had not yet finished. He was determined to give his city all the protection that wise men could devise. On the swampy wasteland between the hill and the river he marked out a circle with his divining staff. Every man of his following was ordered to throw within the circle a handful of earth from his original home. Many citizens had foreseen this need and had brought a pot of earth with them; but Marcus was not the only spearman who gathered a handful of mud at random, in token that before he became a citizen of Rome the wide world in general had been his only dwelling-place.

When the pile of earth was complete Romulus made magic over it, and decreed that henceforth it would be known as the Mundus; for it was the essence of the whole inhabited world. Then, while nervous spectators clutched at their amulets, he took a bronze pick and dug down through the pile deep into the swamp below. Presently he had gone far enough. He called to his assistants to hand him a sealed jar. This was quickly lowered to the very bottom of the pit, where it would be safe for all time; then a great stone was brought to seal the mouth of the hole. Romulus explained that this was now a passage between Rome and the Underworld. In general it was a good plan to keep the gate shut; but there were occasions when it should be opened, to remove spirits from the living world to their true home. The King would decree when the time had come to open it.

So now they were in touch with all the gods, above and below. The sacred things in the storehouse brought down to them the influence of the sky; the Mundus could open, or close, communication with the Realm of the Dead. The new city was well protected.

They did not neglect the affairs of this world, for Romulus believed in keeping his followers busy. During the first summer they felled beech trees, and hauled the timber to the top of the hill; soon the bank and ditch which defined the settlement had been strengthened with a stout palisade of upright stakes. One result of this was that, although Romulus insisted that his city ought to be called Rome after its founder, the citizens usually spoke of the hill on which their huts stood as the palisade, the Palatine.

Another palisade crowned the steep outlying hill known as the

Capitol, where that magical bleeding head had been dug up. A small garrison lived there permanently; for as a fortress it was much stronger than the Palatine, though it was too small to make a city.

All summer the men worked at building palisades or huts, or by turns guarded the common herd of oxen, sheep and pigs. In autumn all hands were needed for the harvest; when that had been gathered they had barley enough to last them with care until next year. By working hard every day from dawn to sunset they could just keep themselves alive.

There was discontent among the common spearmen. This city was all very well for Romulus, for his bodyguard of heavy-handed celeres, for the young men who had been appointed chiefs of the new clans. They were rulers in this new community, much greater men than they would have been at home. But the ordinary men in the ranks were living no better than landless labourers; they had gained nothing by leaving their fathers' farms, where on the evenings of festivals they used to drink wine and court the girls of their village. Men who had bravely left home and kin to win a fortune by the sword were expected to sweat all day in the fields, and in the evening sup frugally on porridge and onions. That was not how they had pictured the lives of successful bandits.

Marcus shared a little round hut with five other unattached warriors, and every evening they quarrelled about whose turn it was to boil the porridge. Cooking was women's work, but there were no women to do it. Common sense warned Marcus that soon he must beget children to care for him when he grew too old to plough or fight. In the end he laid his worries at the feet of Aemilius, his adopted patron whose duty it was to solve all the problems of his client followers.

Aemilius made light of the trouble; but then Aemilius had prudently brought a young slave-girl among his baggage.

"You see, my boy," he said airily, "we are a band of warriors. If you wanted to take a wife at once you should have joined a Sacred Spring, made up of all the boys and girls born in a particular year."

"I couldn't join a Sacred Spring, because my father made me leave home immediately," Marcus answered sulkily. "So far your band of warriors has not gone out on a single raid. Band of labourers would be nearer the mark."

"Before we start raiding we must build a fort, and make sure of food for the winter. But raiding time is coming, sooner than you think. Four days hence a party will cross the river to steal some Etruscan sheep. Quite soon you will be feasting on roast mutton, and then you will see the point of all this building. We would look silly if we stole sheep and then had nowhere to cook them in safety."

"I suppose that's true. But I didn't come here to steal sheep. I thought I was joining a band of desperate young men who would pillage the richest cities of Etruria."

"That will come; give us time. At present we are only three thousand strong, and that's not enough to sack a great city. After we have done well for a year or two others will join us. When we have a really big army we shall devastate all Etruria."

"Unless the Etruscans wipe us out first, I suppose. All right, patron, I'm not really grumbling. It's just that at present I work harder than I used to work on my father's farm, and get less for my labour. Perhaps brigands always begin slowly, with a lot of hard work at the outset. But that isn't how it sounds in the old songs about jolly robbers in the greenwood."

"It's harder work to live by the spear than to live by the plough. I suspected as much before I left home, and now I know for certain. But don't let the King hear you talking in this strain. Though you and I came here to live by robbery, King Romulus thinks that all his followers want to found noble families in his grand new city."

"And that's a good joke, sir, when you come to think of it. How are we to found these families when in this place there are ten men to one woman?"

"Perhaps that holy jug in the storehouse will prove to be a fountain of wives; one day dozens of beautiful virgins may pop out of it. Seriously, the King is so set on making this an enduring city that he must have some plan for getting wives for us. And in the meantime we are much more comfortable, behind our strong palisade, than an ordinary band of robbers hiding in a damp cave."

When Marcus left his patron he felt a little comforted. It was something to know that his misgivings were shared by a distinguished young nobleman who had the ear of the King. He would be patient, and work hard until better times came. At least he could sleep soundly, guarded by the palisade.

The first raid undertaken by the new community was only a modified success. They captured a flock of sheep, but in their retreat they were overtaken by the Etruscans, who killed several Romans. King Romulus announced that they must wait until their army had grown stronger before they again provoked their neighbours.

Chapter 2

SABINE WOMEN

★

There were a few women in Rome. Some of the young citizens had been married before they came to the new city, and these brought their wives; but men so young must be newly married, and it would be many years before their daughters were old enough to marry fellow-citizens. One citizen, who happened to be a little older than the general run, had been a husband for some years; but Tarpeius held himself aloof from the common herd, and guarded his ten-year-old daughter as though men were savage beasts. Because no one else wanted the post he had been appointed commander of the garrison on the isolated Capitol; there he lived with his wife and only child in unnatural seclusion.

A few whores had arrived, as was only to be expected in a settlement of lusty young warriors. They were not allowed to come inside the palisade, but plied their trade in little shacks set in the marshy ground by the river. They had come to a poor market, where they must take their pay in pork and barley instead of silver and bronze. They were a slatternly crew, plain and elderly. No citizen would admit that he frequented their shacks, and it was good manners to look right through any man encountered there and pretend that he was invisible.

But in the second year of the city men began coming to Rome who did not care in what low haunts they were seen, shameless men without dignity. King Romulus was obsessed with the dangerous weakness of his army, though to his followers it seemed that three thousand Latin spearmen should be able to defend their home against any number of Etruscans. He would do anything to increase his forces. After some opposition he managed to persuade the spearmen to open their ranks to any newcomer who could fight. In the Asylum, a collection of flimsy huts below the Palatine and outside the true city, any able-bodied man was welcome and no questions might be asked about his past. Some of the new recruits bore brands which marked them as runaway slaves; others were fugitives from justice, criminals guilty of incest or sacrilege, misdeeds which brought down on them the wrath of the 'gods. But if they looked like stout fighting-men King Romulus admitted them; his celeres bullied the original settlers, decent Latins who had come only to better themselves, into making room for these scoundrels.

When the time came round to celebrate the fourth birthday of its foundation the new city was ready to burst apart from the stress of long disappointment, uncongenial companionship, poverty, hard work, and enforced celibacy. In particular the lesser spearmen came to the assembly which opened the holiday celebrations determined to make a protest. They would insist that the army march out to undertake the siege of Veii, the nearest and weakest of the wealthy Etruscan cities but regrettably, in addition, a very strong fortress. Otherwise they would withdraw the allegiance which the King had obtained from them by false pretences, and march north in a body to take service as mercenaries in the everlasting war between the Etruscans and the savages of Liguria.

They started to proclaim their grievances as soon as the King appeared; it was an additional grievance that nowadays he went surrounded by gimcrack emblems of royal state borrowed from Etruria, emblems which meant nothing to true Latin spearmen. But it was difficult to carry a public meeting against King Romulus.

From the start the King had governed by the simple method of dividing his followers; he could count on the support of every man who had been promoted by his favour. The hundred heads of families whom he had called into his Council of Fathers were solid for him; so were the three hundred young men of property who formed the cavalry of the army, for the horses which lent them distinction were the private possessions of the King. In addition there were the three hundred celeres. No one liked these young toughs, but a great many timid spearmen were afraid of them. In an unorganized assembly of three thousand voters seven hundred of the most weighty citizens were ranged in support of the King.

The opposition soon saw that to make speeches against the King would get them nowhere; but Romulus, that experienced leader, knew that it was better to persuade discontent than to crush it. He spoke frankly.

"Spearmen, you have endured without complaint four years of hard labour. Don't throw away the reward of your work by weakening at the last moment. I know what you want. You want plunder, and women with whom to share your plunder. Well, soon you will have both. This year we shall be strong enough to sack an Etruscan city; and within a month I shall send an embassy to the Sabine villages to seek wives for my warriors. It's no good asking Alba again. They refused last year, just because I had that unfortunate trouble with my brother; they say our whole city is polluted by fratricide, too unclean for intermarriage with god-fearing Latins. One day we'll show them their mistake! As though by defending the wall of our holy city, at the cost of family affection, I could anger the gods who guard Rome! When we flourish they will beg for our alliance! But all that lies in the future. What you want are wives, this summer."

"We shall get them from the Sabines," he continued. "They are our cousins and neighbours. Their ways are not exactly our ways; they squat in villages and don't appreciate the advantages of city life. But they worship our gods, and they speak our language—even though they speak it very badly!"

The last words came out in a comical Sabine accent. The crowd laughed, and Romulus knew he had won.

"So that's decided," he went on. "You should shout Yes to show that you agree with my plans." Roars of agreement. "Now today we shall march in procession through our city to the templum where no less than twelve vultures appeared to prophesy our foreordained success. Let your worship be reverent and dignified, worthy of this city founded by the son of a god, in furtherance of the expressed will of the gods."

In ritual silence they marched to a splendid sacrifice, which promised a fine feast of roast beef at supper time; that put them all in a good temper. Romulus intoned the prayers with an eloquence and conviction which was enough in itself to hearten them. All the same, Marcus felt that in some way he had been bamboozled. That evening, sitting replete by the cooking-fire, he felt brave enough to grumble to his neighbour.

"It's funny how in the end we always agree to something that we don't really want. No one could call us the slaves of a tyrant. King Romulus always explains his proposals, and promises that if we disagree with his plan he will try something else. But somehow when it comes to the point you can't go against him. I don't want to crawl to the Sabines for the right to woo their daughters, a right they should feel flattered to grant to Latins as soon as we ask for it. I don't want to sit down under that insult from our own Latin kin. Perhaps we would do wrong to make war on the cities of our fathers; though that's what they deserve. But there's no reason why we shouldn't raid the Etruscans tomorrow and carry off a few of their women. I'm sick of lying alone in my blankets, listening to five other men snoring in the hut. If we had one girl for half a dozen of us it would be better than nothing. Yet when the King had spoken I voted for him. Do you think he has us all bewitched? They say he is something more than an ordinary mortal man."

"Who say so? Only a few soothsayers and old women," answered his neighbour. "I come from Alba, and I can remember him as a boy; he's only six years older than me. But he's a cunning leader, and I'm content to follow him. It's easy to see why he always persuades the assembly. It's because he never permits anyone else to make a formal speech. Oh, he doesn't forbid it. At every meeting he invites anyone who has something to say to come up on the platform. But somehow there's always an obstacle. This morning, if you had tried to incite us to immediate war against the Etruscans the King would have cut you short by reminding us that the gods were waiting for our sacrifice. Before the next meeting those celeres of his would have beaten you up, unless they charged you with some crime that would earn you a formal flogging before the whole assembly. We never hear the opposition, and so we always agree with the King."

"I hadn't noticed that until you said it, but now I see it's true," said Marcus in some surprise. "But do you think my idea is a good one?"

"No," the other replied. "There isn't an Etruscan city we are strong enough to sack, and we can't afford to have them attacking us in return. Besides, warriors lose their courage if they lie with women."

"That's what the elders said in my village, but I don't believe it. We had a brigand living in the woods, such a mighty warrior that none of our men would face him; and he was always raping women he found in the forest."

"He might have been even stronger if he had lived chaste. It's not a thing you can prove, one way or the other."

"Well, if I can get hold of a girl I shall lie with her, even if there's to be a battle next morning. If I had stayed at home I would be married by now. It doesn't harm your courage if you are properly married."

"I would have been married, too, if I'd had the sense to stay at home," said his neighbour gloomily. "I came here to better myself, and after four years I'm no richer than on the day the city was founded. We have built a fine palisade, though. One day this may be a real city."

"A real city! That's what you all say, and I'm sick of hearing it. I joined what I thought was a band of brigands; and all we do is build for a posterity which can never exist until we find men willing to let us marry their daughters. I've had enough feasting for one day. I shall take a jug of wine to my hut, and drink myself to sleep where I can't hear these fools cheering for King Romulus."

But as the spring advanced Marcus felt more content; for

SABINE WOMEN

Aemilius had been chosen one of the envoys to the Sabines, and Marcus was to go with him as a spearman of his bodyguard.

It was an imposing embassy, even though it came from a city of young men, a city just four years old. The twelve envoys were lavishly bearded, though their beards showed no grey hairs; the escort were tall warriors, well armed, and Marcus displayed proudly the fine iron sword he had taken from a dead Etruscan who had failed to guard his sheep. They brought no present of gold, for there was hardly any gold in Rome; but they drove before them a troop of fine bulls, laden with skins of strong wine. The Sabines ought to be glad to see them.

The Sabines were a nation of tough, old-fashioned warriors who thought it unmanly to sleep huddled behind a wall. Their villages, scattered among the glens of their wooded mountains, were moved every two or three years as the soil became exhausted. But in other ways their manners and customs were those of their Latin neighbours, and they spoke a dialect of the same language. Such old-fashioned but respectable rustics should be proud to intermarry with the citizens of a thriving and lucky new city.

Standing in an open glade, the council of Sabine chieftains listened impassively to the speeches of the Roman ambassadors. They prodded the beasts that made up the present, and commanded that they be led away for sacrifice; but they did not praise them. Finally they withdrew to consult together, and when they returned it was announced that the answer of the whole Sabine nation would be given by a single spokesman.

The spokesman who came forward was a gnarled, burly warrior, his eyes peeping out from a tangle of brown beard. The Romans noticed a twinkle in those eyes as he began, and nerved themselves to agree to a pretty stiff bride-price; evidently the Sabine knew he was about to say something outrageous.

His first phrases were elegant, and must have been carefully composed; although his outlandish dialect made them hard to comprehend. He explained that the Sabines were gratified to see such a fine new city on their borders; they admired the spirit of their Latin neighbours, who had at last decided to retaliate against the raiding of the greedy Etruscans. Of course such a city must not be permitted to decay, for lack of children to replace the original founders. But the mighty King Romulus had the remedy in his hands, and it was odd that he had not seen what was evident to mere rustic Sabines, notoriously slower in their wits than clever Latins. Already King Romulus had set up an Asylum for fugitives from justice, to the great benefit of his noble and broadminded city. Let him found another Asylum, a refuge for unsuccessful whores, runaway wives, and other female castaways. Thus his new citizens would find worthy mates, and there would be no need for the daughters of respectable Sabine villagers to go abroad and marry foreign husbands. The speaker stepped back into the group of chiefs, to show that he had no more to say.

Aemilius turned to his bodyguard. "We are envoys. We may not draw our swords," he muttered savagely. The Romans retired from the clearing with exaggerated dignity, in silence.

When this was reported to the assembly of Roman spearmen there were angry shouts for immediate war against the whole nation of the Sabines; but King Romulus himself seemed more amused than annoyed at the insult. He told his people that for the present they had affairs of more importance than a war undertaken on a mere point of honour. The spring sowing must be finished, then they would raid the flocks of the Etruscans (though they must be cautious, for they were not yet strong enough to capture a walled city), and after that would come the harvest. Not until they were sure of food for the winter could they start once more looking round for wives.

During the summer, while spearmen sat idle in the sun, watching their barley grow, rumours began to spread that there was something lacking in the religious ritual of the city, something that must be put right without delay. At first these stories irritated Marcus; for he thought they already spent too much time on religion, and that for all their prayer and sacrifice the gods owed them more than a bowl of daily porridge and a thatched roof, which was the most any Roman had got out of the new city so far. Then he noticed that the celeres were the source of these rumours, and he listened more carefully. The ideas of King Romulus should be taken seriously.

The celeres were saying that this year they must hold a proper harvest festival. Certainly they had tried earnestly to thank the gods after each harvest in their new home; but last year the yield had been poor in spite of their efforts. They must be omitting something of vital importance.

When earnest students of religion had got that far the next step followed inevitably. In the Latin villages where most citizens had been reared women and unmarried girls played an essential part in the annual harvest festival. It was common knowledge that once upon a time the sowing and reaping of grain had been entirely the affair of the women, as it still was among the savages of the south; only the coming of the new-fangled plough had made it man's business. At a proper harvest festival married women ought to sprinkle on the fields whatever it was they kept in those mysterious baskets of theirs, and a choir of young girls ought to sing the hymn of the unsown field.

Since in Rome they lacked women there was only one way to put things right; they must beg help from their neighbours. At the next meeting of the assembly, when the idea was already lodged in the minds of most of the spearmen, King Romulus outlined a plan. In the autumn they would hold a great festival in honour of the god Consus, who looks after everything kept in store; and to this festival they would invite their neighbours. If the Sabines, and the people of three little nearby towns, mongrel Latins ruled by an Etruscan nobility, accepted the invitation they were to bring their wives and daughters. In the morning the women and girls would bless the fields in their secret female way which no man can understand; in the afternoon they would watch a horse-race in the marshy ground below the city; and in the evening there would be a banquet, with plenty of wine.

When someone objected that it might be dangerous to invite crowds of foreigners to wander about their strong places the King answered that everything would take place outside the palisade. The visitors would of course come unarmed, and both

35

the city proper and the Capitol would be strongly garrisoned throughout the day. In that case, Marcus wondered, would the Sabines be rash enough to come?

Yet on the 17th of August, when the last of the crops were being carried to the barns where Consus would guard them, it was definitely known that the guests, with their womenfolk, had started and would arrive on the next day. Already keyed up by the annual excitement of harvest, the Romans felt the added excitement of entertaining strangers for the first time in the history of their new city. It was considered only appropriate when King Romulus suddenly proclaimed that the evening would be spent in solemn fasting; every spearman was to remain within his hut, tending a sacred fire and praying for the continued fruitfulness of the Roman fields.

In the hut which Marcus shared with five others they kept a jug of wine hidden for emergencies; when all had agreed that this fast was an emergency someone produced a pair of dice, and they settled down to get through the dull evening pleasantly enough. The sudden arrival of a celer alarmed them, for he might denounce them to the assembly as breakers of the fast. But the man came to announce instructions for the morrow, most exciting instructions.

"You are to watch the horse race with swords hidden beneath your cloaks; if you can hide your spears and shields nearby so much the better. When the King gives the signal you are to seize the unmarried girls among the audience, and carry them within the palisade. That's simple enough, but there's more to come, and these instructions are important. You must obey them on pain of death. Listen to me carefully."

After a solemn pause the celer continued: "You are to grab only unmarried girls. No married woman may be molested. There must be no bloodshed. Use your swords to frighten the Sabines, but don't stab them. Finally, and most important of all, we are seeking wives, not concubines. No man may take more than one girl (there won't be enough to go round, anyway), and he may not lie with her until the King has married her to him in due form. Do you all understand? The point is

36

that we don't want undying war with the Sabines. If we treat their daughters honourably we may be able to fix up a peace. Now these are the most stringent commands imaginable. Think them over tonight, and tomorrow carry them out to the letter."

Next day Marcus was surprised to see that more than three thousand men could keep a secret. As the visitors arrived they were welcomed by smiling and peaceful citizens, ostentatiously unarmed. The Sabines admired the frowning palisades which crowned Palatine and Capitol, palisades which looked all the more threatening now that the stakes had been darkened by the weather of four winters; but they did not try to enter the fortifications and showed no surprise at being kept outside. It is not the custom to allow strangers to wander through your strong places.

In the morning all the men, hosts and guests, worked together to prepare the racecourse by the river; in summer the marsh was mostly firm land, and would make good going for horses. The main task was the erection of two masts to mark the turning-points of the oval track, but in the middle they also constructed a platform of turf from which the ladies could watch the sport in comfort. Meanwhile sentries had been posted to keep all males away from the barley fields, where the visiting matrons and maidens performed rites known only to women, rites which would make next year's barley grow thick and plentiful.

At midday everyone gathered by the racecourse, and handsome young Romans offered wine and cakes to the visitors. But little was eaten, for no one was accustomed to more than one main meal in the day, and the feast would begin after the race had been run and the right-hand horse of the winning pair had been sacrificed to Consus. When King Romulus took his stand on the cairn of stones which marked the finish everybody settled down to watch the chariots.

The spearmen had been eyeing the girls, but no more than was to be expected from warriors notoriously starved of female society. There had been no unpleasant incidents, and after more than six hours of peaceful entertainment the visitors felt at ease and secure. The Romans waited for the King to give the signal. But they knew that first the race must be run and the winning horse sacrificed, lest the gods should be cheated of their due; the excitement of the race was warrant enough for the excitement they could not control.

Marcus had picked a good place near a Sabine family of father, mother, small boy and marriageable girl. He had it all planned in his mind; when the signal was given he would make a dash at the girl, and at once carry her off to the security of the Palatine. If he was quick about it her father would still be busy defending his wife, and it seemed that he had no grown sons to help him. With any luck he would be safely inside the palisade before the fighting started, if fighting there was; and with such a prize to guard he would not be expected to return to the race-course to help his fellows find wives for themselves. Even with his concealed sword to help him, he did not wish to thrust himself unshielded among a crowd of angry Sabines.

That should do the trick, he told himself. But, really, what a scoundrel was this King Romulus whom he had served, more or less by accident, for the last four years! Was there any chance that his city could prosper, burdened as it must be by the wickedness of its founder? There was the death of Remus, and the death of Faustulus, which was something very like parricide. Murder of a brother, murder of a father: those were the worst crimes known to man, the crimes most severely punished by the gods. Could there be anything worse? His thoughts turned naturally to incest, because that was notoriously the crime most likely to bring down supernatural vengeance. No one had ever accused Romulus of incest; it was not a sin an unmarried man could easily commit. All the same, incest came into the story, for it was probable that Romulus himself was of incestuous parentage. Not everyone in Alba believed the story of his divine descent. The more prosaic explanation was that King Amulius, wearing full armour and with his face hidden by a great helmet, had raped Rhea Silvia as she returned from the holy well. He had planned, of course, that she should be put to death as an adulterous priestess; and thus there would be an end of the race of King Numitor. But after she had persuaded the citizens that she was the victim of divine lust he had not dared to speak out. All the same, that made Romulus the offspring of a union between uncle and niece, which was generally held to be incestuous. Incest, murder, parricide, now the betrayal of guests under cover of a religious festival; was there any wickedness from which Romulus would draw back?

But in its fifth year the new city was still standing; which showed either that the gods are very patient, or that Romulus enjoyed such powerful supernatural protection that he could break all the divine commandments with impunity. The second explanation was the more encouraging, and Marcus hoped it was the true one.

Now the chariots were pulling up at the end of the race, and a muscular young man pushed through the throng bearing a pole-axe, ready to sacrifice the winner. Marcus fingered the hilt of the short sword concealed under his left arm; then rubbed his sweating hand in the dust, to make sure that his grip would be firm when the trouble started. He wore his cloak wrapped round his waist, with the end thrown over his left shoulder. That left his right arm free for fighting, and at the same time would mark him in the crowd as a Roman; for the King liked every Roman to wear his cloak in this fashion.

Suddenly Romulus leapt down from the cairn, shouting a warcry. The Romans hurled themselves on their astonished guests. Snatching at his sword, Marcus ran to the family he had marked down.

All fell out exactly as he had planned. The stocky, solid Sabine father faced him with doubled fists, and never flinched when the naked sword flashed before his eyes; but his broad back was not broad enough to shelter two women. Marcus dodged, and the blow aimed at his face landed on his shoulder; then he had seized the girl by her hair, and kicked himself free of the little boy who tried to sink his teeth into his calf. The Sabine, quite naturally, devoted most of his energy to defending his wife, who was not in any danger. Marcus hauled his prize into the middle of the racecourse. Gripping his sword in his

39

teeth he twined both hands in her hair and dragged her up the hill to the Palatine.

As he entered the palisade a celer directed him to wait with his captive in the central square. The celer helped him to bind the girl's hands behind her back; when he had also tied her ankles he could be sure of keeping her until the King arrived.

From the middle of the flat-topped Palatine he could not see what was happening in the plain below; but fresh arrivals, streaming in through the gate with their spoils, brought word that the woman-stealing had gone off without a hitch. The first thought of the unarmed visitors had been to get away before they were all enslaved; they fled up the left bank of the river towards the wooded hills of their own country. By great good luck, no one on either side had been killed or seriously injured. Nearly a thousand maidens had been stolen, though some were still too young for immediate marriage. Marcus could not decide whether he ought to be proud of his leader's cunning or ashamed of his treachery.

Presently King Romulus strode into the square. He came in his full state, a purple robe flowing from his shoulders and an ivory rod in his hand; before him marched twelve celeres, bearing bundles of rods strapped to an executioner's axe. To the assembled spearmen this was something new; but ever since the foundation of the city celeres had flogged and beheaded at the command of King Romulus, and as a ceremonial escort for the sovereign of Rome it seemed a worthy piece of pageantry.

Standing on a stool Romulus addressed his subjects.

"Spearmen, you have taken women enough to ensure the continuance of our city. Now we must treat them with such courtesy that they become the proud mothers of worthy Roman citizens. First, these ladies are the wives of their captors, not bondmaids or concubines. My attendants will come among you with baskets of barley-cakes. Each man will break a cake and share it with his lady, at the same time vowing that where he is husbandman she is housekeeper. That is the most binding form of marriage that has ever been devised by learned servants of the gods, and it will endure until death parts you; for it is guarded by the Cornmother who gives us her barley, as well as by Mars my father and by the holy things I have stored in this city. While your wife lives you may not take a second wife, nor may you put her away. If any spearman fears to enter into such a contract with a stranger let him now withdraw, and we shall find some other Roman to take his place."

No one offered to withdraw; for to these celibate young men a woman was a great treasure, on any terms.

"Next," the King continued, "you will treat your wives as friends and partners. You may not set them to work in the fields; such labour is prohibited to Roman wives. If a wife has time to spare from her household duties let her spin wool, indoors. The husband must show deference to his wife, allowing her to go out on her private affairs, recognizing that she rules the kitchen. Don't laugh. I know that at present we live in little round huts; but a time will come when we shall own houses with many rooms. As soon as a family has two rooms, and I hope we shall soon enjoy that luxury, then one room will be the wife's, and the husband may enter it only as a guest. *But*", he paused for emphasis, "the husband is the head of the family. He may put his wife to death, and no one may question his reasons. This right is granted you to maintain your authority, and should be exercised only in the direst emergency. Now you all know how your wives should be treated. . . .

"There is one other practical point. We can't have a married couple sharing a hut with a crowd of bachelors. When the communal wedding is finished my celeres will allot a house to each husband; and if need be the bachelors will sleep in the open until more huts have been built. Now be silent and cover your heads while I pray to the gods on your behalf. Then remain seated in your places until you have broken and eaten the barley-cake."

There was a stir and a rustle as the crowd squatted and the men pulled their cloaks over their heads. Romulus prayed aloud, using the old-fashioned pronunciation in which it is proper to address the gods. He spoke first in his own words, begging the Cornmother to look with favour on these weddings;

then he continued with the ritual invocation they had all heard as children when marriages were celebrated in their native villages. While he spoke the celeres distributed the barley-cakes.

Marcus jerked once on the rope to make his girl squat beside him; then he untied her. The King had given no definite orders concerning such an obvious matter, but no one would blaspheme against the gods by marrying a woman while she was tethered like an animal. All round him his comrades were freeing their captives.

For the first time he looked carefully at his prize.

She was short and square, like most Sabines, with broad shoulders and clumsy hips. Her breasts were small, for she was not much older than fourteen. Her hair was black and straight, abundant but not very long; but her eyes were grey, and her skin white where it had not been tanned by the weather. She had a straight nose and a small mouth. On the whole her regular features might be called pleasing, though she would never be famous for her beauty. She would do.

He spoke to her, for the first time since he had grabbed her. "You heard what our King said. We are to be properly married. My name is Marcus. I am a Latin, and a client of the Aemilian clan. As a free spearman I have been allotted a ploughland and a yoke of oxen; the slaves of the clan help me to look after them. Besides my shield and spear I own an iron sword, and three clay pots. The King will put us in a hut by ourselves. What is your name? Are you content to marry me?"

Anger and disgust showed on the girl's face, but not a trace of fear. She answered readily, as though she had already made up her mind. "I shall marry you, if that's what you want of me. Now that I have been pawed by Roman bandits no decent Sabine would take me to wife, so I may as well make the best of it. I shall not tell you my name. It is a part of myself, and a part I do not choose to share with you. Besides, it would be better if you do not know the name of my clan. Then it will be easier for my kin to take vengeance."

"As you wish, wife," Marcus answered cheerfully. "Keep your name to yourself, by all means. Since I must call you something I shall call you Sabina. Among the neighbours you will be known as the wife of Marcus Aemilius, and that will be enough. By the way, are you a virgin?"

"That's a disgusting question!"

"No, it's not. A bit direct, perhaps, but I want an answer."

"Of course I am. Among the Sabines every girl is a virgin until she marries. But I am old enough to have been instructed in the mysteries, if that is what you mean. I know what will be done to me tonight."

"Look here, Sabina. The King has called on the gods to unite us, and until death parts us we shall share a hut. We are more or less the same kind of people. There's no reason why we shouldn't get on together. Why not be friends? Then we shall live more comfortably."

"So long as I am kept in Rome I want to be comfortable. I shall cook for you as well as I can, and keep our hut clean and warm. Death will part us soon enough, when my kin avenge the wrong done to me. Then I shall be a widow, free to marry some decent Sabine."

"That sounds fair enough. You seem to have been properly brought up. But just go on remembering that vengeance is the duty of your kin, and leave it to them. Will you promise not to poison me, or stab me while I sleep?"

"That much I can promise. The gods punish a wife who kills her husband."

"Splendid. In a few minutes we shall be married. Perhaps you wouldn't mind beginning your household duties straight away? Do you see the rawhide knot on this scabbard? It's meant to slip through that loop on the baldric, but my clumsy fingers have made it too big. Can you tighten it and make it look neater?"

As he laid his scabbarded sword on her lap Sabina smiled. It had been smoothly done. He had wronged her; but they were partners in the adventure of living and they would never know peace unless they trusted one another.

The celer, coming round with his basket of sanctified cakes, saw with surprise a Sabine captive who held her captor's sword as she chatted with him.

43

Chapter 3

THE FIRST REINFORCEMENTS

★

The Sabines were villagers, living scattered among the wooded mountains on the eastern skyline. Those who had escaped from Rome were very angry, but it would take them some time to muster their full strength. But the men of the three half-Etruscan townships, Caenina, Crustumerium and Antemna, could be mobilized by a trumpet-call, and Acron, King of Caenina, had long been a famous warleader. He was not a man to reckon odds when his people had been injured and insulted.

Therefore, from the Roman point of view, the first war of the new city began gently, with small battles against weak foes while the mighty Sabine army was mustering. King Acron marched boldly against them with the few hundred spears that made up the levy of his little city.

The destruction of that little band was the first regular engagement at which Marcus was present. Of course he had often been out with the raiders, but this was not at all the same thing. Raiders want to get home with their plunder, and feel no shame in fleeing faster than the enemy can pursue. For this onslaught the spearmen were drawn up in close ranks, where speed of foot would be of no advantage; and all must fight with no thought of retreat. It was a little frightening.

But the encounter, when it came, was a simple and one-sided affair, which might have been devised to encourage nervous recruits. Since Marcus had neither corselet nor greaves he had been placed in the third rank, where his spear could barely reach the foe; he had been told that his chief duty would be to push hard with his shield and perhaps get the hostile line moving backwards. But even in the third rank he had a good view of the famous deed of King Romulus.

It was a very pretty ambush. As more than three thousand Romans showed themselves on the crest of a hill the little column trudging down the floor of the valley halted and prepared to receive them. King Acron saw at first glance that his little band was in grave danger, and gallantly took the only chance that might save his men. Several lengths ahead of his tiny group of horse he charged against Romulus and the Roman cavalry. If he could kill their leader the Roman charge would falter. In his time he had killed many horsemen; but his time as a warchief was past. When the champions encountered the mighty King Romulus, the full-bearded burly young son of Mars, was more than a match for the elderly hero. With one hand he lifted the King of Caenina bodily out of the saddle, and with the other plunged his sword into his belly. At sight of this exploit the Romans broke into a headlong run. The foe was already fleeing when they crashed into their dissolving ranks.

Though the enemy fled right back to their little city Romulus halted the pursuit in the open. He could not tie down his army in a siege when so many other foes were preparing to attack them. Instead of finishing off Caenina he led his men back to the battlefield and set them to gathering the spoil. They found enough shields to prove that the enemy had fled shamefully, and Marcus picked up a leather helmet with a bronze knob for crest. But Romulus was intent on preserving the memory of his exploit. It was rare for a King to kill with his own hands another King, so rare that it proved once again that Romulus was under the special protection of Mars his father. Such a deed must be worthily commemorated. A tree was cut down, and the weapons and armour of King Acron were arrayed on it; the armour was of the finest Etruscan workmanship, and the corselet had been fashioned from wide sheets of gilded bronze. King Romulus fixed the trophy upright in a four-horse chariot, and rode beside it into his city of Rome. When everyone had seen it the pole, still erect in its chariot, was removed to the storehouse of sacred things.

Thus on the very evening of the battle the victorious army feasted at home. Marcus found his bride standing impassive in the doorway of his hut. But her dignity vanished when she recognized with delight the great joint of sacrificial beef he had brought home for supper.

"Meat again, and we had it only three days ago, on our wedding night! You Romans live well! I shall be sorry when my kin sack the city and kill the lot of you. In my father's village we eat barley-porridge and nothing else, nearly every day of the year."

She smiled in childish greed, and there was a little of the grin left over for her husband. "That's a new helmet. Is it any good? Did you kill anyone? Why do they make such a fuss about the armour of King Acron? He was an old man, and it was no great feat to kill him."

"On the contrary, it was a mighty feat," Marcus answered cheerfully. "King Romulus accomplished it, and anything the King does is a mighty feat. If you doubt it you have only to ask him. He will admit, with a modest blush, that he happens to be the greatest hero the world has seen."

"You don't think much of your King, do you? Why do you stick to him? Are you his born subject?"

"Indeed not, sweetheart. I came here of my own free will, I suppose because I wasn't bright enough to know what was good for me. But it's only an accident that I follow King Romulus. I came here in the train of his brother, King Remus. Romulus had him murdered on the day the city was founded."

"Then let's both go away, now."

"What? Leave Rome, after all the work I have put into building the place? It was the blood and sweat from my raw hands that made the palisade weather to such a fine colour. Besides, I have my own land, and my own oxen. You haven't seen them yet, but they are fine beasts. When ploughing-time comes round you will help me to drive them."

"Certainly not. Roman husbands may not set their wives to work in the fields. King Romulus is a treacherous scoundrel and a pompous bully; I don't think any more of him than you do. But he has sound ideas of the respect due to married women."

"I had forgotten that silly decree. The King would abolish it if he wanted his own wife to weed his onions. No, he wouldn't, though. He would keep it in force for the rest of us, and break it himself. He never bothers to keep his own laws."

"Indeed he doesn't," said Sabina more seriously. "The only decent thing about your Roman wife-stealing was that your King decreed that only unmarried girls should be seized. At least that gave us the chance of honourable marriage, instead of slavery. But one wife was kidnapped. She is called Hersilia and she's married to Hostilius. Your King liked the look of her, and he told those ruffianly celeres of his to snatch her up and pop her in his bed."

"I didn't know that, but I'm not surprised to hear it. All the same, he may be ashamed of what he has done. He has kept it pretty quiet."

"Every woman in Rome knows it. We talk together, by the spring and at the washing-place. Hersilia doesn't mind. She didn't like Hostilius, and I think she is fascinated by her Roman brute."

"If the women knew it, the men will know it in a few days," said Marcus reflectively. "What ought we to do? When my father threw me out I ran away to be a brigand. I planned to make a great fortune by robbing the Etruscans, and then go home and astonish the neighbours. Instead here I am, under a ruler wicked enough to be a robber chief, and yet he expects me to scratch a living from the land just as my brother does at home. Now that I have a wife I can't join a more enterprising band of brigands, and anyway I should be sorry to leave Rome. The soil isn't bad, and that palisade is something to be proud of. Besides, we have a storehouse full of sacred things; and they are truly very sacred, Romulus didn't lie about them. Then there's the bleeding head they dug up on the Capitol; that ought to mean something if it's true. But the strongest tie of all is that I don't want to admit that I have wasted four years of my youth. Perhaps it would be best to stay here and see what will come of it."

"My dear husband, we already know what will come of it. My

47

kin will break down your palisade, destroy your huts and your storehouse of sacred things, and sow salt all over this hilltop as a sign that it is forever accursed. Don't you remember? On our wedding night we agreed that such would be the end of Rome."

"And you promised that when I am enslaved by the Sabines you will see me kindly treated. That was the most important part of the agreement, wasn't it? Very well, we won't think of the future. Anyway, so long as this war lasts I must stay by my leader. To leave Rome now would look like running away. Meanwhile, there is supper to be cooked, and after supper bed. By the way, the enemy ran away before I reached them, and I did not poke my spear into anyone, so I am not polluted with blood. This is a nice helmet, but I found it on the ground, where some fugitive had dropped it."

"Caenina is not my city, but I'm glad you didn't kill anyone. Now you must chop some firewood, and then we'll have supper."

The only way to live happily in that kind of marriage was to treat the situation as a joke.

Within a few days King Romulus had defeated the levies of Crustumerium and Antemnae, catching each little force in isolation. These again were almost bloodless battles, the scattering of weak columns by the sudden attack of greatly superior numbers. Though he might be wicked and impious, there was no doubt that King Romulus was a worthy son of Mars.

There was still no move from the Sabines, the most powerful enemies of Rome. They were farmers who put the welfare of their fields above any other consideration. It seemed that they had postponed their revenge until after the autumn ploughing.

Now that the three little cities had been defeated the levy of Rome might stand down. At the next meeting of the assembly some young hotheads clamoured to be led to the sack of Caenina, whose citizens had lost so heavily in their defeat that they might be unable to hold their wall. But Romulus, dominating the meeting from the tribunal which no ordinary Roman might mount, would not agree.

"Don't take it for granted, comrades," he said, "that Sabines will move so slowly that you can capture a city while they are gathering their army. We should all look very silly if the Sabines were to sack Rome while we were busy sacking the miserable little town of Caenina. Let us stay at home and drill, to be ready for the great battle that must come when the Sabines attack us. But don't think that our victories over the three cities will be wasted. I am in touch with their rulers. We may get a reward from them more valuable than any plunder we could win in a sack."

His hearers were puzzled; surely the King was not suggesting that the defeated cities would pay tribute to Rome? Savages, and even some civilized villagers, occasionally paid tribute to a conqueror so that he should not ravage their crops; but it was not the sort of thing any independent city would do. Besides, if the enemy offered tribute, what would they get in return? Only a promise from Romulus that he would leave them in peace, and the promise of such a wicked man seemed hardly worth buying.

Yet, as usual, the assembly voted to carry out the policy proposed by the King. It was hard to vote in any other way, when Romulus never allowed his opponents to state their case properly.

When Marcus reached home he talked over the events of the day with his wife, and Sabina told him the rumour current among the women. She explained that, as often happened, Romulus was concealing his plans from his followers. He was not trying to get tribute from the beaten cities, but a negotiated peace. The intermediary was Hersilia, who had kin in Caenina; she had told the other Sabine wives all about it.

"Between them Hersilia and Romulus have thought of a very strange proposal," said Sabina. "They suggest that the defeated cities should be reckoned as part of Rome, and that their spearmen should fight in the Roman levy."

"That's absurd," answered Marcus. "A city can't be in two places at once. How can two cities meet in one assembly? The men from one would face a long walk after the day's ploughing.

We can't stop the war halfway. Either we sack Caenina and enslave its citizens, or the place remains an independent town "

"Must you always kill your enemies? Couldn't you sometimes
make peace with them instead? These people have been beaten,
and so they must lose something. But there's no need to take
their lives, or their liberty, or even the whole of their wealth. If
this scheme goes through they will be permitted to live in their
own homes; but they will have to fight when Rome fights, and
obey the decisions of the Roman assembly. I suppose if they feel
strongly about some question they might walk all the way here
and vote on it; as a rule they will do what you tell them. That's
better than having their throats cut, and they will be grateful for
your mercy. They may even be loyal, after they have got used
to Roman rule."

"Yes, it's the mercy that surprises me. It isn't like Romulus
to be so merciful. His father is not a merciful god. And I didn't
think he had the brains to invent such a novel kind of peace."

"He didn't think of it. Hersilia was anxious to find an excuse
for sparing her kin. She devised it, and told Romulus."

"Well, I never heard of anything like this before. But I suppose it can be done."

"It will be done, you can be sure of that. Hersilia has told
Romulus to get it done, and he will tell the Romans to do it."

"We must obey Romulus, I know. I didn't know that he must
obey Hersilia. But I believe you."

Sabina was right. At the next assembly Romulus expounded
his plan. He had to talk at great length before the novel idea
sank into the minds of his hearers; to control the foreign policy
of other free men seemed oddly bizarre. You might conclude
an alliance with a foreign city, an alliance that usually failed
when it was most needed; but spearmen must decide for themselves questions of peace and war, for if an unwilling army went
out to fight it was sure to be beaten. Yet the men of the three
cities (for Crustumerium and Antemnae were included in the
scheme with Caenina) were to be bound by the decisions of the
Roman assembly even though they lived too far off to vote in it.

"But you must not think of these places as separate communities," Romulus continued. "Their walls and their holy places will remain unchanged, for a city is a good thing in itself. I founded a city, and I want to be remembered for it; I don't want to be remembered as the man who destroyed half the cities of Italy. But though the towns will remain standing half their citizens will move to Rome, to be replaced by an equal number of Romans. In that way our new fellow-citizens will never form the majority, either in Rome itself or in our new colonies. You, the original settlers, will still control the assembly. Now are you all satisfied? Don't forget that this arrangement will just about double our military strength. The whole levy of Rome and the colonies will amount to about eight thousand men; we shall need every one of them to meet the Sabine attack. In the end we shall beat the Sabines, we must beat them. Don't forget the portents, and especially the bleeding head on the Capitol. Rome is destined to rule. Your destiny is to help in the accomplishment of the destiny of your city. If you neglect your plain duty the gods will punish you. That much I know, for a god was my father."

The assembly ratified its King's proposal. Citizens were chosen by lot to settle in the new colonies, and they went willingly enough for in the foreign towns they would be richer than at home. But Marcus was glad that he was not among them; he had come to be fond of his hut, with Sabina crouched over the cooking-fire; the stakes he had planted in the palisade were old friends who helped him to sleep secure at night. There were things in Rome that he would miss if he left it.

"I wish", he grumbled to Sabina, "that the King would talk less about his divine ancestry. That's always the clinching argument, when he wants to persuade us to do something we don't like. 'I know the will of the gods, because a god was my father.' It isn't easy to believe, though now I think there is some truth in it. That's why he can commit every kind of wickedness, and the gods don't punish him. They are making allowances for a disreputable nephew. Certainly he's as big and brave and ruthless as a son of Mars ought to be, and now he has rather oddly shown himself to be merciful as well. But I wish that he would sometimes try to persuade the assembly as he used to in the old days, instead of bullying us into agreement by boasting of his influence with the gods."

During the midwinter feasting Sabina told Marcus that she was with child. "My kin have delayed their vengeance too long," she added with a shrug. "When at last I see them breaking in through your palisade I shan't know whether to tell them to spare a young Sabine, or to dash out the brains of a little Roman."

"Perhaps he will be a girl," answered her husband, "and in that case it won't matter. Among the Sabines no one can tell the difference between a slave-girl and a free matron, since both work all day in the fields. Only here in Rome do we honour our wives, and spare them any toil more arduous than spinning."

"Spinning is hard enough, when you all insist on wearing those enormous cloaks to show you are citizens. You wrap up more warmly to go down to the assembly than a Sabine setting off in midwinter to look over his sheep. All the same, you know how to treat your wives. One day I shall visit the ruins on this hilltop and regret the pirate city where I lived with a kind husband and bore his children. This one will be a son, I can tell from his size. Already he is nearly as strong and rough as King Romulus."

Of course they must talk continually of the terrible vengeance which one day her kin would exact. For her pride's sake, Sabina could not admit that she was content with the life that had been forced on her. But Sabines were notoriously slow to move; there was still no sign of their great army when in April Sabina gave birth to a strapping boy. On the same day he was enrolled in the Aemilian clan, and given the name of Marcus after his father. He was one of the first native-born citizens of Rome, but that was not a very rare distinction; for during that spring most of the women stolen from the Sabines produced their first babies.

As the days lengthened Marcus was busy in his ploughland for as long as the light lasted. He found it very pleasant to walk over his own land, seeing the sprouting of his own seed, weeding and draining his own furrows. Dislike of the monotony of an agricultural life had made him join a band of brigands after he had been driven out from his father's village. Now, with Sabina as partner, he followed exactly the same life on the Palatine and found it enchanting. But now he was working his own land, which his own spear guarded from his enemies.

To make the barley grow was a tricky business. Emphatically there was a right and a wrong way of doing everything, from sowing the seed to cutting the last sheaf; but no one knew why the right way was effective, or indeed why seed grew better in ploughed land than on turf. Ultimately seed became barley because such was the will of the Cornmother; therefore the Cornmother must be kept in a good temper. There were many different methods of pleasing her.

The Romans, gathered from so many differing backgrounds, liked to compare one another's spells. It was interesting to try out a new magic while you watched your neighbour, only a few furrows away, doing something else to encourage his barley to grow. Most of these rituals seemed to work. Without noticing the change, Marcus had settled down to the never-ending round of a hardworking farmer.

Only when the sun set did he put away his tools and stroll up the hill to the palisade. On the flat summit of the Palatine there was now a strong family atmosphere; the new wives, with their new babies, sat by the cooking-fires to welcome home the breadwinners. Rome was becoming a friendly place. Marcus felt that he would not mind very much if he stayed there for the rest of his life, working in his fields every day and never growing rich or famous; presently his son would be old enough to take over the plough, and he might pass his old age on a stool by the warm hearth. Such was the accepted pattern of Latin life, and there was no reason why it should not be reproduced in this new settlement of brigands.

But if the Palatine was now a thriving village the outlying fort of the Capitol still kept its masculine atmosphere. The men who guarded it were paid a small monthly allowance in barley and beef as recompense for their extra duty; but they lived in cramped and uncomfortable quarters, so that only the poorest citizens, those too lazy or too careless with magic to be successful farmers, were willing to stay there. Among these poor and shiftless bachelors there was only one family, that of Tarpeius the commander. His daughter was now old enough for marriage, but so far her father had not chosen a suitable bridegroom. The only desirable girl among a crowd of rough warriors, she was so carefully guarded by her parents that she might have been living alone in the forest.

The source of the trouble was that a year ago Tarpeia had been the only marriageable girl in Rome; her ambitious father had expected her to make a very grand match, so that in the beginning none of the young men who offered for her had been good enough. Now Tarpeius could not adjust his expectations to changed conditions. All the eminent young nobles, the companions of King Romulus, had taken wives from among the stolen Sabines; and the immigrants from the new colonies had brought with them a flock of half-grown daughters. Young men of good birth had plenty of pretty faces to choose from; and though Tarpeia was a strong, buxom girl she was undoubtedly plain. As spring passed into summer she grew lonely and restless. One evening Sabina spoke of her to Marcus.

Like a prudent wife, she began with an indirect approach. "What would they decree in that precious assembly of yours if a Roman maiden presented them with an unexplained baby? Would you drive her out to starve, or kill her for adultery? Or would you be so pleased at the arrival of another recruit that you would accept the child without asking awkward questions?"

"What's all this?" asked Marcus in surprise. "*You* can't produce an unexplained baby. I would have to take the credit for any child of yours, no matter how much I might reckon on my fingers in private. And surely all your Sabine friends are also married, with stout husbands to take responsibility for their children? I hope you haven't been talking to the whores down by the Asylum. They are miserable friendless creatures, and I don't want to see them driven away when they have no other refuge. But they must carry on their trade without producing children, and they must not ask respectable matrons to plead for them."

"Of course I have not been talking to the whores. I didn't know that such creatures exist until you Romans stole me; they would never be allowed to settle near a Sabine village. No, I am thinking of an unfortunate Roman girl, the daughter of that noble commander on the Capitol. It's time Tarpeia was married, or at least betrothed. The poor creature sees all Rome a nursery of crawling infants; and yet her father won't choose a man for her. Time passes, and she is afraid that she may die a virgin. One day she might start a baby, just to force her father's hand. Couldn't you speak to Tarpeius, and remind him of his family duties? It seems absurd that the poor girl should pine for marriage while there are still not enough women in Rome. King Romulus keeps on saying that the number of citizens must be increased."

"Oh, so that's it. I'm glad it's nothing to do with you or your friends. No, I can't speak to Tarpeius. He wouldn't listen to advice from a poor spearman. Perhaps I might ask my patron to speak for me. Tarpeius might take the advice of Aemilius, a fellow-noble. But if he doesn't the girl must just control herself. She's not a savage, to do what she likes when she likes. Civilized girls don't give themselves to men outside marriage; if Tarpeia tries it on she will be punished."

Sabina dropped the subject. She had been married long enough to begin to understand something of the queer masculine attitude to adultery. She knew that Marcus himself would gladly take advantage of any willing virgin, and despise himself for ever after as no true male if some scruple held him back. If privately he stumbled on an illicit affair he would willingly join in a complicated intrigue to keep it secret from the world in general. But if in the assembly he had to judge a blatantly guilty woman he would vote for heavy punishment, public retribution for her grave indiscretion in being publicly found out.

All the same, Marcus was a dutiful husband. He duly spoke to Aemilius, who spoke to Tarpeius. But nothing came of it for the moment, and soon a new excitement put the matter out of mind.

The new excitement was the sudden appearance of a strange army. All that year scouts on the Roman boundary had been looking out for the threatened Sabine invasion; but it seemed that the Sabines would get in their harvest before they marched against Rome. This army, reported coming down from the north-east, seemed to be a homeless band of plunderers.

Then the scouts reported that the strangers were not hostile after all, and in fact had asked to be allowed to send envoys to King Romulus. In full assembly these envoys explained what they wanted.

Their army was in fact a very numerous band of mercenaries, who had been fighting for several years in the perpetual war between the northern Etruscan cities and the savages of Liguria. This spring the Ligurians had offered peace and tribute, and for the present there was a truce in the plain beyond the hills. There were many thousands of these unemployed mercenaries, so many that their wages would be very costly. But, and the envoys made a great point of this, they were led by civilized men who would keep their engagements. Though the common soldiers came from every race in Italy the officers were all Etruscans; their general had been Lucumo, or chief priest, in the Etruscan city of Solonium until civil war had driven him into exile.

Without even consulting the assembly, but in the hearing of all so that he could not be accused of negotiating behind the backs of his followers, Romulus answered that he could not afford to hire mercenaries. There was very little silver in his city, and presumably such gallant soldiers would not fight merely for rations of beef and barley. The chief envoy replied, also speaking to the assembly as a whole.

"That's what they all say, lord King. We are so many that no city can afford to hire us. In one sense that is a compliment to our Lucumo. He is a successful general, and recruits flock to him. But we must eat, and we give value for our pay. You are at war with a powerful enemy, and you need us. If we are driven to it we shall fight you for a share of your ploughland; but the Sabines drove us out of their land and we don't want to help them. Here is another plan, if you will agree to it. Why not let us join you, as Roman citizens? Give us land, and huts within your palisade. Then we shall fight in your army, and live as loyal citizens of Rome until we die."

There were murmurs of disapproval from his hearers. Rome might have begun as a nest of brigands, but that did not mean that absolutely anyone was welcome. These men would not boast that their leaders were civilized Etruscans unless a good many of the rank and file were savage Ligurians or runaway slaves. Such mercenaries might be good comrades on the battle-field, but no prudent man wanted to have them living next door to his wife and children.

Then, before the assembly could proceed to a formal decision, a mounted messenger came galloping along the river-bank. He brought urgent news from the scouts on the border. At last the Sabines were on the move. In two or three days their army would be before Rome, and their numbers were much greater than had been expected. King Romulus spoke to his followers.

He pointed out that a decisive battle would be fought within a few days. That made all the difference. If the Sabines won, it would be the end of Rome, and there would be no need for further planning. If the Romans won they could expand their boundaries, and so make room for these new arrivals. Besides, it was obvious that Mars had sent them as timely reinforcements; the god would be angry if they rejected his aid.

"Father Mars again, and King Romulus as his mouthpiece," Marcus muttered in disgust. "Why can't he persuade us that what he wants is right, instead of threatening us with the anger of heaven?"

All the same, when the time came he voted for admittance of the followers of the Lucumo, the Luceres as they called themselves. King Romulus could always get what he wanted from the assembly.

In the evening Marcus poured out his troubles to Sabina, but she saw only that here might be more suitors for the unfortunate Tarpeia. Marcus had forgotten that point, but he was inclined to agree.

"After all," he said cheerfully, "though most mercenaries are low ruffians there is usually among them a sprinkling of young noblemen with too many elder brothers at home. The Lucumo himself must be well born, by Etruscan standards; and he may have brought friends with him."

"Let's hope something comes of it. I'm sorry for the girl. But your King Romulus seems to be frightened of this war against my kin, though he started it with his eyes open. I'm a little bit frightened myself. If the city is sacked someone may hurt my son. Couldn't we slip away to the coast, and hide until the fighting is over? If you haven't borne arms against us, after the war is over and Rome has fallen I might get you a hut in my village. Then little Marcus will grow up among reputable decent Sabines, instead of in a crowd of brigands and mercenaries."

"I can't run away before a battle, as you know very well. I am a spearman, free born of free parents. It's a pity that I must fight against your kin, but there it is. I don't want to be polluted with the blood of my father-in-law; but probably I won't meet him. Since I have no corselet they won't put me in the front rank, and it will be a great battle, with crowds of people on both sides."

"Let's not talk about it. Whoever wins, my friends will be beaten. Of course my husband can't run away; I couldn't bear to be married to a coward. But I wish they would make peace."

"They can't. Your honour must be avenged, my darling. That's why free men carry spears."

Chapter 4

JUPITER STATOR

★

All the spearmen of Rome were thinking of the coming battle, and most of them with apprehension. No one could be angry with the Sabines, who so clearly had right on their side; and even if right and wrong did not come into it, no one could expect the single city of Rome to destroy the great army of the Sabine confederation. It was reported that nearly thirty thousand fierce hillmen were on the march. Romulus tried every desperate expedient to fill the ranks of the defenders.

The situation was saved when it was discovered that the band of the Luceres was very much more numerous than had been supposed. It became apparent that half of them had been lurking in the neighbourhood until they knew how their leader's proposal would be received; but now that they were to be citizens of a strong city they eagerly rejoined their comrades. When the whole army of Rome paraded in the marsh below the Capitol Romulus found with surprise and relief that he led twenty thousand foot and nearly a thousand horse. But a full half of the spearmen were mercenaries or strangers from the colonized towns, and there was an obvious danger that they might take over the city and expel the original settlers. Aemilius comforted his clansmen, when they spoke of this peril, by answering that the Luceres were a gang of very mixed origin, Etruscans, Latins, Samnites, and stray savages from the far north and the far south. They were not a community, and would never combine except for the most immediate robbery.

The marsh below the hills had dried out in the summer heat,

leaving only one patch of morass which might be dangerous to a stranger. Every morning the whole levy of Rome mustered on the flat ground, prepared for battle against the invaders; and every evening they were dismissed, to sleep safely behind their stout palisade. The Sabines were slow in coming. Perhaps they hoped that delay might dissolve the motley forces of the new city.

Then one evening the Sabines were sighted, marching in a solid column down the left bank of the river. It was too late in the day for a battle, and the Romans retired behind their palisade. The Sabines bivouacked nearby, and all knew that the great struggle would come on the morrow.

But at midnight trumpets blew the alarm. Marcus got up reluctantly, with a last look at his sleeping son. Sabina handed him a cup of warm porridge from the pot simmering by the fire; but he did not ask her to fasten his baldric. Probably he would be fighting her kin before he took it off, and she might be tempted to lay a spell on him as she passed it over his shoulder.

Inside the palisade there was hardly room for the levy to form, and they had to open a gate before the horsemen could muster on the slope beyond the ditch. No one knew why they had been called from their beds, for there was no sign of a Sabine attack. They began to grumble at the unnecessary false alarm. Then, across the valley, they saw torches flaring on the Capitol.

Now torches in plenty blazed on the Palatine also. King Romulus was easy to pick out as he stormed through the ranks, with a groom leading his warhorse behind him. The King was in a furious rage, swearing and bellowing at the top of his voice. He kept on demanding whether anyone had news from the Capitol. Apparently nobody had, and that made him angrier than ever. But something important must be happening over there.

The cavalry went forward to scout in the plain below, while the foot rested in their ranks and hoped that they would not march off without breakfast. As someone whispered to Marcus, lounging in the third rank of the line of battle, this was beginning just like all the campaigns Grandfather used to grumble about.

Then a cavalry patrol came in with a fully armed spearman riding double behind the leader. At that moment King Romulus happened to be near Marcus, and he could hear all that was said.

"The Sabines are in the Capitol, my lord," called the leader of the cavalry. "Most of our fellows were killed, and the rest skipped out over the palisade at the back. We found them wandering on the hillside, most of them in their tunics. But this one at least was awake when the Sabines broke in. He's fully armed. So he must have seen it happen. He can tell you about it."

"That's Tarpeius, commander of the fortress. Put him down gently. You should have saluted and asked him for orders," answered the King, who never forgot military etiquette. "Well, Tarpeius," he continued, "the Sabines got over your palisade. How did that come about?

"My lord, we were betrayed," answered the tired old man. He was not really old, but everyone else in Rome was young; he was not really tired, but everyone else was fresh from sleep. It made him look useless and miserable.

"We were betrayed," he repeated. "Someone opened the gate secretly. My men never had a chance. I saw the traitor, my lord, and that makes it harder to bear. My own daughter opened the gate of our fortress to the enemy."

"Did she now? That's most peculiar. I have heard of you as a stern father, whose daughter obeys him in everything. It's odd, too, that you should be fully armed when most of your men were sleeping. Let me see. There are rings on your fingers, and that's a big silver brooch. A wallet at your girdle, too. It's as though you had expected to leave home suddenly, and wanted to bring your valuables. Most curious. Where is your daughter now?" The King's drawling voice changed to a sudden bark.

"I saw her, my lord," called one of the troopers. "At least, I saw a girl, and it must have been Tarpeia. The main gate stood open, with torches blazing beside it. The Sabines were pelting a girl who had fallen on the threshold. It was as though they

were stoning her, if you know what I mean; but what they threw
at her were not stones but their shields. I saw her go down. She
must be dead by now."

"But her father is alive, and unhurt, and with all·his possessions by him," said the King in a musing voice. "Tarpeia lost
her life. I lost my fortress. But you, Tarpeius, have lost nothing.
It seems to me about time that you lost your head. Here, you
and you; make this man kneel, and cut his head off. That's
what happens to Romans who betray their city. As soon as we've
finished with this ugly business we must assault the Capitol,
before the new garrison have learned their way about it."

Tarpeius was a proud man, and in the grip of the celeres he
had no hope of escape. Of his own motion he fell on his knees
and stretched out his neck, so that at least his kin could claim
that he had faced death without constraint and without flinch-
ing. A celer hacked off the head in three hearty swipes; though
the first blow must have been fatal, for the victim made no
sound. As the severed head bounced on the ground the King
seized it, whirled it in the air to get rid of the blood, and then
reached over to stick it on a stake of the palisade. "Spearmen,
follow me," he bellowed. "Unless by sunrise we have won back
the Capitol we shan't have a city to live in."

"Oh dear, oh dear, Mars be my protection, and Jupiter, and
the Mother, and whatever power rules in this patch of ground,"
Marcus whimpered in great distress. "May all the gods avert
the omen. I'll sacrifice a pig if I get out of this alive. Did you
see?" he added, turning to the man on his right. "A splash of
blood from that head fell right on my tunic. Can you conceive a
worse omen, just before a great battle? What makes it worse is
that I know Tarpeius was unjustly condemned. He watched
fully armed every night, because he took his responsibility so
earnestly. His daughter was mad for a husband, any husband;
and not especially obedient to her father. She must have betrayed the place for love of some young Sabine. I'm going into
battle under a load of bad luck! Someone ought to tell the King
about it. At least we should wait to give Tarpeius proper burial
before we begin."

"Be quiet, my little hero, or the celeres will shut your mouth for you," answered his neighbour. "Before an hour has passed this whole army will be splashed with innocent blood. Tarpeius isn't the only virtuous man who will meet death today. I've seen warriors killed in all sorts of ways. I once saw a strong man killed by a woman with a stone. But I've never seen anyone killed by a bad omen."

Marcus said no more. He had a hut to fight for, a hut marked with the memories of his married life; his son slept in it now. His place was in the third rank, and he carried a broad shield. Unless he was willing to fight for his share in the city he had no business to live in it.

That unprepared attack uphill in the dark was a bad introduction to serious warfare. There could be no question of surprise, for the Sabines were still plundering their newly captured fortress. As the Romans pushed up the slope they were met by a shower of javelins and sling-stones. To shielded men such missiles were a nuisance rather than a danger, but in such a press a few warriors were bound to be unlucky; it was most disheartening to lose good men while there was still no way of damaging the foe. The charge faltered as it neared the crest of the hill; and came to a dead stop when it encountered a steady line of Sabine spears, projecting between the stakes of the high palisade.

King Romulus set an example. He advanced alone, covered by his great shield, until he could poke his spear through the palisade. But at once he must defend himself against the darting points of half a dozen Sabine spears, and even the superb shield of a rich leader could not keep off so many attacks. He jumped back out of reach to save his life; and where their leader dared not stand the Romans were disinclined to follow.

All the same, the full levy of Rome greatly outnumbered the small force of Sabines who had crowded into the little fort. The enemy dared not leave their palisade, and now the Roman slingers pelted them until they must cower in shelter. After half an hour both sides acknowledged the stalemate. King Romulus withdrew with most of his troops, to eat breakfast on the

Palatine. A party remained on the slope of the Capitol, where they could contain the invaders.

The Aemilian clan were among the unlucky ones who must keep in their ranks while their comrades breakfasted and armed at leisure for the coming battle. It seemed an unfairly long time before they were relieved, and Marcus could hurry back to the meal Sabina had waiting for him. Between mouthfuls of salt pork he bewailed the misfortune which had befallen Rome.

"We must fight all day with an enemy post on our flank, our right flank, the unshielded side. If our line breaks those Sabines on the hill can run down and catch us before we can get away. We must win the fight, or we shall all perish in the retreat. What makes it so maddening is that it isn't the fault of our leaders, or of any individual Roman. No one took precautions against that kind of treachery. Why should they? I don't know whose side you are on today, my dear, and I deliberately don't want to know. If you feel a sudden impulse to let the Sabines into the Palatine you can be sure some Roman spearman will be watching you. We remember where you came from. But Tarpeia—damn it all, she came here with the original founders. She must have been with the baggage, down by the marsh where we shall fight today, while King Romulus was tracing the line of the palisade and seizing the opportunity to have his brother murdered. If anyone is on our side, she ought to be. Why on earth did she betray us, and why did the Sabines murder her as a reward for her treachery?"

"If you live in a stable it doesn't make you a horse," said Sabina. "Poor Tarpeia saw Rome from the beginning, and hated all she saw. She did not come here of her own free will, she was brought by her father. All she got out of your new city was a miserable lonely life, surrounded by men who knew they might not marry her and therefore never bothered to court her. I'm not surprised she tried to take a Sabine lover."

"All it shows is that you can never trust unmarried girls. Even so, why did your countrymen kill her?"

"Why indeed? We shall never know. I suppose they are ordinary manly warriors, who loathe traitors even when the

traitors work for their side. Would you love me if I had helped
Rome against my own people? You might be glad of my help,
but that isn't the same thing. So now I send you off to battle,
with a clean tunic and a nice bit of pork in your wallet. I shall
pray that you come home safely. But I shan't tell you for whose
victory I shall be praying at the same time."

Although Marcus had never been present at a pitched battle
he thought that everything ought to be familiar, from the
descriptions in the old songs. This would be a field of the old-
fashioned kind, where there could be no manœuvres, no tactical
surprises; incidentally, he noted with a qualm, there would be
no room to run away. Twenty thousand Romans were jammed
between the Palatine and the river, filling the cramped plain;
and behind them rose another steep hill, the Aventine.

Looking northward towards the enemy the river bent away
to leave a wider space of level ground. That was the plain known
as the Field of Mars, because in the second year of the city
the Dancers of Mars, carried away by enthusiasm, had pranced
all over it instead of remaining inside the palisade. A patch of
swamp in the middle might catch a few Sabine strangers, but
there was plenty of dry ground on either side.

Marcus was in the third rank of the Aemilian clan, the proper
place for a poor spearman who did not own a corselet. He was
cheered to find that the Aemilians as a whole were in the second
line of the army; for there was not enough room for such a great
host to draw out in a single line. Fifty yards ahead stood another
triple rank of spearmen, and ahead of that a loose scattering of
slingers and archers; men who were too poor to come shielded
to battle and who by rights should have no vote in the assembly.

From his reasonably safe place he could not see very far forward, and only a clamour of defiance from the ranks in front
told him that the Sabines were in sight. Then he made out a
cloud of dust, and lurching through it the standards of the
enemy. Most of these standards were mere tufts of leaves fastened to tall poles; but he saw one little figure of the wolf of
Mars. That angered him, for the Romans were especially the

children of Mars; the same wolf figured on the standard carried aloft in the midst of his own Aemilian clan.

Presently warcries rang out, and he knew that the front lines were engaged. Still he could see nothing of the fighting; nothing but a cloud of dust billowing high, and looming through it a few horsemen, showing clear above the mass of struggling infantry. He understood with a shock that his future was being decided within a few hundred yards of where he stood; and he could do nothing.

The suspense endured for a very long time. Marcus stood where he had been told to stand, feeling his feet grow tender as the ground beneath them baked in the glowing sun. If this went on much longer he would be unable to run swiftly, whether back or forward. It was impossible to tell how the battle was going; no wounded men hobbled to the rear bringing rumours, for in front the press was so thick that the wounded must die in their ranks. But the Roman front line did not yield ground, so for the moment they must be holding the attack.

At last Aemilius, who was mounted, rode along the front of his clan bidding them prepare for the charge. The trumpeter beside the wolf-standard blew down his long brazen tube, and the bellowing grunt was taken up farther down the line. The whole Roman reserve moved forward at a shuffling and reluctant trot.

They did not charge with dash or enthusiasm, for they could not see the foe. They were advancing, with levelled spears, straight at the backs of their own comrades. It was the wrong way to use a reserve, but in that plain cramped between the river and the hills there was no other way they could come into action.

Aemilius rode steadily at the head of his clan, until just before they reached the first line he drew aside and pulled back level with his men. His followers lifted their spearpoints and slowed to a walk, for there seemed to be no room for them in this battle. That was not what their leaders wanted from them. Shouting, Aemilius ordered them to run in and push.

Marcus kept his spear carefully upright as he ran in behind

his shield, left shoulder forward. He settled the shield against the back of another Roman, and pushed; the man did not seem to mind. Then he remembered that he ought to be in the third rank of the reserve, and that there ought to be two men in front of him. He looked for them, and saw them both a little to one side, filling gaps in the front line. Those people in front had lost a great many dead.

There were Romans on each side of him, fellow-clansmen, pushing as he pushed. He grunted over his shoulder to the man on his right: "How long do we keep this up? And how does it help our men in the front ranks?"

"We keep it up all day, or until the Sabines have had enough. When you are in the front rank you'll find that it helps to be pushed from behind. If you can make the enemy go backwards some of them stumble and lower their guard."

The new phase of the battle seemed to last for hours; in fact it did actually last for hours. Every man on both sides was now fully engaged. There could be no manœuvres, and with the lines so closely locked together the army which first turned to flee would be massacred before it could get clear. Both Sabines and Romans knew this, and concentrated on keeping steady on their feet. Few men fell. Nearly everyone was too busy pushing to be able to use spear or sword.

There were no gaps in the struggling mass, save where some mounted leader forced his way to the front to get at a mounted champion of the enemy. Those heroes on horseback sometimes rode down their own foot; but at least they were striving to kill, not to push. The half-dozen single combats between these cavaliers seemed to be the only deadly fighting in what was otherwise a wrestling match.

On the whole the Romans were getting the better of it. From time to time they surged forward, and they never went back so much as a step. But they could not get the Sabines on the run, moving so fast that they would be tempted to turn and expose their backs; and until one side or the other succeeded in that aim it seemed that the pushing must continue.

At last, when everyone was exhausted, the bronze trumpets of the enemy blared out a signal. At the same instant every Sabine spearman ran back for at least twenty paces. So quickly and unexpectedly was it done that the whole line got clear of the Roman spears. It was now midday, and after fighting since sunrise the Romans saw once more before them an unbroken line of Sabine spears, lowered to meet the charge.

"That's a good bit of drill," Aemilius shouted cheerfully to his clan. "You oafs couldn't manage it, not if you practised for a thousand years. But it has its bright side. They only tried it because their leaders think we are too much for them."

"Hallo," he added a moment later, "they didn't get away scotfree after all. Some horsemen have got stuck in the marsh. The riders can scramble clear, but the horses will smother. That's what comes of running away a bit too quickly. Now you boys try and get your wind before the next clash."

By mutual consent there was a pause in the fight, while exhausted men adjusted damaged harness and regrouped. There was room between the armies for King Romulus to ride out where all his men could see him. He spurred his tired horse until it pranced, and prepared to make another rousing speech. But before he could begin an enemy horseman charged down on him.

"Watch this, boys, they have something to fight about," Aemilius called to his followers. "That man riding against the King is Hostilius, the Sabine husband of the lady Hersilia. Tonight she will be a respectable woman, with only one husband, whichever way it goes."

By this stage of the battle every horseman had thrown all his javelins; the champions encountered with drawn swords. Hostilius aimed a sweeping blow at the King's head, and Romulus, instead of using his sword to guard, gave proof of his daredevil courage by thrusting as the blow fell. The crest of his bronze helmet was shattered, but the leather padding beneath it was just thick enough to save his skull; before the Sabine could recover the point of the King's sword was deep in his belly. Hostilius toppled from his saddle, to lie dead on the ground; while King Romulus, blinking, shook his buzzing head and reined his frenzied horse.

The Romans cheered in ecstasy. But the King, sitting motionless and half-stunned on a motionless horse, was an easy target for enemy marksmen. A shower of sling-stones rose in the sky, and one hit Romulus square on the side of his battered helmet. Unconscious the King slumped forward on the neck of his horse. As a Roman ran up to grab the bridle the Sabines charged all together, with a cheer.

Marcus was not the only Roman to be dismayed by the injury to his leader. All day the citizens had fought stubbornly because they thought that under the leadership of the son of Mars they could not be beaten. To see him dazed, perhaps mortally wounded, drained the confidence from them. Under the impact of the Sabine charge the front rank gave ground; and the rear ranks, instead of pushing forward to hold their comrades in place, turned to flee.

Marcus had been taught again and again, ever since he was old enough to exercise with spear and shield, that at close quarters to turn your back on the foe was not merely disgraceful, it was the quickest way of getting killed. It was unlikely that an armed spearman could run fast enough to outdistance pursuit; and once you had turned your back you could not protect yourself with your shield. All the same, seeing his fellow-clansmen turn to flee, he also whipped round. He found that he was too tired to run very fast.

He was staggering along, and whooping for breath, when he was aware of a horseman beside him. A hand came down and clutched at the neck of his tunic. Expecting death from a Sabine cavalier he looked up, to see the anguished face of King Romulus. "Halt, you, and turn round," shouted the King, shaking him as a dog shakes a rat. There was something in the grasp of a royal hand, the hand of a son of Mars, which made him think it would be better, perhaps even less painful, to meet death with his face to the enemy. He turned about, covering himself with his shield.

Other Roman horsemen rode through the rout. Aemilius rounded up a group of fugitives as the King seized a second flying spearman. Where Marcus stood a rank formed beside him;

until the Roman reserve once more formed line across the plain.
The front rank, still engaged with the Sabines, gave ground
slowly, so that their comrades behind had time to form in good
order.

King Romulus, sitting his horse in the midst of his army,
pulled up the end of his cloak to veil his head as he prayed.
"Jupiter, Skyfather, ruler of all," he called, so loud that his
men could hear, "Jupiter, fount of all law and good order,
whose will keeps warriors firm in their ranks, Jupiter, Stay of
Armies, inspire my citizens to fight for their city. If now you
inspire them to rally, so that Rome endures, I vow to mark out
for you here in the plain not only a templum of holy ground,
but within it a house of brick where your image shall dwell in
splendour. Jupiter, Stay of Armies, help your city of Rome."

Now the remnant of the front rank was running back; but
they halted when they reached their supports, and the Sabines
coming after them hesitated.

"Here it is afternoon, with hundreds of good men killed on
both sides; and the battle is just as it was before we made our
first charge," Marcus thought to himself in dismay. He wondered whether they must stay in that narrow plain, surging up
and down between the Capitol and the Palatine, until one side
or the other had been killed to the last man.

Neither army was anxious to renew the battle, though neither
was willing to leave the field. Romans and Sabines stood glaring
at one another, a hundred yards apart, while the leaders busied
themselves in thickening the front rank by bringing forward
unwilling men from the reserve. One of the mercenary Luceres,
who had no business among the Aemilian clansmen, suddenly
rounded on Marcus and pushed a battered shield in his face.
"Here, look at that," growled the rough hairy giant. "See the
fresh scars on it. And your bit of leather, big enough to hide
two little shrimps like you, hasn't a scratch. You'll change
places with me, or I'll shove this spear down your throat until
it comes out at your backside."

Marcus made a virtue of necessity, since he dared not defy
this ruffian. "Why, certainly, comrade," he said with a sickly

smile. "Of course I will take your place in the front line until you have recovered your breath. Let me know when you are ready to rejoin your own clansmen."

"The minute you are dead I shall step into your place, dear comrade," the other answered with a leer. "That's how we do it among the Luceres."

"As you wish. Don't accidentally stab me in the back," was the best rejoinder Marcus could think of.

"Not accidentally, I never do that," said the other; which did not leave the situation any more comfortable.

At last Marcus found himself in the front line. He levelled his spear, took a firm grip of the shaft, and waited with set teeth for the Sabine charge.

Suddenly on his right he heard shouts of amazement, and the Sabine line before him seemed to waver. He craned forward to look to his right, even though the movement brought him a little in advance of the front rank. He could not understand what he saw. There seemed to be a crowd of women, descending the slope of the Palatine with wreaths on their heads and green branches in their hands.

The column of women flowed between the two armies. All were clad in clean tunics, as though for a festival, and their hair was carefully dressed. Most of them carried babies. At their head walked the lady Hersilia, for the last hour the lawful wife of King Romulus. His face blank with stupefaction, the King rode to meet her.

Marcus, carrying his son in his arms, trudged up the steep path to the Palatine, while Sabina beside him carried his shield and spear. His wife had just finished telling him the whole story of the exploits of the women; now she anxiously awaited his response.

"Well, it must be a good idea, or King Romulus would not have consented to it," he said doubtfully, and Sabina sighed with relief. "But why", he continued, "was Hersilia so late in starting, if from the beginning she intended to make peace between us?"

"Can't you guess her reason? Every woman must be either an untouched maiden, or else the wife of some reputable man. Unless she is properly married she soon sinks to the level of those miserable harlots by the Wolf's Lair, 'she-wolves' as you call them in your jolly manly jokes. Through no fault of her own Hersilia found herself with two husbands. One day Romulus might cast her off, since she was not properly his wife; but Hostilius could not be expected to take her back, after she had shared the bed of another. She very sensibly made up her mind to wait until she had only one husband alive. She knew Hostilius would seek out the King and challenge him to single combat; any injured husband must do that. As soon as she knew that Hostilius was dead—we could see it all from the watchtowers on the palisade—she led us down to make peace, a peace that would leave her the undisputed wife of a great King."

"And if Hostilius had won the duel, what would she have done?"

"She would still have made peace, but on different terms."

"I suppose she would have found a way to make Hostilius King of Rome. It seems she can do with us what she pleases. Oh well, she has persuaded the King; and his followers must obey King Romulus. For myself I welcome peace, on any terms that are not downright disgraceful. When I have met your kin and paid over a reasonable bride-price you and I can live openly as the comrades and lovers we have been in truth ever since our wedding night. I had grown tired of helping you to pretend that you wanted Rome to be destroyed. Now there is no guilt between us, and I can look forward to meeting your father."

"And little Marcus will grow up among friends, with two clans to guard his back from his enemies. Perhaps that is the best thing of all. By the way, I know he had to be named Marcus, after his father; that's the custom of the Sabines as well as the Latins. But are there names preordained for his brothers and sisters? I should like some day to name a child of mine for my brother."

"What? Number two on the way already? I shall have to ask Aemilius to get me more ploughland. Well, the Latin custom is that all your ten daughters are called just Aemilia Prima, Secunda, and so on; but for your ten younger sons you may choose the first names, though Aemilius must come second. That makes twenty-one children in all, which is as many as I shall be able to support. I hope that after that you will stop, if it is convenient to you."

"We'll see what I feel like in twenty years' time. At present I want to bear your children. In Rome there will be room for them."

"Room enough. But it will be a queer sort of Rome. Five years ago we founded a Latin city. When we put up that palisade there were only three thousand men in the levy. With the Asylum, and the colonies, we grew to ten thousand, mostly Latins. To help us fight against your kin we took in those mongrel Luceres, another ten thousand of them. Now we are to bring in ten thousand Sabines. I wonder where it will end? Thirty thousand men will make a great city; yet it's spreading the luck very thin. In the beginning Rome had a lot of luck, for all that there was murder done on the day of the foundation. That bleeding head on the Capitol, and a son of Mars for our King! I doubted at first, but now I know we had luck. May the gods make it endure!"

"They will. Look, little Marcus is laughing. That's a good omen."

Chapter 5

THE COMING OF THE SABINES

★

A whole people were on the march. So many were the ox-waggons, so dense the throng of cattle, that a stranger might have supposed the convoy to be a migration of those eastern savages who dwell always in carts and have no fixed abode. But dotted through the columns were pairs of oxen yoked together, though they pulled nothing; and crowning each pile of household goods on the sturdy waggons was a wooden, iron-tipped plough. These people were not nomads; they were farmers.

It was a peaceful journey, with no need for military precautions. Thus Publius, though he was a spearman of the first rank, might march by his own waggon. As he plodded through the dust, almost deafened by the squeal of ungreased axles, he had leisure to think, since he could hardly see or hear.

There was plenty to think about, for this move would be the most important change in his life. Not that he had changed his manner of living frivolously, at his own whim; his chief was moving house and all loyal clansman must follow, whether they looked forward to the new customs as an improvement or thought them a regrettable mistake.

That made it easier, Publius reflected. It is always easier, especially for a Sabine spearman, to perform an obvious duty than to reach a difficult decision. There was a great deal to be said against the move, and he might have said it; but he had not been consulted, so there he was in the column.

He supposed, gloomily, that this uproar, this stink of dust and sweat, this sense of being hemmed in by a short-tempered crowd, would be his lot for the rest of his life. Tonight they would all sleep behind a crowded palisade, lying almost touching one another. Of course the hut he came from had been crowded enough, with his wife and children huddled as close as they could get to the little smudge of fire. But there had been only four other huts in the village; and then the unbroken ranks of the beech-forest, hiding even the smoke of the next hamlet. Tonight he would feel, as he slept, the nearness of hundreds of crowded huts.

He would have to sleep knowing that a barred and guarded gate shut him off from the greenwood. That would be very nearly the most unpleasant part of the new experience, at least until he got used to it. It would not actually be the most unpleasant part, he reminded himself with a scowl; the most irksome restraint, as he knew very well, would be the unremitting necessity to keep on friendly terms with all these crowding neighbours. He had past experience of that distasteful obligation, when he was exploring a lake beyond the mountains. Three companions had come with him, in a single small canoe. They must sleep huddled together like fledgelings in a nest, and in the morning be considerate to one another at a time when any normal freeborn Sabine wanted to go off by himself and sulk until he was fully awake. That one voyage had been enough for him. It had ended suddenly, when he knocked out the teeth of the clumsy fellow-clansman who had accidentally spat on his knee. There was good hunting to be found among the lakeside cliffs, but he had never gone that way again.

In the new settlement he would never be out of spitting range of his neighbours; even when they went to war they would march in close-packed ranks, like Latins. What was that joke he had heard during the last inconclusive campaign? That if you knocked a hole in a Latin shield you would be set on by the three spearmen hiding behind it? He would never again wander alone under the canopy of beech-leaves. That was no life for a free Sabine.

The wild idea that he might stay behind had been dismissed

from his mind without hesitation. Tatius would live in this new city, and wherever Tatius went it was the duty of his clansmen to follow. Latins could not see what lay behind such unquestioning obedience. They thought of Tatius as a king, and wondered that his followers never thought of deserting him, as those flighty Latins themselves would leave one king to follow a better. They did not understand that Tatius was something much greater than a king; he was the head of his family. Long ago, so long ago that no one could fix the date (though the reckoning by generations in the pedigree was clear enough) there had been only one Tatius, and his wife. Then his six sons had married, and the headship had remained with the eldest. Now Titus Tatius was rightful head of the whole extended family, and he, Publius, descended from the younger sons of younger sons, must give his chief the same obedience that even Latins (for even they had an inkling of decent behaviour) rendered to their grandfathers. If Tatius chose to live behind wooden palings like a milch cow, his relations must follow him.

They had come to an awkward place in the track, a hole which in winter was a slough and now in the summer heat had dried to a bottomless cushion of soft dry dust. The oxen lurched obstinately, scrambling up the far side as though they wanted to pull the wheels off the waggon. Publius steadied them, waving his spear before their eyes. In theory he travelled unarmed on this peaceful journey, as Tatius had commanded; his sword, corselet and helmet were among the bundles on the waggon. But he carried his spear and shield, partly to show that he was a freeman of his clan, partly because there was no other safe way of transporting such valuable objects without a risk of breakage.

With a rattle and groan the waggon lurched out of the hollow; the baggage swayed and toppled. Publius glanced up at his wife and children, perched beside the precious plough which must be saved from damage. Through the dust-haze he could make out his family but dimly, but he could see that there were still three of them; so nobody had fallen off. At the rear of the waggon the ploughman and his woman were freeing a leafy branch which had been caught up in a wheel. His household was complete. There was no more than usual to worry about.

Of course his family was always a worry; that was the natural penalty of being a free spearman with a family to look after. He did not like to contemplate how much life in a city might affect them. Claudia, his wife, could of course be trusted absolutely; she was a free Sabine lady, wife to a free clansman. All the same, she would be continually meeting strange men, smooth artful Latin men, accomplished seducers. She might grow discontented. Worse still, she might complain that one of these strangers had insulted her. Then Publius did not know what he would be expected to do. The first rule for living in a city was that you must never fight your fellow-citizens; but did that outweigh the other binding rule, that you instantly killed anyone whom your wife pointed out as deserving of death?

In the middle of a crowded city slaves would be hard to control. That ploughman and his woman would be always dodging off into strange huts—impossible to keep an eye on them in such a throng. If they ran off they would not at first be missed, though there was no reason why well-treated slaves should run away; any stranger who sheltered them would naturally enslave them afresh. But probably in this new city there would be arrangements he had never thought of; for many years the Latins had been living in cities, and they must have devised some method of keeping their slaves steadily at work.

The children were the greatest worry. Publius was thirty years old, but he had been married only six years ago; and of the five children born to Claudia only two had survived infancy. Young Publius was now four, and Pomponia two. They were lively brats, and not particularly well behaved. In their native hamlet they would have grown up shielded from temptation, a stout spearman and a modest bride; amid all the wiles of a city, and a Latin city at that, they might bring disgrace on the Tatian clan.

There was nothing to be done about it. Tatius had decided, and his cousins must follow. All the same, it had been a very queer decision, and if he had heard of it as the act of a stranger

Publius might even have considered it dishonourable (of course the act of his own chief could never be dishonourable). To make peace in the middle of a battle, while there was still every hope of victory and no particular danger of defeat, seemed on the face of it to show a lack of spirit. To make peace on the advice of a parcel of women was even more odd. To alter your whole way of life and become a city dweller among your Latin enemies —that was frankly eccentric. And among sturdy barley-growing, boar-hunting, forest-dwelling Sabines to be convicted of eccentricity was to be condemned. The path of duty led an honest spearman to strange destinations.

There was something familiar about that outcrop of rock above the path. Of course—the army had halted there for breakfast on the morning of the battle. They were getting near the end of their journey; but for this horrible cloud of dust Rome would already be in sight. Publius considered. He recalled that just before the track reached the isolated group of hills it swerved very close to the river. When they reached that point he would tell Claudia to get down from the waggon, and they would all wash and put on clean clothes so as to make a good impression on their new fellow-citizens.

Presently a message was passed down the line, bidding the spearmen form in their ranks for the ceremonial meeting between the two kings. Wives and children might look on, if they wished; waggons and baggage could be left in care of the slaves. Claudia lowered the heavy bundle of armour to her husband. He was proud of the full equipment which had earned him his post in the front rank. He had inherited corselet and helmet from his father; both were made of thin bronze over stout leather padding. A lucky skirmish with a band of Etruscan raiders had brought him a pair of greaves, solid bronze held in place by straps of woven linen. Greaves were rare on this side of the river, though many well-to-do Etruscans wore them. They were not very useful to a spearman who must scramble over mountains on foot, and Publius seldom wore them for serious campaigning. But they were just the thing for a state procession.

THE COMING OF THE SABINES

When all the straps had been fastened he slung over his corselet a gay baldric of embroidered wool. This supported a very fine sword, which he had bought from an Etruscan trader during a rare interval of truce. Though it came to him by way of Etruria the blade had been forged farther north; it was a leaf-shaped, double-edged weapon, longer and heavier than the common swords of central Italy, excellent steel which kept an edge even in damp weather. It had cost him three cows and a big jar of wine; he could not have bought it if he had not just captured more cattle than he had the right to graze in the common pasture. When he was armed he made such an imposing figure that it seemed surprising he should march on foot; there were mounted nobles who wore less valuable harness.

With the halting of the waggons the dust-cloud gradually dispersed, and it was possible to see the surrounding country. To Publius it was familiar ground, but it seemed odd to be looking at it without the taut nerves and dry mouth which come even to the bravest spearman before imminent battle. There, just beside him, was the flat boulder on which he had sat to fasten his greaves. Just ahead lay the bend in the river, below a cluster of steep-sided hills. He was already abreast of the garden-covered mount which the Romans called the Pincian; due south, in line, he could see the little knoll of the Capitol and the spreading, smoke-blackened palisade on the Palatine. They were on the edge of that wide marsh where the stubborn battle had been fought. A tough fight it had been, and once the Sabine line had been forced to retire (he could make out the bog where Curtius had lost his warhorse). But they had rallied and come again, to see the backs of those Latin woman-stealers. If Jupiter had not answered the prayer of King Romulus they would have stormed the palisade before evening and Rome would have disappeared. Romulus, that king from nowhere, certainly enjoyed more than his fair share of luck; perhaps there was some truth in the legends about his divine parentage.

It seemed that King Romulus would welcome them on the very site of the battle. He sat there, on horseback, with all his men behind him. If they wished they could begin again that interrupted fight, and perhaps find out whether Jupiter would help the Romans a second time.

No, they could not fight, after all. The Romans were standing in line, drawn up in the usual three ranks (and doing it very well too; they must have been drilling recently). But they were unarmed, dressed in clean tunics and very large cloaks, all worn in the same way with the end thrown over the left shoulder. Standing thus, in clean white wool, they looked quite a pleasant set of men.

It was a graceful compliment, and Publius felt his heart warm to these Latin interlopers. To a meeting of ceremony the Sabines had of course brought their best armour and weapons, because in public a spearman carries his spear to show his status and anyway they none of them had long white cloaks of that fashion. To show that you trusted the truce-oath of strangers by coming unarmed to a conference was an elegant excess of politeness that would never enter the head of a plain, blunt Sabine spearman. All the same, it was a very good idea.

The two lines halted at a little distance, the two leaders embraced without dismounting, then King Romulus urged his horse forward so that all the visitors might hear his speech of welcome. But first he pointed to something on his right, and the Sabines craned to see it. At the foot of the Palatine stood a little square building of brick. It must be a storehouse of sacred things, for surrounding it they could see the peeled wands, stuck upright in the ground, that marked the limits of a consecrated templum. What a curious place to choose for the storage of sacred things, thought Publius; right out in the open, beyond the palisade, where any foe could break in.

King Romulus was explaining. "Friends, that building marks the spot where you nearly overcame me, when last you came to Rome. There I prayed to Jupiter the Stay of Armies, and he inspired my men to rally. In return I vowed to Jupiter that I would build a house for him to dwell in. That is the house, the dwelling of Jupiter Stator. Do you understand? Of course Jupiter has a templum, which I marked out with my own very lucky divining-staff. But within the templum we have built that house, of lasting brick, with the end open so that the god may come and go as he pleases. Inside an image of Jupiter reclines on a couch, and from time to time we carry in a table and put a good dinner before him. Jupiter seems pleased, for when I watch the birds he sends good omens. So now you know. That building is the house of a god, the first house built for a god in these parts. Don't go in if you have done anything that makes you ritually polluted. But whenever you look at it you can remember that it is a memorial to the courage of Latins and Sabines alike, who fought a drawn battle on this very plain; and that only a King who sees into the mind of a god as I do could have thought of building it. Your new home is under the special protection of the gods, and I interpret their will. This is a lucky city, ruled by a lucky King."

Ruled by a long-winded King, Publius thought privately. But it was a sound idea, all the same, to persuade the Stay of Armies to live in Rome and keep an eye on Rome's levies; and the building of the house on open ground below the palisade proved that King Romulus had confidence in the ability of his men to keep enemies at a distance. Perhaps this new plan of living cooped up with a lot of Latin foreigners would turn out better than he had expected.

King Romulus was speaking again. "Friends, you are very welcome. But my palisade is not big enough to hold us all, and I am sure you will feel more at your ease in a place of your own. For the present my people will remain on the Palatine, and you will build your huts and palisade on the Hill of the Spearmen over there, the Quirinal as we call it. But the two villages will remain one city, for our assembly will meet in this plain and all will be bound by the common decision. Here we are neither Latins nor Sabines, we are mere Romans. To prove it, let us gather at the assembly as individuals. Don't let me see men marching in a body from either hill. I beseech you," he added more gravely, "in this lucky meeting-place, beside the house of the god, be Romans, not Quirinals or Palatines. Only thus can our city endure."

"What about the ancestors?" called a voice from the Sabine

ranks. "The guardians of our clan may be served only by true clansmen. We don't want Latins sharing in our sacrifices."

King Romulus smiled candidly. "I had thought of that already. I have devised a plan, if King Tatius approves. We shall divide our citizens into three tribes. My followers are the Romulans, you will be the Tatians, and the rest, who are neither Latins nor Sabines, will be called Luceres after the Lucumo who is their most eminent leader. In these tribes you will manage your religious affairs. But the tribes will be concerned only with religion. When you gather here in the assembly, still more when you face the foe in arms, you must be Romans and nothing but Romans."

There was a murmur of approval. The service of the gods is a private thing, best managed by the kindred without interference from strangers. But in other matters, especially since they were not to be compelled to live cheek by jowl with foreign Latins, the Sabines would feel all the stronger for their membership of this double city.

Then the two leaders dismounted and walked apart to discuss practical affairs in private, while soothsayers said and did some very odd things to bring luck to the new union. Presently King Tatius sent messengers to summon a hundred men from among his followers, while the rest were dismissed to go with their families and baggage to the top of the Quirinal, where they might start building the palisade.

Publius saw that he must leave the choice of the site of his new home to Claudia, who would have chosen it anyway even if he had been beside her; for he was one of the hundred spearmen summoned to the presence of the King.

Tatius was flustered, which made him also a little angry. He was older than Romulus, and a more experienced warrior; but as chief of a Sabine clan practically his only duty was to lead his followers in battle, and he had no experience of ruling a community in peacetime. For the last half-hour he had been breathlessly trying to understand the novelties proposed by his younger colleague.

"Now, cousins," he barked stiffly at the hundred clansmen

who had come at his call, "this morning you were just spearmen, like all your other cousins and mine. From this moment you are elders and fathers. It's very sudden. Perhaps not all of you are the men I would have named if I had been given more time to pick and choose. But I know you will do your best. You see, King Romulus has a council of a hundred elders, who advise him how to rule his city. He suggested to me that the council should be doubled, so that we shall be leaders of a joint council of two hundred. He then asked me to have my advisers ready for the first meeting this afternoon. I didn't care to explain to him that in our clan there is only the chief and a great many equal spearmen. So I picked the hundred of you, and you must back me up. I don't think there is any more I need tell you. Of course you won't offer me advice unless I ask for it, and then I shall let you know what kind of advice I want to hear. No impudence or insubordination. Just because the Latins want us to form a council that's no excuse for weakening the authority of the head of the family. But you can pass on my orders to the rest of our cousins, and if anyone questions your right to command you can tell them that I, Tatius, chose you as elders. That's all, unless I have to remind you that when we join these Romans in their council you vote together, and vote as I tell you. Now go and build your huts, and sharp about it. Oh, one other thing. Has anyone a spare hacksaw he can lend me? My fool of a bailiff seems to have left mine behind."

No one had a spare hacksaw; they were costly imports, made only by foreign smiths beyond the eastern sea. Someone offered the loan of a chisel, and that would do nearly as well. Tatius, as head of the family, could command absolute obedience from his cousins; but they were sprung from the same ancestors, and it would not have occurred to any clansman that he ought to work for his ruler like a servant. Tatius must build his own hut, with the help of his slaves only; or sleep in the open.

The Quirinal was another steep-sided hill with a flat summit, like the Palatine; but it was larger, a long spur linked to the plateau on the north. There was plenty of room, even for a community of Sabines who did not care to live crowded together like Latins. Publius found Claudia and the ploughman trying to hammer in a cornerpost, while the slave-woman looked after the children. He approved the site they had chosen for the hut, and told them that he had been promoted to be some kind of Latin chieftain; then he left them to their dull and boring work while he went over to help with the construction of the palisade. That was a task for warriors, in which the help of women and slaves would be improper.

Women and children must have weather-proof huts, and in a few days the Sabines were soundly covered. The spearmen were more interested in the allocation of new ploughlands; unless their fields were more fertile, and larger, than those they had left in their native woodlands the move must be pronounced a mistake. On the whole they were satisfied with what had been provided for them.

Publius was more than satisfied. His allotment was two full ploughlands of cleared ground, and a section of forest which he might clear whenever he needed to grow more barley. It was more than twice as much as he had possessed at home, and he thanked King Tatius most gratefully.

"You should thank those fine greaves of yours," the King answered with a grin. "It's the standard allotment for a Father and councillor, as these Latins call you. I don't think King Romulus understands that my following is a single clan; their Latin clans are much smaller. He told me he had a council of a hundred heads of families, and invited me to add a hundred of my own advisers. There was no time to explain that all my warriors are equal, so I picked my hundred then and there. To make up the number I had to hunt around, and your fine greaves caught my eye. A man who wears such armour must be important, or so any Latin will suppose. I hope you enjoy your new dignity. Now don't take offence. Of course you deserve it, at least as much as those Latin boys who follow Romulus. He's a good leader, and we get on well together; but he has an absurd liking for pompous names. His advisers must be the Fathers, the Council of Elders; and not one of them is forty years old.

At that I suppose they are the eldest Latins in Rome. Well, you elders hold office for life, and I suppose eventually time will mend it."

"As far as I can tell after these few meetings," said Publius, "the Council really discusses things, while the assembly only listens to speeches and then votes Yes or No. We are partners in the government, the common citizens can only obey."

"They could disobey, of course," answered the King. "But I don't see why they should, unless we do something that really annoys them. We can always manage them, so long as we let them hear only one side of every question. But to manage the assembly the whole Senate must stick together. Don't you begin to think up ideas of your own."

"Of course not, cousin. You are head of the family. Every Tatian will vote as you desire, in the Senate or in the assembly. That means that we Sabines will in fact govern Rome. Our vote is solid while those flighty Latins are often divided."

"That's broadly true, but you mustn't push it to extremes. We can't control the third party, the Luceres. We haven't any of that ragtag in the Senate, but they all vote in the assembly. They feel no loyalty to anyone, least of all to the Lucumo who led them here. It boils down to this: we are in control, but we must go very gently. Let the other fellow have his way if he feels strongly and you don't. That's a good maxim for the rulers of any city; but especially good for the rulers of a mixed community gathered from all the ends of the earth. Heed my advice, cousin, and think it over as you plough your land. I expect you want to be ploughing now, and I won't detain you. Remember, back me up when it comes to voting in the Senate."

"Good-bye, cousin. You can always count on my vote," answered Publius cheerfully. Romulans and Luceres addressed their kings as 'my lord'; but a free Sabine spearman was the cousin of his ruler. The thought was comforting.

The soil of the Latin plain was not quite the same in texture as the hilly clearings which had been the homeland of the Sabines. Properly managed, it was even more fruitful; but the newcomers were glad to listen to advice from the earlier settlers. The land over the southern border of Publius' holding had been allotted to a Latin named Marcus Aemilius, a friendly unpresuming little man who did not try to hide the fact that he was an Aemilian only by adoption; though he claimed that he had been born into one of the lesser Latin clans. He was very pleasant—correctly deferential to Publius Tatius the eminent Sabine Senator, and condescendingly kind to the ploughman, himself a Latin who had disgraced his manhood when he accepted servitude instead of death in battle. Marcus walked through the fields with their new owner and his servant, and gave very practical advice on draining and weeding. Only at the end of the day did he mention shyly that his wife was one of the stolen Sabine women, perhaps even a relation of the distinguished Publius. "For when I married her by force she would not tell me her name. I had to call her something, so I called her Sabina. Now we are very good friends, and she has no secrets from me. But still I don't know the name of her kindred, for she says that she likes the name I gave her on our wedding night and does not wish to change it. She will be Sabina until she dies. Perhaps your wife, noble Publius, will call on her and tell her the news of her old home."

"Certainly I will ask my Claudia to visit her. I can't do more than ask, you will remember. Here in Rome we must obey Roman laws, and I may not control my wife's visits. Even if I meet her among the huts I must make way for her." Publius smiled at the absurdity of this law, which none the less he obeyed as a loyal spearman should.

"It isn't exactly a law, it's the King's decree. King Romulus promulgated it as some expiation of the wrong we did in stealing our wives. It's a good law, all the same, and we live quite comfortably under it. I suppose your presence here shows that the wrong is now forgiven, but we need not change a custom which works well."

"You Romans are so gentle with one another!" said Publius, with a laugh that had an undertone of exasperation. "In my village the five householders were all cousins, bound by ties of blood. But if two cousins quarrel, as happens often enough, they may fight with their fists, or throw stones; though of course they may not strike with deadly weapons. Here if you give a fellow-citizen a black eye you will be hauled before the assembly. It's hard to remember that a few years ago you started as a collection of brigands."

"I expect it's always like that in a city," answered Marcus. "In fact a city could not endure under any other way of life. Latins have been living in cities for centuries, and we know how it must be done."

"Well, what do you get out of living in this city? We work just as hard as any villager, and we never go raiding as I thought we would. We have to waste time at these talkative assemblies, and then when we are at home we can't do as we like for fear of annoying the neighbours."

"I don't know," said Marcus slowly. "I have no other home, and I rather like living here. The children are safe from slave-raiders, and they grow up with plenty of friends. I wouldn't go back to my village even if my father sent for me. You get used to the crowd, and it's pleasant always having someone to talk to. Besides, here in this city we share in all the wonderful luck that marked its foundation."

"Oh yes, that luck. I suppose there's something in it. But we don't seem to share it much. Generally we go off to placate the gods separately, in our clans and tribes."

"There are ceremonies for the city as a whole. Most of them come at the opening of the year, and you won't see them until winter is ending. But we try to share the luck among all the citizens."

"I've heard of your chariot-race. Every Sabine has heard of it. I wonder you have the nerve to repeat it every autumn as you do. As for the other ceremonies, I shall wait until I see them. If they seem to me suitable to the dignity of a Sabine spearman I shall take part, if not I shall leave them alone."

"They are good ceremonies. I am sure that when the time comes you will be glad to join in."

THE COMING OF THE SABINES

As autumn merged into winter Publius found that living in a crowd was not nearly so irksome as he had expected. His hut was private enough, except that his neighbours could hear all that went on inside. But no one entered without an invitation, and he soon discovered that it was not good manners to refer to anything overheard from outside. Even when he had occasion to flog his ploughman no one spoke of the loud groans which must have been heard on every side. In fact there was more privacy here in Rome than in his native village, for here there was always so much going on that the people next door had something else to interest them; in the village everyone discussed any activity out of the ordinary.

There was ample space on the Quirinal, and his hut had two rooms besides a lean-to for the slaves. These slaves disliked one another, for the woman was a Ligurian savage and the man a low-class Latin and their habits were widely different; but of course they must sleep together, since the woman was still young enough to breed. It was bad luck that she so hated her mate that so far no child had appeared. Slave-women often cheated their owners in this way; it was said that they used a secret spell, unknown to the free, which kept them sterile.

In the hut proper the first room contained the hearth, the corn-bin, and the racks for weapons and armour; this was the general living-room, where visitors were received. The inner room, with its great marriage-bed, was the private domain of Claudia and the children; even her husband asked permission before entering it, and no other man was admitted. But, in accordance with the free customs of Rome, she might entertain ladies there without first asking her husband.

Claudia had struck up a close friendship with the wife of Marcus, whose only name was still Sabina. "She's a nice little thing, and a good mother; two children at her skirt, and a third on the way, for all that she looks such a baby herself," Claudia told her husband. "Of course I thought to begin with that she must have something to hide. It seems odd not to tell your true name to fellow-countrymen, even if you want to keep it secret from Latins. But now I am sure she is a genuine Sabine, and free born. Her manner shows it. She sticks to it that she won't have her name known because her father and uncles have never formally made peace with Rome, and she doesn't want them to continue the blood-feud. That seems reasonable. If her kin never hear of her they will forget the vengeance due. I shall keep on calling her Sabina, even though the name hardly makes sense with so many Sabines in Rome."

"I suppose you are right," said Publius doubtfully. "A wife joins the clan of her husband and breaks with her father's kin. The odd part of it is that she should consider Marcus her lawful husband, when you recall how shamefully he stole her."

"I doubt whether he had to run very fast to catch her, at that chariot-race which they keep on telling us we must forget. Perhaps she didn't like any of the boys in her own village. Anyway, she is quite absurdly devoted to her foreign husband."

"What's this? I don't see anything absurd in wifely devotion. When we lived at home we took it for granted. And if they keep on telling you to forget the treachery of the Consualia, you ought not to need telling that we mustn't call our Latin fellow-citizens foreigners."

"You're just as bad," Claudia answered cheerfully, "calling our old village home. We have a new home now, where our children will live after us."

"If the place lasts. There isn't much sense in founding a city here, right on the border of the Etruscans, unless we are going to sack Etruscan cities. But the Kings won't let us go raiding. We shall have to rely on that famous luck which seems to be the private possession of King Romulus. Perhaps that will see us through. Certainly the Latins here take enough trouble to propitiate the gods with their queer ceremonies."

There were a number of these ceremonies, and presently one of them nearly led to a quarrel between the two palisaded settlements which were trying so hard to become one city. The worst of the winter was over, the days were lengthening and the ground drying. Every farmer could see that it was time for the barley to show above ground.

Publius felt excited and unsettled. His ploughlands were in

good shape, clean and adequately drained; but only when the barley began to sprout would he know for certain that this earth had accepted him. It was not the first time he had felt this tension; three times since his childhood his native community had shifted to fresh ploughlands among the beech-woods, and on each occasion there had been this period of anxious waiting, until the old men announced that the rites of growth had been satisfactorily performed. He was waiting for King Romulus to make the announcement. It was due. For the last ten days women and girls had been weaving baskets of plaited osiers and putting into them things which no man might see.

Claudia must know when the time of purification would be officially proclaimed. Her face bore a secretive smile; she was always washing herself all over, putting on clean clothes, and going off to meet the other women by the spring. Once she had taken the slave-woman with her; though that disobliging wench still showed no sign of fruitfulness, and would surely set a bad example to any field in which she made magic. Publius would not ask indiscreet questions of his wife, and if he did she would not answer them. There is a life of men and a life of women, and they should be kept separate.

The morning came when he knew that something must happen; for both Claudia and the slave-woman got up early, washed carefully, and dressed in their best clothes. They made no effort to leave the hut, but stood about in the doorway, apparently waiting for something.

Publius had planned to go down to his ploughland and poke about with a stick, ostensibly to check how the drainage was working but really because he could not be happy at this critical time unless he was handling the earth he would presently harvest. Now he decided to wait and see what the women would do.

Claudia did not seem to mind his presence. He sat on a stool, pretending to tighten the rivet on a spearhead and watching her. She was listening for something; from the cock of her head she was listening for a distant sound, not for some noise just outside the hut.

They all heard it together, the howling of wolves beyond the palisade. The children began to whimper. Publius reached over for his shield, and for a better spear. He looked longingly towards his fine greaves glistening on the arms-rack. While chasing wolves you could not wear greaves, for they hampered your running; but if the wolves were chasing you, as seemed now to be the case, they might be a most useful protection.

He listened again, and called softly to his wife: "When I am gone bar the door and hide little Publius at the bottom of the corn-bin. That's not wolves howling. That's men, using the wolf-howl for a warcry. I can't understand how they got so close without being seen, but they seem to have pulled off a neat surprise."

He was trying desperately hard not to betray his fear. It was one thing to get ready for a charge, with warcries and magical rites and plenty of time to let the idea sink in; and quite another to hear the shouts of the enemy unexpectedly, while breakfast was still on the table. But when a palisade is attacked the only reply is to defend it; it is already too late for flight.

Claudia answered him calmly: "Yes, it's men, and we have been expecting them. They did it so well that for a moment I mistook them for real wolves, and felt frightened. This is the service of the gods, and nothing to worry about. Now we all stand outside our huts, and the Wolf-men bring us luck. It's women's business, that's why I didn't warn you earlier."

At once relieved and angry, Publius moved slowly to the door of the hut. The women, more eager, crowded before him. It annoyed him that his family had seen him surprised and perhaps dismayed. He had a good mind to beat his wife, or flog the slave-woman. But he knew that in fact he would not, once he had got over his surprise; and he had sense enough not to make any threat that he could not carry out in cold blood.

The alley filled, as its inhabitants poured out of their huts to see what was going on; but by this time the Sabines were used to living in a thronged city, and without instructions they left a narrow passage in the middle. Publius heard a roar of joyful cheering coming nearer and nearer; then whatever it was came round the corner into view, and he craned to look.

To his horror, he saw four naked youths leaping towards him. They were not entirely naked, for on their heads and shoulders were the tattered remnants of goatskins, and they waved other bloody strips in their hands. But below the shoulder they wore nothing.

Howling like wolves, the young men bounded up. One stopped before Publius, turning to face him. Publius naturally tried to stand in front of his wife and baby daughter, to spare them from shock. But the women stubbornly pushed in front of him, even little Pomponia and the slave-woman. They smiled up at the naked figure, their arms open as though to embrace him.

The young man bounded obscenely, waving his strip of new-flayed skin until drops of blood fell all about. Publius dived back into the hut to fetch his sword, but when he came out again the figure had moved on. Now all the women on the Quirinal were howling like wolves, the naked youths darted from alley to alley, and bewildered Sabine fathers of families stood about helplessly, trying to shoo away the indecent intruders.

It was over as suddenly as it had begun. With a final howl the naked men fled out by the farther gate; they could be seen crossing the valley on their way back to the Latin settlement on the Palatine.

Publius wasted no time. He picked up his spear, to show he came on public business, and went at once in search of King Tatius.

Already a group of angry spearmen stood round the royal hut, and more were arriving every minute. When the King came out Publius, remembering that he was a Senator, spoke up for all the men of the injured clan.

"Cousin, you must lead us at once to the sack of the Palatine. Those Latins have insulted every respectable wife in our clan. Their young men pranced naked all over the city, thrusting their revolting nudity into our faces. They howled like wolves as they did it, as though to proclaim that they behaved as wild animals rather than men. We must have vengeance at once, today."

Tatius grinned. It was a deadly insult to his clansmen, but there was no other word for his expression. "Be easy, cousins," he said with a chuckle. "That was a most sacred religious ceremony. The Latins do it every spring, because it makes their women fruitful. They run about like wolves, since they are the nurslings of the she-wolf. That blood from the goatskin gives children to any woman on whom it is sprinkled. The young men must be naked; it's part of the rite. Now it won't happen again until this time next year. Surely there's nothing in that to make you wage war on your fellow-citizens?"

"Cousin, I won't have it," Publius repeated stubbornly. "We know, every husband knows, that women have their private ceremonies to make them fertile, and that some of these ceremonies are unseemly. The women go apart to do these things, where men cannot see them. But this is a matter of Latin strangers running up to our wives in the presence of their husbands and children, before all the city. It is an insult, and must be punished. If you command us to keep the peace, we shall obey the head of the family. That is to say, we shall obey you this time, in case the Latins did not realize that their conduct would be resented. But next year, if those naked sons of the she-wolf come here again, I shall stick my spear into the belly of the first rascal who goes near my wife; and I shall do so even if you have ordered me to keep the peace."

"Very well, cousin, if you are so earnest in this unimportant matter," said the King with an anxious frown. "I am the head of the family, but I cannot override the opinion of all my kindred. I shall speak to King Romulus about it. Now tell me, which part of the affair seems to you objectionable? We must keep up something of the sort, if we want our wives to have babies. Is it that the men come uninvited, or that they are naked, or that they sprinkle the women without first asking permission from their husbands?"

"None of these things," shouted another angry Sabine husband. "They are Latins—foreigners. That's what I can't abide."

"And why should they call themselves especially the sons of the she-wolf?" Publius added. "The wolf is the beast of Mars, and Mars is not the private god of the Latins. He's just as much the father of the Sabines."

93

THE COMING OF THE SABINES

"If that's the main trouble I can easily alter it," said King Tatius, relieved. "Next year we shall have two lots of Lupercals, sons of the she-wolf. The Latins can bring fertility to their own women on the Palatine, and we on the Quirinal shall welcome young Sabines as luck-bringers. Will that suit you, cousins, and persuade you not to destroy this promising city by civil war? Though, mind you, I would be happier if you would permit the Latins to perform the rite on behalf of us all. I don't like to see two of everything in one city, as though we were allies and not fellow-citizens."

"Then why have two kings, if the Latins are to be our leaders?" shouted a rough anonymous voice from the back of the crowd. King Tatius could not think of a crushing answer on the spur of the moment; with a frown of anger he went back to his hut. Even the head of the family must endure a great deal of backchat from free and independent Sabine spearmen.

The new arrangement was solemnly ratified at the next assembly. Henceforth there would be two sets of Lupercals, Latin and Sabine. In addition, just to remind posterity that Rome had begun as a double city in which two nations had equal rights, there would in future be two teams of the Dancers of Mars. These were the young men who in springtime danced about the city with shield and spear, to ask a blessing on the campaign of that summer.

The more responsible leaders disliked this emphasis on the double origin of the city. In particular, the two teams of Dancers were likely to urge their supporters to embark on separate campaigns. But the Tatians would not be content with less. They were not getting on very happily with the Latins, and if there had not been a third party, the Luceres, to help in keeping the peace, there might have been another stand-up fight on the old battleground.

The Lucumo let it be known that he would lead his men against whichever party began a civil war, and that just kept Rome united. Things jogged on, uncomfortably.

94

Chapter 6

ENVOYS FROM LAVINIUM

★

Five years later Publius Tatius was at last chosen one of the Dancers of Mars (the choice was made by Mars himself, who arranged that his chosen candidate should draw a marked pebble from a pile of little stones in a cooking-pot). He was delighted that the choice should have fallen on him before it was too late; for in his thirty-sixth year he was growing a little old for such an energetic ceremony, and it had begun to look as though Mars would pass him over. When he came home elated to tell Claudia she guessed that perhaps King Tatius, supervising the draw, had helped Mars to make his tactful choice.

Publius at once went into strict training, determined that when the time came he would dance as well as any of his younger colleagues. It was towards the end of an unusually severe winter, but nevertheless he ate sparingly and went out for runs in the open country. When the Lupercals next ran through the settlement on the Quirinal he watched their performance with a critical eye. These young men were now his Sabine kinsmen; though he still felt a shock when a naked youth wagged his belly at Claudia and the slave-woman he accepted it in good part as necessary for the continuance of the city. The ceremony had proved its worth; the slave-woman was now the mother of three brats, and in his own hut two sons would carry on his line and two daughters would presently by marriage extend the bounds of his kindred.

So many things were necessary to assure the continuance of

Rome; though now it seemed that the city had achieved permanence. After twelve years of existence it was already older than most of the villages among the Sabine hills, quickly built and soon abandoned in the search for fresh soil. Walking back from his exercise in the waste Publius looked up at the weathered palisades, and thought that the sere stakes crowning the grass-covered earthen banks might have been there since the beginning of the world. Grooves worn by waggon-wheels and the sharp hoofs of oxen scored deeply into the hillside. The track leading to the ford in the river had been repaired with stone in the Latin manner until it looked almost like a wall laid on its side. In the valley the little brick house, which it was hoped might be the favourite residence of Jupiter Stator, had lost its rawness; the citizens no longer thought it odd to visit a god who lay on a couch as though taking his ease at the dinner-table. Beside the templum the many meetings of the assembly had left their mark on the earth; a trampled circle showed bare, with in the midst a platform of turf from which the kings might address their obedient spearmen. Publius found it hard to believe that when he was one of the older boys in his village, trusted to guard cattle, all this valley had lain unpeopled.

Yes, Rome had come to stay. But it was not the kind of city he had thought to join when he brought his family and his cattle from the Sabine woods. He had come with reluctance, solely because there seemed to be no other way of ending a savage blood-feud with a powerful neighbour. Either the Tatians must avenge the stealing of their women by perpetual war, a war which would leave them no time to harvest their fields or tend their cattle; or they must seize this unlooked-for chance of an honourable peace. There had been a third course open to them, to admit defeat and conclude a dishonourable peace; but no one had been bold enough, in the council of the spearmen, to propose such a disgraceful treaty.

Sabine daughters, interceding for peace between their fathers and their husbands, had been potent ambassadors; the prospect of peace without dishonour was tempting; but no one would have agreed to the migration but for the further hope—that they would be welcomed as reinforcements by a successful band of brigands. Here was this new city, founded by desperate ruffians who had been cast out even from those ruffianly Latin settlements; daringly, they had built their palisade on the very border of the rich Etruscans, beside the easiest ford in the river. Only brigands would choose to live in such an exposed fortress; but for courageous brigands it might turn out to be a rewarding base.

The first spring in their new home had brought disillusion. The Dancers of Mars went out, capering and casting spears into the air; but no matter in which direction the fallen spears should point, King Romulus declared that the enemy who lived over there were too strong to be raided. Or if the enemy were not too strong, then they were not the enemy; for these Latins were hemmed in by kinsmen from whom they refused to steal so much as a pig. To the south, on the marshy coast, lived only a few very poor Latin shepherds; south-east were the Latin cities; to the north-east was the great range of the Sabine hills. If you might not raid kinsmen, that left only the Etruscans. It soon became evident that King Romulus and his mongrel subjects were afraid of the wealthy Etruscans, skilled in magic.

King Tatius also was to blame. Instead of stiffening the spirits of the odds-and-ends who obeyed King Romulus, he had meekly followed his colleague's lead. He also spoke in the assembly for peace, telling his disappointed cousins that they should live by growing barley on the rich Latin plain, so much more fertile and easy to work than the clearings in their native forests.

For five years a clan of free Sabines had been living by the plough, eating only the fruit of their own labour. All summer they sweated in the fields beside their slaves; and in winter they ate carefully, measuring the corn-bins that must last until the next harvest. In the hills other Sabines, warriors who had been wise enough to refuse the deceptive shelter of this tall palisade, feasted on beef and wine, which tasted the sweeter when it had been bought with blood. That was the right life for a warrior. Someone ought to propose in full assembly that the Tatians drop the proud ancestral title of Spearmen, and call themselves the Ploughmen of the Tatian clan. That might shock the lazy youngsters into a sense of their unworthiness.

Publius had devised an even better plan. Mars had chosen him to be a dancer. He would dance to such effect that an army must follow him.

When spring was well advanced the great day came round. Long ago Mars had shown the ancestors how free men should pass the summer. The barley was in the ground, and could be left to grow by itself; the army must be home for harvest, but now was the time to raid your enemies. First you must honour Mars, so that he would protect your fields in your absence. But this annual dance was in intention only a prologue; the rite would not be complete until the army had taken plunder.

This year, when the Dancers would be led by a veteran warrior who was also a Senator of this new-fangled town, the rite would be carried to completion.

At cockcrow, when the first streak of light showed low in the eastern sky, Publius slipped silently out of the great marriage bed and in silence tiptoed from his hut, wearing only the loincloth in which he had slept. His whole family knew that he had been chosen as leader of the Dancers, and after the lots were drawn friends had congratulated him on his luck; when Claudia awoke she would know why he was missing. Even so, the Dancers were not individual spearmen; they were the Tatian clan in arms, seeking help from their supernatural protector. He was no longer Publius, a middling farmer and one of the poorer but more respected of the Senators; he was the embodiment of his clan, forgotten ancestors and unborn children as well as his own contemporaries. It would seem unfitting, it might even be impious, if he took leave of his wife and went openly to take his part in the rite.

Silently he crept through the shadows until he reached the gate; it stood ajar, and the watchman gazed at the sky as he slipped out. His bare feet made no sound as he drifted like a ghost down the hillside. Already the magic of the day was working in him; he felt himself to be not a particular man but a representative of helpless humanity, wandering unarmed through the dark to seek the help of his advocate in the sky, the advocate who would grant him weapons and the courage to face his enemies.

It was mildly distressing that he must cross the wide, bare place of assembly, and creep in through the half-opened gate of the Palatine. He would have felt better if he could have gone to array himself in the sacred insignia in a wholly Sabine storehouse. But everyone agreed that Romulus was endowed with exceptional luck, and that he knew more about the ways of the gods than anyone else in those parts. In the double city of Rome there was only one storehouse of sacred things, and that stood next door to the hut of King Romulus.

The storehouse was a tall round building, whose roof sloped to a point. There were no windows; the door, set high in the wall so that it could be reached only by scrambling up notches cut in a tree-trunk, was so small that you must crouch to enter. But since the storehouse was constructed of thin poles set close together, without clay or plaster, in the daytime enough light entered by the chinks for a man to see what he was doing. Now, with dawn breaking outside, the interior would have been pitch dark but that King Romulus and King Tatius each held a torch as they climbed about the narrow gallery high under the roof, taking down the sacred things which hung in clusters from the rafters.

The Dancers arrived punctually, clambering in one after the other. There were twelve of them in all, six for each half of the community. Publius no longer felt himself to be a mere man alone, seeking help from the gods against a dangerous world; he was now part of the army of the Tatians, with kinsmen to guard his back. But still he was not Publius the father of Publius; he was any spearman of the clan, or rather all the spearmen.

The kings remained on their high perch, handing down sacred things to their own followers. Each dancer received a little leather cap with a bronze knob on top; that had been the helmet used by the ancestors, in the days when every fragment of metal was precious. Then the kings gave each man his dancing-spear; these were purely ritual objects, which even the ancestors could not have used in battle. Their leaf-shaped heads were of bronze, chased into intricate patterns; the shafts, too short even for javelins, made them look like divining-staffs rather than weapons.

Last of all came the most important and sacred piece of equipment, the twelve bronze shields, said to be copied from the shield carried by Father Mars himself when he goes to war. They were heavy metal objects, two discs joined one above the other to form a figure of eight; the bronze, green with age, had been hammered into a pattern of writhing serpents with terrible open jaws. With a solemn expression, and solemn thoughts, Publius passed his left arm through the upper grip and grasped the lower in his hand. He had never held such a thing before, and he feared that the unusual weight might unbalance his dancing. But now he was truly a Dancer, a link in the chain of generations that handed on the favour of Mars from the first ancestors to unborn posterity; for all that he was terribly excited, he could feel the strength of Mars stiffening his muscles and filling his lungs with deep unhurried breath.

Within the storehouse not a word was spoken. All the Dancers were perfect in their ritual, and they needed no instruction. As soon as they were equipped they scrambled outside, and when the last had emerged the kings drew up the notched pole. During the ceremony they would remain alone in the storehouse, hoping that the mind of Mars would speak to their minds and inspire them with sound plans for the next campaign.

In silence the six Sabines trotted through the Palatine, across the valley, and into their own settlement on the Quirinal. Everything had been done punctually, and as the sun rose they were in position at the edge of the open templum in the midst of the huts. They stood in silence, waiting for Publius to give the signal.

Sunlight, moving over the beech-woods below, crept nearer; at last it flashed in his eyes. Publius gathered himself together and bounded high in the air as he leaped inside the consecrated templum. As he leapt he drummed on the bronze shield with the haft of his dancing-spear.

Behind him his comrades leaped. The smitten shields pealed like thunder. The spearmen of the clan hurried from their huts to watch the luck of Mars brought down to their settlement.

Unto noon the strenuous ceremony continued. Wherever two alleys met the Dancers drummed on their shields and called on Mars while they leapt exactly twenty times. Publius kept careful reckoning, and only once was he compelled to repeat the rite because a Dancer had shouted Mars when he should have used his other name, Marmar. Between leapings they trotted silently to the next crossroad, until the whole settlement had been blessed and they must descend to bring luck to the ploughlands. With never a pause for rest they ran or leapt, and the bronze shields were heavy; but Mars gave them breath to carry out their duty. At last they reached the farthest field, a new clearing ploughed for the first time. Publius was drenched with sweat, so dizzy with fatigue that he could hardly see, his lungs labouring. But this was the most important rite of the day, the final performance from which the clan would draw omens for the coming year. He would give them a worthy omen, one that even the cautious King Romulus could not ignore. His twentieth leap was as high and vigorous as his first; his strokes on the shield kept time with the chant, and he pronounced the right words in the right order.

The crowd of spectators fell silent. Gathering his remaining strength, he hurled his dancing-spear into the sky.

Mars, he had decided, must be helped to make up his mind. The rite demanded that he throw the spear upwards, so that it should fall wherever chance, or the will of Mars, might decree. But if you did that a malicious ghost would sometimes make nonsense of the whole ceremony by turning the spear-point towards your own hut, or making the sacred weapon fall butt downwards. The dancing-spear had been in his hands for nearly five hours; it was a badly balanced toy, too heavy in the head, but he thought he understood it. The weighty head made the spear turn end over end as it flashed through the sky, but Publius had judged its flight correctly. It fell with the point embedded deeply in the soft earth, and it pointed unmistakably to the south-east.

There was a gasp of satisfaction from the assembled clan.

The next meeting of the Senate was noisy and bad-tempered. As soon as the Fathers were in session King Romulus proposed that for this year again there should be peace with all their neighbours. Young men, if they wanted to, might steal cattle on the Etruscan side of the river; but they must not raid under the wolf-ensign which was the communal standard of Rome. If the Etruscans caught them they would not be avenged by the city. On the Sabine and Latin frontiers not even this private raiding would be allowed. The programme for the summer, the thirteenth of Rome's existence, would be peace and sound farming, and a welcome for newcomers capable of bearing arms. Let the spearmen be patient a little longer; presently they would be strong enough to sack a rich Etruscan city.

As he finished half a dozen Sabines clamoured to be heard. "The Dancers," they shouted, "the Dancers of Mars. The god commanded us to make war. He showed us our prey. We must obey the omen."

Anxious to still the confusion, King Tatius looked down the ranks of his cousins and called on the sound and obedient Publius to address the meeting. Publius, not a good speaker, normally stood silent in the Senate; but today he was so full of what he knew must be done that words poured out of him.

"Mars has shown us the way, assembled Fathers. I was chief Dancer, I carried the wise spear. I saw the omen. You must believe me, it was the doing of the god. The spear came down with its point completely buried in the earth. That is the signal for all-out war, war to the knife, as we all know. It pointed south-east, to Latin land. I have checked the line, and now I know that it pointed straight at the pastures of Lavinium, a city no stronger than Rome, a city rich in cattle. If we raid

Lavinium Mars will grant us riches; if we remain disgracefully
at peace we shall be disobeying the command of our protector
in heaven. Now, what shall we recommend to the assembly?
It is for you to decide, Fathers, after you have heard the advice
of the Kings. King Romulus has already advised us. What is
the advice of King Tatius?"

King Tatius frowned. This was not what he had expected
when he called on a level-headed middle-aged father of a
family; he had picked on Publius as a speaker because usually
he bored the Fathers and that made them willing to do whatever
the kings suggested.

"King Romulus and I did not see this omen," he began
slowly, choosing his words with care. "All that morning we
remained in the sacred storehouse, in silent meditation. In the
storehouse Mars said nothing to us, so the omen may not have
come from him. If my young cousins want to steal a few Latin
cows I shan't object, but I won't lead the Tatian clan to war
against these neighbours who have never harmed us."

"My men won't even raid them," Romulus interrupted
brusquely. "We are as much the kin of these Lavinians as you
Tatians are kin to one another. To make war on them would
be impious. It would be bad policy as well, for our best hope
of gathering recruits is that adventurous Latins should join us.
If we quarrel with the Latins we shall never be strong enough
to invade Etruria."

"But Mars commanded it," Publius objected. "The spear told
us to make war on Lavinium. That is what happened. But the
spear must point somewhere at the end of the dance. If you had
already decided that this summer we must live in peace, why
did you send out the Dancers to seek a propitious enemy?"

"Perhaps that was a mistake," answered Romulus with a
cheerful shrug. "You Sabines take omens so seriously. Of course
every year we must dance for Mars, or he might forget us when
one day we need him. But we shan't make a campaign every
summer of our lives; for this year peace suits us better than war.
There's no need for further discussion. Let's vote, and then
recommend our decision to the assembly. I advise peace,

Publius is for war. Do you agree, King Tatius, that we have debated this question long enough?"

"I think it's time we had a war, King Romulus. We'll never get anywhere if we just sit quiet and reap our own fields. But I can't expect your men to rob their own kin, and in fact it would be disgusting if they did. So since your men won't fight the Lavinians we can't have this particular war. I'm sorry, cousins," he added in an aside to his own followers, "but on this occasion only I must vote for peace. Perhaps next year we can have a nice little war."

"You see that King Tatius supports me. As a rule the majority vote as I recommend. You have heard both sides and there is no more to be said." Romulus spoke hastily, as usual stifling debate when it seemed that it might go against him. "We'll take the vote straight away. Remember that you are all bound by the decision, whether you agree with it or not."

In fact they did not vote by show of hands. The Senate very rarely divided, even to settle the most controversial questions; for men troubled with conflicting loyalties do not like to declare themselves openly. Instead all the Latin Senators, and a fair proportion of the Sabines, moved over to stand behind the kings. Publius and a group of his friends remained stubbornly in their places until it was obvious that they were outnumbered; then they also moved over, sulkily, so that it might be proclaimed that the Senate had decided unanimously.

At the next meeting of the assembly the decision for peace was ratified without trouble. Many spearmen did not like it, but no one was hardy enough to oppose two kings and the unanimous verdict of the Senate.

For Publius that was the end of the matter. His duties as a citizen of Rome and as a loyal follower of King Tatius pulled in the same direction, and the double obligation was too strong for his private wishes. In sad disappointment he went back to the weary round of farming, weeding his fields, tinkering with his drains, taking his turn at guarding the communal herd of oxen.

But he did not consider it part of his duty to warn the kings that a raid was being planned in defiance of their orders. Romulus had his three hundred overbearing celeres to tell him of approaching trouble; perhaps King Tatius would not be grateful if early information compelled him to prevent a raid of which he did not really disapprove. There were daring young men among the Tatians who were determined to follow the omen of the spear. Quietly, more than a hundred of them stole out of the city; ten days later they returned, driving a herd of raided cattle.

Everyone who lived on the Quirinal, with the doubtful exception of King Tatius, had known all about the raid before it began. The returning warriors were greeted by an enthusiastic crowd, while sullen Latins looked on in disapproval from the Palatine. The beasts came from Lavinium, as anyone could see from their brands. These Tatians had openly defied a resolution passed in due form by the assembly.

At the next meeting of the Senate King Romulus talked of nothing but ritual preparation for the coming harvest. No one suggested that the lawbreakers be punished, and the raid was not mentioned. However, the subject was glanced at in passing; no one could mistake the reference when King Tatius said casually, ostensibly while discussing the place of family ties in the harvest rejoicings: "The bonds of kinship are a strong force, as we all agree. The family must support all its members, even when some of these members are in the wrong. But there is another force, stronger than the tie of kinship, the bond that unites fellow-citizens. To save the city I would, if need be, turn even against my kin. I hope such a painful dilemma will never be forced upon me."

"In other words, the raiders are forgiven but they mustn't do it again," whispered a young Latin Father who stood near Publius. The unfortunate affair seemed to be decently buried.

It was not. While they were all at work in the fields, getting in a very good harvest, look-outs reported the approach of strangers. There were not enough of them to be raiders, and they walked openly along the track; presently it could be seen that they carried tall staves, wreathed in greenstuff. Closer scouting made it certain that they were an embassy of ten envoys, with a number of servants.

In theory every spearman knew all about embassies, the etiquette of their reception and the privileges of envoys; that was part of the education of every warrior. In fact an embassy was a rare event; none of the Tatians had seen one since the disastrous occasion when the Latins of Rome had come in search of Sabine wives. When the facts were known all work stopped in the fields, and the spearmen were called to the muster by the roaring of bronze trumpets, as though an enemy were in sight.

The citizens mustered in arms, because that was how you answered an unexpected summons in the middle of the day. Then a few celeres bustled about, proclaiming that it was bad manners to receive envoys fully armed, and that everyone must climb the hill again to put his shield away. But there was no time for the double journey, since the embassy was already in sight.

Armed, the citizens formed automatically in their ranks, because that seemed to be the obvious thing to do. The nobles were mounted, and the two Kings also appeared on horseback. When the envoys stalked into the place of assembly they saw before them the whole levy of Rome, ready for immediate battle.

The envoys were not dismayed. They looked a little angry, for this was not a courteous form of reception; but their leader at once began his speech, in the Latin language that was close enough to Sabine to be understood by all his hearers.

"King Romulus," he said without preamble, "we are sent by King Aulus of Lavinium to inquire whether you and your Romans are at war with us, or whether you wish to remain at peace so that you may come unhindered to our festival. If you are at war with us, you have committed a grave fault in not sending heralds to proclaim the opening of the campaign. But we shall excuse the ignorance of the rulers of a new city, and defend ourselves with all the means in our power. But if you desire peace with our city, a city which no god-fearing Latin should injure, then you must at once return the stolen plunder, and in our sight punish the robbers."

King Romulus frowned at the ranks of his followers. "Go away, all of you," he called angrily, "and come here this evening, decently unarmed. This is a grave matter, and I must take the advice of my councillors. Sir," he turned to the envoy, "I go now to decide on my answer, with my Senate. This evening our decision must be ratified, or perhaps rejected, by the spearmen of the city. If you will pitch your tents here, just outside the templum dedicated to Jupiter Stator, you will receive my answer in the morning. Come with me, Senators. Get your friends to carry your arms back up the hill. We must talk about this at once, and it won't look decent if you come armed to a meeting of the Senate."

Publius had of course taken post among his nearest kin of the Tatian clan, for when preparing for battle it is always wise to have a faithful cousin on your unshielded right side. This cousin could be trusted to take home his weapons, even the precious greaves; he handed them over and went straight to the Senate House.

The Senate House, in spite of its name, was a mere unroofed enclosure; no one could roof a room big enough to hold two hundred councillors. But there would be no point in picking a council of elders to discuss grave matters in private if any casual spearman could overhear their deliberations. In the valley between the Palatine and Quirinal, some distance from the river-bank, stood a stout enclosure of hurdles, higher than a man; behind these woven hurdles the Senators could argue and differ without spreading dissension among the common people, while patrolling celeres kept eavesdroppers out of hearing. Within the enclosure tree-stumps and billets of wood were arranged in rows as seats, and at the end was a platform of turf from which the King could speak.

Or rather the two Kings. Latins sometimes forgot that Romulus shared power with an equal colleague; the Sabines never forgot it for a single moment.

Publius, sitting on his stool among a clump of Sabines, was

annoyed to see Romulus alone on the tribunal. But after a few minutes King Tatius bustled up beside him, and in fact the Sabine King was the first to address the meeting.

"Well, young men—I mean reverend fathers, of course," he began, with a smirk at the old, stale jest about beardless Senators, "it doesn't much matter what we tell these envoys from Lavinium, so long as we all stick to the same story. I'm quite ready to make war on them if you are, and I don't think we would get the worst of it. Or if you prefer it we can have peace. We can get that by a graceful apology and the offer of a few lumps of copper in compensation. What I won't sanction, on any account, is that we give back the booty my young cousins won at the risk of their lives. This is the Age of Iron, and there is far less justice in the world than there used to be; any soothsayer will agree with me there. If these silly Latins want to keep their cattle they must guard them more carefully; and if we guard our own cattle carefully no one can take them from us."

He might have said more, but a roar of cheering made it unnecessary to continue. He grinned broadly and sat back on his stool.

When the noise had subsided King Romulus rose to his feet.

"Fathers," he said gravely, for he had never been able to see the funny side of anything connected with his city of Rome, "Fathers, what King Tatius proposes seems to me dishonourable; it is even worse, because it is faint-hearted. If we think only of this city perhaps our wisest course would be to make war on Lavinium. But we can't, because we can't fight our own kin. So since we can't make war we must make peace. It should be a true peace, with compensation for all wrongs done; stolen property should be restored to its rightful owners. We don't want a state of affairs in which our Latin neighbours are technically at peace with Rome, but all the time harbouring a grievance against us and ready to help any of our enemies. Peace is good, and there is something to be said for war. But enmity without open fighting is about the worst state of affairs there is in the world. Let us return the stolen cattle, and pay compensation for any Lavinian killed or injured in the course

of the robbery. Of course if they ask us to hand over the robbers
we must refuse. We can say quite truthfully that we don't know
who they are. Now do you all agree to that?"

"I don't for one," shouted King Tatius, without even bothering to rise from his stool. "The men who lifted those beasts are
cousins of mine, and I won't see their hard-earned plunder taken
from them."

"But we can't fight Lavinium, I tell you. My followers won't
make war on the holy place," Romulus answered at the top of
his voice. "We must make peace on the best terms we can, and
for that we must at least return the plunder."

"We Tatians keep our plunder, or we go home to our own
country. That's final, and I won't budge from it. Why are we
in Rome, anyway? I thought we came here to live by plundering our neighbours."

By this time Latins and Sabines were cheering and counter-
cheering, until the Senate was as noisy and factious as any
meeting of the full assembly. King Romulus saw he was beaten.

"Fathers," he began again, "in the hearing of the common
spearmen we must speak with one voice. I think we ought to
give these envoys their stolen property; but if I can't persuade
you of that let us at least agree on as much as we can. I want to
remain at peace with Lavinium. But I can't do anything to
punish the raid, because as ruler of the city I know nothing
officially about it. Is that what I am to tell these envoys? Mind
you, we shall probably have to listen with patience to a very
rude reply. But at least we shall remain at peace with our Latin
kinsmen."

The compromise did not satisfy either Latins or Sabines; but
it was evidently the greatest common measure of agreement,
and not one of the Senators spoke against it.

When the compromise came before the assembly, on the
other hand, it was well received. The Sabine warriors who had
profited from the raid might keep their plunder, but there would
be no war. That pleased everyone. After King Romulus had
laid the decision of the Senate before the meeting no one
offered to speak; it was carried unanimously.

In the morning the assembly was summoned again. These frequent meetings kept busy farmers from their fields; but embassies were rare, exciting events, and no one grudged the time. The spearmen came unarmed, with their long cloaks over their shoulders in the characteristic Roman fashion. They made a fine show as they stood in an orderly crowd, waiting to hear the Kings deliver the answer of Rome to Lavinium, and the reply of the envoys.

That reply was short, and insulting. The chief envoy spoke without preparation, his eyes blazing with rage.

"We shall not wage war for a few head of cattle," he began contemptuously. "I suppose the wretched loafers of this new city often go hungry, since they are too lazy and ignorant to till the ground. If you had begged for food because you were starving we would have given you alms. Keep the cattle, and be grateful for our kindness. In future our flocks will be guarded, as a precaution against further petty thieving; but whenever you ask we shall give you a few dry old cows. Furthermore, you have begged for peace, I suppose because you fear our warriors. We grant you that peace, since you are not worthy to be our foes. Such is our forbearance that we shall even receive your embassy at the festival. But I ask King Romulus to see to it that he is accompanied only by decent attendants, if there are enough respectable men in his new city to furnish him an escort. I have no more to say."

In silence the embassy left the meeting.

As Publius climbed the hill to his hut anger raged in his breast. He had left his own village and moved into this crowded noisy, fatiguing collection of huts because the head of the family had ordered him to move. This was what he got for his outstanding obedience: to be insulted before a crowd of foreigners by a pompous Latin city-dweller. As he panted upwards he thought for a moment of leaving his clan, and setting up for himself on some isolated hill in the greenwood. But to leave the protection of his kin would be to live like a hunted animal; his family would be exposed to constant danger. He had made his bed and he must lie on it.

When he reached his hut he heard voices chattering excitedly. He remembered with a frown that Claudia, to celebrate her birthday, had invited that Latin who farmed just beyond their boundary to have dinner with them. He was not in the mood for company, but it was too late to cancel the feast. Oh well, it might be worse. Sabina was a decent young matron, even though she acted as though she were ashamed of the clan into which she had been born; Marcus Aemilius was a friendly little man, with as much breeding as you could expect from a Latin. As he entered he stretched his face into a smile of welcome.

"Peace, it's wonderful," Claudia greeted her husband, with a giggle. "I hear the envoys gave you some rude words to swallow; but now we can grow our barley without everyone being called away for picket-duty or patrolling. When we came here I knew we were coming to a different life, but I never thought to see the day when my man would listen quietly to insults from a Latin. I suppose that's one of the new customs of city life."

"Yes, everything you say is true," answered Publius between his teeth, "but do you mind talking about something else for the time being? Here we live under new, un-Sabine conditions, as you have just pointed out. For example, I am not supposed to beat you when you tease me. There are grave disadvantages in living in a city, but we must take the rough with the smooth."

"Peace really is a good thing, you know," Marcus put in with a humble smile; he was awed by these warlike Sabines, and a little shy when he spoke to such an eminent Senator. "At the beginning I thought, we all thought, that we would live here by raiding our neighbours. That was twelve years ago, though it seems like yesterday. Now I have got into the habit of growing my own grain, and my ploughland is in splendid condition. I don't want to see the weeds growing in it all summer, while I sit in a watchtower with a helmet on my head."

"Then there is nothing to complain of," answered Publius sharply. "You Latins want peace, the whole lot of you. You've got it. A few decent Sabines must endure insults which no foreigner would dare to utter among the hills where I was bred; but that doesn't matter. The Kings say we must endure it, and we can't argue with Kings. There's only one thing I don't understand. Why are you Latins so horrified at the idea of making war on Lavinium? I've heard it called a holy city, but that doesn't make sense. I can't imagine a city whose inhabitants are all servants of the gods. Who would do their work for them? Anyway, those envoys seemed to be ordinary spearmen like you and me."

"Lavinium is not a holy city," Marcus answered quickly. "As you say, that would be a very odd kind of place. There is a very holy shrine there, but strictly speaking the shrine has nothing to do with the city; it's much older, for one thing. The shrine has been there from the beginning, and later a city was founded on the same hill. All the same, it would be difficult to make war on the city without risking damage to the shrine. That's why every Latin is glad to see peace confirmed."

"Is the shrine sacred to all Latins?" asked Publius, not very interested in the answer. Religion was to him a family affair, and if everyone else in the world went off to worship some holy rock he would still stick to the ancestors of clan Tatia. "I thought you fetched your gods with you to Rome, as we did. What does Romulus keep in his storehouse, if his gods live in Lavinium?"

"We brought our own gods, of course. We didn't bring all the gods there are. At Lavinium, or rather on the hill above the city, is a rocky cleft in which a god answers questions. Once every twelve years the rulers of all the Latin cities meet there to study the omens. It's a great festival. After the sacrifice they settle disputes and arrange the marriages of their daughters. It's a very splendid meeting, and until you have taken your place there you are not truly a King of the Latins."

"Ah, I understand. King Romulus must be there, or there will be a slight on his honour. No wonder he wants to keep on good terms with the guardians of the shrine. By the way, you say the meeting is held every twelve years. Did your King attend last time?"

"The next meeting is a year ahead. That means that the last one was eleven years ago. That was the year after the foundation of the city, and at that time we were a poor and unimportant little place. King Romulus did not go to the meeting, for fear that when he got there the other rulers would not recognize his kingship. So of course he must go next year, if he claims to be as good as the other Kings of the Latins."

Sabina spoke for the first time. She squatted by the hearth stirring a complicated stew; she was delighted to get back to a kitchen where they understood the full rigours of Sabine cookery. "King Romulus would have avoided a lot of misunderstanding if he had explained all this when the embassy arrived. If his dignity is in the hands of these Lavinians of course he must keep on good terms with them. It's lucky for him and his followers that all the insults were directed at us Sabines."

"They were not directed either at Sabines or at Latins. There are no such people here. We are all Romans, and our city has been insulted. Nevertheless our Kings advised us to make peace, and the assembly ratified the proposal. There's no more to be said. We must obey the Kings and the assembly." That was Marcus, putting the point of view of all right-thinking citizens to this group of savage hillmen.

"Yes, there's no more to be said," Publius agreed. "Any one of us is entitled to avenge an insult to clan Tatia; but if our King tells us to ignore it there's no shame in following his advice. . . . That Latin festival must be a remarkable gathering. If I get the chance I should like to see it."

Then dinner was ready, and afterwards the men sat sipping wine while the women cleared away. Marcus was really a very nice little man, for all the lowliness of his birth. The three Sabines were happy listening to his chatter, and felt that they might pick up useful hints on how to live in a city; he enjoyed spreading civilized views among these backward villagers. Each side felt itself superior to the other; until sunset they talked pleasantly and lazily.

Next morning Publius rose early, ready for a long day on his land to make up for yesterday's idleness. But as he was leaving his hut trumpets sounded on the Palatine, to be answered by the trumpets of the Quirinal. At first they blew the alarm, but before Claudia had finished strapping on his greaves the call changed to an urgent summoning of the assembly. Unarmed, he hastened down the hill to the meeting-place.

King Romulus was already there, though King Tatius had not yet arrived. Behind the King stood his three hundred celeres, fully armed; at most meetings a few of them stood ready to count the votes, and the rest mingled unarmed with the ordinary citizens. Publius was not the only Sabine to take note of this sinister departure from precedent; he saw a group of young boys hurrying down from the Quirinal with their fathers' shields and weapons. He wished he had thought to hide his own sword under his tunic; but now it was too late to fetch it, for King Tatius arrived at that moment. King Romulus on the tribunal looked round anxiously for an omen. Soon a sharp-eyed celer pointed out a pigeon on the right, the lucky side. With this evidence that the gods were still favourable the assembly might begin its session.

King Romulus stood silent and erect until all eyes were fixed on him. Then, still without speaking, he made a sweeping gesture of grief, both arms outspread; and stooped to pick up grains of dust which he sprinkled on his head. When his hearers were on tiptoe with expectation at last he spoke.

"Spearmen," he shouted, "last night the envoys from Lavinium pitched their tents a few miles from the city. This morning they were found with their throats cut. They were ambassadors, dismissed from the city in peace. There is no more to be said. I know, and you know, who killed them. My celeres will now arrest the guilty."

He waved to the armed men behind him, who began to march purposefully into the unarmed crowd.

King Tatius pushed him aside, calling for attention.

"Cousins," he called, "I'm talking to you, not to the foreign spearmen who happen to be here also; though they will be wise to heed my advice. *I* don't know who was responsible for the murder of these ambassadors, and King Romulus doesn't know either. They may not have been murdered at all. Perhaps the gods struck them down, as punishment for their insults to brave Sabine warriors. That's just as likely as anything else, and King

Romulus can't contradict me; unless indeed he was there when they died, and if he was that will take a bit of explaining. Because of this handful of unexpected sudden deaths, it seems that King Romulus has ordered his celeres to arrest my kinsmen. That is a rash and improvident step. There are three hundred of these celeres, while my kin number about seven thousand spears. So whatever the merits of the case the King enforces his will in a most clumsy fashion. The rest of the Latins may help the celeres, or they may not. If they do, well, some years ago we had quite a good battle on this very patch of ground. The end was a draw, as near as no matter, and I for one am willing to fight it all over again. I'm going now to fetch my sword and shield. I propose that the meeting adjourn until I get back. Now, King Romulus, will your men make these arrests?"

Romulus stamped with rage. Then he pulled himself together, standing erect, grave and still.

"Thirteen years ago I founded this city," he said in a quiet, carrying voice. "The omens that were then granted to us made me think that my city will one day rule the world. I *am* the son of Mars, those omens *were* granted to us. You do believe me, spearmen, don't you? You *must* understand, it's so terribly important. Now for those thirteen years the city has grown and prospered until we are nearly ready to begin the conquest of Etruria which will make us great. We are so nearly there—if only you will have patience it will be so easy. Yet here you stand, threatening to smash the most important city in Italy just because you stick by your kinsmen even when you know in your hearts that they are utterly in the wrong. Very well, you bloodstained Sabines, have it your own way. To me Rome is the most important thing in the world, more important than law and right dealing and the sanctity of envoys. You murdered those men—everyone knows it, *I* know it. But rather than destroy Mars's own city I shall permit your crime to go unpunished. You are shameless, and I must be shameless also. We will offer no satisfaction to Lavinium. No one will be punished for this atrocity. In return grant me this much. If the wronged citizens of Lavinium are willing to live in peace with us, do them no further harm. The wolf was my foster-mother, but I have seen my spearmen behave more savagely than wolves. Don't become wolves in all your dealings. Don't be wolves to every civilized Latin who worships the gods of the Latins, the gods who have promised us unimaginable prosperity."

Overcome with grief and shame, he sank down on the tribunal, his head buried in his hands. Grinning, King Tatius came forward.

"Now, you celeres, you heard what your master said. Why not go home and put away your weapons, instead of starting a war against twenty times your numbers? As for the rest of us, and my cousins in particular—the best thing we can do is to let bygones be bygones. Those men are dead, aren't they? Killing other men won't bring them to life. We shan't send a message of any kind to Lavinium. They sent one to us, and it turned out most unluckily. If they make war on us we can deal with them, if they are willing to keep the peace we shan't do them any further harm. That seems to me fair and straightforward. There's one other thing I want my cousins to remember. You know very well that you are completely in the wrong. I've saved you from the punishment you deserve. That's what the tie of kinship means, saving your kin from what they deserve; you would save any stranger if he were to be punished unjustly. So remember this: I've done my duty, fulfilled all my obligations. Next time you do wrong you take the consequences—that is, if you get found out. You silly fools, why couldn't you wait until they were a bit farther from Rome before you cut their throats?"

He turned on his heel and left the tribunal. The celeres, or most of them, had already vanished. The assembly dispersed.

Publius slouched away, his hands clasped behind his back. He was almost ashamed to be a Sabine. But he was proud to be the kinsman of King Tatius, a gallant warrior who stood by his cousins through thick and thin. It was comforting to know that such a faithful leader would guard you when you were in danger.

Chapter 7

MURDER BREEDS MURDER

★

All the Sabines on the Quirinal were unhappy and ashamed. Even those who had taken no part in the murder understood that their support had enabled the murderers to escape punishment, which meant that every Sabine shared in the guilt. But autumn was on the way, and there was no time for idle repining.

Rome had fallen into the unresting rhythm of an agricultural community. After harvest came the ploughing; then the seed must be sown, the most important event of the farming year. But before the sowing the fields must be prepared to receive the purifying influence of heaven. In that task everyone helped, warriors, soothsayers, craftsmen, even slaves if they had something to contribute from the magic of their own countries; but it was especially the responsibility of the women.

The Sabines realized the full enormity of their guilt when they discovered that Latin women from the Palatine would not join them in the sacred task. It was all the more bitter in that many of these Latin women were Sabine by origin, wives stolen at that notorious mass-marriage. But now, mothers of Latin sons, when it came to choosing sides they sided with their husbands.

The women of Rome were always meeting one another, at the springs from which they drew water, at the washing-place on the river-bank, on the bleaching grounds where cloth was spread on the grass. If King Romulus had thought that by forbidding Roman wives to work in the fields he would keep them separate in their huts that only proved that no man understands the life of a wife and mother. Claudia saw Sabina nearly every day, and at first could not understand why this unfortunate and ill-treated Sabine girl always had some urgent engagement which made it impossible for her to join in the women's rites below the Quirinal. At length Sabina lost patience, and explained in blunt words.

"It's no good, my dear. As you say, I am a fertile mother, just the kind of woman who can show the barley how to increase in the ground. But this year I can't help you at all. Your man did not murder an envoy, but he helped the murderers to escape justice. That would be in my mind while I danced among the furrows, and the seed-corn would know my thoughts. The barley would learn from me that the slayers of envoys, and their supporters, deserve to go hungry. Nothing at all would come up where I trod in your fields."

"But we are in danger from these Latins. You were born a Sabine, and in this crisis all Sabines must stick together."

"No, Claudia. It's because Sabines stick together that your men have got themselves into this mess. Besides, I'm not a Sabine any longer. Marcus is the father of my sons, and with him I make offering to the ancestors of the Aemilian clan. I would be unprotected beside a Latin hearth unless I forgot my Sabine kin."

Claudia consoled herself by recalling that even if Sabina had once been a Sabine she had never been a member of clan Tatia, never of the kin that really mattered. Now that the truth was out the Sabine wives resigned themselves to performing all the rites of the women without help from their neighbours on the Palatine.

Rome was deeply divided. Some of the younger Sabine spearmen hinted that it might be profitable to expel those Latins and take over the Palatine as a Sabine settlement. But the leaders of the clan knew that if they were disliked it was the penalty of past wrongdoing; they kept the peace because they must admit that any punishment which came their way was no more than they deserved.

All the same, civil war nearly broke out at the time of the

autumn horse-sacrifice. This was a queer and novel rite, no part of the wisdom of the ancestors; because horses themselves were new-fangled beasts, and no one was quite sure how they should be employed in the service of the gods. The Etruscans beyond the river, learned men and prosperous besides, which proved that they knew how to call down the favour of heaven, these Etruscans raced in chariots on great festivals. At the end of the race you knew which were the best horses; then you cut the throat of the right-hand horse of the winning pair, because the right is in general the lucky side of anything. That was how the Etruscans sacrificed horse to their gods, who were not the gods of the Latins; but heaven was pleased with the sacrifice, for the Etruscans grew richer every year. King Romulus had introduced the ritual to Rome. No one was quite sure which god was being honoured, but that did not matter. There are many gods, and a wise man pleases as many of them as he can.

A dead horse is a cumbersome thing. The wise Etruscans did not carry the whole carcass over their fields to bless the seed. The important part of an edible sacrifice must be the entrails, in which grass is turned into flesh; but horses are servants, not food, and the important part of a servant is his head. The Etruscans stuck the horse's skull on a pole among their furrows, and their barley always sprouted vigorously.

Under the guidance of King Romulus the Romans followed in every particular the Etruscan rite. It was not until the race was over and a hefty celer had hacked off the head of the dead horse that the Tatians realized there was only one skull, which the selfish Latins intended to stick up among their own fields. The Sabines might have organized another chariot-race of their own, but it was nearly sunset on the one day in the year which was right for this festival. It seemed simpler to take the skull from the Latins.

Luckily everyone had come unarmed to the joyful festival. A few eyes were blacked and noses bloodied as the spearmen struggled together; but boxing was no part of the training of a warrior and most of the contestants merely wrestled with their adversaries. The Tatians worked off a great load of resentment as they pushed those horrid Latins about, and since they were lucky enough to gain possession of the skull they felt in a much better temper when the riot was over. The Latins withdrew in anger to the Palatine, where some of them could be seen getting out their spears and shields. But before deadly war could break out King Romulus hastily summoned the assembly and made a speech which could have come into the mind only of a born politician.

"Spearmen," he said cheerfully, surveying the angry crowd, "you have been inspired by some god to add a most valuable rite to our annual sacrifice. Rome is one city, and therefore only one horse can be offered. But just as the effort and weariness of all the other horses in the chariot-race add to the merit of the chosen victim, so do your efforts, the pain and weariness of the contest, and indeed the bruises so many of you display, add to the value of our offering. For one city there can be only one victim. But in the city are two settlements. Each year, after the race, the men of the Palatine shall struggle against the men of the Quirinal for possession of the trophy, pleasing the gods with an offering of their own bodily strength. By next year the virtue of this skull will be exhausted, but there is no reason why the winners should not keep it as a memorial of their success in a most enjoyable sport. So far it's one up to the Quirinal. Perhaps my kinsmen will have better luck next time. Anyway, when our children look at the row of skulls, they can see which hill has bred better muscle. For remember, Rome is destined to endure as long as the world. What we begin, you and I, the founders, will be done by our children until time ends. Now we are all comrades together, and the Quirites have shown themselves the stronger. To make next year's match more interesting, why don't some of the Tatians move to the Palatine? Then we can bet on a nice open contest."

The Sabines went home content. Some young Latins picked sides to begin an early practice for next year's match.

That evening King Tatius went calling on his Senators. Publius and Claudia were sitting by the fire when he dropped in unannounced, and he would not hear of the lady withdrawing to her room. "No, I want you all to hear this," he said with a smile. "I would call a meeting of the clan, but then the Latins might think we are planning some move against them. I've come to tell you that King Romulus is a splendid fellow, and we must all support him. He really believes that stuff about Rome being something special, a city destined to endure until the end of the world. As far as that goes, he may be right; I shan't be there to contradict him when the world comes to its end. Anyway, so long as he has the running of this place, it will last. He took one look at a very ugly faction-fight, and in a few words turned it into a sacred rite, pleasing to the gods. He's the man to follow, and while you obey me you will follow him. Now have you got that straight, and are you willing to do as I say?"

"When you give orders, cousin, I must obey them," answered Publius with a worried frown. "I suppose King Romulus is all right, if you say so. I wish those Latins of his were more friendly. They won't even help us to bring luck to our fields."

"We have not deserved their friendship. Some of our men murdered those envoys, though you and I were not mixed up in it. Even there we got our own way in the end; I was able to protect my kin from punishment. So there it is. I want Rome to continue, because I like the place. It can't endure if Latins and Sabines are at loggerheads. You must make friends with your fellow-citizens, and if they seem to despise you remember that some of our kin did in fact put themselves utterly in the wrong. As head of the family, I have come to tell you that."

"I do as the head of the family tells me," Publius answered curtly.

"But, cousin, there's one other thing you must bear in mind," said Claudia, talking quite brazenly to a male visitor as though a woman were as good as a spearman (but then city life was spoiling the good manners of the old days). "King Romulus is a very fine fellow, as you say. But in Rome there are two kings, or there ought to be. Don't let Romulus take the lead in everything, or the people will forget that you are his equal."

"My dear she-cousin, you aren't the first of my advisers to

make that point, though you are quite right to tell me what is in your mind. The answer is that I am not the equal of King Romulus, and I never can be. So why struggle for what is beyond my reach?"

"Not equal to King Romulus?" Publius stuttered with anger. "Why, that was the agreement. We would not have come here without it. It's bound to be awkward coming into a place after it's been founded. It wouldn't be safe unless we had our own King to protect us, a King fully the equal of King Romulus."

"Ah, but I haven't the magic of King Romulus," Tatius answered with an easy smile. "I'm not the son of a god, and I haven't a storehouse full of sacred things brought long ago from oversea."

"You have what Romulus lacks," said Claudia, "the devotion of subjects born to obey you. He rules over Latins who have chosen him for King, and who may one day choose another. We Tatians cannot desert you."

"That's true, as far as it goes," the King answered. "But today Romulus has more followers, though they may not follow him always."

"What is this luck with which King Romulus has been endowed? What do you think of it yourself? Do tell us your opinion. Look, I have put the Lar into his cupboard and shut the door. We are all cousins here and no god is listening. We are quite private."

Claudia knew that no woman should speak so frankly to a man; but her husband would never dare to ask this question, and she really wanted to know the answer.

"Well now, I don't know what to say, I suppose because I haven't made up my own mind. Romulus is a queer creature. He made himself King by his own efforts. He wasn't born to it, as I was. But he inherits from his ancestors those staffs with bronze snakes on them; odd things, I never saw the like of them among the Sabines. Perhaps whatever he keeps in those tall earthenware jars is equally odd. I don't know what it is and I don't propose to find out. It may be something dangerous or it may be a silly bogey. But it isn't worth the risk, to challenge him to do magic just to see whether his magic works. Some magic works, we are all agreed on that."

"Yes, but magic is not the most important of his claims," Claudia persisted. "He says he is the son of Mars. Do you believe him?"

"Perhaps he is and perhaps he isn't," Tatius shrugged. "His mother was a priestess, vowed to virginity. When she gave birth to twins she told such a convincing story that her fellow-citizens spared her life. But I never heard her tell the story, so I am not wholly convinced. Anyway, my dear lady, no man can say of his own knowledge who was his father. Can I prove that my father was not a Ligurian slave? Can you prove it of yours? We can go only by hearsay, the opinion of our elders; and they are often mistaken. Gods exist, and they can beget mortal children. There are dozens of pedigrees to prove it. Romulus says that Mars was his father, and he behaves as though he believes it. He may be right. Life is easier if we grant that he is right. Let's leave it at that."

"But we can't leave it at that," said Publius, at length catching the drift of his wife's questions. "You are the leader of our clan, and you are leader of our clan because you were born to it. But that doesn't make you the equal of King Romulus. You are a warchief, he is a divine ruler. Unless you want him to outdistance you, you must try to seize some kind of divine power for yourself."

"I haven't forgotten that aspect." King Tatius winked, and then put on a solemn expression. "I spend half my time representing my people at religious festivals, and then by sticking close to Romulus I try to pick up some of his supernatural endowment. That's another reason why I want my cousins to be friendly with the Latins. Next spring there will be something really important. The great festival of Lavinium has come round again, as it does every twelve years. The priests who manage the shrine have invited all the Latin kings to attend, and that means all kings who rule Latin cities. I shall go to Lavinium with Romulus."

"But that's madness, cousin," Publius cried in alarm. "If

there is one place in the world where the avengers of blood will be waiting for you, it's Lavinium. They have right on their side, too, which makes it more dangerous. Our kin murdered their envoys, there's no denying it; and you saved the murderers from justice."

"Yes, yes, I know. But Romulus tells me the festival has no connection with the city. It's just that the shrine happens to be on the same hill. I need not enter the city, nor have any dealings with the Lavinians. Anyway, it's one of those farming festivals, to make the crops grow; so no one is allowed to bring a weapon inside the sacred enclosure. I shall have friends with me, and unarmed Latins cannot harm unarmed Sabines. If they start any trouble we shall knock them down and sit on their heads."

"All the same, why go where you will find deadly enemies? What do you gain by it?"

"That I don't know. But I gain something. I want to find out in advance what will happen at this festival. It's for kings specially, so they must do something to make kings more sacred and powerful, or the kings wouldn't take such trouble to go there. You are friendly with this Latin, Marcus Aemilius, the man who persuaded his Sabine wife to become herself a Latin. I know what goes on in my clan, and I know he's always in and out of your hut. I want you, Publius, to find out all he knows about the rites of Lavinium. They do something there which brings great luck and power to kings, I'm sure of it. If I know what it is they can't cheat me by not doing it to me. They can't turn me away as a Sabine foreigner, you know. They invited the kings of all the Latin cities, and I'm King in the Latin city of Rome. I shall hold them to their duty. But I must know what to expect, and you must find out for me. I ask as your cousin."

"I must help my cousin," said Publius cautiously. "But I shall be quite open with my friend Marcus. I shan't try to trap him into revealing religious mysteries. I shall tell him what I want to know, and why I want to know it. We Sabines have enough on our conscience already, especially when you remember that we consider ourselves simple bluff countrymen compared to those wily Latins."

"All right. Be honest if you insist. After all, it's good news that I have one honest man in my clan. I hope your Marcus doesn't think it his duty to inform Romulus, because if all the Latins get together they can cheat me. Just ask Marcus frankly, and pass on his answer. At the same time you can tell him that I have ordered the whole clan to be loyal to Rome and its founder, King Romulus. That happens to be the truth, and it will make him more willing to tell all he knows."

On the next day Publius went in search of Marcus. For more than one reason he disliked the whole scheme, but he did not think that gave him the right to disregard a direct order from the head of the family. He disliked the scheme first because it was dangerous and second because it seemed to be sharp practice of the kind that upright Sabine warriors considered low. A general invitation to the rulers of all Latin cities was not meant to include a Sabine clan-chief, and if Tatius went to Lavinium he would be behaving in a pushing and discourteous fashion. But his third and strongest reason for disliking it was that it might prove too successful. Tatius was by birth the head of his clan. But he was of the same blood as his followers, a warrior leading free warriors. A man commissioned by the gods to rule lesser men, a sacred King Tatius, would perhaps become a powerful tyrant.

When consulted, Marcus willingly told all he knew, though that was not a great deal. "At Lavinium the shrine is the important thing," he explained. "It has been there from the beginning, while the city is quite modern. The shrine is the dwelling of a powerful god, and whenever you want to consult him you go there and make an offering."

"But if it's an oracular shrine and no more, though I am sure a very potent one, why don't kings go whenever they like? Why do they hold this great festival only once every twelve years?"

Marcus shrugged carelessly. "That's how it's always been done. It's hard for the rulers of all the Latin cities to get away at the same time, so I suppose an annual meeting would be a nuisance. There is something, you know, in the number twelve.

Soothsayers maintain that there are twelve great gods, though no two of them agree when you ask them for a list. I expect you Sabines have the same feeling. The kings visit the shrine, and seek divine guidance; but it's really a conference of Latin rulers as much as a religious rite."

How like Latins, thought Publius. All their religion was a matter of doing what had been done last time, without bothering to think of a reason for it; and no outsider could tell whether what seemed a religious occasion was really a meeting for secular business.

"Then it's not a private affair, for Latins only?" he persisted. "The priests in charge of the shrine would admit a Sabine?"

"They would welcome him, if he brought a good offering. But why are you so anxious to go? Is there trouble on the Quirinal? Can I do anything to help?"

"I'm not especially anxious to go, though I shall probably make one of the party. It's a whim of King Tatius, and as far as I know he wants to go only because he is King of a Latin city and therefore entitled to attend."

Marcus looked worried. "Well, that's fair enough. This is a Latin city, and he is King in it. But the Etruscan chiefs who rule in some Latin cities never go to Lavinium."

"They worship different gods, we don't. It's like this. Romulus must go, to make sure that his kingship is recognized by the other kings. So King Tatius must go also, to make sure that he is recognized as the equal of King Romulus."

Marcus looked even more worried. "It's a very holy shrine. If a man should bring bad luck into it the bad luck would be turned against him. No one may visit it who is polluted. Even a man who has killed quite honourably in war must be cleansed of bloodguilt before he approaches the holy place. All the kings are purified as soon as they arrive."

"Then Tatius must go, to demonstrate his innocence before all the Latins. I know what's in your mind. You think he is polluted with the blood of those murdered envoys. Well, he's innocent. When he has been welcomed at the shrine everyone will be compelled to admit it."

"Yes, I see," said Marcus, "but the shrine stands just above Lavinium."

"You mean he might be murdered? He will take a body-guard."

"He can't. No one brings arms into the templum, and if there is any suspicion the priests search you."

"Then the avengers also will be unarmed."

"It sometimes happens that an unarmed man kills another unarmed man."

"It won't happen to King Tatius. He's as strong as any Latin, and he will have a group of cousins with him."

Marcus still looked unhappy. "It's not the right place for a Sabine King. Latin blood has been wrongfully shed. There will be bad luck about."

"Nonsense. This makes it all the more important that he should go. I shall tell him so. If you like, I shall also warn him that some Latins consider it unsafe. Then he will look out for himself. But go he must, to demonstrate that he took no part in the murder of the envoys."

In a gloomy city the winter dragged on. The weather was unusual, because in every winter the weather is unusual; but whenever rain or wind menaced next summer's crop the Latins on the Palatine complained that the gods were angry with blood-polluted Sabines, and the Sabines on the Quirinal complained that of course things went wrong when those selfish Latins hoarded their good luck and would not help their neighbours to put the fields to rights. Nobody discussed war and conquest and great wealth won easily from raided cities; Rome was a community of farmers, or rather an uneasy alliance between two communities of disgruntled farmers.

But in the spring green barley showed above the scratched earth, and after all the city would be fed for another year. In a more cheerful spirit the citizens began to prepare for the embassy to Lavinium.

This would mark the formal reception of Rome as a city among the ancient Latin cities. It must be splendid and glorious and dignified. Everyone contributed willingly to the show. The two Kings would wear purple cloaks and ride in chariots. Romulus already had a chariot, brought among his ancestral possessions from Alba; the Tatians collected a great herd of cattle to buy one for their leader from the Etruscans beyond the river. Any carpenter could make a war-chariot, a pair of wheels and a flimsy basketwork frame; though in fact war-chariots were seldom used now that horses could be bred big enough to carry an armed rider. But only Etruscans knew how to make a ceremonial chariot. This new one was a very splendid object, the frame of solid planking under a thin sheet of bronze on which images of the gods had been worked with a hammer; the carved seat was embellished with strips of a hard white substance called ivory—it came from beyond the sea and no one knew whether it was a stone or a metal. The Tatians gave a hundred heifers and five bulls for it, and had to humble themselves before the craftsmen of Veii to get it even at that price.

The purple cloak was more easily come by, though in Italy no one had discovered a good purple dye. A merchant happened to arrive from the south with a roll of the stuff, bought from foreign traders; he was prevailed on to sell a length for ten times its weight in silver, made up from the ornaments of Tatian women.

Each King was to take ten councillors, who would ride on horses beside his chariot. These companions must of course be unarmed, since they were to visit the festival. They were dressed alike, in long white cloaks worn hanging over the left shoulder. Publius, who was among the ten chosen Sabines, gave his greaves as security for the loan of a pair of red riding-boots, reaching to the knee; they were foreign work, but their present owner was one of the brigand Luceres, who had murdered a solitary traveller to get them. For the journey the councillors would wear shady straw hats; they brought with them a slave skilled in making wreaths, which they would put on for the festival.

In addition each King brought a bodyguard of a hundred picked warriors, fully armed. These men came unwillingly, after strong persuasion, for they would have a weary journey for nothing. They must be left by the roadside ten miles from Lavinium, because no man might bear arms within sight of the sacred assembly.

There were gifts for the shrine, and beasts for sacrifice. It would be the most splendid and costly embassy that had ever left Rome since the city was founded, thirteen years ago. The citizens regretted the expense, but they were consoled by the honour to be shown to their city.

It was high summer when the delegation set out. To the Sabines especially the journey was a great adventure. Never before had they seen the long-settled Latin land, farm touching farm throughout the plain, walled cities built of stone or brick.

Publius hoped that they might ride through a city, but he was disappointed. King Romulus explained that it was contrary to etiquette to bring armed men within a city unless they had been specially invited; and there was strong distrust of the Romans in every Latin city because of the murder of the Lavinian envoys. Even so there was much to be seen from the track: steep citadels, close-set hearths under a cloud of smoke, in one town a building roofed with thin slabs of baked clay instead of thatch, a remarkable innovation.

Presently they left their armed escort in camp by the roadside, and soon after Lavinium came into sight. Now they encountered other Latin rulers hurrying to the conference; more than a score of them, for Rome was not the only Latin city ruled by colleagues. Each King was clad in purple, but many of them rode horses; Etruscan chariots were at once useless and costly. That Rome could furnish two chariots proved that the new city was already more wealthy than some members of the ancient Latin League.

Lavinium climbed a steep hillside, and its interior could be seen from the plain below. At first glance the city seemed to be composed of many fortresses; its square houses were made of solid masonry, their thatched roofs projecting beyond sheer white-plastered walls. Publius was worried to think that his kin had murdered the envoys of such a mighty town. Then he noticed a few Lavinian spearmen scowling from the open gate at the passing Sabines, and saw that they were only common little Latins, slightly built and with high reedy voices. Such people might be rich enough to build brick houses for themselves, but they were puny folk when it came to push of spear in the open.

Above Lavinium the hill towered to a bare rocky crest which was the shrine. The Romans had come to the end of their journey. Good manners demanded that they approach the god on foot, and with relief they left horses and chariots near the city gates. To men who by choice fought on foot riding seemed to jerk their legs loose in the sockets, and a jolting chariot was less comfortable than an ox-waggon.

All the hilltop was a consecrated templum, its boundary marked by flimsy wands set in the ground. The summit was carpeted with green turf, grazed short by a herd of sacred goats. Just below it lay the rocky cleft which was the oracular shrine; a mere crack in the cliffs, twisting so that its far end was hidden. At the entry stood an altar of unmortared stone. Latin Kings were already pressing round it, and behind each ruler was led the bull which he would offer in sacrifice.

"We have to wait our turn," Romulus said casually, "but we must get the sacrifice over as soon as we can. We can't do anything until the god has sniffed his roast beef, but I want to talk to some of these Kings before the conference opens. I shall go first, if King Tatius will permit me. Put the offering of silver on that flat boulder over there; then dedicate the bull to the god in the shrine—without naming him, because if you give him a name you may get it wrong. Lead the beast forward and give it a tap on the head. The professional servants of the shrine will do the rest. They cut the throat and take the hide off and burn the thighs on the altar; they also steal some of the beef, but there will be enough for all. Leave it all to them; they are speedy, because they do this so often. Other Kings are waiting their turn, and we don't want to put them in a bad temper by delaying them."

He hurried on with his group of Latin councillors, while the Sabines waited quietly until the altar should be free.

When their turn came Publius noted with regret that no sentiment of religion entered his mind. He had never before witnessed sacrifice on this scale; he was aware of nothing but the stink of blood and burnt flesh, the bellowing of bulls waiting for death, flies, and the stream of animal excrement that fouled his borrowed riding-boots. He thought only of his own discomfort as two brawny attendants seized the bull, and King Tatius strode forward alone to give it the ritual blow on the head with an archaic bronze axe. The bull would bawl until someone cut its throat, then it would sink to its knees, then they could all move away to the cleaner air of the hillside. He knew what would come and there was no need to watch.

Suddenly he heard a shout, the warcry of his clan; it faded into a bubbling gurgle even as he lifted his head to look. He saw the bull bucking, its tail in the air, while instead King Tatius sank to his knees. The King's throat had been cut with the sacrificial knife, and for good measure one of the spits on which bulls' thighs were immolated was sticking out of his back. For a moment the councillors gaped, too amazed to move. King Romulus was running to join them.

Publius groped at his waist, and his hand came away empty. In this sacred place he carried neither sword nor knife; there was not even a stone handy on the smooth turf, and his long cloak hampered his movements. The dozen servants by the altar carried cleavers or spits or long butcher's knives, and they had closed up together like veteran spearmen awaiting the charge. The ten Sabines were outnumbered and unarmed; even with the head of the clan lying dead before their eyes they could not summon the resolution to run in and avenge him.

"No fighting in the holy place," shouted King Romulus as he panted up the hill. "The Latins will kill us if we pollute their sanctuary. Stand still. Let the Lavinians deal with the criminals."

A patrol of armed men, shields and spears at the ready, hurried up the slope. On their arrival the murderers laid down their butcher's tools, meekly holding out their hands to be bound.

Someone was already removing the peeled wands from this place which was no longer a templum dedicated to the gods.

"All of you, go back to your baggage," shouted the leader of the Lavinian spearmen. "Our elders will judge this crime, and publish their verdict before sunset. All foreigners must go down to the valley at once. The dead man will be delivered to his countrymen as soon as we have got him on a bier."

"All out, all out," Romulus added his authority. "Every Roman will muster by my chariot in the plain below the city. No revenge here, on Lavinian soil. The assassins are already bound and awaiting judgment."

A Sabine spread his hands and shrugged his shoulders. Publius echoed the unspoken advice with another shrug, re-arranging the cumbrous cloak on his shoulder. In the first moment of horror he could have nerved himself to attack armed men with his bare hands; once people began to make speeches that kind of excitement ebbed away. His leader was dead and could not be restored to life. The murderers were under arrest. If the Lavinians spared them there would be time for vengeance later.

In a few minutes the hilltop was deserted; Kings and their councillors hurrying down to the plain passed a procession of soothsayers issuing from the upper gate of the city to purify the desecrated shrine. The service of the god who lived there would not be intermitted for a single day.

As soon as they had reached the baggage Romulus jumped into his chariot and hurried about from one Latin King to another; but the Sabines mounted and rode hard for the encampment of the bodyguard, ten miles away over the ridge. They spent an uneasy afternoon, with the bodyguard under arms and the waggons drawn up to form a barricade. At sunset Romulus joined them, escorting the corpse of Tatius on a fine Lavinian bier, borne by Lavinian elders. The Sabines must guard the corpse all night, to keep the King's ghost inside it until burial; so the councillors, waking in turn to take over the watch, had no chance to consult together.

Next morning, riding back to Rome, they could discuss the

future. But no one would take a definite line until he knew the opinion of the spearmen on the Quirinal, and nothing was decided. Publius rode in silence. After all, he reflected, he was not truly a leader of clan Tatia; he had been appointed Senator because there were not a hundred eminent men available and he had happened to be wearing those fine greaves.

By the time they reached Rome, slowed up by the pace of the spearmen who carried the bier, the King's body was already stinking. Romulus urged them to burn it by the roadside, and bring home the ashes for burial; but burning was a Latin custom, unfitting for a Sabine, and the Tatians would not hear of it. Rubbish and litter might be burned, but the body of a great warleader must lie complete in the earth, lest its spirit should need it again.

A grave was ready when they reached the city. Since the dead man left no son the pig sacrificed at the grave-closing was killed by the oldest Tatian present.

The dead man left no son. All the Sabine councillors had been thinking of that as they rode home from the murder. There was indeed a daughter, now married; and in ordinary circumstances a son-in-law had a fair claim to succeed. But the husband of Tatia had three elder brothers living, which meant that he must be poor; and by blood he was not a Tatian. A Pompilian could not be the leader of clan Tatia.

After the funeral the leading clansmen met in what had been their King's hut to discuss the situation, and it soon became apparent that there was no logical successor. Earlier chiefs had been potent in battle but not in bed. The late King had been the only son of an only son; he left neither uncles nor cousins.

Of course every Tatian was descended from the first Tatius, and could recite the names in his pedigree. But in these pedigrees seniority was left uncertain; no one could swear that his great-great-grandfather had been older than his brothers. After discussing the matter back and forth, the councillors concluded that the next chief must be elected in a general meeting of the clan.

Publius took no part in the discussion. He was not a skilled genealogist, but he knew that his birth gave him no claim to the succession, and he did not support any other candidate. But regular attendance in the Senate had taught him something of practical politics, and just as the meeting ended he made a startling proposal.

"Look here, cousins," he said awkwardly, "do you want to go on living in Rome? I do, on the whole. It's crowded, and it smells bad in summer; but it's safe, and lucky, and often amusing. If I went back to a little hamlet I should miss the throng of neighbours. Well, if you want to live in Rome why have a clan-chief at all? Our late chief commanded us when we lived by ourselves, and he was the undisputed heir of his father. Coming to Rome was his idea, and we followed him. But a new, untried leader will never live content as the colleague of King Romulus. He will want to take us back again to the hills. Some of us won't follow, and then the clan will split. I propose that we make King Romulus our warchief, as we might appoint any good warrior if the head of the family were a child or a cripple. The clan can still sacrifice to the ancestors. The elders will teach the ritual to our children, and our Latin fellow-citizens will help us to keep alive the spirit of the tribe of the Tities, as they call us in their odd pronunciation. But if we remain in Rome we don't want another King of our own. I propose that we do not elect another leader, and that except for religious affairs we merge ourselves with the other citizens."

"It hadn't occurred to me, but I agree with Publius," said the eldest of the Senators. "I also want to stay here. I like this palisade, and I'm too old to run up a cliff when raiders attack my undefended village. Let Romulus rule over us all."

For that night the council left the matter undecided, but at the general assembly of the clan next day it soon appeared that no candidate for the chieftaincy could win a clear majority. After long haggling and argument it was resolved to end clan Tatia as a political organization, keeping the tribe only for religious purposes. King Romulus was chosen as warleader. Nobody's honour had been slighted, and Rome was now peacefully under the rule of a single man.

MURDER BREEDS MURDER

Within a few days an embassy arrived from Lavinium. The envoys brought with them, in fetters, the murderers of King Tatius. The Lavinians declared that it was for the Romans to judge these men and inflict the due penalty. At once the assembly of the people met to try the case.

Marcus Aemilius had arranged a supper party. There were only two guests, but they had never before come to a formal meal, though they had sometimes dropped in for a friendly visit; that was because the Senator Publius Tatius and his wife the lady Claudia were socially much higher than a client of the Latin Aemilians. It was a festival; there was wine and pork even for the slave-woman who cleaned the pots (Sabina herself did the cooking), and the Lar was decked with flowers.

Marcus had taken trouble. He had borrowed Etruscan couches for the men, which left his two chairs free for the ladies. The food was as Latin as a Sabine wife could make it, but there was more meat than usual, and barley-porridge was served only at the very end, in case someone still felt hungry.

After they had eaten the wine-bowl was filled with the lavish mixture of equal parts of wine and water, and the company settled down to conversation.

"Let us drink to Rome," said Marcus, spilling a libation to the gods. "I was here when it all began, more than thirteen years ago. At first we were a Latin city, with a few refugees from all over the place. Six years ago you and your cousins came in; but you didn't exactly join us. Rather were we a double city. Now at last we are united. No more Sabines and Latins, just Romans, living in one city."

"My Publius was the first to suggest an end to clan Tatia," said Claudia proudly. "Of course he never told me about his speech, husbands never remember to tell their wives that kind of thing. But I heard about it all the same, and I think all his friends ought to know."

"It's not a secret, my dear, though it's not important. All my cousins agreed as soon as it was put to them. After all, it's silly to keep up two kingdoms in one city. After all these years in Rome I want to stay. If we had chosen another King he would have taken us back to the hills."

"Yes, a city is the place to live in," said Sabina. "No one led me here, and I felt very surprised when first I was carried into this hut. But the children play in safety behind the stout palisade, and there are always plenty of neighbours."

"The city gives us safety," Claudia agreed, "and it doesn't really interfere too much with our freedom. Roman wives have more privileges than my mother ever enjoyed, and I am used to neighbours watching me all the time."

"Don't forget that in addition this city enjoys divine favour," said Marcus.

"Oh, that," answered Publius with a shrug. "Lavinium must enjoy divine favour in plenty, with that shrine just outside the gate. It hasn't saved the Lavinians from a certain amount of trouble lately."

"Something brought them great good luck today, anyway," said Marcus. "It would have been hard for those envoys to watch the execution of fellow-citizens at the hands of foreigners, even though it was deserved. Now they can take them back safely to their own city."

"I think the people decided rightly," Publius pronounced. "I myself voted for acquittal, even though the murdered man was my cousin and leader. Those unfortunate Lavinians cannot be blamed for avenging their own kin, but the blood-feud must stop somewhere unless we are always to be at war with all our neighbours."

"I seem to be the only Tatian left," said Claudia with a nervous smile which seemed to apologize for her daring. "If the blood-feud is an obligation, and I think it is, the Lavinians were right to murder our King, but you were wrong to let the murderers go free. If the blood-feud does not excuse murder, then they did wrong to kill within the sacred shrine. Whichever way you look at it, they should have been put to death."

"It's your memory that is at fault, my dear, not your reasoning," said Publius indulgently. "You didn't go back far enough. Our cousins did the first wrong, when they murdered the

Lavinian envoys a year ago. Since we Tatians shed first blood we have the right to end the feud."

"You are all very civilized and highminded and modern." Claudia was growing angry and she spoke more sharply than was fitting in a dutiful wife. "You took no vengeance when the men who had killed your King were brought bound before the assembly. If strangers can kill your fellow-citizens and you do not avenge them, where is the famous security of this new city? Vengeance is the first duty of a warrior. That's what I was taught, and if nowadays it isn't true you must carry a sword wherever you go, for you will not be safe anywhere. Our King put his duty to his kin even before justice. That's why he would not allow Romulus to punish the killers of the Lavinian envoys. Now he's dead, and no one can be bothered to kill his murderers. It makes me ashamed to be a Sabine."

"It was the only sensible course, if we are to stay here," answered Publius, speaking gently because pride would not let him rebuke his wife before strangers. "King Romulus wants peace. He is the only King left in Rome, and if we had thwarted his wishes he would have found some way to get rid of us."

"Yes, there's a difference between the two Kings, isn't there?" Claudia replied sweetly. "Tatius stuck by his kin, and it brought him untimely death. Romulus won't avenge his colleague, because peace is so much less trouble than war. Poor Tatius lacked the natural advantages of Romulus. His father was a mortal man, not Mars; and he was an only son, so he couldn't murder his brother."

"There is right on both sides," said Marcus, hoping to calm the quarrel. "I'm glad the assembly voted to send back the Lavinian murderers unharmed, for the murderers had only followed the commands of honour. It's magnanimous, and will increase the glory of Rome. As to King Romulus, perhaps he should have done more to avenge his colleague; he left the decision to us, but we all knew how he wanted the verdict to go. He's a queer man, perhaps more than a man. I was there when he killed Remus, though it all seems a very long time ago. There were faults on both sides, you know. Anyway, Romulus has prospered ever since. If he's guilty of fratricide and still prosperous, that only shows that he enjoys exceptional divine favour."

"Perhaps, but let's see how he ends. Sometimes the gods wait a very long time before punishing the wicked. But he is our King now, since we are all Romans; so I suppose I mustn't ill-wish him." Claudia was still unconvinced, but willing to drop the argument.

"Let's drink the toast again," said Sabina, glad at the chance of peace. "To Rome everlasting, and to you and me and all of us, and to all the other Romans who will come after, until the world ends."

Chapter 8

THE FUGITIVE

✭

Even in this desperate crisis the service of the gods might not be neglected; when the city was in such need of divine assistance it was all the more important that they should be served with due devotion. But there were barely enough warriors to man the wall, after the heavy losses of that earlier defeat. The priests and diviners were all under arms, and only one young man, with an elderly cripple to help him, could be spared to offer the morning sacrifice.

Perperna, aged seventeen, had never before conducted a sacrifice; but then he had never fought in a battle either, though he had been trained as both warrior and haruspex. The chief priest had decided that he could be spared for an hour, to kill a ram and look at its liver. A recruit would be no great loss to the outnumbered garrison, and his education ensured that he would read the omens rightly, while not even careful training could make certain that an untried spearman would be of much use in battle. It was an important trust. For an hour the luck of the city would lie in his hands. He must remember all he had been told, and not scamp the ritual.

The holy place was in the oldest part of the city, the flat-topped rocky crag encircled on three sides by a sinuous river which had been the fortress of the original settlers. Now it was the only quiet part, for the attackers could not approach its water-lapped walls. A brisk dawn wind carried off the sound of the fighting, and the early sun left most of the lower town in shadow. To Perperna, looking out southward over the river, it seemed for a moment that all was as it had been, and that the city was still at peace.

Carefully he removed his iron corselet; the gods do not care for innovation and it is bad manners to bring the new-fangled metal within their holy place. In addition he took off his helmet and greaves. They were of blameless bronze, which the gods know and like; but the haruspex must approach the altar barefoot, and greaves seemed to infringe that rule. He must also veil his head in a special cloth woven from pure linen, and he could not do that while he wore a helmet.

Stripped to his tunic, he bent down and picked up his sword. He slipped the baldric over his left shoulder, and then hesitated. It was a very fine sword, and a free Etruscan should go armed while his city is under attack; but there was no doubt that it was made of iron. Keeping carefully just outside the sacred furrow he edged along to the spot nearest the altar, then laid down the sword with its hilt towards the holy ground. He would cross the furrow undefiled by iron, but in two strides he could once more be an armed free man.

The ram stood by the altar quietly, as they stood always. As was customary, the attendant had fed it with grain soaked in wine until it was drunk and cheerful; for a ram which showed reluctance to be sacrificed would be about the worst omen it was possible to imagine. The old man, standing crooked on his injured leg, was not strong enough to lift it to the stone of sacrifice. Perperna must do that himself, with one easy motion of his smooth young shoulders.

Now the ram lay on his back, with the attendant pulling hard at his hind legs. In this position it looked so like a bent old man that for a moment, standing with the bronze knife bare in his hand, Perperna felt that he was about to do murder. That was as it should be. He knew that the ram was a substitute for a man. The gods would be better pleased if a human being were sacrificed to them; but it would be murder to kill a fellow-citizen and much too expensive to kill a slave every day; so this ram must fill the gap. He stabbed downward into the windpipe, and then sawed at the veins.

Now the beast was dead, its blood smoking on the stone altar to please the gods and persuade them to help Etruscans hard-pressed by the attack of northern savages. Perperna took a fresh grip of the bronze knife, and after a tussle laid open the victim's belly. Before the next operation he hesitated; to plunge his hand into those reeking entrails and grub about for the liver was still disgusting to him. But it was one of the most important duties of a haruspex, and in time he would grow accustomed to it. The chief priest, who was always clean and neat, could pull out a liver without getting a single spot of blood on his gown.

From the lower town came a sudden outburst of shouting, the haphazard lowing of a single bronze trumpet, the rhythmic clashing of sword against shield with which the savages heartened themselves for the charge. Normally the savages were late risers, so that in the besieged town dawn was the quietest period of the day; just for this once they seemed to be trying a dawn attack on the walls. The noise was so loud and threatening that Perperna was tempted to snatch up his arms and run down to his station by the north gate. But he knew that what he did was more important than anything a single warrior could do on the wall. With a shudder of repugnance he forced his right hand into the slimy mass of guts.

He could feel the liver, just where he had been taught to look for it. Even though this was his first performance as chief haruspex he would not pull out some other organ by mistake, which would be a very unlucky thing to do. The liver came out, a horrid bloody brown lump in the palm of his hand. He held it aloft, so that Skyfather should see it first; then lowered his extended arm and waited for the attendant to take it from him.

Without conscious thought he pronounced the ritual prayer, his eyes fixed on the sky as was proper. But he did not at once feel the attendant taking the liver from him. How tiresome. This was the very first time he had been trusted to perform the sacrifice by himself, and he had done his part just as it should be done. Now the rite would be marred because this veteran attendant, who had done it thousands of times before, was woolgathering when he should be ready.

The attendant was staring at the lower town. "The fighting is very noisy, my lord," he said nervously, "and there are roofs burning. Perhaps some of the savages are over our wall. We have given the life of this ram to the gods above, and that's what matters. Shall we go straight down and join in the fight?"

"Is this a religious rite or a chat about the progress of the siege?" Perperna asked angrily. "You know as well as I do that within the sacred enclosure we must speak only the words of the ritual. But since you have broken that rule I may as well break it also. Of course we must complete the rite before we leave. Skyfather wants only the life of a ram, and that we have given him. But the city needs divine guidance, to tell us how to beat these savages. Hold that liver steady, while I inspect it and read its message."

The attendant took the liver in his cupped hands, making a clumsy little bob as he held it under the nose of the young man; by rights he should have presented it on bended knee, but his stiff leg excused him. Then he glanced down casually at the bloody fragment in his hands, just like all the other livers he had held out for inspection during long years of service. Perperna saw his face fall.

Generally speaking, one sheep's liver is very like another; skill and care are needed to spot the tiny wrinkles, warts, and other irregularities which tell of good fortune or ill. Perperna had studied the science for years, with a clay model to guide him; but he was prepared to find, when he examined the sacrifice, that it would indicate nothing in particular. He would have to report that today the gods had no message for their devout worshippers. There would be no harm in that, for no news was reckoned as a favourable omen.

But this liver was like nothing he had ever seen before. It was hard, shrivelled and at the same time rotten; thin threadlike worms writhed within it and already it stank. It was horrible, and frightening.

"As bad as can be," muttered young Perperna. "After such an omen we ought to do nothing at all, except sit quietly with our heads covered until the bad luck has begun to wear off. And instead we are fighting a desperate battle! Come with me. We must get hold of the chief priest and see if he can't stop the fighting before the anger of the gods destroys the whole city."

"Too late, young master. That liver was rotten all through, as a sign that our city is finished. Listen. The fighting sounds closer all the time. And look behind you! The savages are climbing into the citadel itself, and there's no one here to throw them out!"

The attendant pointed to the wall. Perperna looked quickly round, to see three leather helmets bearing the bull's horns of the savages rising above the low curtain which, with the rocky river-bank, was the only defence of this high plateau. The precipice below was steep and exposed, though not quite unclimbable. A single sentry was here an adequate guard; but now, with the battle raging in the lower town, the sentry had slipped away to join his comrades.

The lame attendant hobbled downhill, shouting and waving his arms to summon help. Perperna ran to his sword. There was no time to pick up shield and spear, if he was to reach the wall before the invaders were within.

A hairy face gazed into his eyes, all long moustache and beard under the fantastic bull's horns. The savage wore a stout leather corselet and carried a great oval shield. But just at that moment a swordsman covered only by a linen tunic might take him at a disadvantage; for his left arm with the shield on it was hooked over the top of the wall, and his right hand, encumbered by the sword, clutched a knob of rock outside the citadel. Perperna had never been in battle, but this seemed easy. He lodged his sword in one of the ridiculous bull's horns which made the gaudy helmet useless for serious warfare; the leather cap flew off, and a heavy downward stroke sent the savage toppling to the river far below. Perperna peered over the edge, to watch the body spinning down.

In the same glance he saw a dozen other savages clambering up the rocky face. A small party was evidently trying an escalade while the defenders were busy fighting in the lower town. Even a dozen invaders on the level platform of the citadel would mean irreparable disaster. But the lame attendant would send help as soon as he reached the warleader, and in the meantime one active man standing securely on the summit might be able to hold the wall against a weak and disjointed attack. Perperna ran swiftly to the right, where another savage was climbing in.

He was just too late. This second attacker was not actually over the wall; but his feet were on firm ground, and while holding the coping with his left hand he still kept his shield in a useful position. His body was encased in hairy rawhide which would turn a swordcut. Perperna fenced with him cautiously, hampered by the lack of his own shield.

It was novel to feel the jar of a strong blow strongly parried, and to know that the stroke had been aimed to kill him. It was so absurdly like a fencing-lesson that he had to remind himself that one mistake would be his last. Really these savages fenced very clumsily! That was a long sword, but the man used it as though he feared it would break if it met a parry. Fighting in deadly earnest was not nearly so difficult as one might expect; he could keep this up indefinitely, even if he could not kill his adversary.

It was most unfair that other people should join in, just when he was doing very well in his first fight. As he stepped back to disengage he heard footsteps behind him, and out of the corner of his eye saw the glint of a sword raised to strike. He leapt aside to avoid the blow. A quick turn of the head showed three other savages closing in on him.

This must be the end—of the city, of his friends and family, of himself. The savages had won the citadel, and it hardly mattered how the fighting went in the lower town. Even the bravest warrior might now think of saving his own life.

Perperna ran swiftly to an angle of the wall. The savages were after him, but he was stripped to his linen tunic while they were burdened with shield and corselet. With the point of an enemy sword at his back he leapt the low wall exactly at the spot he had chosen. As he sailed over with room to spare he heard a shout of triumph and derision from his pursuers. To all the savages on the citadel it must have seemed that this panic-stricken Etruscan had jumped down a sheer precipice, avoiding their swords only to be dashed to pieces in the rocky river-bed below. There would be no pursuit.

He landed, as he had planned, with his heels digging into a narrow funnel of loose scree; the stones slid with him, but they slowed up his fall. He was not the only young man in the city who knew of this private way out; but since it was impossible to climb back up the shifting scree there had been no obligation to report a weakness in the defences. Once on the river-bed he dodged among the boulders, waded the shallow summer stream in the middle of the wide channel, and climbed out on the southern bank. Crouched behind a bush, he looked back to see the end of his city.

That it was the end there could be no doubt. The town was burning all over, and capering savages danced on the walls. Many of them carried armfuls of human heads, and none drove captives before him. These invaders sought only plunder and trophies, being too brutal to value slaves. No citizens would survive the disaster, unless there were a few other lucky fugitives like himself.

The threat had been there for years, since before Perperna was born; but the end had come suddenly, so suddenly that still he could not adjust his mind to knowledge of it. The city had been an outpost, the only Etruscan settlement north of the river; all around were barbarous Ligurians who complained that Etruscan ploughs ruined their hunting-grounds. That had continued for three generations, and Ligurian enmity had never been dangerous. The natives were too poor to use decent weapons, and too barbarous to combine into proper armies; they might pounce on strayed citizens, but they feared to attack stone walls.

Three years ago a new foe had come down from the unknown lands beyond the mountains. These men had iron swords and bronze armour, and they moved about in real armies that did nothing but fight; after a victory they took their plunder back over the mountains, so that nobody knew how they lived in their homeland. The few tame Ligurians who would talk to Etruscans said that this new race of warriors called themselves Celts, and that beyond the mountains they owned all the land as far as the edge of the world. The Ligurians, in abject terror, were fleeing from their hunting-grounds in the level river-plain and taking refuge in the jagged hills to the westward.

Last year a Celtic army had trespassed on Etruscan territory, a large army, too strong to be repelled in open battle. The citizens had shut themselves behind their wall and waited for the savages to go away. Before snow had closed the passes the savages withdrew; but first they destroyed the standing crops, so that the citizens went hungry that winter. When another army appeared in the spring there was nothing for it but to go out and fight them or face starvation. Perperna had been one of the youths left behind to hold the walls; which was perhaps a stroke of luck, for few spearmen of the citizen levy survived the encounter. Perhaps he had not been so lucky after all. It might have been better to die in battle, with his comrades round him and his city still standing, rather than to drag out a few more months of life as a hopeless and solitary fugitive.

But at the time of the defeat no one had thought the disaster irreparable. There were still enough old men and boys to garrison the walls, and it was common knowledge that these savages could not break into a fortified place. The city would be very hungry indeed, after the loss of two successive harvests; perhaps in the spring they would have to abandon their hearths and move south of the river to the protection of the main Etruscan League. But for the present all they had to do was to stand firm and man the wall. They had underestimated the skill of the savages, who were learning by experience.

Perperna lay behind his bush until late afternoon. Then the long shadows made it possible to slip away southward, unobserved by watchers on the citadel. It was likely that the town was already deserted, for the savages would not stay long in it after they had sacked it. In any case he was hungry and thirsty and exhausted, and must prepare for the night before darkness fell.

He had a linen tunic and an unscabbarded iron sword, and nothing else in the world. But mentally he was well equipped for survival, even in these conditions. His training as priest and haruspex had taught him to think coolly, and he was used to cold and fasting. Luckily he had not seen the horrors of the sack. Though he knew that all his friends and family had been barbarously slain, he could not picture their bodies lying unburied and disfigured; they had merely left this world for the next, and it would be his duty, as soon as he found a safe refuge, to see that their spirits were properly tended. He could think clearly, without disabling fear.

With his sword he cut a strip from his tunic to serve as a sling, and at his feet were smooth waterworn pebbles. Presently he was lucky enough to find a jagged piece of flint. Tonight the glow of a fire might bring the savages on his trail, but now he could warm himself when he judged it to be safe. He journeyed for several miles, and slept, cold and hungry, in a rocky cleft where a range of hills bounded the southern edge of the plain.

As dawn broke he killed a wild goat, and lay up for three days while he roasted the flesh and made a more serviceable sling from the hide. He made also a baldric to carry the naked sword, and rough sandals for his feet. When he wore these accoutrements he stank horribly, but that was not a grave handicap; passers-by might smell him out, but the mixture of he-goat and man would puzzle sheepdogs. On the fourth day he broke off a branch to serve as a staff, put a little sun-dried meat in his goatskin wallet, and set off to look for another city. He had not seen a single man; the Celts had not crossed the river, but fear of them had driven the local peasants into hiding.

He journeyed slowly, keeping always in narrow valleys where he could not be seen from a distance. It was ten more days before he came to cultivated fields, and hid behind a rocky outcrop to see what kind of men lived there. It was the beginning of harvest, so there were men in the fields. But harvesters work in groups, and it was not until evening that he saw a man alone.

The man was repairing a road, levelling the ruts and filling the puddles with stones. It was obviously hard work, but it called for some skill; it was not the sort of task that would be left to an unsupervised slave. Besides, the man looked intelli-

gent; there was on his face the indefinable expression of responsibility and self-control that marks a free citizen who judges
issues of peace and war. Perperna did not want to approach a
slave in the first place, for slaves were often so frightened of any
stranger that they could not talk sense. This was a good person
to interrogate.

The stranger worked along the track until a low rise of ground
hid him from the nearest harvesters. Now was the time. Perperna
had been crawling cautiously on his belly; he stood erect, his
right hand open in sign of peace, though the sword dangling
from his baldric showed that he was not defenceless. He called
a greeting.

The stranger started, and gripped his hoe as though it were a
spear. Then he saw that Perperna was alone, and answered his
greeting in the correct and grammatical Etruscan of the nobility.

"You made me jump, young man," he said easily. "Lucky
for you that I carry no arms, or I might have struck first and
spoken after. You seem to be in a very bad way. If you seek food
and shelter you must come with me to the city."

"I need help," Perperna replied, "but I would like to know
more about this place before I enter its walls. I wasn't even sure
that it is an Etruscan settlement. I suppose it must be, since you
speak the language so correctly."

The stranger bowed. "My parents taught me carefully, and
I am glad to know I have not forgotten their training. But this
is not my native place, and here their tongue is more barbarous.
I suppose you are a fugitive from one of the northern cities,
destroyed by the Celts. So am I. I have been here two years."

"And is this a good place in which to seek refuge?"

"It's a lot better than wandering over the plain, with no roof
to your head and no hope of a hot meal. The rulers are Etruscans of sorts, though the common people are Italian. Unless
you have kin in some safe city who will give you a fresh start I
advise you to come here. The council will protect you, and you
will sleep safe at night. But unless you have silver you must earn
your keep. Do you know a trade?"

"That will be all right. I am trained in two skilled crafts. I can read the omens in a liver; and I can use all the weapons of a free man, though at present I have only this sword."

"No good at all, I'm afraid. No foreigner may follow either of those callings. The priests here don't welcome competition, and of course they won't let strangers bear arms. That's only prudence."

"Then what will they expect me to do? I don't want to live on alms."

"You won't get alms, after the usual three days of hospitality. If you want to eat regularly you will be expected to work in the fields, as I do. In the morning they will give you a task, and a dinner when you have finished it. Then next day they will give you another task, and so on."

"But that's the life of a slave," Perperna protested. "Haven't they given you a ploughland? Aren't you working your own field?"

"Indeed not. There isn't enough land to go round, especially now that the Celts are driving us out of the north. I'm not a slave, you know, even though the life is pretty hard. I am a free refugee, a ward of the city. I sleep in the porch of the council house, and they give me a warm tunic every winter. Nobody is supposed to beat me, though it isn't tactful to complain at every whack across the shoulders. Perhaps it isn't much of a life, but then I don't deserve much. My city was sacked, and my kin are dead. I'm lucky to have escaped formal slavery, since I possess nothing."

"Then why not move on, to some place where you would be more welcome?"

"Where would that be? Here they speak my language, and worship the gods I knew as a child. It's my own fault. I should have fought to the death when the savages broke into my city. Now I have food, and a safe place to sleep in. If I moved on to the Italian cities they would make me a slave, working in chains and shut up at night."

"If you are strong enough to work you are strong enough to fight. You could join a band of brigands, and perhaps gain silver enough to buy land of your own."

"I have thought of that, naturally. But it's not a life that would suit me. I'm old, and stiff in my joints. Probably I would be killed by some angry farmers, and if not the other brigands would steal my plunder. Here I am safe, and that counts for a lot when you have been chased as I was."

"Then you advise me to do as you did, to go as a suppliant to the city council?"

"I don't give you advice. You must do as you wish. If you enter the city you will be granted the three days of hospitality due to any wayfarer. But if they suspect that you plan to join the brigands they will crucify you before you can get away. In these parts we don't like brigands. When the three days are up they will put you to work. What more can you hope for? By rights you should be dead, killed in the defence of your city."

"Thank you for the warning," answered Perperna. "I shall be a brigand. In fact from this moment I *am* a brigand. You see this sword? Have you anything that would be useful to me?"

"You have decided for yourself," said the old man with a weary sigh. "Don't pretend afterwards that I advised you. Here you will have bread and wine, with a bit of meat on feast days, and you will sleep safe while a sentry guards the wall. As a brigand you will eat beef every day, except when you eat nothing; and it's just possible you will gather riches, though more likely that you will be stabbed in the back as soon as you are worth robbing. If you have really made up your mind I won't hinder you. Let me see. Here is a hunk of bread and cheese, and this little knife may be useful. Please don't take my shoes. They are my only pair, and no better than your goatskin sandals. After you have gone I must raise the alarm, to explain how I lost the knife they lent me. So don't raid our sheepfold tonight, when the sentry will be looking out for you."

"Very well. I don't know when I shall taste bread again, so I'll take yours; also the knife, but you may keep the shoes. By the way, one day I might meet some of your kin. Will you tell me your name, and the name of your city?"

"I am a fugitive. I have no name, and no city. When I am dead no one will tend my spirit, and as my ashes cool I shall be utterly forgotten. That's what it is to be a fugitive. Perhaps you are right to choose the brigands. Now get into hiding. I shall count to a thousand before I shout for help."

It was not difficult to join a band of brigands. Perperna carried a good sword, and was not himself worth robbing, so the leader made no objection. This leader was himself an Etruscan fugitive, a nameless man whom his followers called Mor, a barbarian word meaning Tall. There were four other Etruscans in the group, and a score of Ligurians and Italians. They lived rather by petty thieving than by armed robbery, for since they had only six shields among twenty-five men they dared not face real warriors; but they had a lair in a narrow glen, where they slept in huts of turf and cooked openly over big fires. During the winter Perperna sheltered with them rather than try to live alone in the open. When spring came round he had a thick sheepskin cloak and sound shoes, and plentiful roast mutton had built up his reserves of strength.

As soon as the weather was warm enough for sleeping in the open he left the band and wandered southward alone. He felt the need for companionship, but the brigands could not give it to him. Even the Etruscans among them had degenerated into slow-witted oafs, thinking no farther than the next meal; and their customs embarrassed him. Three frowsy women lived in the camp, survivors of many stolen from outlying fields; but at the end of winter Mor's private concubine died, and the leader seemed to think that the latest recruit, a handsome youth in his nineteenth year, would make an adequate substitute. It was time to be moving.

He could look after himself. His nerves were steady; he could feast or starve, doze or watch, huddle by a fire or endure the frost, with an equal mind. Night and day he was in danger of death, but he was seldom afraid though he avoided unnecessary risk. The sword which was his only link with home was clean and sharp, and with a sling-stone he never missed. Anyone would find it hard to kill him. That was why he was still alive.

He travelled slowly, for he must hunt or steal his food; and when he had killed a sheep or a deer it would be wasteful to move on until it was eaten. But he kept moving in a definite direction, with the coast on his right and the high hills on his left. He knew, from what he had learned in the old days, that beyond the Etruscan settlements he would find other peoples who also lived in cities; they might be more generous to penniless fugitives. But when the first frosts of autumn warned him to seek shelter he was still in lands ruled by Etruscans, though most of the men working in the fields were commoners who spoke only Italian.

Once, while he dozed on a hillside, a troop of mercenaries marched noisily through the valley below. He crept up behind the rearguard; when he had been recognized as a solitary outlaw he approached boldly and asked whether they had room for another recruit. They were willing to take him if he wanted to come, though at present they were unemployed and so not very eager to increase their numbers. For a few days he ate well and slept soundly, with a sentry watching over him and comrades to guard his back.

After ten days he slipped away from the band. He had drawn no pay and they did not bother to chase such an unimportant deserter. The life did not suit him, chiefly because his pride would not allow him to fill the place appropriate to a mere swordsman. He had no shield and no armour; since he could not stand in the line of battle he was inferior to the basest Ligurian who had picked up a full panoply. He was told that when they fought his post would be somewhere on the flank, where he might use his sling; and that in the meantime he might as well get on with cooking and fetching water, tasks beneath the dignity of fully armed warriors.

During his second winter as a fugitive he actually worked for his living, like a peasant. In these more settled southern lands he could not find a suitable band of brigands; the few and hunted outlaws were as likely to murder him for his sword as to welcome him as a recruit. During a heavy rainstorm, which reminded him that soon he must find a permanent shelter, he came on a solitary sheepfold high among the hills. So late in the season he expected it to be deserted, but before he could enter he was bayed by two fierce dogs; an old shepherd came out to investigate the noise. The old man knew him at once for what he was, a dangerous outlaw on the run; but that did not worry him. He was a slave, and the sheep belonged to his master. The young stranger could take a sheep if he liked, for there was nothing else worth stealing; but if he was seeking safe harbour for the winter let him stay and work for his food. Perperna, cold and wet and miserable, looked towards the glowing hearth and closed the bargain.

After years of solitude the old man was very like a sheep himself. In these southern districts the flocks were left out all winter, and he did not expect a visit from his master until spring at the earliest. He spoke a few words of Etruscan; but his own language was Italian, and he talked softly to himself all the time he was awake. Time had stopped for him more than fifty years ago, when he was stolen by slave-raiders; he chattered of his childhood in a Sabine village, never of anything later. When Perperna had helped him with the lambing, and it was time for him to be on his way again, he had learned a fluent, ungrammatical Italian besides the elements of caring for sheep.

This kind of life could not go on for ever. He was clear-sighted enough to realize that he had been very lucky; in the summer it was not very hard for an outlaw to pick up a living, and so far for each winter he had found a safe harbour. But sickness or an accident might leave him starving and helpless in some hidden cave, or an enraged farmer might get him with a lucky javelin; there had been narrow escapes already. He was entirely alone. That was the trouble.

He might steal a girl, though as a rule there were warriors within call when village maidens took the pigs to pasture in the beech-wood. In theory, once he had caught a girl and raped her no other man would touch her and she would have to be faithful to him. But in practice things did not always work out like that; the girl might still hate him enough to betray him. Besides, the gods disapprove of such behaviour, and Perperna himself did not like it.

If he joined a large band he would never be more than a scullion; a shieldless swordsman was not the equal of true warriors. Besides, a large band, its members bound by long comradeship, might regard him as an outsider and sell him into slavery. He could go into partnership with another solitary outlaw; there were plenty about, though it was not easy to get in touch with them. There the tiresome obstacle was his youth and good looks; his partner would always be trying to climb into his blankets.

All the same, this summer he must find companionship, if it could be managed; and preferably in a large community, where he could sink unnoticed into the background until he had learned his way about. If there was no other chance he could at any time enter an Etruscan city, to lead the serf-like life of a penniless fugitive. But he had been told that beyond Etruria the Italians lived in some kind of imitation city they had copied from their more civilized neighbours; if he found himself near one he would try its welcome first, before he resigned himself to what his countrymen offered to their fellows in distress.

Shortly after harvest-time he came to another river, flowing southward to the sea on his right like all the other rivers he had encountered. On the western bank the land was fertile and closely cultivated; but there were patches of scrub and woodland, and a single man, long practised in these evasions, could work down unseen to the bank of the stream.

In the river below him, by a little island, a bend slowed up the current and left a ridge of gravel which was evidently a much-used ford. On the farther bank a cluster of low but steep-sided hills rose from a flat plain of beech-woods and scattered cultivation. Two neighbouring hills were crowned with palisades, and in the valley was a dusty hollow with a few buildings scattered about it, perhaps the common meeting-place of the two villages.

For though the two settlements were crowded and populous they could not be called cities, at least by an Etruscan. They were defended by stakes on top of earthen banks, not by proper stone walls; and the houses within were round huts, thatched with rushes. It looked as though some lesser race of villagers had tried to copy the great cities of the Rasenna as well as their limited technique and limited intelligence would permit. Perperna guessed that this must be one of the new Italian cities; in the good old days when he was himself a citizen he had heard of them. Here he might find a better welcome than in a real city inhabited by civilized men; at least the experiment would be worth trying.

The strangers had some tincture of civilization. That short stretch of road by the ford was better made than anything he had seen in his own country. As he looked closer he saw that the ford itself was paved with great slabs of flat stone. The fields were neatly cultivated, and vines grew as well as barley. He might find a good home in these alien villages; but not if they made him a slave, or even a labourer working all day for the night's food and shelter. He must inquire cautiously, and not let himself be captured before he had decided to enter of his own free will. He settled down to wait in hiding until he had a chance to talk with one of the natives alone.

These people were well organized. Towards sunset he could see them all coming in from the fields, while a guard of fully armed men marched out to watch over the cattle penned in the valley. Then a trumpet blew, and the gates of the palisades closed. Now he dared not approach, for a stranger prowling by night would be treated as an enemy. There was cold bacon in his pouch, but he dared not light a fire. Wrapped in his cloak, he settled down to wait for the day.

At dawn the trumpet sounded again, and the gates opened. Perperna was preparing to cross the river when he saw a party splashing through the ford towards him. It was a patrol of a dozen fully armed spearmen. He waited for them, since they were exactly the kind of people with whom he could safely make contact. They would not be afraid when he sprang out before them, but if they were hostile he ought to be able to run away from men who carried shields and full armour.

Better still, when the patrol reached his side of the river the men spread out to search the bushes. One man came quite close to him, where he crouched among the thorns. He could talk to a single man, as he had planned.

The approaching warrior was stocky and bearded, apparently in his middle thirties; his armour was plain but serviceable, with more leather in it than bronze. He did not look as though he enjoyed patrolling, but he did his duty carefully, without scamping it. Perperna stuck his head out of the bush and called quietly: "Can I speak to you? I come in peace."

He spoke in Etruscan, because in moments of stress that was the language which came automatically to his mind. The other luckily understood it after a fashion, though he answered in Italian.

"Peace it is then. What do you want?"

"I am an Etruscan and a fugitive," said Perperna in Italian. "My city has been destroyed by savages, and I am looking for a new home. What is the name of your town, over the river? Do you allow strangers to join you?"

"Our city is called Rome, because it was founded by King Romulus, son of the god Mars. You may not have heard of it, for it's no older than you are, about eighteen years I suppose. Some strangers are welcome among us, and others are not. We need warriors, but we have thieves enough. Stand up and let me have a look at you. If you look all right to me I shall call my commander and you must tell him your story."

Perperna stood, threw his sword at the other's feet, and held out both hands to prove they were empty. "I'm harmless enough, as you can see. But I don't fancy being captured by a patrol of foreigners of whom I know nothing. Don't call your commander, or I shall run off faster than you can follow me. Can't I talk to you alone, and find out more about this place before I put myself in your hands?"

"Certainly, if that's what you want. I'm not afraid of you. I'm not hunting for slaves either, in case you are afraid of me. We can't keep discontented slaves in our place, so near the Etruscan boundary. Unless you have been robbing among our farms, on the other side of the river, we won't do anything worse than chuck you out if we decide not to keep you."

"I have never in my life crossed this river, so I can't have robbed Romans on the far side. You can see that I live as a robber, but that's not really my trade. I am a fugitive, and if I went to an Etruscan city they would keep me a landless labourer all my life. I stole to stay alive; though sometimes I worked, and I'm willing to work again. I want to join a city, or a village, or a clan, anything where they will let me fight in the army and perhaps give me land of my own to plough."

"Then you have come to the right place. If we accept you, you will have your station in the ranks and a vote in the assembly and a ploughland of your own. But *I* can't make you a Roman. Not even my commander can do that. First you will have to speak to King Romulus, and then if he recommends you the assembly of spearmen must accept you. But only the King matters. The assembly never goes against his wishes."

"Must I enter your palisade, and be your prisoner, before I know whether you are willing to accept me?"

"You sound very cautious, for a bold, wicked, single-handed robber. Do you think we shall cook you for supper? Look here, I'll take an oath if you like. My name is Marcus Aemilius, and I came here as one of the original founders of the city, eighteen years ago. I've lived here ever since, and I have a wife and children up on the hill. Now then, I don't know anything about your complicated and powerful Etruscan gods, so I shall put my hand on this rock. I swear that if you speak to King Romulus no harm will come to you, and that if we don't accept you as a citizen you will be free to leave. My oath is as firm as this boulder, and if I break it may all the rocks in the world fall on my head."

"That's a good oath, and I trust it. My name will be Perperna when I am a proper spearman again, but since my city has been destroyed it would be unlucky to name it. Will you carry my sword as we cross the river? By the way, what are you doing on this side of it?"

"Looking for traces of Etruscan raiders, as we do every morning. The river is a boundary, and we don't want to be caught napping. Now it's time to go back again. You keep close to me, and I'll see you're not bothered until King Romulus has decided your case."

Perperna came willingly, carrying his sword since the other did not seem to want it. There was an aura of practical honest kindliness about this Marcus. He was not a gentleman and he was shamefully ignorant concerning the gods, but it was obvious that his word could be trusted.

They found the King just on the other side of the ford, in the valley between the two fortified hilltops. He had been performing some kind of sacred ceremony in a templum marked out near the river-bank, though Perperna thought privately that this son of Mars went about the service of his relatives in a very amateurish way. Surely while sacrificing he did not carry iron weapons, or keep his armed bodyguard within the sacred enclosure? Yet it seemed he had done so.

Romulus was a tall, imposing warrior in early middle age; his bushy beard and the fine carriage of his head gave him a presence. But he was running to fat, and when his paunch grew he would cease to look dignified. There were lines on his face as though he frowned often, though he greeted his subject with a cheerful smile. It seemed a lax kind of court. Anyone could come up without notice and consult the King on public or private affairs. There were no servile prostrations, no preliminary search for hidden weapons. Yet the armed and suspicious bodyguard of surly young men remained within hearing, their swords loose in their scabbards.

"So another man wants a share in the celebrated luck of Rome," the King said affably, as soon as Marcus had explained his errand. "Well, we used to take anyone, anyone who chose to seek refuge in our Asylum over there. But since we prospered we have closed it, and now we pick and choose. However, we still have room for stout warriors; and a man who can live as a solitary brigand, with no comrade to guard his back, must be worth his place in the battle line. We have other Etruscans here, a number of them, and some are well born by their own account. But Latin is the language of the city, so it's just as well you can understand it. You seem to be the kind of man we want, and if you answer my questions satisfactorily I shall ask the assembly to accept you. All the same, these questions must be cleared up. To begin with, have you any reason to suppose that the gods are angry with you?"

"My city was destroyed by savages from over the mountains," answered Perperna, "which makes it seem that the gods are displeased with me. On the other hand, I got away safely; which more or less cancels it out."

"That isn't what I mean. Cities rise and fall. Except my Rome, of course, which is destined to endure for all eternity. Have you yourself done anything to anger the gods, incest, or sacrilege, or the murder of a kinsman?"

"Never."

"You are very certain in your answer. Sometimes these crimes can be committed unaware, as dozens of stories tell us."

"Yes, my lord. It is possible to anger the gods by accident, though only when the gods are already hostile can the accident befall. I might have done some forbidden deed, not knowing that it was forbidden. But if heaven were hunting me for some crime I should immediately be aware of it. I am of pure Etruscan birth, true Rasenna on both sides of the family; and I have been trained as a sacrificing priest and haruspex. I am not accursed, for if I were I should hear in my mind the snuffling of the Old Women as they followed my trail."

"Don't speak of the Old Women here, in this lucky place. But I understand that you know what you are talking about, and I accept your word that you do not bring bad luck into my city. There is still one other question. You are an Etruscan of pure race; but the Etruscans live just across the river. Will you fight honestly for your city, if we go to war against your own people?"

"Certainly. If those Etruscans were my people I would not be here. They make fugitives into landless labourers, and the League never helped us when the savages were battering our wall."

"Very well. Now one last point. You are quite alone? No comrades, no kin, no wife or concubine, no children? I see.

Then go up that path there to the Palatine and ask for the royal hut, the Regia. My servants will look after you until the assembly meets this evening. They will also lend you armour and a shield, so that you make a decent show at the meeting. Come down here in the evening and let the citizens see you, and I shall recommend that you be accepted."

Chapter 9

RELIGION AND WAR

★

By the autumn Perperna had settled into his new life until it was hard to remember a time when he was not climbing up and down the steep path to the Palatine. He attended the assembly when it met, which was nearly every day; and on the rare occasions when a vote was demanded he had his place in the tribe of Etruscans and other non-Latins, the Luceres. He had been allotted a ploughland, though he could not begin to cultivate it until spring. When the spearmen mustered in arms he took his place in the front rank with the best warriors. He assisted at the sacrifices, because his early training had taught him how to behave in a consecrated templum. In law, in religion, in military affairs, he was a free Roman citizen.

And the whole business was a sham, as he reminded himself whenever he felt too cheerful. He had no weapons of his own, no plough or seedcorn, no beasts to offer in the daily sacrifices. He might go through the motions of citizenship, but in fact he was as completely the servant of King Romulus as if he were a bought slave. His arms were borrowed from the King's store, from the King he must seek all the equipment of a farmer, every day he ate the King's bread and at night he lay by the King's fire. (These Romans made a fuss about the King's fire; it must burn continually, which meant that the girls of the King's household spent most of their time tending it.) At first the King demanded nothing in return, which made the position all the more unpleasant; for the borrowed shield, even the borrowed shoes, might be taken back on any excuse or none. It was a relief when King Romulus suggested that he might care to serve him as a celer.

That was a queer, busy life; but in a way it was reassuring, for he was giving value for his weapons and the King was his friend. Every morning he must report for orders. He would be detailed for the bodyguard, sent on an errand, or, occasionally, given a day off to attend to his private affairs.

There were in all about three hundred celeres, past or present; for many senior members of the band were practically retired. These seniors were quiet elderly Latin spearmen; they had followed Romulus all his life and defended him from his wicked uncle in the old days before Rome had been founded. Perperna felt at ease with them, as much as any young Etruscan could feel at ease with elderly Latins. They were sensible, honest veterans, with wives and children and well-tended ploughlands. They were absolutely loyal to their lord, and would defend him against any foe; but they had their private self-respect, and there were things they would not do, even at the word of command.

The younger men were not such pleasant companions; they reminded Perperna of the brigands he had met on his travels. They were brave warriors, and so poor that they would have found it difficult to remain free citizens without this steady employment. Nearly all of them were also fugitives from some disaster in the outside world, strangers utterly dependent on the King's bounty. Some were rogues who bullied timid citizens and pilfered from their property; though, like brigands, they would not steal from a comrade and Perperna was safe from their depredations. There were cut-throats among them, who boasted of the evil deeds that had sent them into exile. Taken as a whole, the younger celeres were the rowdiest and least reputable of the citizens, and it seemed odd that the King had chosen them for his close companions.

Perperna would have liked to make other friends; but there were few Etruscans of good birth in Rome, for all that the tribe of the Luceres, one-third of the community, was called by an Etruscan name. The Lucumo, their leader, no longer appeared in public; he was still a young man, but some past blow on the head had brought ever-increasing damage to his wits. When Perperna called on him formally in his hut the unfortunate noble greeted him politely; but within five minutes he had forgotten the name of his guest and once more greeted him as a stranger. He had found a safe refuge, but he could not lead the Etruscans of Rome.

Some of the other Luceres had been born in Etruscan communities, which made them Etruscan in the eyes of their Italian neighbours. But in the cities of southern Etruria only a small ruling class were true Rasenna; most of these mongrels of mixed blood were as foreign to the well-born Perperna as any Latin.

When he was not standing, fully armed, behind King Romulus, or carrying out the royal commands, he led an aimless and lonely life. There was only one home where he could drop in uninvited; for in general the Romans, strangers gathered from every quarter of Italy, kept themselves more private than the citizens of other cities. The friendly family was the household of Marcus Aemilius, the spearman who had persuaded him to try his luck in this uncongenial settlement. But for that cheerful fireside, where a handsome matron presided over a brood of young children, he might have moved on to seek another refuge before winter.

Marcus was not a lively companion or a witty talker; in fact he was a bit of a bore. But after listening to the boasts of vicious young celeres Perperna was glad to visit the family so that he could bathe himself, for a change, in an atmosphere of simple goodness. Sabina did not scuttle into a back room at the approach of a strange man; if she was cooking, or washing the children, she joined in the talk, and if for once she had nothing to do she pulled up a stool and took her share as the wine-bowl passed round. It was obvious that husband and wife were friends and partners. Even a visitor could see that these people were governed by a moral code; unlike the young celeres, they would not do anything at all merely because the King had commanded it.

That was the real trouble about Rome, Perperna thought to

himself; the lack of a moral code. This place was not yet truly
a city, though in time it might become one; and the reason was
that the inhabitants had not yet made up their minds whether
they were farmers or bandits. Even Marcus was always talking about the wild plans for universal rapine which had brought
the original settlers to this exposed cluster of hills on the frontier.
It was odd to see his wrinkled farmer's face and his stiff, weather-
beaten ploughman's body, and to hear coming from those
bearded lips speculations about the great raids they would
undertake next spring. His stocky bow-legs would never carry
him over an Etruscan wall, yet he talked like a bloodthirsty
pirate. But when Perperna inquired about the profits from last
year's raids it gradually emerged that Rome was at peace,
though there had been a few skirmishes soon after the founding
of the city. When Marcus genuinely made plans, instead of
talking idly about what he hoped might happen, all his projects
were for the improvement of his land; next year he would plant
vines on the steeper slopes, for already there was more than
enough barley in Rome.

That seemed to be the general opinion, when the time came
for everyone to turn out to gather the harvest. Only the younger,
landless, celeres remained under arms to man the outposts,
while citizens and slaves, women and children, worked in the
fields. Perched on his watchtower, Perperna felt out of things;
but next year he would have his own land and go harvesting
with the rest of the community.

At nightfall he went back to eat supper in the King's hall as
usual. As soon as he reached the Palatine he saw that something
was wrong. Harvest is a time of rejoicing, but everyone looked
gloomy and frightened. The first slave-girl he met in the hall
told him the reason. "Haven't you heard? There's no yield to
the barley. It looks all right until you cut it, but then there's no
grain in the ear. All day I was reaping, and I don't suppose I
gathered enough for supper."

"You'll get by, sweetheart," a young celer put in. "A strong
woman will always fetch a good price. If the King can't feed
you he will sell you for foreign corn, and in the winter you will

eat bread every night while we are boiling nettles. But the rest of us may be hungry before next harvest."

"*You* won't go hungry, young man, while there's food in Rome; not with a sword like yours," the girl answered impudently.

"You see, Perperna? Even slaves mock me. That's because I am only a simple Latin ploughboy, not a ferocious Etruscan noble."

"I never raped three sisters in one evening. If I had I would not boast about it, as you do. The girl is angry only because you haven't yet raped her, and that will soon be put right."

These ruffians must be answered in their own language.

Supper was as plentiful as usual, for they were still eating last year's grain. When the wine-bowl had begun its travels the King himself entered the hall and called for silence. As a rule he gave his orders at the morning parade, and the celeres listened quietly to this unexpected speech.

"Something seems to have gone wrong with our luck," Romulus said easily. "It's nothing to worry about. The gods aren't really angry, or I should know it. All the same, we need more barley than has grown in our fields this year, so we shall just have to take it from those who have it. Mars has already put a splendid plan into my head. I want twenty volunteers who can ride over rough ground in the dark, and perhaps slit a throat in the morning. Now don't all shout at once."

This King Romulus might be a bit of a brigand, Perperna thought to himself, but he was certainly a cunning warleader. The men of Fidenae had been wrong to rely on those new-fangled gates in their city wall. Most gates move on a stone pivot which fits into a stone socket; but a stranger who came to Fidenae had shown the citizens how to hang their gates from leather hinges fastened to iron hooks. Such gates were more easily opened and shut, stray pebbles could not jam the workings, and the few inches of clearance above the ground made a novel spyhole from which to watch besiegers; besides, leather hinges were the latest fashion among the more cultured cities beyond the eastern sea. But leather can be cut by the sword.

Romulus, or possibly his father Mars, had thought out the scheme. The little party of celeres, creeping up in the dark, cut through the leather hinges without disturbing the city watch. When the main gate was unbarred in the morning both doors at once fell outwards to leave a broad gap in the stout wall; and a few minutes later the whole citizen-levy of Rome was maching steadily for the entry. The outnumbered men of Fidenae must fight in the open, with no help from their massive wall. Rather than accept slavery for themselves and their families they would die fighting; but they very wisely offered to negotiate before blows struck in anger should bring undying blood-feud between Fidenae and Rome.

Romulus had no time to waste. Tomorrow, unless peace was made at once, Veii and perhaps the whole Etruscan League would be on the march to help Fidenae. The terms offered were generous. Fidenae must forsake the Etruscan League and acknowledge the leadership of Rome; her stored barley would be shared (but the Romans would pay in cattle for what they took); a number of the citizens must emigrate to Rome, leaving their houses and ploughlands for the Romans who would replace them.

Fidenae accepted these terms. Before midday the Roman garrison was installed in its new home, and the main army was marching back to the Palatine.

When next Perperna dropped in to see Marcus the talk turned naturally to this latest stroke of foreign policy. Of course Marcus was pleased to know that there would be food for the winter; but he was not so sure, now that it had happened, that he approved of unprovoked aggression against a peaceful neighbour.

"They had done us no harm, and they thought they were at peace with us," he said unhappily. "It's not like the old days, in the beginning, when everyone knew we were at war with the whole world. Now it's going to be very difficult to trade with foreign cities."

"It was a dashing exploit, all the same," Perperna said cheerfully. "It was clever of the King to spot the weakness in these new gates."

"It's over and done with, and can't be altered," Marcus continued mournfully. "This bread I am eating was stolen, and if I didn't eat it I should be hungry. But I wish we hadn't been so hard on those people, whom we overcame only because we took them by surprise."

"Hard on them?" Perperna exclaimed in genuine surprise. "The King's terms were a miracle of generosity. We had Fidenae at our mercy. Any other army would have sacked the place, slaughtered the warriors, and sold the women and children for slaves. I had never imagined that you could capture a place and then permit it to exist. If the King treats the conquered with such leniency other cities will yield when he attacks them, and the power of Rome must grow."

"I'm glad you think so," said Sabina, coming forward with a bowl of stew. "Dinner's ready, and no one ever feels scruples about eating stolen mutton. Somehow sheep and cattle are fair game, though I agree that it *feels* wicked to steal a harvest. But it's amusing to hear a noble Etruscan excusing conduct that shocks a mere Latin villager—and shocks a simple Sabine housewife into the bargain. We forget that for two years you were a bandit, my dear Perperna. You must get hold of some innocent Roman maiden and marry her. Then your wife will recall you to a proper sense of right and wrong."

"Yes, when will you marry?" asked Marcus. "Shall I look out for you, among the men with growing daughters? You will need children to help you in clearing your ploughland."

"You are very kind, but I won't bother you. My family on both sides are true Rasenna, and I don't choose to marry until I can find a maiden of the same blood."

"Dear me, you won't find one of those in Rome," said Sabina with a laugh. It was impossible to snub her, just as it was much too easy to snub the kindly Marcus. Perperna could never get the emphasis right when he tried to close an awkward subject of conversation.

"You will have to look sharp to get a wife of any kind," she continued. "We haven't nearly enough women to go round. Now don't ask Marcus if you can borrow me for a night. That isn't really an old Latin custom, whatever you Etruscans may say."

"I'm not the marrying sort. Two years of brigandage spoiled me for domestic life. Now tell me: when I have land of my own am I allowed to kill goats that stray on my fields?"

The best way to stop these dear people from intruding into his private life was to get them talking about the laws of their new city, a subject in which they took a deep interest and pride.

That evening a gale blew from the south, and in the morning there fell a rain of blood over Rome.

Even the vital work of harvest was abandoned. The look-outs on the border were doubled, in fear that enemies should take advantage of this terrible calamity; but otherwise all the citizens stayed under cover in their own huts to avoid the ghastly pollution. About midday the weather cleared. At the first gleam of sun the King, accompanied by a great crowd, went to the templum on the Palatine to sacrifice. There was nothing odd about the liver of the dead bull, and after it had been exposed to public view the general excitement diminished. Romulus announced that he would seek divine guidance, alone, in his storehouse of sacred things. On such an unlucky day no work should be done, and the citizens would be wise to stay at home until evening. At sunset the assembly would meet, and the King would make public the advice he had received from father Mars.

Perperna was among the half-dozen celeres who loitered below the ladder at the entry to the storehouse. His comrades were uneasy, edging away from the shadow of the holy building; but he leaned casually against a post, whistling. Little odds and ends of lucky charms picked up by ignorant Latins could not harm a true Rasenna, a learned servant of the great gods. King Romulus must have seen him through the cracks of the building, for suddenly he put his head through the door and beckoned him within.

"You don't seem to be impressed by this portent, or even by

the sacred things brought by my ancestors all the way from uncanny Samothrace," he said crossly. "Who are you? Oh, that's different, you are the young Etruscan. You haven't my luck, but you may well have more knowledge. I want a private chat with you."

The interior of the storehouse stank of badly cured hides, and there were fleas hopping among the rushes. Perperna remained unimpressed.

The King peered at him sharply. "Yes, it's time we had a private talk. Your luck is not nearly so strong as mine. Even if you don't grant me that, good manners ought to make you respectful to my family shrine. Besides, I have three hundred celeres to cut throats for me, and you haven't. So when I ask your advice you had better give it frankly. Now then, can you tell me anything about this rain of blood?"

"It isn't really blood . . ." Perperna began, but the King interrupted.

"I know that, of course. I'm not a fool. If this morning Sky-father had bled all over us something pretty terrible would have happened by midday. The blood wouldn't just stop, with nothing coming after. So when I was sacrificing I took care to get a spot of bull's blood on my tunic, just beside this mark made by the heavenly rain. As you see, now both are dry the colour's quite different. But if it isn't blood, what is it; and what does it mean?"

"It falls occasionally." Perperna spoke easily, as one equal to another. "In the south it's rather more common. Our learned men have noticed that it comes always on the heels of a strong south wind. So we suppose that on the far shore of the southern sea there must be a red, dusty country. Sometimes the wind picks up this dust and carries it to fall on Italy. That's the explanation that our wise men give, and it's true as far as it goes. But I am a trained priest and haruspex; and I can tell you that this perfectly natural dust falls only when the gods are angry. Now what have you and your Romans been doing to anger the gods?"

The King scowled, clenching his fists and drawing himself

erect. Then he smiled and shrugged his shoulders. "We are alone here, and I told you to speak freely. Anyway, if at present the gods are angry, I know how to wheedle father Mars into a good temper. Let's try and think calmly. Of course everything we have done since the foundation of the city has been an outrage on ordinary morality. But there must be something special. I can't think of any particular recent crime."

"Incest? Sacrilege? Parricide?" asked Perperna calmly, and the King shook his head at each question. "Then it's not the gods above who are angry, but the spirits of the underworld. Murder of kinsmen? Corpses left unburied? Neglect of the blood-feud? Murder in time of truce?"

"That's it," Romulus struck in, "or rather, the last two, both of them. I thought those troubles had been forgotten. It all began some years ago, with the murder of the Lavinian envoys. But only last year my colleague was murdered, and I have certainly neglected to avenge him."

"Then you will have to appease the neglected spirits, whose anger has brought this portent on Rome. Luckily that's not so very difficult. You need not actually avenge the murdered King, or put to death all the murderers of the envoys. Just do something to show you have recognized your duty."

"You don't have to teach me my own business, young man. I have been King here for the better part of twenty years, and I know how to comfort my subjects. I can easily atone for those two errors of judgment. But I shall have to invent some striking ceremonial to make plain to the people that the rain of blood has left no permanent pollution."

"There's no better way of getting rid of bloodstains than by washing, my lord," said Perperna, for the first time addressing Romulus by his title. "Let them wash themselves, and their clothes, again and again in clean water. If you want to make the ritual impressive you could first consecrate the water, and perhaps sprinkle it over the whole city."

"That's a good idea. You Etruscans understand these things. Mind you, I believe in the gods, as I'm sure you do. I have my luck, which was put into me when I was born and which I have done nothing to deserve; that helps me in tight places. But even so the gods demand a certain bare minimum of honest dealing, and I am careful not to provoke them. I shall quite genuinely appease those angry ghosts. As for this blood, and the washing of it away, I shall compose some moving prayers, and mean every word as I say them. But the real object will be to calm my people, not to placate the gods. There's nothing wrong in that, is there? Now I suppose this public washing is an Etruscan rite. Can you give me any hints on the most solemn way of doing it?"

On the next day there took place the first ritual lustration of Rome. The King sprinkled his sacred water on every gate and every street-corner, and a few drops were poured into the water-pot of each household, for the cleaning of polluted garments. When all the citizens had been cleansed, and knew themselves to be cleansed, there was a long and argumentative session of the assembly. In the end it was agreed that those Sabines who had been implicated in the murder of the Lavinian envoys should be deprived of their citizenship. They were given ample time to get away, and in fact many of them had gone back to their native hills soon after the murder of King Tatius; so nobody was executed or put in danger of death. But right had been done, and publicly. The spirits of the murdered envoys had no justification for further molestation of the living.

It looked as though the murder of King Tatius could be avenged only at the cost of a troublesome war. Luckily the Lavinians, themselves terrified at news of the awesome rain of blood, did justice of their own free will. They in turn sent their murderers into exile, and the whole matter could be decently forgotten.

All the same, news that the gods were displeased with King Romulus spread widely throughout the countryside. The luck of Rome had been weakened; there might be plunder to be picked up by the adventurous. While the Romans were still occupied in getting in the last of their meagre harvest, sentries gave warning of the approach of a hostile force.

The army which poured down on them, without a declaration of war, was soon recognized as the levy of Camerium, a minor town in the Etruscan League. The invaders had crossed the river by a ford upstream of Rome, and as the citizens formed their ranks they could see smoke rising from their stackyards in the open country. King Romulus had been caught unprepared, and the enemy hoped to pick up a few waggonloads of barley without fighting. But the habit of meeting in a daily assembly made the citizens swift to mobilize. By mid-afternoon the spearmen were marching up the left bank of the river.

In battle King Romulus kept a small bodyguard beside him, but the rest of the three hundred celeres were scattered through the whole levy, to inspire the main body of citizens and set an example of willing obedience to orders. Perperna found himself detailed as a front-rank spearman among the Sabine Tatians, who might well begin to act independently unless a few strangers were brought in to break up their sense of forming a separate community. He went a little unwillingly, though he did not dare to refuse. It seemed a dangerous business to march into battle among strangers, who might perhaps desert him on the field and would feel no obligation to save him in a tight place. His safety depended in particular on the steadiness of his right-hand neighbour, whose shield must guard his shieldless right side. He was pleased to see that the man appeared to be a decent veteran spearman; as soon as they were on the march Perperna began a conversation.

"I have never fought in a set battle against civilized men," he said with a placatory smile, "though I have faced throngs of savages, and for two years I lived as a brigand. In my youth I had the usual military training of an Etruscan citizen, so I ought to be able to protect myself; but I would be glad if you will tell me when you see me doing anything wrong."

"That's not the way most of the King's celeres talk before battle," answered his neighbour with a frosty glance at the King's device on Perperna's shield. "I'm glad one of you can be civil to a veteran. If you like I shall keep an eye on you, but you won't find anything difficult. Just keep in your place, beside me. Don't try to get ahead, and I need not tell you that you mustn't hang back. The great thing is to meet the enemy with our spearpoints in a level line. Just dodge the spear of the man opposite you, and don't bust a gut trying to kill him. It's quite enough if you push hard and get him moving backwards. I shall look after your right, and remember that Pontius on your left depends on your shield as you depend on mine. Push steadily, and trust in the luck of Rome. If that is stronger than the luck of Camerium we shall break their ranks. If not, they will break ours."

"You don't speak as though you were longing to kill these dastardly invaders, who have treacherously ravaged our crops," said Perperna with a grin of encouragement.

"I want to get them off our land, but the less killing the better," said the other. "There's no call to start a lot of blood-feuds, especially since our King Romulus doesn't seem to know how an honourable man carries on the blood-feud. There! I've only said what every man of my kindred is thinking, and I don't care if you report it. I'm a Senator, and I have influence with my own people. If the King tries to bully me I shall just go home to the Sabine hills and let Rome get on without me. My name, by the way, is Publius, of the Tatian clan. I came to Rome because the head of my house commanded it, and I still haven't made up my mind whether he decided wisely. Why did you come here, and why are you a celer? I suppose because the men of your own city wouldn't put up with you any longer."

"You don't like celeres, I gather. I'm not sure that I like them very much myself. I serve the King because I want to know there will be a dinner waiting for me tomorrow as well as today; and I didn't come to Rome because my city threw me out but because my city was destroyed."

Publius answered with a noncommittal grunt, a discouraging response for a young man burning to tell the story of his life. All the same, Perperna went on to relate the terrible end that had come to his city, and all his adventures as a brigand during two dangerous years. Publius heard him out without interruption. Then he answered, in a grudging tone:

"So when you had nowhere else to go you came to Rome. All right, you'll do. You won't run away and you won't join the enemy. But I wish I could meet someone who had come to Rome because Rome was the place he desired, not because to him one place was as good as another."

"Give me time. In the north, where I was born, we had scarcely heard of your Latin cities. Rome is at least very lucky. I was trained as a haruspex and I can see that. In the end I may come to like the place as much as any Latin."

"Luck! That's all the young men talk about these days, as though when you have found a lucky city you can sit down and let the gods work for you. Anyway, a King who neglects to avenge his murdered colleague isn't likely to stay lucky to the end of his days. The gods don't like a man who won't fight to avenge his comrades."

"You and I will do what we can to help the luck of Rome, when we meet the enemy," Perperna answered peacefully. Then he marched in silence. If he encouraged his neighbour to grumble the crusty veteran would presently say something so disloyal that a paid celer must report him, and that would never do. There was no sense in making enemies in this foreign community.

Presently they came upon the levy of Camerium waiting for them, drawn up on a gentle ridge; and the luck of Rome held. At the first charge the invaders were pushed back, and once they had got them on the move the Romans went on pushing. Then a Camerine spearman turned round to get away faster, there was a confused eddy in the close-packed line, and as each man began to fear that he could not depend on his neighbour he would also turn to flee. Perperna speared two fugitives in the back, and then did not bother to catch any others; it was too exhausting, and the battle was won anyway. Altogether in this pursuit the Romans killed about six hundred raiders.

When they had stripped the slain and collected the spoil the Romans prepared to return home; but King Romulus had other ideas. The celeres were ordered to get the whole army on the move; the spearmen might drink from a nearby stream, and eat any food they might happen to have with them, for they would march all night to attack Camerium at dawn.

Even Perperna the ex-brigand and Publius the veteran were amazed at this energy, though like the rest of the army they obeyed. They had gained a great victory in the field, very easily and almost without casualties; now it would be proper to march home and hold a great feast to celebrate their good fortune. Besides, there was the plunder to be divided, and it must be stored in safety. After a victory every far-seeing warrior spent at least one evening by his fireside, boasting to his family; so that his children should remember the glorious deeds of their ancestors. Now King Romulus was making them get on with the war as though they had not already won it.

"I suppose Mars, his father, put him up to this prank," said Perperna with gloomy resignation. "It's warlike enough, and he will frighten the Camerines. But if he thinks that after a day and a night of hard marching we shall have the energy to assault a fortified wall he will have to think again, that's all. I am a celer, so I can't very well disobey him. But when he gives orders for the attack I shall just wait and see what the rest of the army does."

"It may possibly come off," answered Publius as they hurried along in the dusk. "It's a great prize if we can win it. All these years we have been dreaming of the sack of a rich Etruscan city. Now there's a chance of it. The excitement may carry our men over the wall."

"It isn't worth it, even if we succeed," Perperna went on. "The men who fled today will be back behind their wall tomorrow, and I know the strength of proper Etruscan fortifications. If we had cut their line of retreat, or destroyed the field army to the last man, we might get in without too much bloodshed. As it is even a victory will cost us more dead than any amount of plunder can make up for."

"You are yourself an Etruscan, and you don't value Etruscan wealth as do we poor Italians. If half the Roman army is killed the other half will think themselves well rewarded. Sabines seldom attack walled cities, because we don't know how to go about it. But if Romulus and his Latins show us the way we shall follow cheerfully."

All through the night the weary army scrambled up hills, floundered through swamps, splashed across shallow fast-flowing streams, and blundered in the knee-high heath of un-cultivated plains. King Romulus and his few horsemen bustled them along as dogs bustle a flock of sheep. The men caught the feeling of urgency, and instead of complaining began to boast of their toughness. When dawn showed them the wall of Camerium crowning a low but steep hill they cheered raggedly, shouting that only Romans could have accomplished such a march.

At the King's orders they halted to rest; they were also per-mitted to eat breakfast, but no one had brought anything to eat. It was a cheerless way to prepare for a stiff fight. "Never mind," said Publius gallantly, "the Camerines will be just as tired as we are."

"I'm so tired that I can hardly hold up this shield," sighed Perperna. "But it's the King's shield that I carry, and if he orders me to charge I must obey him. One charge is the most I can do, though. Unless we succeed at the first try we must hurry straight back to Rome."

"It looks as though we won't have to charge even once," called Publius in great excitement. "Look, they are opening the gate. Here comes an embassy in full state, with olive-branches and trumpets."

Some Romans cheered, others flopped down to seize this unexpected chance of another rest. It was hard for King Romu-lus and his celeres to get the weary men once more into battle order, and Perperna felt himself to be a fraud as he nagged at the loungers. But the envoys themselves were exhausted, and the Roman army by the time they reached it was once more upright and in rank, though most unwilling to fight.

No one wanted to begin the war again if a way could be found to an honourable peace; so much was clear from the outset, and the envoys seized their chance. They had barely stated their terms when the celeres were summoned to hear a message and carry it through the army. Perperna limped slowly to the eagle standard that marked headquarters, until a glance from the King's fiery eye made him stiffen. When his suite was assembled Romulus issued his instructions.

"I have accepted the surrender of Camerium, but the spearmen must ratify my decision. So when you tell them of the agreement you must make sure they know which way to vote. Silence anyone who wants to fight to the bitter end for the sake of plundering the town. It won't be difficult to silence him, for we are offered a great deal of plunder without any more fighting. The rulers of the city have agreed to desert the Etruscan League and serve Rome. They offer us as plunder the property of exactly half the citizens, to be chosen by lot. The unlucky ones will move to Rome, and receive a share in the public land. The place of every man who leaves will be filled by two Romans, who will keep their own property and in addition divide what they find here. Of course the buildings and holy places of the city will suffer no harm. There will be no sack, merely a change of ownership. Also there will be no more fighting, and we may march home in peace as soon as we are rested. Now get the men to vote Yes, and take the names of any volunteers who are willing to stay on as Roman settlers. If there are not enough volunteers we can draw lots to make up the remainder. Come back and report to me as soon as you have a favourable vote."

With the celeres to persuade them, all the Roman spearmen greeted the proposal with shouts of delight.

Quickly the Etruscans piled an altar of unshaped boulders, and a white heifer was led out of the town for sacrifice. Together King Romulus and the Etruscan chief priest poured barleymeal on the victim's head, and her blood was sprinkled over both armies; now Rome and Camerium were one kin, and it would be parricide if the war began again. The new peace was as binding as political forms and religious ritual could make it. The Romans had nothing further to do but go home.

Yet King Romulus, who ruled by prestige, must first enjoy the trappings of victory. He would lead his men into the city, and offer sacrifice in its templum. Camerium was a small place, and inside the steep Etruscan wall the houses were rough and poor; but in the holy place stood a monument that made the Romans gasp in admiration.

This was a life-size model of a war chariot, cast in pure and precious bronze. The chariot stood empty, its pole resting on a yoke borne by four crude clay horses; whenever Mars wanted to amuse himself he might mount into the empty car and play at driving the toy horses. Mars is known to be rather a childish god.

The leading files of the conquering army gazed on this masterpiece with awe. They had an uncomfortable feeling that Mars might be standing there now, to make sure that his worshippers were not massacred after they had yielded on terms. Perperna, and his Sabine companions, were even more frightened and impressed when they saw King Romulus jump off his horse and climb without hesitation into the empty chariot.

"It's up to my weight," he called gaily, "and the wheels work. It can move like a real chariot. We shall bring it back to Rome, and put it in my storehouse of sacred things. When we enter the city I shall ride in it. All right, I know it is sacred to Mars, and no mere man should ride in it. But I'm not a mere man. Mars is my father, and he won't mind lending his fine chariot to his favourite son. Come on. Let's get the thing off its stand and hoist it on one of the baggage waggons."

"Oh dear, and we have to march home behind this impious leader," sighed Publius. "No good comes of sacrilege, and Mars may take vengeance on the whole army."

"Nothing has happened so far," Perperna replied with a grin. "Perhaps the King really has enough luck to avert the anger of the gods. But in any case you need not share the dangers of his return to Rome. I shall volunteer to stay here. Why don't you do the same?"

"No, we are Sabines, all my family. My wife wouldn't like to live among foreigners. Besides, I know my ploughland, and I would not care to change it. But you are right to stay, since you are a newcomer to Rome and unmarried. Find a local girl, and breed more Romans to guard our winnings when we are too old to fight for them."

"That's just what I'll do. Rome is a good place, and I'm willing to fight for her. But I shall be all the more loyal if I don't have to live among a crowd of Romans."

It took most of the day to get the sacred chariot mounted on an ox-cart, and to check over the civic property of Camerium which now belonged to Rome. King Romulus decided that the conquering army should remain one more night in the town, and that the first Roman settlers should be installed that very evening. An assembly was held in the market-place, and before a large crowd of interested onlookers the practical, brutal, cold-blooded business was brought to a satisfactory conclusion.

To begin with the surviving ablebodied citizens of Camerium were divided into pairs. Then the gods decided, by means of the sacred knucklebones, that the left-hand man of each pair should leave his native city and all his possessions, to start life again as a penniless citizen of Rome. The emigrants were permitted to take with them their wives and young children, their aged parents if any, and a single change of clothing. All else, slaves, pots and pans, domestic animals, farm gear, houses and furniture, must become the property of their supplanters. Even though the exiles would be granted full citizenship in their new home they were not allowed to take their weapons, save for one sword for each head of a family; shields and armour were to be left behind. Of course chance had parted brothers and close friends, and many of the defeated Camerines wanted to change places; but this King Romulus would not permit. He did not wish to transplant groups of friends, but rather individual settlers who would look to him for protection from their new fellow-citizens.

After the exiles had been marched off under guard, to camp for the night outside the city which they might never re-enter, it was the turn of the new settlers. Nearly enough volunteers had been collected from the Roman army, and the King had detailed others to make up the number. They were formed in rank, and it was arranged that each pair should draw lost for the property of one exile and then divide it between them. But first there was a rather amusing function, something to make an interlude of frivolity in this solemn business of transferring the ownership of land. Anything to do with women must be funny in itself, since women are comic creatures; that was the assumption of King Romulus and of every serious Roman. A mass-marriage would put the weary troops in a good humour, and at the same time settle a number of tiresome problems.

The six hundred Camerines slain in the pursuit had left a quantity of widows, and the population contained the usual crop of unmarried maidens. These were drawn up in line facing the army, and the bachelors among the volunteers were invited to choose among them.

Perperna was one of the first to choose. As a young bachelor without family ties he was eligible, and as a celer and adherent of King Romulus he was privileged above the majority of his fellow-citizens. For of course there were still not enough women to go round. Rome was full of surplus males, since the fugitives and outlaws who continually flocked there were all men without women of their own.

He would look ridiculous if he walked up to the first woman in the line and seized her; but it was even more ridiculous to examine them carefully, as though he were buying a cow. What were the qualities you sought in a wife? And once you had decided on that, how did you spot the external signs of them? In fact, did he want a wife at all? But he must look as though he were choosing with care, so he peered closely into a row of strange faces.

Most of the widows were weeping, or staring ahead in stony-eyed endurance. A few maidens tried to smile provocatively; though they were more frightened than pleased. It had better be a widow. He was not looking for a pretty girl to share his bed. He was a homeless exile, who had accepted Roman citizenship only because it offered him security; he had no ambition to found a family, and it might happen that later on he would move away. He was seeking a wife only because in Rome such creatures were rare and valuable, and it seemed silly to throw away this unexpected chance of getting one for nothing; he did not seek affection, he wanted a sensible partner to manage his household while he worked his land. This thirty-year-old widow looked sensible; she was plain and strong and could control her emotions. She wore a long tunic of unbleached wool, and her black hair hung unbound in sign of mourning.

"Where are your children?" asked Perperna, trying to smile as though he were talking to an equal.

"I had three, but they died as babies," the woman answered in a matter-of-fact voice, lifting her head to stare indifferently into the empty sky.

"Do you know how your husband died?" he continued.

"They tell me he was wounded at the very beginning. Since after that he couldn't run fast he stood his ground until a Roman knocked him on the head."

"Then I am not polluted with his blood. I killed two Camerines, but both were fleeing. So since that impediment is out of the way and you must marry one of us, are you willing to be my wife?"

"Why not?" said the woman, glancing at his face for the first time. "You don't look any worse than the others. My name is Vibenna, and my father was Etruscan though my mother was Italian. What do I call you?"

"I am Perperna, though my family need not be named since they have all been killed by savages. We are of the same race." He spoke in Etruscan, glad to think he would be able to speak his native tongue in his new home.

The woman answered casually in Italian. "It's no good speaking the language of the Rasenna to me. I don't know it. My mother was just a concubine. My dead husband was a citizen, but we were not ruling nobles. Everyone here speaks Italian, except when they speak to the gods."

"Very well, Vibenna. My name is Perperna and we shall speak Italian together. You shall be my wife, not my concubine. Roman wives are protected by good laws. This is a new start in life. Make the best of it."

"It's better than being a slave. I can cook, but my children die. If you have chosen me I will lead you to my house."

"Not yet, my dear. We must wait until King Romulus marries us, in a solemn ceremony which calls on the gods to protect our hearths and our happiness. But I don't want you to stand here to be looked over by all the other young bridegrooms. So come with me while I say good-bye to my friends."

He took her by the wrist and led her to his place in the ranks, where she squatted on the ground without a word. Publius lounged on a sack a few feet away, and he strolled over to tell him all about it.

"Phew, that was an unpleasant job. I think our gallant King Romulus is rather beastly. I feel like a slave-dealer. But I've got a wife who says she can cook, and who will bring me some sort of a house. So I haven't done badly out of my first battle."

"Unpleasant job you call it, young man? Perhaps it was a little brutal and cold-blooded. But if you see it in the proper light it's really most humane and merciful. We could have carried Camerium by assault, raped the pretty girls, slaughtered the warriors and then sold the survivors. The town was at our mercy. Instead of that, some of the citizens keep some of their property and the women suffer nothing worse than honourable marriage. Is it harder for them to be picked out at a public parade than to marry the man chosen for them by their parents? If your woman had screamed at the sight of you, wouldn't you have moved on to choose someone else? So you can comfort yourself by saying that in fact she chose you, as much as any woman can choose the man she will marry. You will shake down together, depend on it. I think you are a very lucky man, and the best part of your luck is that you can't serve as a celer while you live in Camerium."

"You may be right. It's true that you Romans are generous and merciful. But you go about your deeds of kindness so ungraciously that you seem more brutal than savages. Well, good-bye and thank you for the protection of your shield. Now I must line up with Vibenna to be married by the King."

Chapter 10

THE COLONIST

★

Camerium had a long history, though it had never been important or powerful. The wall was made with great stone blocks, neatly fitted without mortar, and the houses inside were of brick, at least in the lower story; for many had an upper floor, built for lightness with beams and wicker. At the local brickyard they had just begun to make roofing-tiles, thin curved bricks which could be laid in ridges on the roof to carry off rainwater; as the old thatch decayed more and more of the houses were being roofed with baked clay. The narrow streets had long ago been paved with round cobbles, in which grass grew and puddles abounded. It was all quite unlike the raw newness of Rome.

Vibenna kept the house which had been her late husband's; though she was compelled to divide her possessions with another Roman who had brought a Roman wife with him. It was not the kind of house Perperna was used to, the kind they built in his ruined city far to the north. Here everything was cramped and a little flimsy, as though when the place was founded they had first laid out the walls and then found they had not left enough room for all the people; but it was more or less in the Etruscan style, and he could feel at home in it.

That was just as well, for in other respects the new Camerium was not a homely place. The Roman colonists, though they were twice as numerous as the old citizens, felt awkward and guilty about being there, which made them boisterous and quick-tempered. The citizens were not allowed to meet in their own assembly, though in theory they would be welcome in the assembly at Rome if they had the time to visit it. In everyday matters they were governed by a council of ten elders, who had been elected in the Roman assembly—or rather nominated by King Romulus. It seemed unnatural to live behind a wall and lack the privileges of self-government. The citizens were always quarrelling among themselves, especially now that their ploughlands had new boundaries; but they must take their disputes to Rome for settlement. Like citizens anywhere, they spent most of their free time lounging in the market-place; but since they were forbidden to hold a public meeting they gathered in hostile cliques. To Perperna the whole place seemed very like an encampment of bandits. But at least it was a sternly ruled encampment, where a man's life was safe.

Worst of all, to a trained Etruscan haruspex, was the absence of religious worship. The right to inspect sacrificial victims, and so to learn the sentiments of the gods towards the city of Camerium, had been transferred to King Romulus with all the other attributes of sovereignty. Perhaps he remembered to offer sacrifice on their behalf; but if so he did it in Rome where they could not see it being done. The templum was never used, and the storehouse of sacred things had been emptied. That marvellous chariot, made all of cast bronze, the pride of the town, now stood on the Capitol in Rome, and its treatment there was a subject for hushed and horrified comment. Men said that King Romulus had placed the clay image of a man in the car which had been dedicated for the use of Mars alone. Then, before all his people, he had breathed into the face of the image and proclaimed that henceforth it would represent himself, riding in the chariot of his father Mars. Such presumption must bring its own punishment, unless in truth King Romulus was something more than a man.

Meanwhile the colonists of Camerium, as a community, paid no corporate worship to the gods. What must be done was done for them in Rome. Perperna knew that was not enough, and tried to fill the gap with private and unofficial offerings. But he saw, uneasily, that the new colony must survive without divine favour, by its own human resources.

THE COLONIST

He had a good ploughland, with a team of oxen and an elderly slave to look after them. The land had been carefully cultivated and he stepped straight into the shoes of his predecessor, Vibenna's first husband, without any of the bother of clearing unbroken land which usually went with the grant of a new farm. His home also was in running order, and housekeeping was easy; but his home brought him no comfort.

He had enough to eat; the hearth blazed with a clear bright fire on cold mornings, and gave off clouds of smoke when the insects were troublesome; his bed was clean and soft, and Vibenna shared it without tiresome protestations of false modesty. But through all the shared intimacies of married life she treated him as a stranger.

She never opened a conversation, though she answered his remarks briskly and intelligently. She still maintained that she did not understand Etruscan, and replied always in the common Italian dialect; though he suspected that she knew more of her father's language than she would admit. She possessed hardly anything of her own, and practically nothing that spoke of her past; all her property she kept in a wooden box whose lid was closed with a hook, and he did not wish to appear a bully by searching through it. She owned two woollen tunics and a cloak for cold weather, a bronze necklace, silver earrings, and a fine comb carved carefully from boxwood. These treasures appeared gradually, as they were needed, and he never saw them all at once.

It was odd that there were no sacred things in the house, either her own or those of her late husband (whose name he never learned). Most housewives had at least a little clay image to guard the store-cupboard, and something lucky by the hearth to make the baking go right. When he questioned her she answered willingly that once there had been a Lar, and an object belonging to her husband which he kept covered with a cloth, which she supposed to be the skull either of an ancestor or of some great man killed in battle by an ancestor. Those things had been there, and sometimes her husband had poured wine before them; but in the confusion of the conquest they had disappeared. Someone must have stolen them. She herself was a simple woman, brought up by her Italian mother; she did not understand the complicated service of the high Etruscan gods.

At first Perperna tried to make friends with her, but after a time he gave up the attempt in despair. If she had hated him there might have been a chance of changing her feelings, but she seemed to have no feelings at all. He was inclined to put down her lack of interest to sheer stupidity; until one day, almost without thinking, she told him her philosophy of life. He had come in from the fields to find her quietly weeping by the hearth, and he asked her whether anything special was the matter. He never forgot her reply.

"No, there's nothing the matter. I am a woman, so from time to time I weep. That is the life of a woman. First you are a child, and that's all right. Then you grow up and some man does something to you and you cry. Then the same man, or another, does something else, and you cry again. In the end they stop doing things to you, and you die. But you yourself never do anything, you just wait for the next thing to be done to you. If you are sulky about it they beat you; if you let them do what they want no one bothers to hurt you. But in any case you cry quite often. If you command me to smile I shall try to obey you; but I wish you would allow me to do the only thing that a woman ever does of her own free will."

"Well, if that's how you see life you do well to weep, and I shan't command you to stop," he said brusquely. "Here, put my dinner in a bowl, and I'll go out to the market-place and eat it. I used to wonder why men lounge there in the evening, when they have warm houses waiting for them. Now I wonder only how children get begotten, to continue the human race. Good-bye. I shall come in again when it's too cold to stay outside any longer."

After that he did not try to win her affection. He was kind to her, as he was kind to his oxen; but he thought of her only as cook and bedwarmer, and did not pry into her thoughts.

She had been unlucky. All the same, he reminded himself, King Romulus had undoubtedly shown great mercy to the surviving inhabitants of Camerium. Most of them were still free, and eating regularly, either in their own city or in Rome. They were poor, of course, and their daughters had been forcibly married to strangers. But then they had started a war and lost it. It was hard to imagine anything more terrible than defeat in war. He was lucky to have been accepted into a city which seemed likely to get the better of all its enemies.

He himself was not happy, though at least he was secure. He worked hard all day, to harvest just enough barley to feed his family of two persons and a slave until next harvest. But no one would stab him in the back as he drove his plough, and on the hills trustworthy sentinels watched for hostile raiders; at night he might hang his sword on a peg and sleep by a blazing fire. For two years he had slept sword in hand, after smothering any embers that might betray his hiding-place.

All the same, he wished he could find a friend. Even little Marcus Aemilius, or the rustic Publius Tatius, had been better companions than these ruffians who had chosen exile in Camerium. The men who surrounded him had failed even among failures; for only failures tried their chance in Rome, and these colonists had found Rome too difficult. They were surly and quarrelsome and not very honest in small things, though serious robbery was rare in face of the King's bloody justice. They could not talk about anything except food and women, save when they boasted of their deeds in battle; and that was the most boring subject of all, for you could not believe a word they said. Not one of them knew anything about the gods, or about how a man should win their favour.

That was really the worst thing, to live in a city where the gods were ignored. Something unpleasant would happen very soon, if nobody offered sacrifice or even thanked the gods for allowing men to go on existing. It is the nature of the gods to plague mankind, and unless skilled priests devote a great deal of time to placating them they bring down famine or pestilence or armed invasion just to remind mortals that there are beings in earth and sky more powerful than any man. Perperna hoped that his private devotions would save his life when disaster struck; but he expected disaster to strike Camerium.

Therefore when the colonists were summoned to war he put on his armour with a heavy heart. It was a just war, in defence of their own territory; but all the same he expected no good of it. The gods would not be gods if they did not seize this chance of revenge on mortals who ignored them.

Out here in Camerium it was impossible to learn the rights of the quarrel; but it seemed that the Etruscans of Veii had suddenly remembered that Fidenae had been entitled to protection by the Etruscan League. Since it was too late to save the liberties of Fidenae, by now an obedient colony of Rome, the Etruscans demanded that it become a colony of Veii. That was obviously an unscrupulous and selfish demand, which made the Veientines little better than pirates. Perhaps it was not really what their envoys had suggested to the Roman assembly; but it was the version of the negotiations given out by King Romulus, and there was no way of learning the exact truth. All that anybody knew was that the main army of Veii was marching against Rome, while a subsidiary Etruscan force prepared to attack the disputed prize, the Roman colony of Fidenae.

The colonists of Camerium were directed to march on Fidenae, as reinforcements for the garrison. That was a little depressing, as though all colonists were reckoned to be second-class citizens, not quite worthy to fight in the main Roman army. But orders must be obeyed, and it took them far away from the decisive battle.

Fidenae was another of those stone-walled Etruscan towns, perched on a steep hilltop, which Perperna knew to be a death-trap if once the foe got over the wall. It looked strong, from the outside; but there was no way of retreat open to beaten defenders. In addition, it was not a pleasant station for a large garrison; there were not enough stores for a long siege, and the only spring within the walls sometimes ran dry. Luckily King Romulus recognized these disadvantages, and may also have feared that a close investment might tempt the garrison to change sides (for the detachment contained many of the original Etruscan citizens of Camerium and Fidenae). To the relief of every thoughtful Roman he gave orders that the colonists should march out and engage the invaders in the open field.

On a cool and pleasant autumn morning the levy of colonists marched to a gentle ridge, over the stubble of the harvested ploughlands, and at leisure prepared for the encounter. To Perperna it seemed very like the only other battle in which he had taken part, the overthrow of Camerium; he felt much braver than when he had been shut in the town. On a fair field in the open they would be sharing the luck of Rome with the main body of the Roman army; they would not bear the burden of divine disfavour which must cling to the neglected altars of Fidenae as of Camerium. If the worst came to the worst he could run away as fast as any fully armed man could pursue. Best of all, the last battle in which he had fought had been an easy victory, and everyone expects the next battle to be like the last one.

The Roman force had no single commander; in the absence of King Romulus it was led by a council of Senators. But that was not a handicap, for in an affair of this kind there was no room for manœuvre or tactical finesse. Every man on the field was a heavy-armed spearman, there were no cavalry or light troops, and the only method of fighting possible was to form a thick line of overlapping shields and keep on pushing until the other side ran away. The Romans had leisure to array their line, they held the higher ground, and they stood on the defensive. These were all reckoned to be advantages. They might expect to win.

Such a set battle as this was a rare and hazardous adventure, and no one was in a hurry to begin it. When the Romans had taken up their ground the foe were not yet in sight, and they had time for an ample breakfast; each man had a good share of strong wine, besides the usual bacon and barley-porridge. Then they carefully and comfortably adjusted their armour, and shuffled into their close-packed ranks. Perperna, well armed and in the prime of his strength, was placed in the front rank. But on each side of him were competent and trustworthy veterans, and his rear-rank man was another dependable Roman; it might have been very much worse.

It was already mid-morning when the Veientine army came into sight. They also were a detachment from the main force, with few ensigns and no important battle standard. But they were unmistakably an Etruscan army; the shape of their helmets and the bellowing of their trumpets identified them, even though most of the lesser men in their ranks were probably Italian. For the first time Perperna realized that he would be fighting against his own people, perhaps against his own kin. Well, that was not his fault. If Etruscans treated homeless fugitives with greater generosity he would not have been driven to seek refuge in alien Rome.

The Romans rammed down their helmets and took a fresh grip of their spears. There could be no mistake about the moment when they must advance to meet the Etruscan charge with all the impetus of a counter-charge downhill. The leaders had thoughtfully placed sticks in the turf about fifty yards ahead; when the enemy reached them, and not before, all the defenders must run down in a close-packed line. This sensible device gave them courage; they were in competent hands.

But no one had offered sacrifice, for that was the privilege of King Romulus. As usual they would call on Mars as they charged, reminding the wargod that his favourite son was their ruler; but they had not done their part, and there was no reason why he should help them. The Veientines were not the children of Mars, but surely today they would not have neglected the service of the gods?

Then the warcry was raised, and they stamped their feet to its rhythm, so that when the time came they would all charge together. Perperna felt himself caught up in the surge of common excitement. Here were the children of Mars about to fall on their foes; stout warriors, who for twenty years had defended their pirate-city against an encircling sea of enemies—undaunted veterans, who time and again had clashed head-on in just such a charge as this—proved comrades, who had willingly made room in their ranks for a homeless fugitive with no kin to guard his back. They were a fine dependable band of ruffians, and he would prove himself worthy of their fellowship.

THE COLONIST

As the Etruscans passed the line of sticks the Roman warcry ended in the high wailing hunting-call of the she-wolf. There was one final thud as greaved legs beat the ground in unison, and they charged.

Perperna pounded down the gentle slope, keeping as straight a course as the jostling of his neighbours would permit. The enemy also had broken into a run. He braced himself to keep on his feet when they met, for in the scrimmage that was coming a fallen man would be a dead man. Even when the lines were only ten yards apart he could not be certain which Etruscan would meet his spear; on both sides close-packed shields forced the warriors to lurch and stagger. But even more important than keeping on his feet was to make sure that he was not forced out in advance of the line; anyone who reached the enemy before his comrades would be spitted on a row of Etruscan spears.

That was why the shock, when it came, was much less fierce than Perperna had been expecting. In the last few yards every man on both sides checked his stride and hung back to keep in line; the lines themselves hesitated, until the leaders must shout again the command to charge. When the two armies collided it was at a gingerly shuffle, not in a fierce and reckless swoop.

Perperna found himself opposed to a tall and splendid warrior, whose short black beard and arched eyebrows marked him as a Rasenna of pure blood. He tried to ram his spear into the grinning mouth, because that was the thrust which came naturally to his inexperienced mind. Of course he did not reach his goal; the shield came up as the head went down, and he felt his point glance off bronze and lodge itself in stout leather. His opponent had not attempted such a clumsy thrust, which any active man must parry instinctively; the Veientine spear had been aimed at his guts, but just because he was holding his shield rather too low the point caught in its bronze rim.

For half a minute they all stood still, pushing with the stout ash spears. Perperna saw no blood and heard no cries of pain; it seemed that the initial meeting of two armies had not harmed anyone at all. Then he felt the shield of the Roman behind him placed flat against his back, and the five rear ranks of the array began to shove. He was borne forward unwillingly, right among the Etruscan spear-points. In terror, he doubled up behind his broad shield. He could see nothing, but with relief he felt his unseen spear-point plough free of the enemy shield. Now it was darting harmlessly in the air; but he dared not expose his face to aim it properly, for he was jammed against his adversary shield to shield. All round him was a forest of interlaced spear-shafts, stretching at every angle so that he could not distinguish Etruscan from Roman. He crouched even lower, and felt the pressure on his shoulders as the men behind him pushed their spears forward on either side of his helmet. He was wedged in the press, unable to see, unable to strike an effective blow.

He dropped his useless spear, which remained entangled among other spear-shafts and did not fall to the ground. With his right hand he groped for his sword, but when it was drawn he made no attempt to use it. Instead he braced his right hand on his knee, holding the sword behind his shield. In this attitude he might perhaps endure the growing pressure without being knocked off his legs and trampled to death by indifferent feet.

The position was stabilized. This was desperately hard work: no one was pushing a sharp spike at him, and suddenly he recovered his nerve. Why, he was fighting gallantly in the front rank of the Roman army! It seemed that he would come out alive, and then for years afterwards he might boast of his exploits. Set battles were not nearly so dangerous as the casual frays between brigands and shepherds which he remembered from his wandering days. He took a firmer grip of his sword and looked about him. Below his own shield he saw an inch or two of brown thigh, with an Etruscan greave below it. He thrust awkwardly, using only the strength of his wrist; for all his force was needed to keep him in his crouched posture.

He heard a grunt above his head as the bloody leg flinched away. There was a momentary easing of the pressure, until the ranks behind forced him forward and his left foot fumbled for purchase on a writhing body. His shield was now engaged against another solid obstacle, so that he was in no danger of falling on his face. He looked down to see that he was standing on a fine woollen loincloth, whose protective leather apron had been thrust aside by his toe. A quick downward stab, and he had killed his first foe in open battle. He could not see the man's face, but he supposed he must be the Etruscan noble who had engaged him when the armies met.

He had advanced a few feet; so, luckily, had his comrades on either side. But as a whole the battle was still undecided, though now it was becoming more deadly as men dropped their spears and began to rip at bellies with their short stabbing-swords. Yet a wall of shields was still opposed to another wall of shields; no one was free to move forward, and only the rear ranks were free to retire.

Yet the lines were never still. A commotion far away to left or right set them eddying and swirling, as men lurched in the throng. Trumpets sounded above the warcries, there were bellows of rage and shrieks of pain; and under all the noises a steady trampling of feet, as unwounded warriors strove desperately not to be knocked over. It was deafening and exhausting, and far more dangerous than it appeared to be.

But Perperna had grown accustomed to his dangerous surroundings. Sword in hand, he guarded with vigilance the only vulnerable point in his panoply, the lower edge of his shield. Once a spear-point flickered there, until he trod it underfoot and the unseen foe dropped it; several swords appeared, to be warded aside. Then the pressure seemed to be easing. He straightened himself cautiously, looking over his shield to see if victory had already been won.

It had not, as he realized when he saw the Etruscan helms thronging close. He had more room because the Romans at his rear were falling back. He might have been left behind to be hacked to pieces by innumerable swords, if his rear-rank man had not tugged at his tunic. "Get back, you fool," his comrade gasped. "We must keep the line unbroken or they will be all over us."

Without turning he took four long paces to the rear, stumbling over the wreckage of the battlefield. Then he was snug again with sheltering shields on either side, and felt ready to begin the fight once more.

But now that the line had begun to move back it was very hard to bring it to a halt. The slope favoured the Romans, but even so the Etruscan advance gathered impetus. The pressure grew once more strenuous, and every Roman had the idea that another long step back would set him free to move and give him a chance to find firm footing. Perperna could not feel the support of a shield at his back; obviously he could not be expected to stand alone against six ranks of Etruscans. The only thing to do was to move faster and catch up with his retreating comrades. The line was now falling back at a steady walking pace.

As he walked backwards he stumbled, and saved himself from a fatal fall only by a quick sidestep which strained a muscle in his thigh. The clods of stubble-strewn earth seemed to be meeting his feet at the wrong angle, and he wondered for a moment whether some hostile god were attempting to trip him. Then he understood, and was even more afraid. The retreating army had been driven back to the summit of the slope, and henceforth the Etruscans would have the ground in their favour.

All the Romans were aware of their deadly danger. For a few desperate minutes the retreat was halted while swords and spears prodded across the short space of level crest. But men who have once begun to give ground find it hard to stand firm. With another surge and a great blast of trumpets the Etruscans got them on the move again; and now it was more difficult to keep a footing on the steeper reverse slope of the ridge.

Thus far Perperna had not been scratched, while many combatants in either side were losing blood from cuts on arm or leg. But his thigh ached from the sprain, and he knew that if it came to a rout he would not be able to run fast. Very well, then. He had survived the destruction of his city, only to die in a skirmish between detachments from the main armies of two remote provincial states. In his second battle he would be slain, and there was no striving against fate. He still had one last duty, to his ancestors and his kin. Since he could not flee he must die well, leaving a corpse which the victorious enemy would treat with reverence; a corpse fully armed, even to the shield, and bearing all its fatal wounds in front.

Slowly he walked backwards, still covered by his shield, his sword darting out beside it to keep attackers at a distance.

The Etruscans were leaving him alone. For the first time since the armies had clashed, and that seemed long hours ago though in truth it was not more than forty minutes, no one was trying to get past his guard and stab him in the heart. He could lower his shield and look about him. He saw the explanation. On either side the Roman lines had broken, with the warriors of the front rank turned about and trying to run from the field as fast as they could. Thanks to his sprained thigh and his natural reluctance to turn tail he had become the apex of a little wedge of resistance when the rest of the army was broken. Behind him a score of sober and sensible veterans were rallying, level-headed men who knew that even in a lost battle panic flight was the most dangerous expedient.

Of course he was far from safe. Since there were no cavalry on the field the Veientine foot were all engaged in the pursuit, and none had leisure to deal with this last knot of defiance. But already there were Etruscans behind him, though they had not yet turned to attack his little party from the rear. He wondered if there were still some way of escape, and at the same moment someone behind him called out: "You are the outlaw from the north, aren't you? You must have been in other fixes like this. I won't run away, but have you any idea what we ought to do next?"

Perperna had been looking round for someone to command him. Now he realized that these lost Romans looked to him to bring them to safety. That he could not do, of course; but at least he could show them how to end a defeat with dignity.

"Run away if you want to," he called back. "I can't, because I am lame. But the Veientines are behind us. There's no escape, and we may as well die fighting. If some of you will guard my back we may kill an Etruscan or two before they make an end of us."

He set off resolutely to the crest of the ridge, and after a moment's hesitation the score of Romans followed him. The fighting was already a furlong or so behind them. They had leisure to search for unbroken spears among the litter of the battlefield before they sat down in a circle, facing outwards.

Perperna was gratified to note that he was quite calm. He was setting an example to hardened veterans. It was unfortunate that the enemy did not know his name, and that in any event he had no kin to hand down his memory to posterity; for this was the kind of end out of which poetry was made. Perhaps in the underworld his deeds would be known, and when he entered it he would be welcomed by the heroes of old. He looked round the deserted field to see if he could spot any of the Choosers of the Slain, the maiden daughters of Skyfather, who ought to be busy here just now.

Over there was a crow, which might very well be one of them; if she came within earshot he would tell her his name and ancestry, and remind her that he was about to die like a hero in what was only his second great battle (he might add that in his first battle he had killed more than one of the foe). But she remained tearing at a fresh corpse, presumably doing her duty, and came no nearer to the little group of living men. It was odd that he should see only one bird that mattered in augury, and that one on the lucky right-hand side. In this pass it was hard to imagine what a good omen might promise, but it was undeniably a good omen.

"The pursuit has gone clean out of sight," someone remarked cheerfully. "If we keep to the north side of the slope, where they can't see us from a distance, we may be lucky enough to get away unharmed."

"That's the straight road to Veii, isn't it? Well, they won't be looking for us in that direction. How many are we? Twenty-four? Perhaps we shall reach the town before the Veientine army, and capture it all by ourselves." Perperna also spoke cheerfully; for now that he knew he would be dead in a few hours nothing seemed to be really important or depressing.

There seemed to be no living men in sight, though they knew that among the wounded some would observe their flight. There was no hope of escape, but to keep marching seemed somehow more gallant and heroic than to wait for death sitting still. On the far side of the ridge they soon left behind them the wreckage of the first encounter, and their spirits rose as they moved over clean untrampled grass.

They were only a few miles from the city of Veii, in which there must be some kind of garrison. Soon they would be surrounded and attacked. If the enemy were in a bad temper after heavy losses the last survivors might be knocked over alive and then killed painfully and slowly. Perperna decided to place himself in the front rank once again, and to guard himself carelessly. It would be prudent to get a spear in the heart while everyone was busy fighting at full stretch.

They marched for more than an hour, and must have been getting near Veii when the last man in the group shouted a warning. After looking round Perperna gave his orders, for by now he had been accepted as unquestioned leader. "Draw up across the track here, in four ranks of six men each. Get the formation as tight as you can, and remember that flight won't save you. Hold your spears well up; aim at the rider, not at the horse. But where did those horsemen spring from? In the battle I saw no Veientine cavalry."

Galloping hard behind them came a knot of armed horsemen, their ensign of dyed wool streaming from a gilded pole and their trumpet pealing the charge. The Romans answered the challenge with their own warcry, the sobbing call of the hunting she-wolf.

Suddenly the riders sawed at their reins, pulling up in a spatter of clods and turf. One man alone rode forward at a walk, and then shouted in amazement.

"So you really are Romans? I thought those Veientines couldn't get our warcry right, even to save their lives. But what are you doing here, all by yourselves? Do you plan to take Veii alone, all twenty-four of you? I thought we had only two armies in the field. Where have you come from, and who is your leader?"

All speaking at once, they told of their adventures. Soon the young noble cut them short. "So you follow this Perperna, though the King has not given him any regular authority? Very well, sir, that promotion on the battlefield makes you my equal. I am Aemilius, a commander of horse. I'll get you a mount, and you must come with me to report to the King. This is a famous deed. I was sent out to see if there was anything left of the colonists after their shocking defeat by the Veientine detachment. After riding for miles over the bodies of Romans stabbed disgracefully in the back, and persuading terrified fugitives to climb out of the tree-tops, I find a score of undismayed veterans setting off to attack Veii on their own. Heroic, that's what it is. But if King Romulus hadn't destroyed the main Etruscan army you'd all be food for crows by now. Not only are you brave men, the gods must be very fond of you."

His words came tumbling out, in undisguised admiration. But the greatest compliment of all was that he ordered a sulky noble to dismount and give his horse to Perperna.

The main Roman army was halted before the gate of Veii. But the gate stood open, hung with olive-branches in token of peace. Etruscan councillors were bringing out the chests of tribute, and less important Veientines, Italians of the populace, were bargaining over skins of wine with those Roman spearmen who had a little silver. Quickly Perperna understood. In the same hour in which the colonists of Fidenae and Camerium had been heavily defeated the King had gained an overwhelming victory. He was told that Romulus himself, with nothing but his personal bodyguard, had destroyed a whole band of spearmen nearly fourteen hundred strong. At once, fearing that they could not survive an assault on the city wall, the Veientines had offered terms of peace. They would pay tribute, they would give hostages, they would surrender their precious salt-works at the mouth of the river, they would hand over anything—if only the dreaded Romans and their all-conquering King would go away. Then the city of Veii would remain free and independent, even though depopulated and poor.

The victorious Veientine detachment, bearing trophies taken

from the colonists, was even now marching in by the western gate, too late to save their city.

King Romulus sat on his famous ivory stool beneath an awning of purple cloth. He was obviously tired to the limit of endurance—a middle-aged man, almost an old man, who had fought for a long day like a lad on his first campaign. But he was also obviously at the very summit of happiness, drunk with satisfaction as though with wine. Now here was another item of good news, so that his pleasure might overflow. With a broad grin he embraced Perperna.

"The disgraceful behaviour of the colonists was the only blot on this wonderful day, and you have redeemed the squalid story by your heroism. People will forget that my men ran at the first charge, and instead remember that when all was lost a score of Romans showed themselves willing to fight the whole army of Veii. And it was your doing. Your comrades are brave men, and I shall reward them; but they would have straggled away if you had not held them together. It's all the better that you are one of my old celeres. That will show the world that I can pick out good warriors. Now what can I do to make you as happy as I am? You will come back to Rome, of course, and bring your family and all your household. I'll give you a good house on the Palatine, and twice the ploughland of an ordinary citizen. If that isn't enough you can also manage the salt-works at the river-mouth. The works were designed by Etruscans, and it will take an Etruscan to manage them. And even more important, I shall make you a Senator. I have just decided, this very minute, to add a hundred Senators of the tribe of the Luceres to the hundred Latins and the hundred Sabines. It won't be easy to find a hundred respectable Luceres, but you are one man who deserves the promotion. Now is there anything else I can do for you? No? In that case you may go home and get ready to move your household. Keep that horse. It's one of mine anyway, and it won't harm my proud young cavaliers if one of them has to march home on his feet for a change. Now be off with you, before I give you the half of my kingdom and then begin to envy your prosperity."

THE COLONIST

Vibenna was pleased at the change of affairs. She managed to stretch her face into a cold and perfunctory smile, the first her husband had seen. "I shall be glad to get away from this unhappy town, where everyone remembers that I was taken as spoil of war in a forced marriage. Perhaps in Rome they will think of me as a real matron, whose husband was correctly chosen for her by her parents. Anyway, they all say that in Rome wives are well treated. And it is a healthy place, or healthier than this; so your child who has started to grow inside me will stand a chance of living. It will be wonderful to see a child of mine crawling about, after three of them dead in their cradles. Yes, I know you are surprised at my news, men always are. But all the same it's true, and I'm not sure that I don't love you."

For the first time since he had met her, she was speaking in Etruscan.

Everyone enjoyed the splendid victory celebrations, except the Veientine commander, who had been captured in the field. When Romulus gave thanks to Mars on the Capitol this prisoner followed behind his chariot, dressed as a child. Afterwards he was slowly whipped to death with the light canes used for punishing children; though whether this was done as a sacrifice to the gods, or merely to give pleasure to King Romulus, no one could say.

Chapter 11

BLOODGUILT

✴

The citizens were gathered in the assembly. If all the spearmen in Rome had attended the valley would have been uncomfortably crowded; and if all the colonists had come too, from their outlying cities, the King would have been compelled to choose some other site. In fact Romulus faced only a small audience. The assembly was summoned tò meet on most evenings, and its business was never announced beforehand; most citizens could not be bothered to come. Thus the King could boast that he ruled with the assent of all his subjects, and yet there was a very slight risk that anyone would vote against him.

This evening there was nothing of importance to be decided. A few young men had reached military age; they must be presented by their fathers for enrolment in the tribes. More pigs were needed for sacrifice to the gods below, who do not care for oxen. The pigs would be bought with silver from the common treasury, which could amply afford it; but the expenditure must be agreed by the assembly, so that the sacrifice might be offered on behalf of all the citizens. There was one clear case of damage to growing crops; but the owner of the straying sheep had already acknowledged his fault, and the amount of compensation had been settled between the parties. The assembly pronounced on it only to put on record that the dispute was at an end.

King Romulus glanced down with pride at the clerk squatting below him. It was a sign of culture that nowadays there was so much official written record in the business of the city; a sign that the place was wealthy also, since these clerks were expensive.

But it was worth the expense. The clerk took down every decree on his tablet of beech-wood, and months later even another clerk could read what he had written in the simplified version of the Greek alphabet which Rome had borrowed from the Etruscans.

There was no more to be done in this assembly; all had passed off very well, without a single difference of opinion. The people were united behind their monarch, at least when he had his armed celeres with him to impress the doubtful. The King stood to pronounce the formula of dismissal.

As the small crowd ebbed away he saw that his work was not yet finished. At the edge of the assembly ground, near the house of Jupiter Stator, a stranger leaned against his tall traveller's staff in the queer attitude which some foreigners found as restful as sitting down. In these days the King could not boast that he knew each one of his subjects by sight; there were too many of them. But this man must be a stranger, for his cloak was not thrown over his left shoulder in the characteristic Roman manner.

He was a young man, not a Latin, perhaps from the dressing of his hair and beard one of the new Greek settlers from the south. There was no bundle or pack beside him, though he must have come a long way. He stood calmly, making no effort to attract attention. He had plenty of time, and his business was important; somehow his bearing, a mixture of patience and self-assurance, conveyed that as clearly as if he had spoken.

King Romulus beckoned to a celer. "That young man must be waiting to speak to the King of Rome. Find out what he wants, and tell him that now I am free to hear his petition. That is, of course, if what he wants is reasonable."

What happened next was very odd indeed. As the celer approached the young man came to life; he swung his staff in a horizontal circle and shouted urgently. One word was repeated again and again, though the King was too far off to understand it. Then the celer came back, alone.

"He won't allow me to go near him, my lord. He says he's polluted, too dangerously polluted to be touched by a common

202

man. Only a true King can approach him, and you must go and talk to him by yourself. He says even you may be affected by the pollution, unless your divine protection is strong enough to overcome it. So if you are afraid to go near him he will leave Rome and seek some greater King."

"That sounds rather impudent. Why should I bother to remove pollution from this stranger?" said Romulus, nettled. But of course he must interview the fellow at once, or the celer might think he was frightened. The young man had planned his approach with skill, for all that it sounded insolent.

"Hi, you," he shouted briskly, swaggering up to the youth who still leaned on his staff, "I am the King here. I am also the favourite son of Mars, the wargod. No pollution can injure me. I can cleanse you, if I want to. But first you must tell me what brought about this defilement. For all I know you may deserve every bit of trouble that afflicts you. What have you done, and why did you do it?"

"I killed my brother. There is a long story behind it. I have seen the Old Women, though only in a dream. That's why I wouldn't let your messenger come close. I am careful not to infect others. Will you help me? Only a great King, who enjoys the favour of the gods, can cleanse me and bring me back to the life of everyday." The stranger spoke in Italian, but it was not his native tongue. Romulus knew him to be a Greek from the south.

"Killed your brother, did you? That's bad, even if you had an excuse. But for the matter of that I killed mine, a good many years ago; and look at me now. If the gods really favour you these things always come right."

"Then will you help me?"

"I shall help you to start with. Between us we can do something to make your pursuers leave you alone for the time being, so that you may enter my city without bringing danger with you. Then we shall talk over the whole thing. When I know your story I shall decide whether you stay here or move on. We mustn't waste time." He turned to the celer. "Run up to the Palatine and fetch down a ram. I shall want a bronze knife as well, and dry fuel and a couple of flint firestones. That's a load for two men. Get one of your comrades to help you. Say it's the King's order."

He had spoken carefully and distinctly, so that the stranger would understand his Italian. Now he addressed him again. "You understand what I intend to do? It ought to be enough for the present. But it will take time to get ready. You will feel cold as the sun sets, but we had better not risk setting your bad luck beside a Roman fire. Just be patient and stay where you are. Behind you is Jupiter's house, and this place of assembly is also a consecrated templum. So you mustn't move, or I shall have to consecrate one of them all over again. You were clever to stand in the only open part of the valley, the only place that isn't part of the city or part of a templum. You must know something about religious affairs. Now tell me your story. Who are you, and where do you come from?"

"I know enough, Lord King, not to speak my name aloud," the young man answered. "Ears listen for that name in every blade of grass, in every puff of wind. For a very long time I have been hunted, and now if I am careful the hunters will lose me. So I shall not tell you anything about myself until the ram has done his work. When I can sit under a roof once more I shall explain everything, and I hope you will permit me to remain in your city. I am not a murderer."

"Very well, I shall wait," Romulus answered graciously. "I don't really care what you did in the past—except for your disability, that is. We have murderers in plenty in Rome, and thieves besides. What they did before they came here is nobody's business. Of course if they break the laws of my city they die. But once I have freed you from your pursuers you can make a fresh start. I must know the whole story before we accept you as a citizen, and if it's too bad we may send you on your way. That's the worst that can happen."

They fell silent, inspecting one another. The King drew himself up and tried to look impressive. To be accepted as a Roman citizen was a great privilege; too many of these hunted fugitives seemed to take it for granted that any ablebodied man would be welcome. This fellow must realize that he would be weighed in the balance and might be found wanting. He looked very sure of himself, but then it was said that every Greek believed himself to be superior to all Italians. Romulus felt himself grow peevish, as he stood there waiting awkwardly for his servants to bring him the ritual paraphernalia. It was a familiar feeling and he tried to fight it down. The truth was that now he had grown old he envied vigorous youth; the mere proximity of a young warrior would put him in a bad temper. But he needed the support of young warriors to maintain his power. He must master these foolish sentiments.

Presently the two celeres arrived with the ram and the firewood (it was a task too sacred to be delegated to slaves). At the end of a busy day King Romulus was feeling his age, and now he was faced with strenuous physical labour. But it was important work, which could be done only by a King who was also a favourite of the gods, and he buckled down to it.

First the unco-operative ram must be induced to stand still, on a spot outside either templum. The fugitive, who knew this ritual well enough to need no prompting, quickly leapt astride it and lifted his feet so that no part of him was in contact with the ground. It was a tricky moment, for the celeres might not touch the animal, and yet it ought to remain more or less in the same place. Waving his knife, the King sprang at the victim, collared its head under his arm, and began sawing at its throat. Luckily his first snatch had given him a firm grasp, and now strength was needed rather than agility. The muscle of a veteran warrior was enough to make the knife pierce the rubbery throat; as the blood flowed Romulus directed it at the patch of bare earth he had already chosen as suitable. Grasping the fleece with both hands, the young man kept himself clear of the ground.

As the ram collapsed the fugitive still crouched on its back. Now came the most difficult part of the work; but still the King must do all single-handed, without assistance. The beast lay in a puddle of its own blood. It might not be moved, but the firewood must be placed underneath it and the fugitive must remain in position. From time to time Romulus groaned, as twinges of rheumatism caught at his shoulders. But at last the billets of wood were inserted, and the pyre was ready, Holding a twist of tinder between the fingers of his left hand the King prepared to strike fire from his lucky flints.

There was the usual maddening delay, as a little breeze that had not been there before that moment carried the sparks wide of the tinder. After three or four failures Romulus was tempted to send for a glowing brand from one of the hearths on the Palatine. But that might mean the pollution of every fire in his city; for pollution could travel back from a flame to its source, and the hearths of Rome were constantly rekindled from any other hearth that happened to be alight. Muttering angrily, he fought back the temptation; and at last coaxed out a little flicker of glowing light. Then came the business of kindling the blood-soaked pyre.

A horrid stench of smouldering wool and scorched mutton announced that the sacrifice was in a way to be consumed. Coughing, the King leaned into the foul smoke and caught the young man by his shoulders. The burden nearly pulled him off his feet; but the fugitive, strong and athletic, did his part. He had held his position without moving when it seemed as though he would be burned alive, and he was still self-possessed. The King swung him clear of the fire and set him down on his feet just within the templum dedicated to Jupiter Stator. Panting, they once again stared at one another.

"That's done," said Romulus with satisfaction, when he had got back his breath. "It's some years since the last time I did it, but it's not the kind of thing you ever forget. It was well done, too, and I don't think we made a mistake. But, mind you, it hasn't cleared up your pollution. If something is tracking you we have broken the trail, but a good nose could still puzzle out the line. For a day or two you will be safe, while we decide what to do with you. Then I must either cleanse you thoroughly, with the help of various wise men who live with me in my city, or you must go off on your travels again."

"Don't bother to spare my feelings, lord King, by talking of a nose or of something on my trail. For two months the Old

BLOODGUILT

Women have been in my thoughts day and night, and I don't mind speaking of them aloud. They will follow me until they reach that sacrifice, and then the blood and the smoke will make them suppose I have met my doom. But when they look for me in the underworld they will know they have been tricked, and then they will resume the hunt. I know that you have given me a respite, and that it is no more than a respite. But now I can talk freely, will you listen to my story?"

"Not here and now," Romulus answered firmly. "We must get farther away from the sacrifice; and don't speak of the Old Ones so loudly. Over there is the Mundus, one of the entries to the underworld; though for the present I have closed it with some bits of magic of my own. In any case, I alone shall not judge you. I am full of luck and divine favour, but I am not so wise as some of my councillors. You must tell your story to the full council, and then we shall decide what to do with you. Now I think it is safe for you to come into our city, and eat our food. In the morning the council will meet, and you may speak to them."

More than two hundred councillors had crowded into the enclosure, which lay open to the sky but was screened from the populace by walls of wicker. They squatted or stood in a circle, with the King on his ivory chair opposite the entry. In the centre of the circle burned a lucky fire of sweet-smelling wood, and by it stood the young man who sought cleansing from pollution. He began his speech without hesitation; for he had been all night composing it, and in his native city stammering or sentences left in the air were considered evidence, not of sincerity, but of incompetence.

"Councillors of Rome, fathers," he began, in a fluent but mispronounced Italian, "I was born a citizen of Cumae, a Greek city far to the south-east; but still a city of Italy. I shall not tell you the name of my father, or of my kin, or that by which I was enrolled among the citizens. For, as you will understand, I no longer have a father, or kin, or a city. My friends used to call me Macro, the Big Fellow, because I was the tallest youth in my company. That is not my true name, but it is all the name I shall use during my exile."

He went on to relate that he had been the elder son; but when his father died he had been oversea, trading in Greece, and he returned to find his brother in possession of the family farm.

"That is against the custom of my city, by which land goes to the eldest son. But it was not a serious wrong, for I am a trader and my brother was a ploughman. The quarrel came on the day of our annual feast, when we offer sacrifice to the heroes who guard our city. We march in procession to the altar, and we march fully armed. Now my father had been a horseman, and the farm was charged with the maintenance of a warhorse. That is a very great honour. It showed that we were rich and accounted brave in battle. As my father's heir I was entitled to ride our warhorse in the procession. My brother said the horse was his, with everything else on the farm. So we stood, face to face, by the stable. And since it was the morning of the procession we were both armed. When I tried to take what was mine my brother refused me. He struck me with his fist, though I was the elder. Then swords were drawn, and my brother lay dead at my feet. . . . Therefore I have come to your great King, to beg him to cleanse me from bloodguilt; and if I am cleansed I wish to settle in your city and end my life here."

At once an elderly councillor was questioning him. "You say that swords were drawn. Did your brother draw his sword?"

"It came out as mine did. We carried no shields, for we were both armed as horsemen. But I remember the shock as he parried my first blow."

"Your brother lay dead," persisted the councillor. "Can you tell us how he lay, and where was his wound?"

"He lay on his back. His helmet had fallen off. The blood flowed from a great gash in his throat."

Another councillor interrupted, a wizened middle-aged man with a foxy grin. "The quarrel concerned land, and a horse? There was no woman in it?"

"We were neither of us married. I had a concubine in a Greek port, and I think my brother lived with a slave-girl on the farm. There was no woman for us to quarrel over."

"I think that the rights and wrongs of this manslaying have nothing to do with the Senate and People of Rome," put in King Romulus, anxious to end the questioning. "The killing of a brother may well call down the vengeance of the gods. But in this case the gods have not chosen to avenge it, for here is the slayer in good health and seeking to join our city. It is true that he is disabled by pollution. That disability I can remove. We need young spearmen; here is a young warrior anxious to help us. Unless my councillors advise otherwise I shall recommend the assembly to accept him."

There was a murmur of agreement, though some Senators shrugged their shoulders as though they might have argued further if the King had not made up his mind. Then Macro went off with the King to the storehouse of sacred things, for he must be thoroughly cleansed before he entered the assembly.

Next morning he rolled up his borrowed bedding and swept out the corner which had been assigned to him in the guest house. He was no longer a guest of the city, a charge on the public treasury; he was a full citizen of Rome, and if he wanted to eat breakfast he must go out and find it by his own efforts.

He had nothing at all except a tunic, a cloak, a pair of shoes and an empty wallet. But he faced the future with confidence. If this city needed warriors so urgently that it welcomed any ablebodied stranger the citizens must also need hands to work in their fields. He would find employment, and with it food and lodging. One day, when they had taken more land from their neighbours, a farm would be allotted to him. For the present they had explained to him that every field was occupied, and that he must wait his turn.

He strolled down towards the valley, where in the morning the place of assembly was used as a market. There were stalls selling cheese and fruit; if no one had steady work for him he could help to load donkeys and pack up goods until he had earned his keep for this one day. It was wonderful to rub shoulders with a crowd without spreading the pollution of fratricide; to smile at women, to let babies play at his feet, without warning every stranger to keep his distance. Best of all was the feeling that he did not have to keep looking behind him; that bitch sniffing at his heels, the she-goat lifting her head as he passed, were not someone else in disguise. He had committed a terrible crime; but, as King Romulus had pointed out to him yesterday, he had expiated it by embracing the punishment of penniless exile—and also by the supernatural effect of those complicated ritual cleansings.

He was a free man, a citizen of a thriving city; after his haunted journey through the mountains he now had neighbours who would guard his back.

But still he had no food, and no friend in all this strange and crowded city. There was much to be done.

The settlement on the Palatine seemed to be still in part a temporary encampment. There were new houses, their walls gleaming with plaster and their roofs stretching level under clay tiles; but there were also crazy old cabins, huts of unpainted plank, warped and rotting. The narrow streets ran straight, as in a military fortress; they were clean, and the cobbles underfoot made a sound pavement. But the dwellings pressed close on every side; the city was outgrowing its site. Across the valley the other settlement on the Quirinal looked equally crowded, misted with smoke from many close-set hearths. But the place of assembly was clear and uncluttered. There was a law against building on it, and it seemed that these people obeyed their own laws.

As he passed through the gate he looked closely at the palisade. This was now his city, and at any time he might be called on to man its defences. The grass-grown bank was tall and steeply scarped; patches of raw unweathered soil showed that any gullies made by rainwater were speedily repaired. But many of the stakes above were old and beginning to decay, nearly at the end of their useful life; there were no gaps, but the whole barrier looked flimsy and fragile. It seemed that the Romans did not expect to be besieged.

In such a populous city a strange face might go unremarked. No one stared at him, and since he now wore his cloak thrown over one shoulder in the Roman manner there was nothing obvious to mark him as a newcomer. Down in the market he wandered unnoticed, tormented by the odour of apples boiled in honey. His empty stomach complained, but to go up to a complete stranger and ask for work and food seemed unpleasantly like begging. He stood awkwardly, staring at his own feet, trying to summon the courage to begin.

Then someone greeted him, and at once he felt very much better. A slender man of about thirty, with a short but very black beard, smiled down at him as he slouched in his shyness. He noted in one quick glance that the stranger wore a clean, unmended tunic, and fine shoes of soft leather; except for his round, alien face the man might have been a prosperous Greek townsman. He smiled in reply.

"You are Macro, the new citizen from the south, aren't you?" said the other. "My name is Perperna, and I also came here as a grown warrior, though that was more than ten years ago. My parents were Etruscan, so I suppose we shall be fellow-tribesmen. Everyone who isn't a Latin or a Sabine is put into the tribe of the Luceres. That makes a bond between us. If you haven't eaten breakfast will you join me at this stall?"

The market-woman served them with hot porridge and watered wine, and a little bit of goat's cheese to finish. Perperna gave nothing in payment, and noticed Macro's look of surprise.

"No, breakfast isn't free to all citizens, though sometimes after a good harvest we share out the extra barley. I've heard that in some Greek cities they give free dinners to any citizen in need, but here we are not quite so advanced. In fact we have rich and poor, just as though we had been founded centuries ago; and unless you hold land you must work hard for your food. It's just that this stall happens to belong to me. Years ago the King gave me two ploughlands because I had been lucky in a battle, and since then I have done well enough to buy three more. My people run several stalls in the market, and sometimes I breakfast down here to keep them up to the mark. Today I was looking for you. I gather you are in need of work, and I am in need of citizens to work for me. Don't make up your mind immediately. Come to my house and discuss it over a bowl of wine."

It was a fine brick house with a tiled roof, standing on the very edge of the Palatine. The palisade blocked the view across the valley, but a breeze brought clean air from the open fields and the distant fringe of beech-forest. As he reclined on a sheepskin, looking across a stone-paved floor to his host reclining on the other side of the wine-bowl, Macro felt that he had come to a civilization that was almost Greek.

Perperna was talking, pleasantly and fluently, in simple Italian that any foreigner could understand.

"I must begin by explaining our institutions, before you can understand what I want of you. Every family in Rome came here from somewhere else, for the place is not forty years old. So in the nature of things we can't possess a nobility. But we have a Council of three hundred leading men, and I happen to be one of the councillors. No one has yet decided whether this rank shall be hereditary. Also I hold five ploughlands, five times as much land as is held by the average citizen. This land will descend to my eldest son, and it would be natural if he were appointed to take my place on the Council when I am dead. In short, I am trying to found a noble house. For that I must have followers."

"You wish to hire me to follow you. But against whom, and how earnestly? Is it a matter of shouting down your enemies in the assembly, of cutting throats in secret, or of open civil war?"

"It's a pleasure to explain these things to a Greek. You see in a flash what I am trying to say. But your conclusions are rather extreme. I don't quite know what I shall want from my followers. But I know that I shall need followers, for all the other prominent councillors are gathering as many as they can. We have so many of these retainers in the city that we have invented a special name for them. We call them clients. I believe it's an Italian word, though I don't know what it meant before Rome existed. A client has all the privileges of a citizen, a vote in the assembly and a place in the levy of spearmen; but normally he votes the same way as his lord, and follows him to battle. In return the lord sees that his follower doesn't starve, and speaks up for him in the assembly if he gets into trouble with the law. It's quite open and above board. You will find dozens of poor but respectable citizens who will answer, if you ask them, that they are the clients of some great lord. No one is ashamed of it."

"But you still haven't told me how firmly this tie binds. Can I stop being your client when I want to, either to follow some other lord or to set up on my own? And must I fight for you, right or wrong, even if you break the laws of the city? Must I fight for you ever, in armed combat? Or is it rather a matter of shouting abuse and throwing an occasional stone?"

"I can't answer those questions accurately, because they have not yet been determined," said Perperna with a smile. "You must remember that the city is only thirty-five years old, and so far we have not fought a civil war. I'll tell you what I'll do. I'll support you for a few days while you learn your way about; I ask nothing in return except your friendship. Say that I do it because I like Greeks. There will be no obligation on either side. In the meantime I shall introduce you to an old acquaintance of mine, one of the first men I met when I myself came to the city. Marcus Aemilius has been here since the foundation. He's an old man now, officially discharged from the levy; though he still keeps his vote in the assembly, and might help to man the palisade in an emergency. The point is that he's most respectable; everyone admires him as an honest, upright householder. Yet since he came here he has been a client of the chief of the Aemilian clan. His first lord died last year, and he automatically became the client of the heir, who is young enough to be his son. When you know old Marcus you will understand that anything he does must be honourable in Roman eyes. He's the best man to tell you exactly what obligations a client undertakes. He's a real countrybred Latin, of the same stock as King Romulus. The laws of Rome were made by people like him, to bind people like him. He understands them by the light of nature, because they suit all his native prejudices."

"That's a fair offer, and I accept it," Macro answered with gratitude. "While I eat your bread I shall reckon myself your follower, but if I find the obligation too exacting I shall warn you openly and withdraw."

He took another long drink of wine, to nerve himself before speaking again; for he knew that what he was about to say might be considered too frank for politeness.

"Lord Perperna, for at present you are my lord, tell me this. If civil war is a thing unheard of in Rome why do you spend your wine and barley in hiring more followers, especially young unattached followers of military age?"

"Rome is thirty-five years old, and has never seen civil war," Perperna answered with a slow grin. "But there must be a first time for everything, just as once there was a first sunrise. Many things have never yet happened in Rome. In particular, we have never yet been faced with the choice of a King."

At this frank reply Macro buried his face in his cup, and when he spoke again it was to ask for instructions in his daily duties.

"I don't ask anything of you today. Just call on Marcus Aemilius and tell him I sent you. When the assembly meets it will be correct for you to follow me there in company with my other clients. There is food for you in my kitchen whenever you feel hungry, and you may sleep somewhere about the house. Don't sleep with the slaves, though, or you will be despised. The porch would be the best place. By the way, I suppose you don't mind sleeping alone? Or are you still afraid that something may creep up on you in the middle of the night?"

"Oh no, my lord. All my fears are at rest. King Romulus performed a most elaborate ritual, and my past has been buried for ever."

"H'm, it was a Latin ritual, I suppose? I am a Rasenna, and we have a different method of appeasing the gods. But that is a thing we can talk over when we have more leisure. It's getting on for mid-morning, no time to be sitting over the wine-bowl. My steward will tell you how to find Marcus Aemilius. At this hour he should be at home, for he's too old to work in the fields."

Macro understood that his meeting with this old man was really important, and within an hour set out to find him.

In the evening blankets and a pillow were ready for him in the porch of Perperna's great house. Three or four others slept there that night, colonists come up on business from their cities and a tenant-farmer who lived mostly on his remote holding. All were free citizens, and in some measure dependent on Perperna. His slaves slept in an inner room, where their proximity could not contaminate citizens. Macro settled down with a sigh of content. For the first time since that terrible day at Cumae he could sleep easily, without fear of the pursuers. In this strange city he was well established, and the future seemed hopeful.

Marcus Aemilius was a good man, the kind of simple honest rustic you heard about in the songs of nostalgic poets. He had seen the foundation of Rome, and did not deny that it had been founded in bloodshed and guilt; though he was reluctant to speak of these unhappy events, and instead told at great length of the bleeding head found on the Capitol and of all the other omens that had made plain the stupendous supernatural endowment of this favourite city of Mars. Since his youth he had been a client of Aemilius, so dependent that he even took the name of his lord. Without hesitation he had decided that the obligation was lifelong, and had transferred his loyalty to the heir. In the same way he had assumed that in following his lord he could never offend against the laws of the city; for his lord (patron was the Italian word he used) would never command him to do anything unlawful.

In other words, no one had ever thought out the contradictions of this odd institution of clientship. But a Greek mind must think out everything to the very roots. Macro owed a loyalty to the city which sheltered him; he owed another loyalty to the patron who fed him. Before these loyalties came into conflict he must make up his mind which he would put first.

One thing was certain: it could not be shameful to live as Marcus Aemilius lived. Therefore clientship was an honourable status. Another thing was certain: he had shaken off the pursuers. In fact he was a very lucky man.

But he could not sleep soundly; perhaps because after an idle day he was not tired enough for deep sleep. When he dropped off for a minute he saw his brother's white face staring up at him above a gashed and bleeding neck; twice he dreamed of his brother, and woke with a start of fear. But he had not dreamed of the pursuers, and when he looked round him there was no creature that might be one of the Old Women in disguise. So he made a lucky sign with his fingers, mumbled a Greek formula which ought to placate any god who lived in that porch; and composed himself to rest until dawn, even if he could not sleep properly.

In the morning he faced another day of pleasant idleness. He was sure of food and shelter and protection, and again and again he might refresh himself in the delightful proximity of a friendly crowd. That was the keenest pleasure of all. For two months he had wandered up the central spine of Italy, in safety since his pollution was so fearful that even hardened brigands would not approach him; but also in utter solitude. When he entered a village the children were snatched away, any fires burning in the open were hastily smothered, doors were barred and even watchdogs kept their distance. Some responsible elderly man would put out a little heap of parched barley on a green leaf, or a hunk of bread on the naked dust. It was his duty to eat all of it, or to take away any fragments left over; so that his pollution should not remain in the settlement. Of course he must see to it that his shadow did not fall on a house, or even on a cultivated field. He knew all this without ever having been told about it; just as he knew that he must not leave any material trace of his passage, a worn-out shoe or a rag from his cloak or even a splinter from the ragged branch that served him as a staff. Perhaps the most burdensome prohibition was that he must never use fire.

It seemed to him quite natural that strangers should see at a glance that he was defiled by bloodguilt in its most ghastly form. It was the kind of thing that ought to leave some physical mark; very likely an emissary of the Old Women was all the time fluttering above his head. He never understood that his countenance, his manner of walking, the way he held himself, all proclaimed that he was an outcast. Sometimes as he entered a village he shouted a warning; but he was not aware of it, because often he shouted at the top of his voice the guilt which filled his mind, not noticing whether he spoke his thoughts or merely endured them in silence. He accepted the fact that this crime had cut him off from mankind.

Naturally he had not attempted to enter a gated city. To go into such a place would be to bring down pollution on the innocent; but he could not go in if he would, for the guard by the gate would spear him if he came too close.

Now it was wonderful to stand at a busy corner, feeling the impact of hurrying citizens as they jostled him; a child chasing a puppy ran into his legs, and he laughed aloud with delight.

But though his body no longer carried pollution his mind was not at ease. His brother's white face rose continually before his eyes; it was not so much that he feared vengeance as that he could not escape remorse. He knew himself to be worse than other men, even though he had been cleansed from the consequences of his crime.

After the evening assembly he found Perperna loitering in the porch, enjoying the cool night breeze. There was no one else within hearing, and he grasped his opportunity. "My lord," he said, approaching with deference, "you are an Etruscan, a trained servant of the gods. Will you set my mind at rest? Tell me, has King Romulus cleansed me from the guilt of fratricide?"

"Well, has he? You ought to know. If you feel clean you are clean. The vengeance of the underworld affects only the mind. There is no mark on your body, so it must be clean. But then there never was a mark, even when you felt most deeply accursed. Whether your spirit is marked you can tell, but not I."

"I feel that I have been cleansed. There is no pursuit. But continually I see the dead face of my brother."

"Of course. What did you expect? The King can save you from the pursuers. He cannot make you into a good man if you are a bad one."

"Can anyone do that?"

"Someone, perhaps, but not King Romulus. Our King is a mighty warrior, and he rules his city with prudence. But he does not rule as the representative of heaven. What he has is the most astounding luck. He hasn't earned it, it came at his birth. For all I know he may be truly the son of Mars; though that is not a matter in which his own evidence is any proof. Who knows, who can know, who was really his own father?"

"I see, my lord. Very well. Here I am safe from vengeance. I shall live and die a Roman, and not seek out some more powerful priest-king. And I will gladly be your client, to serve you as Roman clients serve their patrons. Have you any commands for me?"

"That isn't easy to say, just at present. In Cumae you were a sailor, I understand, and here we have no ships. Perhaps you could help in my smithy. I employ a first-class armourer, a free man and a fugitive from Etruria like myself. He's always asking for more hands to help him, and it isn't prudent to permit slaves to handle arms. Yes, the smithy would be a good place for you. But your chief duty is to be within call when the assembly meets or when anything unusual happens. You must pick out a good panoply, one that will fit you; and keep it within reach, especially at night. If I knew what was going to happen I could tell you what to do. All I really know is that something will happen soon, and that when it happens a band of armed clients will be useful to the house of Perperna."

It seemed to Macro that perhaps his patron thought to employ him as a hired assassin; but then what employment could be more suitable to a man who had murdered his brother? He agreed with deference, and went off to arrange with the steward about some more private sleeping-place than the windswept porch of his patron's house.

Rome was not a Greek city, but it was not such a bad place

to live in. The work of the smithy was interesting, when he was allowed to do more than fetch and carry. As far as he could gather the iron came from Etruria and was paid for in live oxen. But there was an air of mystery about its arrival. He surmised that somewhere the trade was illegal, though in Rome it was open enough. Probably the Etruscans forbade the export of raw iron.

The smith made nothing but iron swords and flat strips of bronze to be fastened on the leather foundation of a corselet. The corselets were without ornament, and the swords nothing but heavy, ill-balanced knives. But, though ugly and clumsy, they were cheap. There were many other smithies in Rome, enough for the armourers to form a guild of their own; and as a result every citizen owned an iron sword and a complete panoply.

The average smith is a talkative man, and his forge, with its fire which burns all day, something of a social centre in cold weather. But Perperna's smith was a morose and tongue-tied Etruscan, knowing only a few words of Italian. He never spoke to his helpers except to give orders; and when he muttered spells in verse, as he did to hearten himself on a difficult job, they were always in incomprehensible Etruscan. There were no visitors except on business. Work in the smithy was dull.

Presently Macro discovered that he was not expected to work there very hard. It was never stated openly, but he gathered that the job had been found for him so that he should have a visible means of support. In truth he was a hired retainer, an armed guard. That would not sound very well if it was bluntly stated in the assembly, so he could call himself a helper in the smithy. But nobody minded if he took a day off whenever he chose, so long as he was at hand when the doors of the big house were closed for the night.

The big house was the finest private dwelling in Rome, so fine that it had given a name to its builder, who was enrolled in the official records as Domitius Perperna. The whole roof was covered with baked tiles, and where these met the eaves a line of decorative earthenware figures were set upright to prevent the rain driving in. The plastered walls of the principal rooms had been painted in the Etruscan style, which was a very long way after Greek models. Macro could not identify the divinities, and the human figures displayed curious proportions. The roof of the central hall sloped inward to a gap above a tank set in the floor to catch rainwater, which seemed to Macro an ingenious way of dodging the problem of stretching rafters across such a span. That compensated for the shabbiness of the inner rooms, where pictures of gods and ancestors were blackened by smoke from a hearth that never grew cold; these forest-dwelling Italians warmed themselves by burning whole trees in great open fireplaces, where a frugal Greek would have hugged a little brazier.

On the whole the house was comfortable and not unsightly; and the people in it were possible companions for a civilized man. Perperna was an alert, sardonic intellectual; he saw little good in the world around him, but worked for the future of his house as though he had been born to serve his own children. His two sons and two daughters were pleasant handsome young creatures, who liked to hear Macro describe the wonders of Greece. They obeyed their father, except that they often brought into the house amusing young men of doubtful antecedents.

The lady Vibenna, mistress of this great household, was a more complex character. Outwardly she seemed content, attached to her four stalwart children and adored by them in return; she was on good terms with her husband, and the house-slaves did not hate her. But in fact her mind was never in Rome. She walked through life as distractedly as a cook who smells burning while listening to his master. She seemed to be fully alive only when she entered the Black Room, the room which contained the hearth; then her eyes would blaze with hatred as they lighted on the images of the gods. Macro feared her, but there seemed no rea 1 why she should harm him unless he crossed her path.

The citizens of Rome, as he saw more of them, seemed hard-working honest people, sound farmers and careful though uninspired craftsmen. But they were not genuine citizens, as a

Greek understood the term; in fact it was using language loosely to call them Romans.

Hardly one of them thought of himself as a Roman. This was the thirty-sixth year since the foundation of the city, and many of the younger men had known no other home; but almost everyone, if asked to describe himself, would answer that he was a Latin or a Sabine or an Etruscan—and of course a Roman citizen as well. If you asked him what he thought of affairs he would answer with the name of the great lord he followed, never with his own opinion on the policy of the city. But then the citizens did not truly rule their community. They met in the assembly, and voted. But King Romulus had first drawn up the questions on which they were to vote, and the answers to these questions had been settled beforehand in private consultation with the Senate.

If the city was not a republic neither was it a kingdom, as some old-fashioned cities of the Greek mainland were kingdoms. King Romulus had none of the prestige of a hereditary ruler. His men neither followed the ways of the ancestors nor thought out what ought to be done by the light of human reason. They obeyed the commands of King Romulus because he was their warleader.

In fact Rome was an encampment of brigands. The brigands had been settled in the same place for a long time, they dealt honestly with one another, and they earned their bread by farming and not by war. But they were brigands all the same, united under an absolute ruler whom they had not chosen, obeying him only because obedience saved them from the vengeance of resentful neighbours. Such a settlement might well die with its founder.

Chapter 12

KING ROMULUS

*

As Macro became more fluent in Italian he realized that these Romans could never rule themselves like Greeks. For one thing, their language was so crude that nothing intricate could be discussed in it. But it was a splendid tongue for expressing shades of feeling, and was so used at every meeting of the assembly.

Nobody, of course, spoke against the King. But there were some proposals in which he was neutral, and in others it was possible to support what the King desired and still speak against his other supporters. Any meeting of the assembly seemed to proclaim that Rome was on the verge of dissolution.

One cause of the bad feeling, as Macro presently realized, was the division of the citizens into two age-groups. Thirty-five years ago Rome had been founded, chiefly by young men not yet twenty years of age; which meant that now they were between fifty and sixty. They had sons, who were now between twenty and thirty. But there were hardly any men of intermediate age. Two generations were in opposition, with no halfway generation to bridge the gap.

The King was in his early sixties, though he looked older because he ate and drank too much and, since the last war, had taken hardly any exercise. But though in body he belonged emphatically to the elders his point of view was that of the very young indeed. His most faithful followers were the celeres, young warriors with clean spears who had never seen battle. They were energetic and loyal and brave, and thought of nothing but the interest of Rome; from which it followed that they would disregard the rights of any particular Roman if they thought his oppression would contribute to the general good.

There was, for example, the problem of the shortage of land. Every ploughland in Rome had once belonged to some neighbouring city, and in the beginning some Roman citizen had been given it without payment, or perhaps in payment for his services in the levy. But latterly many ploughlands had been sold, and a few had gone out of cultivation. Perperna, with five ploughlands, was one of the largest landowners; but other councillors held two or three, while many spearmen were landless. The young men clamoured for a new distribution, and it was rumoured that the King favoured the project.

"But it's a foolish idea, and I'm against it," said Marcus Aemilius one evening, walking back with Macro from the assembly. "I'm against it even though I am one of the poor oppressed husbandmen these boys say they are defending. I got my allotment at the very beginning, in the stony fields close to the city. When drought hit us and we had no barley I sold the land to my patron. I'm too old to work in the fields now, in any case. But my sons plough for me; we rent the same land from Aemilius, paying him with a share of the crop. If the young men have their way I may get my whole farm back, and Aemilius would be the loser. But then in a few years there would be another division, and my sons would be pushed out to make room for other citizens. Besides, if the harvest failed again there would be no one to buy the land; when once you have robbed the rich there are no more rich to help you next time. I would rather know that I can rent this ploughland, and that no one can take it from my patron, than have the free use of a good farm for a year or two until the assembly chooses to make another division."

"A man isn't a man unless he can grow his own barley," Macro agreed. "My father owned his land down in Cumae, and in the assembly he voted as he pleased. My porridge grows in Perperna's fields, and I vote as he directs."

"That's it. Without property there can be no freedom."

There were enough of these sensible men to discourage the

young celeres, and the proposal was never formally introduced into the assembly. But equal division of land at frequent intervals remained one of the daydreams of the progressive party; and the mere knowledge that many favoured it made elderly veterans touchy and ready to meet aggression halfway.

The young men also wanted to go to war against the whole Etruscan League, hoping to win more of the good land over the river. But here King Romulus did not agree with them, and without his backing they could do little. It seemed curious that a King endowed with such strong luck, a King who believed himself to be the favourite son of Mars, should be content with continued peace; his exploits in the war against Veii were still remembered, and there were veterans who swore that the King had killed fourteen hundred Etruscans with his own sword.

This Macro could not believe, and one day he questioned his patron about it. He was a little nervous as he put the question, for he feared that if it was known that he doubted the King's valour the celeres might persecute him.

Perperna took it calmly. "What a very Greek question," he said, smiling. "You Greeks always try to spoil a good story. Isn't it much better to believe that we are ruled by a hero who can kill a whole army single-handed? Doesn't it give you a warm glow of safety when you think uneasily of those great Etruscan cities to the north of us?"

"It would comfort me if I could believe in it. Since I know that no man can kill fourteen hundred enemies by himself, the fact that lies are told about King Romulus does not increase my confidence."

"Yes, all very enlightened and coldblooded. As a matter of fact there is some foundation for the tale. I didn't see it, because I was at the other fight, near Fidenae; remind me to tell you about that fight some time. But at the battle of Veii King Romulus commanded a special reserve, and he caught about fourteen hundred Etruscans who were trying to get in rear of our army. His charge scattered them. So that you can say truthfully that the King defeated fourteen hundred men; the story doesn't add that he had a lot of Romans helping him."

"Thank you, my lord. I am glad to know that our King is a mighty warrior; and you have only to look at him to see that he enjoys exceptional favour from heaven. But does he really command enough supernatural power to free me from the avengers of fratricide? I still dream of my brother more often than is natural."

"How often does he dream of his brother, Remus, my dear Macro? Surely that is the answer to your question. He murdered his brother, during the holy rites that marked the foundation of this city; yet he has prospered ever since. His luck protects him from the consequences of his crime, and he has enough luck left over to protect others afflicted in the same way. So long as he is your King he will protect you. But that isn't quite the same as if he had removed your guilt. Romulus can't do that, because he isn't the type of man who can cleanse anyone from anything. Luck is all he has. If you want an old age free from care you must seek the blessings of some King who has never himself committed a crime against the kindred. Perhaps a blameless priest would do, if you can find one who is blameless; there are no true priests in Rome, whether blameless or not. But, as I say, there is no hurry. While King Romulus reigns you are safe."

"Of course there are no true priests in Rome. Even I can see that. Patron, why don't you put it right? It won't be very difficult. You have good material to work on, for these Romans deal justly with one another and don't scamp the sacrifices. They are grateful to the powers who help mankind. If they neglect to placate the other powers, who hate us, it's only because they don't know how to go about it. I suspect that you know well enough."

"I am a trueborn Rasenna," Perperna answered complacently. "But would it do any good if I pushed myself forward and upset all my dear ignorant neighbours? Suppose I set up a priesthood, who is to come after me? There isn't another genuine Rasenna in the city, now that the poor Lucumo is dead. My children are one-quarter Italian, though I try to make them as Etruscan as I can. No, Rome has luck, more luck than has ever before been granted to mortals. All the kindly gods favour her. Long after I am dead the gods below may destroy her, unless before then some greater power has destroyed the gods below. I don't know why I babble of these things to you, a Greek who doubts even the warlike deeds of the son of Mars. But it's true, and every haruspex knows it. One day the gods below will lose their power, and man will be left face to face with the Ruler of All. At that, our children may be the worse for it, unless they are granted a mediator. But that's what is coming, in some future age."

"A gloomy prospect. It makes me shiver to think of it—just Man and Heaven, with nothing in between. But we have come a long way from my misfortune, and the pursuers from whom lucky King Romulus will protect me so long as he lives. I suppose I may as well stay here, hoping that things as they are will last my time?"

"My dear Macro, you have been lucky. But then Rome is a lucky place, and all its inhabitants share in its luck. After all, if you kill your brother you must expect to pay some penalty; it isn't easy to wipe such guilt away. Yours has not been wiped away, but you may yet meet someone with power to cleanse you; and in the meantime you are safe."

That conversation explained something about Perperna, as Macro understood when he considered it afterwards. The Etruscan was at the same time gloomy and content; as though he knew that only the second best would come his way, but that he was sure of getting the second best and not the third. His pursuit of wealth shocked many of the Sabines on the Quirinal, and even the Latins thought it rather unmanly; but he did not cheat, and he carried himself with such overpowering personal dignity that it was obvious he was not himself ashamed of his actions. In the same way he treated the lady Vibenna as a true Rasenna, worthy to be his wife; they spoke Etruscan together, and the Lar and the empty jars which represented their missing ancestors were served with purely Etruscan rites. Vibenna would remain half Italian, nothing could alter that; but she was the best wife he could get. It was his policy to pretend that she was better than she was. She hated Rome, and she did not love her husband; but her elder daughter was betrothed to young Aemilius, and the thought that one day her grandson would be chief of the proudest Latin clan in the city seemed to give her a feeble pleasure.

Macro knew that his patron was not a good Roman; in fact Perperna disliked the city and his fellow-citizens. But the welfare of his family was bound up with the welfare of Rome, and for his family he would strive to the utmost.

Macro the Greek lived in the household of Perperna the Etruscan who had never in his heart become a Roman. He saw the city as it were at two removes. What he saw did not satisfy him. There seemed to be no particular reason why Rome should exist. What was the object of all this warfare and hard work? The citizens behaved like villagers; and if they had remained in their woodland villages they would have lived in more pleasant surroundings. There were no public buildings, save for that queer little house in the valley which Jupiter Stator was supposed to visit; no public entertainments, not even the communal thanksgiving after vintage which among Greeks provided such a pleasant opportunity for new songs in honour of dead heroes and new satires on the contemporary great; no public property for the enjoyment of every citizen, no baths, no gardens, no dining-halls; no public religious festivals in which all the citizens might take part.

There were religious festivals of a kind, but they were merely occasions for rough buffoonery, like the silly riot over the head of the October Horse. That kind of thing could not please a god. For the rest, King Romulus sacrificed on behalf of his people, as though he were the only head of a household in the city and his subjects were his slaves.

There was nothing beautiful in the place, though you would hardly look for beauty among Italians. But if they did not want to produce fine architecture, or delicate craftsmanship, or stirring poems, why had they bothered to collect into one place? He could not ask his patron to tell him why Rome had been built; for his patron, like himself, had come there only because no other city would give him a refuge. He knew only one man who had come to Rome when he might have stayed peacefully at home, only one man who was a Roman because he thought that to be a Roman was a high privilege. He called again at the little house of Marcus Aemilius in search of information.

"Why was Rome founded?" echoed the little old man. "Well, it's hard to find an answer. I suppose we came here because Remus and his brother Romulus suggested it; and I stayed on after Remus was dead because Romulus promised to be a great King. But that isn't the whole answer, now I come to think of it. The twins founded a city because the gods had commanded it, and they founded it here because omens prophesied that one day the world will be ruled from the Capitol. You can't get away from those omens, the bleeding head and all those vultures. So here we are, waiting to do anything else the gods shall demand of us."

"Yes, but why do all of you stay here? Why not send a few men to occupy the fort on the Capitol and the rest of you go back to Alba, the town where Latins really feel at home?"

"Long Alba is a splendid place. I never lived there, but I have seen it. You ought to visit it. Now the King has removed your pollution you may visit any city without bringing in the pursuers with you. In Alba you would see holy places and sacred things that go back to the very beginning of the Latin race. But it's a small town, all the same; a mere village compared to Rome. Do you know that the League has agreed that when we put a combined army in the field Rome shall nominate one leader and all the other Latin cities the other? Rome is now reckoned equal to all the other Latin cities combined. I suppose that is your answer. Rome was founded to be a seat of power. At this moment Rome has power; and so she fulfils her destiny."

"That's not a very rational aim. You gather a great army, from foreigners of every sort. Then you say you have accomplished your destiny, which is to gather a great army. What will you do with the army, now you have it?"

"Enjoy security, and impose our will on our enemies. Don't

you see that already we are doing this? Have you once been in fear of your life since you were accepted into our city? As you say, we are foreigners from all over the place—and yet we live together in peace. I shall die of old age, in my own house; my sons will inherit what I leave. That's more than a lot of cities can promise. If you doubt me, ask your patron. Mars has decreed that his children must live in amity, obeying the laws they themselves have laid down. Some of you young men want war, I know; but even then you need a safe place in which to store your plunder. Rome gives us safety, and peace, and an equal law. There isn't another city in the world that can offer the like."

"That's a proud boast, and it's more or less true—while King Romulus lives. When he goes there will be trouble. All the same, thirty-six years of success and security is something of an achievement, even if his city should die with its founder."

But that supposition was more than old Marcus would accept. With an angry snort he went out to the kitchen.

It began to look as though there might be trouble while King Romulus still reigned. Everything he did was for the welfare of Rome, as he explained afterwards; but he took more and more on himself, and sometimes the assembly was unwilling to ratify the measures he had accomplished for their welfare.

Nowadays the assembly was poorly attended. Settled peace meant that there were no questions of foreign policy, and the meetings came round so frequently that often there was nothing else of importance to be discussed. But Macro never missed a session. He had no other interests to occupy his time, and if civil war was coming (as he suspected) close attention to politics might enable him to choose the winning side. Besides, his patron never missed a meeting; and Perperna could not feel happy in a public place unless he was accompanied by a group of stalwart clients.

These meetings of the assembly, though frequent, had become empty forms. The King no longer sat on an ivory chair; instead he reclined on a couch like the image of Jupiter Stator at his ritual banquet. He wore a long robe of the purple cloth which came only from oversea, a cloth so costly that no one else in the city could afford it; his shoes, of a special design, were not remarkably costly in themselves but so peculiarly his own that no common citizen dared to imitate them. His rowdy, brusque celeres crowded about him, ready to overawe any opposition; from their manner it seemed likely that they carried concealed daggers, though it was the law that all should come to the assembly unarmed.

Before each meeting of the assembly there was normally a meeting of the Senate; but Perperna grumbled to his followers that this also had become an empty form. "Our last remaining privilege is that we learn the King's commands a little before the common run of citizens," he complained. "The rule is that no question can be introduced into the assembly until the Senate has discussed it; at least, that was the rule when I became a Senator. Now the King tells us what he has done, and we agree that it was rightly done. Then the decision is made known to the assembly, and they also ratify it. There is no debate, because no one dares to speak. For an important matter he gets our consent before he acts, instead of acting first and telling us after; but that is the last remains of our power. He does that much only out of courtesy to us, not because we could hinder him if we disagreed."

Presently King Romulus exceeded even these bounds. One day the state guesthouse in the middle of the Quirinal stood empty. For ten years it had been inhabited by a score of Etruscan nobles, members of the ruling aristocracy of Veii. The citizens had grown used to seeing these aliens wandering about the streets, peering scornfully at religious ceremonies and searching the market for quaint Italian souvenirs. Sometimes their amused superiority was hard to bear, but their presence was a memorial of the defeat of their city. So long as they were held hostage in Rome the Veientines would not dare to advance across the river.

Now they had gone, and no one had seen their going. In the assembly the King announced airily that he had sent them away at their own request. It was absurd, he added, to continue these precautions. The Etruscans had already proved that they would keep their treaties; or did the citizens think that ten years of honest dealing was not sufficient proof? Now the business was finished. But it would be fitting that the citizens should ratify his decision, taken for the common good.

An angry Sabine rose to reply. He would have liked to climb on the turf platform from which the King had just addressed the crowd, but he could not push his way through the celeres. His cloak bore the coloured edging that was the badge of a Senator; Macro learned from a neighbour that he was Publius Tatius, one of the original Sabine settlers.

"The King has gone too far, spearmen," he called from the floor of the meeting-place, when he saw that the celeres would not make way for him. "This matter touches the safety of the whole city, and such a step should not be taken without the consent of the citizens. But even if our safety were not at stake, the King has no right to squander trophies gained by the valour of all the Romans. Perhaps the men of Veii have shown themselves to be trustworthy, though when I was a child my elders warned me never to trust an Etruscan. Even so, the trophy was worth keeping. We Sabines don't often get the better of Etruscans. It was comforting to see those pampered, conceited, god-fanciers hanging about in our city because they did not dare to disobey us. Luckily the damage done so far is not very serious. If they left this morning they can't yet be home. We must just send a messenger after them, telling them to return. The messenger can explain that there has been a misunderstanding; the King forgot that all matters concerned with peace and war need the consent of the assembly. Now the assembly has overruled him, and the hostages must return. . . . Shall we vote on it now, lord King, or does anyone else wish to speak?"

"There is no need for another speech," the King said firmly, rising with a frown from his godlike couch. "You have heard both points of view. I wish only to add that Publius Tatius is mistaken when he tells you that our victory over Veii was the achievement of all the Romans. Alone I overthrew fourteen hundred Veientines, while my army was busy fighting the rest of them. Poets have sung of that exploit, and every child knows it. Now you will vote, either to confirm my action which wins us the friendship of this powerful foreign city, or to bring back a useless and expensive trophy—merely to gratify the vanity of uncouth Sabines who dare not face Etruscans unless they have a Latin to lead them."

Macro heard a hiss of indrawn breath; as though Perperna, standing just in front of him, had heard something so remarkable that he could not contain his surprise. Otherwise there was no reaction. Soon the celeres brought out the long ropes which formed the voting lobbies. There were two pens, one for Yes and one for No, and each could hold about a hundred citizens. Those who had voted moved over to the far side of the assembly, but today they had not long to wait. At the fourth counting the No enclosure was not filled. The King called out once to inqure whether anyone else wished to vote No. Then he announced that the assembly had ratified his action.

This was the first time Macro had seen a genuine division in the assembly; usually assent was given by acclamation or by show of hands. It seemed to him a reasonably fair way of counting heads, even though it was unobtrusively weighted in favour of the King. Those who would not vote at all were reckoned among his supporters. Those who voted No must do so in the presence of the King, who might perhaps remember their names; but he was entitled to know which of the citizens were his opponents. Perhaps the result might be rigged, in moderation; but if a great majority of the assembly opposed him the King must give way.

The men who had voted No were all Sabines; they had been standing in a group beside Publius Tatius. That made the affair look like organized defiance. But then if opinions differed open defiance was healthier than secret disloyalty.

But Macro, with his memories of the public quarrels and extravagant insults of Greek political life, was the only man present who was not frightened and depressed by the breach. Every other citizen left the assembly with a worried look, and

Perperna was so excited that he discussed the crisis with his clients as they all climbed up to the Palatine together.

"Publius and the King were disputing about nothing," he said with a weary sigh. "It doesn't matter whether we keep those hostages or send them back. As Publius said, they are a comforting trophy; the Veientines will keep faith with us anyway, as the King reminded us. No, the dispute doesn't matter. It's the King's speech that worries me."

"What was wrong with it?" asked Macro, seeing that everyone else was too depressed to keep up this enthralling conversation. "I thought he spoke adequately, in his bullying way; and I have heard Greeks trying to persuade Greeks."

"He got what he wanted, but he was quite reckless in his argument. He behaved as though nothing mattered except getting the assembly to agree with him tonight. Hitherto he has taken the line that all right-thinking men must support him, and that his opponents were an insignificant minority. Tonight he let it be seen quite casually that he regards Publius Tatius as the leader of the Sabines, and that he will overcome Sabine opposition by the votes of his Latin followers. That's the way to civil war, but it would be the end of Rome. At present we are as strong as the combined Latin League, and stronger then the great city of Veii. What will be our strength after the King's celeres have killed the best of our warriors? That was frightening enough. If the King had not insulted the whole Sabine nation nearly three hundred of them would not have united to vote for Publius. But the other point is even worse; it shows that the King is losing his common sense. I suppose if you listen every night to poets singing your praises you begin to believe the nonsense they bellow over your wine-bowl. The King solemnly argued that because he alone had defeated the army of Veii he alone might impose terms of peace without consulting the assembly. Every child knows the song about his deeds—he's quite right so far. But even the children don't believe it, any more than they believe that a real cow jumped over the moon. We all know it's a lie, or at best a slab of gross flattery; all of us except King Romulus. If he believes the flattery of the poets he

will soon be thinking himself divine. It's the end of him. He is
breaking up. We must make plans to face what will come after."

"What ought to come after, lord patron? Is there an heir of
his line? I gather he has no sons?"

"He married that silly bitch Hersilia for her pretty face, and
she gave him only two children. After she died he never bothered
to marry again. No care for the future! A feckless King! His
son Avillius sickened and died. You can hardly say he was
killed by the vengeance of the gods, though of course there were
old followers of Remus who said it. The boy just came out in
spots and died, like a great many other boys of his age that hot
summer. The girl is still alive, but she doesn't count. Prima was
always a bit queer in the head, and she got religion in the silly
unbalanced fashion of these Latins; they don't understand the
true service of the gods. She persuaded herself that her mission
in life is to keep alight the lucky fire in the King's old hut. To
have leisure for that duty she took a vow of perpetual virginity;
She will be past child-bearing by now, though the fire burns
well if that is any consolation. She ought to have been married
to some promising noble, who would succeed when her father
dies. That kind of inheritance is actually more common among
Latins than straightforward succession from father to son. They
think that it's more lucky, or more natural, or some nonsense
of that kind. So now there's no one to come after. I suppose
Romulus has persuaded himself that the son of Mars will live
for ever. He's wrong. He will die quite soon. If he doesn't show
some ordinary prudence he will die at the next assembly.
Challenging the whole Sabine nation! Setting his young louts
to bully Publius Tatius, who was cutting throats before they
were born! I suppose that when he puts on that purple cloak he
thinks he is Mars. But he isn't. He isn't a god, he is one of us.
We shall deal with him."

Perperna had grumbled himself out of breath. Except for a
few snorts, he finished the journey in silence.

All through the autumn there was trouble between the young
Sabine followers of Publius Tatius and the King's celeres. The

duty of the celeres was to arrest lawbreakers, not to punish them. In theory they went unarmed within the sacred pomoerium, though it was well known that they carried hidden daggers. Hitherto they had been able to seize any citizen whom the King wished to put on trial; because there were three hundred of them, all strong young men. Now the young Sabines, also about three hundred strong, would often come to the rescue of their victims.

An offender could not be punished until he had been judged and found guilty by a vote in the assembly. But he could not be tried unless he was physically present before his judges, and custom decreed that no man might be bound or fettered until he had been found guilty by his fellow-citizens. An offender had only to keep out of the way while the assembly was in session, and he would never come to trial. That had not happened hitherto, for the celeres could make his life so uncomfortable that he would either submit to trial or else vanish from Rome of his own free will (which was the customary solution). Now anyone persecuted by the celeres could rely on powerful protectors.

Violence between citizens is the downfall of any city. Another equally fatal distemper is lack of respect for private property. Macro was the first to recognize the danger, for it was a truism of his Greek education; but soon these Italian villagers who were trying to live as citizens recognized it also. Luckily the trouble was slow in coming to a head. There had never been very much serious crime in Rome; for thieves and murderers, who could live comfortably in the greenwood, had no incentive to join this new community. Now valuable tools and weapons began to disappear, and there was an ugly murder—a jealous husband found with his throat cut. Instead of running away the suspected slayer swaggered through the streets, and married the widow immediately after the funeral. Nothing could be done about it, unless the private vengeance of the dead man's kin should bring in the blood-feud to divide more deeply the already divided city.

"Your consecrated pomoerium is not up to its work," said

Macro lightly when his patron referred to this latest scandal. "Isn't it supposed to keep strife from entering the walls? Perhaps the power with which the King endowed it has grown weak after more than thirty years. He should go round it again with his lucky plough."

"It's not the fault of the pomoerium. I've heard accounts of the foundation from old men who saw it done, and everything was performed as it should be. A genuine Rasenna couldn't have done it better."

"But the first man to enter was a fratricide," said Macro.

"Very true, and we all forget it much too easily. There's hardly anyone left who remembers Romulus as an ordinary man. When we think of his crime we think only that the foundation of the city was marked by a peculiarly striking human sacrifice. In a sense, shed blood strengthens a wall; any haruspex can see that. But this city was founded on strife and murder, and strife and murder must dwell within its walls. What has kept it going so far is the luck of King Romulus. I have been looking carefully into the omens, but I can't see what will come to us after he is gone."

"Tell me, patron, what will *you* do when the King dies?" asked Macro boldly. "My work in your smithy doesn't pay for my meals, so I suppose you keep me as a hired spear. Are you gathering mercenaries to make yourself the next King of Rome? If you are, you need more of us, and you must take us into your confidence. I have no ties anywhere, and I will follow you against any foe. But some of the others won't fight against their fellow-citizens unless you prepare them for it."

"Don't dream that one day you will be the favourite of a mighty tyrant. I have no ambition to be King of Rome. I haven't done so badly, for a man who arrived as a penniless fugitive. I want to found a noble family, and to do that I must keep hold of my wealth. That's why I need armed retainers, so that my sons will stay rich even after I am gone. But my family is not worthy to rule in Rome. I am the last true Rasenna of my house; the boys have an Italian grandmother. Land and servants will be enough for my children. As for myself, I would rather be a simple spearman than King of this turbulent city. Rome is a good place to get rich in, but it isn't important enough or civilized enough to be worth the labour of ruling it."

"Yes, it's the home of the second best, isn't it?" Macro agreed sadly. "I want to be a noble horseman more than I want anything else in the world, and here the few horsemen are Italian villagers. I shall never be a horseman of Rome. But here I am safe from the pursuers. I eat cooked food and sleep under a roof. That's enough to be getting on with. When the next war comes I shall carry my spear for Rome."

"You may do better than sleep under a roof. If I continue to prosper you shall sleep under your own roof. It's a pity we are still so short of women, but we shall find you a wife somewhere. But before you found a family we must wipe out your unfortunate past. I could have done that myself in my young days, when I lived in a city where the gods were served correctly. Here, among ignorant savages, I can't order the ritual as it should be performed. What King Romulus has done for you probably won't survive him; and the omens say he will die soon. Well, we must not look too far into the future. Rome harbours us now. When trouble comes we shall surmount it, or move on somewhere else."

In winter Macro found Rome a dull place. Its people were mostly ploughmen, who in their native villages might have displayed a quaint rustic charm; he could recognize the beauty of simple agricultural life, with its ordered round of festivals that were little more than jollifications, and its frank interest in the reproductive aspect of nature. But men of that sort transplanted to a crowded settlement could not cope with their own squalor; their wooden cabins, that might have looked functional scattered among fields and covered with creeper, were mere boxes when set down in rows. On the Palatine there was no unofficial meeting-place where men could gossip together; though the dwellers on the Quirinal, all Sabines connected by cousinship, would drop into one another's kitchens when they had nothing better to do. Down in the valley, where the legendary Asylum had flourished in the old days, there was a tavern for visitors; but it served disgusting food and wine at an extortionate price, and most of the customers were bandits on holiday. When the weather was too bad for work in the fields the true citizens of Rome stayed in their own homes; or if they went into a strange house it was as clients to curry favour with their patrons, not as equals visiting their equals.

He was the only man in Rome who had ever been on a ship. Ever since their successful war against Veii the Romans had possessed the coast at the river's mouth, where salt was made by evaporation of sea-water. A garrison guarded the precious salt-works; his patron Perperna had for a time been manager of the whole concern. The citizens ate a good deal of fish, and garrison and saltmakers passed their spare time in fishing from little boats. But no Roman had ever possessed the curiosity and energy to set about building a real ship, the kind of thing that could sail to a foreign land. That was the Italian peasant in them. Some Etruscan cities were beginning timidly to take to the sea, copying the ships of the Greeks as they copied every other Greek invention; but Italians were land-bound.

There were men in Rome who had seen every part of Italy; but Italy was not an interesting land. In the central hills spear-men grew barley and lived in villages; to the north were stone-built Etruscan towns, almost worthy to be called cities save that they were ruled by a small council of nobles; farther north, all the plain below the high mountains had been overrun by savages, Celts who decorated their helmets with the horns of oxen to prove that they themselves were no better than beasts. In the south things were even worse. Down there lived primitive savages whose only virtue was that they did not understand organized war. Among them metal was a rarity, and for lack of oxen they scratched their miserable garden-patches with hoes of stone.

The only genuine city in the whole land was Cumae, the first settlement of Greeks; and to Macro even his native place was a provincial backwater. For he had crossed the open sea to visit the Dorian homeland. There he had heard tell of wide realms far to the east, where mighty kings ruled from golden thrones and thousands of craftsmen laboured together to pile great buildings of hewn and polished stone. In Argos he had met a man who had visited Sardis.

Here in Rome they spoke with awe of the little house they had made for Jupiter Stator, considering it a great thing to offer a god four walls and a roof; instead of leaving him to squat in a square templum of open grass under the open sky.

But Rome was the best refuge open to him, and he must do what he could to make it comfortable. Privately he did not think much of the intelligence of his patron; Perperna was too wrapped up in his unimportant barbarian pedigree, and too busy placating the gods, to look after himself properly. But that was on the whole useful to a client who had brought down on himself such a grave measure of divine vengeance; and it was easy to flatter the Etruscan by listening with an air of eager interest to his gloomy views on the future.

Macro had resigned himself to a bachelor life. He had seen a few handsome boys, but he kept away from them. In Rome, as in most cities, that sort of thing was forbidden on pain of death; the difference was that in Rome the law was enforced. As for a wife, or even a slave concubine, that was out of the question. There were just not enough women in the city, and baby girls were betrothed in the cradle as the most valuable gift a father could make to his best friend. There was gossip among the celeres and other young ruffians that if you approached a Roman husband in the right way he would lend you his wife for a few nights. The story was told of many other nations, and Macro had never heard of a concrete instance. He would need a great deal of silver before he could buy a concubine, and he would not get a wife until he was nearly ready for the grave.

One other thing still bothered him. In his dreams the face of his brother grew clearer instead of fading into indistinctness. He was not truly cleansed from the guilt of his crime, though King Romulus had thrown the pursuers off the trail.

Then one day in late spring the city nearly boiled over into civil war. At dawn there was a thunder of rushing feet, as all the three hundred celeres of the King ran through the streets in a body. They went fully armed, as though no one had ever ploughed a consecrated pomoerium round Rome.

The armed men seized fifty young Sabines straight out of their beds; they hustled their prisoners down from the Quirinal and up the steep path of the Capitol. At the summit King Romulus was waiting for them, by the altar on which he sacrificed to Jupiter Lord of the Sky. On that day the victim was a he-goat (even in her present prosperity Rome could not afford to offer 365 bulls in each year). The King completed the rite, as was proper; for such a thing, once begun, may not be interrupted. Then he gave orders that the prisoners be thrown down the steep rock which had been named after Tarpeia the traitress. In a few minutes it had been done and the King walked down at leisure to inspect the mangled corpses.

Sabines were pouring out of the Quirinal, all carrying swords and some in full armour. The men from the Palatine came unarmed, since the dead were not their kin; but they also were in a fever of excitement, either rejoicing in a Latin victory over Sabines, or ready to lament the destruction of liberty. All alike rushed down to the place of assembly, where they found the King waiting to speak to them.

Romulus was still clad in the vestments he had worn for the sacrifice; his hair was bound with the sacred fillet, one end of his long purple cloak had been draped over his head, and he was shod with his queer lucky boots. In his hand he carried the curved divining-rod of the augur, though he stood in a permanent templum where there was no need to mark out the quarters of the sky. From head to foot he was all priest; even though he trifled with the gods, as was his custom, by carrying a short iron sword in his girdle.

Round the King stood his armed celeres, lest the armed Sabines should murder him. The Sabines hesitated, in two minds whether to begin a battle in the holy place of assembly, the very place where more than thirty years ago their fathers had fought to avenge the stolen women. They could have started a civil war which would have ended in the destruction of Rome; and they very nearly did.

Romulus the King quelled them—Romulus the favourite son of Mars, Romulus the founder of the city, the heir of grandfather Aeneas who had brought the sacred things of Samothrace and Troy over the sea to Italy. The diving-rod and the fillet on his head played a part; but what made the crowd take their places quietly in the assembly was the innate authority of Romulus the lucky, who knew the ways of the gods. Motionless he stood on his turf platform, praying with covered head for the welfare of Rome; until the last of the clamorous warriors put down his weapons and waited in silence.

Then Romulus spoke. He admitted that he had broken the law and custom of Rome. He had killed fifty citizens without the pretence of a trial. But he had done it to save Rome. That was the office of a King, who to save his city must shoulder the guilt even of grave crimes. Long ago he had taken on himself the appalling burden of fratricide; and because he had not shrunk from it the pomoerium now stood, never crossed by a foe in arms. He would never shrink from his duty. Now duty had commanded him to make an end of these highborn scoundrels. Once the fathers of these wicked men had murdered the sacrosanct envoys of Lavinium, bringing down a dangerous war, and a still more dangerous pollution, on the city which sheltered them. Now the sons wished to destroy the laws of the city, withstanding the honest celeres who enforced these laws. It had been necessary to make an example; and the King, out of mercy for his fellow-citizens, had taken all the bloodguilt on himself. Fifty wicked men were dead; yet no citizen need fear the blood-feud, for the deed had been done by the King alone. Now it was for the assembly to judge; he was glad to see that the law-abiding Romans, whenever a crisis struck them, took their places in the assembly to judge the issue calmly. Let them vote on it without delay. If they held that he had done right the matter would never be mentioned again. If they decided that he had done wrong he would go, leaving the Sabines supreme in Rome. They need not fear that he would resist the verdict of his faithful spearmen; rather than bring civil war to Rome he would go forth at once, taking nothing with him, and that night sleep under a bush alone.

It was a very fine speech, all the better because it was the first time for many years that the King had striven to convince his subjects. Latterly he had not bothered to persuade where he might command, and when he had spoken in the assembly it had been only to tell them baldly what they must do; most of his hearers had forgotten what a fine speech King Romulus could make when he tried hard enough. When it ended there were shouts of approval, and the assembly endorsed his action without a vote.

At this emergency meeting there was no other business; as soon as the citizens had given their assent the King terminated the session with the usual ritual formula. The people drifted away. This terrible and striking event, the sudden death of fifty fellow-citizens, was not a matter to be discussed in public.

A throng of clients accompanied Perperna to his mansion on the Palatine; and then hung about uneasily in the hall, not knowing whether they should go away or whether their patron wished to speak to them. This assembly of the people in the early morning had upset established routine. Did it mean that today was a public holiday, or ought they to go out to the fields as though nothing had happened? But public business was not yet finished. A group of Senators called on the master of the house. Then Perperna came out from his private apartments and addressed his waiting clients.

"There will be no work today; not because it is a feast but because we mourn. Fifty of our fellow-citizens lie unburied. At sunset there will be a great funeral. According to the custom of the Sabines these Romans will be buried in the earth, not burned. But even if the rite seems strange to you I should like all my clients to be present."

Down in the valley Sabines laboured all day, digging a long row of graves. Fifty black pigs were purified for sacrifice, great jars of the best wine were carried down for the libation, the most valuable swords in the community were collected to be buried with the bodies. It was a united effort of all the Sabines on the Quirinal, united in defiance of King Romulus; and when the funeral feast was held more than half the Palatine attended also. Only the King and his celeres remained within the palisade, pretending that this was a day like any other.

Chapter 13

THE SENATE AND THE KING

★

It was a few days after midsummer, the beginning of the hottest season of the year. Macro spent most of his time in the smithy, because oddly enough he found it cooler than working in the fields. He kept well away from the glowing forge, where the slaves who pumped the bellows fainted regularly every noon. In the shade of the porch he wielded a little hammer, engraving designs on bronze corselets and sometimes embossing the frontal of a helmet. He had never worked in metal until he came to Rome; but he knew what a design ought to look like, and he could draw a human or divine figure with better proportions than these barbarous Italians and Etruscans could manage. There was always work waiting for him at the smithy, and no urgent time-limit by which it ought to be finished. He could sit in the shade through all these glowing midsummer days, and yet feel that he was earning the bread he would eat in his patron's hall.

Nearly everyone who could afford the luxury wanted a wolf's head on the frontal of his helmet, as was fitting for spearmen who fought in the army of the she-wolf. At first Macro grumbled at this boring repetition of one design which had taken the fancy of his fellow-citizens; then he found that every grinning mask turned out to be something unique, either fiercer or more supernatural or more protective than the last. The little hammer seemed to have a life of its own; he began to fancy that perhaps Mars guided his hand to make a badge appropriate to the fate of the warrior who would wear it.

It was a pleasant, idle fancy. That last head had come out positively doleful, which ought to indicate that its wearer would be killed in his next battle. Then Macro shook himself angrily, and muttered under his breath: "A spear kills, unless you put your shield in the way. If you ward off the thrust you are unhurt. No god kills you if you keep your guard up. No god saves you if you don't. In battle one man kills another man. The gods do not intervene."

It was absurd. He was a Greek. He knew that two and two make four, that what goes up must come down, that in the end every man will die. Yet here he was playing with these whimsies like a blind harper telling fortunes at a wedding. There must be something in the air of this place, this Italian barbarous place, which existed only because its citizens believed it was lucky. No wonder they were always talking about good and bad luck, they who guided their whole lives by an omen, sitting here in the bend of the river just because someone said he had dug up a bleeding head on the hill of the Capitol.

There was indeed something religious in the air of Rome. The citizens were deeply divided, and almost on the brink of civil war. Yet no blow was struck, no threat was voiced, even in the assembly no one spoke as though he belonged to a faction. Everyone was waiting for some mighty portent, some pronouncement from heaven that would relieve the tension.

Little Marcus Aemilius was no seer. There was no more practical, down-to-earth farmer than Marcus, with his tired wrinkled face and his ankles clumsy from stumbling after the plough. But when he came into the smithy with a damaged sickle, one breathless noon, he spoke to his friend Macro as though both were hardened omen-fanciers.

"It's a bad time, the worst time I remember in Rome," he said in an unhappy voice. "The storm gathers every hour, and soon something terrible will flash from a black sky. I don't mean the real sky up there," as Macro glanced with surprise at the sun flaming from a field of intense blue, "I mean the sky that is the home of Skyfather, our Jupiter and your Zeus. That lowers blacker every day. I'm told that at the sacrifice today the

245

livers were not shaped like livers at all. I heard a heron squeaking most oddly down by the river."

"Do herons squeak? More likely it was a water-rat. It would be ominous if the water-rats stopped squeaking. The saddle of mutton we had for dinner yesterday must have come from one of your ill-omened sheep. The poor beast had probably suffered from a hobnailed liver for the last five years of her long life. Seriously, Marcus, you don't suppose that something awful is going to happen just because the south wind and the heat wave have made everyone nervous? Anyway, if there are omens about why should they foretell trouble for Rome? Why not for Veii, or Alba, which share the same weather? Are we so important, in this little corner, that Skyfather must summon all his storm-clouds to warn us?"

"Of course we are important. When the city was founded omens promised that one day our children should rule all Italy; and we are governed by the favourite son of Mars. When Sky-father changes the weather he is thinking of us, the most important of his worshippers." Marcus seized his mended sickle and walked out of the smithy in a huff.

That was what all these Romans believed in their hearts, even the most matter-of-fact of them. They pictured the gods as thinking about nothing but the fate of Rome; the corollary was that Romans should think about nothing but divine affairs. A sensible Greek, who offered occasional sacrifice so that the gods should leave him in peace, could not keep up with their fancies.

Perperna adopted a slightly different attitude. He was more occupied than a sensible man should be with trying to find out the future, and especially the will of the gods; but he was not particularly concerned with the fate of the city of Rome. It seemed almost as he were trying to contract out of some misfortune which he expected to fall on the community. In the apartments at the back of his great house he conducted his Etruscan rites in private.

As a consultant on religious affairs he was in great demand. The King himself sought his advice on the troublesome matter of his hearth. The King's fire had been consecrated to Vesta, the goddess who looks after the rising and setting of the sun; and word had got about among the superstitious that if the fire went out in the night there would never be another dawn. To keep it going endless precautions were necessary, and the unfortunate lady Prima, the King's only daughter, had very little leisure.

Marco told himself that these barbarians were inventing their troubles because they had nothing better with which to occupy their amazing prosperity. He suspected that the King agreed with him, and that half his ceremonies were carried out only to soothe the vulgar. How much of the rigmarole seemed true to Perperna Macro could not make out.

All the same, if they went on expecting some remarkable interposition by the gods, something striking would actually happen. The stretched nerves of the Romans would see to that, even if heaven remained indifferent. In any case the political situation could not remain as it was, with so many of the King's subjects discontented by his summary punishment of the young Sabines. Macro inquired cautiously about living conditions in the Etruscan cities beyond the river; it might be wise to move a little farther. What he heard made him decide that there was no refuge better than Rome. The Etruscan nobility would not offer full citizenship to a Greek, and they already had so many skilled craftsmen that his amateur tinkering as a bronze-smith would not earn him a living even as a voteless foreigner.

Besides, there was still the matter of his bloodguilt; the pursuers might yet be on his trail. In Rome he felt safe; but he was safe only under the protection of King Romulus. The King's close friendship with Mars could keep vengeance at bay, but a King who had himself slain his brother could not wipe out the stain of fratricide. That led to another, and disturbing, question: what would happen when the King was dead?

He had no home of his own, and not much chance of ever being prosperous enough to build one; no wife, and little chance of finding one in a community where men so outnumbered women; no prospect of ever rising above his undignified employment as a mere hired retainer of a rather sinister foreigner. Therefore he thought as little as he could about the future, trying to squeeze what happiness he could find from the little events of each day.

The King, worried by the temper of the city, took to calling meetings of the Senate in especially sacred places. At these meetings, as Perperna made known to his clients with some contempt, all the Latin Senators debated among themselves about new religious ceremonies to avert the disfavour of the gods; the Sabines contributed nothing because they had come to hate the King, and the Luceres also kept silence because it was really no good trying to show these childish Latins how to go about such a solemn business.

"Romulus may be the son of Mars for all I know," Perperna said with smiling scorn. "Mars is capable of anything; for example he has given victory to these fantastic Romans. But even if Romulus has a divine father he is not himself divine; no one has been so foolhardy as to suggest it. Therefore these meetings to devise some form of intercession for the King's welfare are a waste of time. The King is mortal. One day he will die. I think that day will come soon."

Macro found it curious that everyone should assume that the King's life was in danger. Romulus was an elderly man, but his health was excellent. It seemed odd that seers and wise men should go about to devise ceremonies for his preservation.

One of these ceremonies was to be held outside the city, at a marshy place near the river known as the Goats' Mere. The auspicious day chosen was the 9th after the full moon, during the greatest heat of midsummer. All the citizens were to attend, since the 9th day after the full moon was a regular public holiday; the King would offer a bull to Mars, and the whole Senate, standing round him, would take vows for his continued prosperity. When the magnates had done their duty the common people would contribute their share of good wishes; the celeres would enforce the attendance of every free spearman. In this way a much-disliked ruler would gain the devotions of all his subjects, unless some of them were firm enough to defy the King's command.

Macro would have attended anyway, because this was the sort of characteristically Italian rite which interested him as an onlooker. Rather oddly, Perperna reinforced the King's command, ordering all his clients to march to the assembly with their patron. On the previous night he feasted them all in his hall; but he himself remained in a little templum he had marked out in the yard behind his house, fasting and purifying himself with sweet-smelling smoke and in general invoking all the divine protection that could be called down by a learned and pious Rasenna. That was even more odd. Omens had declared that the King's life was in danger, but there was no hint that harm threatened any Senator of the tribe of Luceres.

At the appointed time they marched in procession to the dried-up marsh. It was a very long procession, for in thirty-seven years Rome had become a crowded city. All marched unarmed, in the white cloaks which had become the regulation full dress of a Roman citizen. But in such a populous community there were many grades of distinction. Senators wore shoes of a special pattern, and their cloaks had purple hems. The noble young horsemen who came next wore rings on their fingers. Among the ordinary citizens fathers of families and veterans of great battles came before the newcomers. Macro saw that in a crowd so careful of precedence Perperna would have little benefit from his lowly clients, who might not walk near him. He had made such a point of their all being present, and had taken such trouble to see that they were all ready for anything, that he must be expecting some disturbance; but he could not expect it during the march.

At the Mere a white bull awaited them, held by the King's herdsmen. But slaves could have no part in such a solemn public sacrifice. Before anything else was done the herdsmen withdrew, and their place was taken by three eminent Senators, one from each tribe. Publius Tatius represented the Sabines, and Perperna the Luceres. For the Latins there stood forth Julius Proculus, an undistinguished warrior but a descendant of the

fabled Aeneas and therefore kin to the King; he had been at the
foundation of the city, but in the last thirty-seven years he had
done nothing of importance. That he should represent the Latins
showed once more that among Latins good birth got a man
farther than personal achievement.

The citizens were drawn up in a rough circle, with the bull
and the altar at its centre; but they were still arranged in careful
order of precedence, Senators nearest the middle, then the
young horsemen, the common herd on the outside. Macro
could not see well over several rows of intervening heads, but
those who could see relayed the information that the present
delay was caused by the bull's irreligious behaviour. A sacrifice
of this solemnity would be useless unless the beast showed himself a willing victim; but for a long time he would not stretch
out his neck and lay his head on the altar, even when attractive
barley-cakes were spread before him.

The weather was oppressively hot, but they were spared the
direct rays of the midsummer sun. Clouds had been gathering
all morning; and now, at midday, they seemed to loom lower
in the sky. Presently there would be a thunderstorm. If the
lightning came before the bull was killed it would make the
whole ritual unlucky and the rite must be postponed; but lightning after a sacrifice signified that the gods were grateful for the
offering and was reckoned to be a good omen. That was one
more reason for persuading this tiresome bull to co-operate.

At last Macro, craning over the heads of the crowd, saw the
gleam of a bronze axe, and heard after the thud of the stroke the
last bellow of the dying bull. Everyone relaxed. The sacrifice
had beaten the thunderstorm, and prayers and vows could now
be recited at leisure.

Then came something quite unexpected. While the great
men, hidden at the centre of the crowd, were presumably occupied in eviscerating the bull to inspect its liver, fog suddenly
swirled up from the river-bank. In Rome fog was rare at midsummer, rarer still at noon. But to Macro there seemed nothing
supernatural in this thick white mist. He knew that mist was
water, drawn up by the heat of the sun. Water was at hand in

the shrunken river-bed, and though the sun was hidden the heat proved that it was shining vigorously somewhere above the clouds.

This was not how his neighbours saw it. That mist should veil the sacrifice just as the King was about to read the omens seemed to them terrible evidence of the anger of the gods. In panic someone shouted: "Get away before the thunderbolt strikes. Jupiter Stator will protect us. We shall be safe in his templum."

That templum, surrounding its genuine tiled house for the god to rest in, lay only half a mile from the Goats' Mere. When one man began to run down the valley others followed, until the whole population of Rome streamed beside the river-bank. Macro went with the crowd, though he was not afraid. A man who has survived pursuit by the Old Women is not easily upset by portents of divine displeasure, and he had noted, as he turned to run, that the Senators were still standing in a close throng round the altar. If those superstitious men, so near the centre of attraction, did not seek refuge the danger could not be very pressing. But it is unwise for a new citizen to stand out against the tide of public feeling. He did not wish to be known for the rest of his life as an unbelieving eccentric. It was easier to go with the crowd.

Presently a breeze sprang up; the mist vanished, and at the same time the clouds cleared from the sky. Soon the sun shone from a field of intense and flawless blue. In the heat birds chirped languidly, the river sparkled in the sun's rays, two magpies flashed their particoloured wings over the Capitol. The populace gathered in the templum of Jupiter Stator saw them as flying to the right, and two magpies together, in any quarter of the heavens, are a favourable omen. At this sign the crowd took heart, until the bravest spearman began to walk back to the place of sacrifice.

Macro, among the first to return, thought it curious that all the Senators should still be clustered round the altar. It seemed a striking vindication of the King's choice of councillors that not one of them should yield to superstitious panic when all the common people ran away; it was even more curious that they should wait patiently in exactly the place where they had been standing when the rite was interrupted. Surely during the wait one of them would have felt an urge to stretch his legs, even if not one had enough sense of responsibility to come and reassure the frightened commons. But what had kept all these men busy while the inferiors were dodging the anger of heaven?

At the approach of the citizens the Senators divided their ranks. Through the gap could be seen the rough altar of piled stones, the carcass of the dead bull, the implements of sacrifice piled in an untidy heap. There was no sign of the King, who should be holding up the liver for all to see, while he announced the message it conveyed to the city.

The first comers halted. To leave the assembly without saluting the King would be discourteous, even if the ceremony was finished. But where was the King? Surely he would not leave privately without dismissing his faithful people? Romulus enjoyed being saluted; it was not his custom to slip away from a function incognito.

Then the three tribal leaders came forward. Julius Proculus was their spokesman; but Perperna and Publius stood just behind him, their eyes seeking out their supporters among the Sabines and the Luceres. Julius spoke briefly, in the tone of one reciting a sacred formula.

"Spearmen, the gods have called our King. The mist covered him, and he vanished. He is now with Skyfather. Go quietly to your homes. Do not mourn him, for he is not dead; he will never die. The Senate will look to the safety of the city until it is fitting to hold another assembly. Then we shall decide on our future form of government. For the present, go in peace—go singly— go to your homes."

This was something too terrible and too unexpected to be greeted with excited discussion. The spearmen took the advice given them; in ones and twos they walked silently to their homes.

Macro had no other home than Perperna's great house. He was waiting by the porch when his patron came in.

"Well, Greek, you see that our omens have a meaning after all," the Etruscan called to him. "Livers and the flight of birds both indicated that something would happen to Romulus, King of Rome; and something happened. Now listen carefully to what I tell you, for there is a great deal you must do. First you must gather all my other clients, and even the ablebodied slaves. If any neighbours come here to seek protection ask them to join the band also. Give every man a sword, and see that he carries it. Let them tuck their swords under their tunics in deference to the law which forbids us to go armed within the pomoerium; but they need not hide them carefully. No harm if strangers see we are prepared. When you have numbered the garrison collect a shield for each man and stack them in the hall near the door. The men are not to carry their shields unless fighting breaks out, for that would be a serious breach of the law. But you must have the shields handy, and they must know where they are. Presently I shall come out and give more detailed orders. But at this moment I carry something under my cloak, something very sacred, and I must dispose of it properly before it breaks loose and spreads its influence in places where it would do no good."

Perperna pulled the end of his cloak over his head, as a man should who is about to enter the presence of the gods; then he walked through the hall to squeeze himself into the narrow cupboard where he kept his sacred things. The doors of this cupboard normally stood open; when he had pulled them shut there was just room for a man to stand within. Macro heard his voice raised in an Etruscan invocation; then there was silence, and after a pause he came out. He looked pale and shaken, as though he had just done something dangerous.

He had left the doors open behind him, and Macro could see that the objects within were now differently arranged. In the place of honour on the principal shelf stood a small clay jar, carefully stoppered with wet mud. There was no design on the jar, not even the conventional circles which sometimes indicate a face it is unlucky to depict. Whatever was contained in the jar was completely anonymous—and very full of power.

"That's got it penned in for the present," Perperna muttered to himself. "If the ordinary rules hold good what I have just said should keep it in its place. It's an honourable place, too, and he ought to be satisfied. All the same, he may not be bound by ordinary spells. Hey, if any of you men dream odd dreams tonight you must let me know at once."

"I must go and bathe," he went on in an ordinary voice. "I don't know whether I have been defiled by a corpse or consecrated by touching something too holy for mortals to handle. But in either case I must clean off the infection."

The lady Vibenna came forward, gloomy and taciturn as always. Without a word she led him to the bath house behind the kitchen.

Later, as his retainers were eating their supper, Perperna addressed them again. He was much more cheerful after several cups of strong wine, and the same medicine had encouraged his household.

"Gentlemen," he said almost gaily, "I'm grateful to you for coming here to protect this fine house; but it looks as though your help may not be needed after all. Tonight Rome has no ruler. I expected pillage, if not open civil war. But it seems that our fellow-citizens have settled down to live in peace together. At the next assembly we shall decide on our future. Tonight we must keep the doors barred, and you must all take your turn as watchmen. Tomorrow, if all is still peaceful, you may go home."

"But what actually happened?" called a voice. "All we know is that King Romulus can't be found."

"That's as much as anyone knows," answered Perperna. "I was beside him, since I represented our tribe at the sacrifice. The mist came down thick, and when it cleared there was no King to be seen. We all know that omens had foretold his end. Now he has vanished. He isn't dead, for there was no trace of a body. I suppose some god called him away. He may come back to us, or he may not. But if Rome is to continue we must devise a form of government. That will be the task of the next assembly."

"Why should Rome continue? It's not much of a place,

except for its fine army. The Sabines hate it. Even the Latins and the Luceres would not be very disappointed if the whole concern were wound up," said Macro. But he said it in a low voice, almost under his breath, waiting to see if any of his neighbours would support him.

But the other clients seemed to be loyal Romans, and all they said in reply to their patron's speech were a few murmurs about Rome's luck. Macro said no more, and quietly changed position so that no one could mark where his voice had come from.

While he stood on watch that night he tried to puzzle out what had really happened to King Romulus. There had been omens, certainly; and wise men trusted omens, at least in public affairs. But even the omens had not foretold that the King would be taken up alive into heaven. When he disappeared the soothsayers had been as surprised as anyone else. Had a god really intervened?

There are gods, dwelling in the sky and in the underworld. There could be no doubt of that, for the gods of the underworld had hunted him from Cumae to Rome. But had any man before been carried alive into heaven? There were stories about it in the dim past, Heracles and Ganymede and a few others; but the heroes so honoured had been from the beginning more than mortal men. It was most unlikely that Romulus had been taken up alive into heaven, even if Mars was truly his father.

That Mars was his father rested on the unsupported evidence of Rhea Silvia, his mother. So much Macro had learned soon after he had reached Rome. True, she had convinced the men of Alba; but then they did not like their wicked King and were probably anxious to be convinced, since the alternative would have been the execution of a popular and wellborn priestess. The mist which had hidden the King's disappearance had been an ordinary river-fog; Macro had tasted it on his lips. Romulus might have escaped under cover of that mist; a few steps would have taken him to the river-bank, and he could have hidden in the bed of the summer-shrunken stream. But why? It was obvious that he enjoyed being King of Rome.

Standing beside the King had been Publius Tatius, his bitter foe; if he had struck down his master Perperna, ambitious and loyal to Rome as a city but not in the least loyal to its King, would have said nothing; the third tribal representative, the unimportant Julius Proculus, would do as his colleagues told him. Tatius might well have killed the King. But in that case what had become of the body? Murder means blood, blood spilled on the ground and crying to the underworld for vengeance; Macro knew that better than anyone in Rome. If the murderers had pitched the body over the river-bank, as they had time to do before the citizens recovered from their superstitious fear, there would still have been evidence on the ground.

Suddenly he saw it all, and for a moment felt faint with the shock of discovery. There had been a murder. It had left plenty of blood. The citizens had seen the blood, since no one had attempted to hide it. The altar stood reeking with the blood of the slain bull, slimy with entrails hacked out in the search for the liver, covered with gobbets of fat from the thighs which were to be burned as an offering to Skyfather. Kingly blood, Mars' own blood, might mingle with it and no one the wiser. Perhaps morsels of the King's flesh lay among the hunks of raw beef.

Of course that was it. They would never dare to leave the King's body lying under cover of the low river-bank; at any moment someone might see it, and how could they get it away? But there were three hundred Senators. If each hid a small portion under his cloak there would be nothing left by the altar but the expected smear of blood. He knew, not only what had happened down by the Goats' Mere that day, but what his patron had brought home in the unmarked clay jar. He glanced nervously towards the cupboard at the back of the hall, and saw with relief that its doors were shut.

Chapter 14

INTERREGNUM

★

It was the time of the morning sacrifice, but there was no King to make the offering. Nevertheless, a routine that had continued for thirty-seven years could not be interrupted. The ten celeres whose duty it was on that day of the month brought the chosen ox to the altar, and then waited to see what the Senate would order to be done. Many Senators were present, for during the last night of alarms there had been time for them to wonder how the new day should be greeted. They stood about, waiting for a lead; until Perperna saw that they looked to him, as an expert in religious ritual who was not a candidate for the vacant kingship.

An obvious temptation flitted through his mind. Why not come forward and announce: "Rome was the city of Romulus, dependent on the luck of that noble son of Mars. Now his sojourn on earth is ended; let his city end with him. Today there will be no sacrifice, for today Rome is no more." If he said that most of the Sabines and Latins would go back to their original homes, and the Luceres like himself would find some other refuge. In the annals of Etruria his name would be remembered as that of the statesman who had wound up a dangerous experiment, an attempt to bring city-life to rustics who could not cope with its complexities.

But he was not strongly tempted. If Rome ceased to exist that might be a good thing for Italy in general, but it would ruin the carefully acquired stability of the Domitian house. The city must continue, and for that Jupiter must receive his due offering.

The obvious solution was to call on the most eminent Senator to perform the sacrifice in place of the missing King. He very nearly did so, but while he was weighing the importance of various Senators he saw the danger. At this juncture an unguarded word might accidentally inaugurate a second King of Rome, a king who would not hold himself obliged in any way to the Domitian house. He must make it clear that the Senator chosen to perform the sacrifice would officiate as the representative of the whole Senate. What he must say fell into place in his mind without further thoughts.

"After due discussion the Fathers will choose a King to succeed our founder, and when the assembled people have ratified the choice he will reign as the second King of Rome. But in the meantime the daily sacrifice must be offered. I suggest that each Senator perform the sacrifice in rotation. But to ensure that the sacrificer holds no pre-eminence over his colleagues let us begin with the most junior Senator. A few months ago our late King nominated twenty Fathers to fill gaps in the order. The youngest man of that twenty shall offer the sacrifice today, and the next youngest tomorrow."

He added in a conversational tone: "You see, Fathers, I have made provision for the next three hundred days. I hope that before every Senator has taken his turn we shall have chosen another King."

A young man came shyly forward and took the axe from the waiting celer. Perperna was pleased to see that he was an insignificant Latin, a youth who had been raised to the Senate only because he was the son of his father. Here was one awkward corner passed. The King of the Sacrifice would not be regarded by the people as having some claim on the kingship of Rome.

Perperna went home while they were still grubbing the liver out of the carcass. He did not wish to be called on to read the omen. He knew very well that it would be announced as promising peace and prosperity, no matter what its shape and texture; and he felt that an ignorant Latin could lie to the people more convincingly than a Rasenna trained to read the messages of the gods.

INTERREGNUM

At home his first task was to dismiss all his clients. That mobilization of all his armed retainers, even though it had lasted only for a single day, had made a great hole in his stores. Now there must be peace, at least for a short time; until two or three popular candidates for the kingship had mustered their supporters. Later he stood before the domestic shrine, and deliberately emptied his mind; but he could hear no inner voice. That was as it should be. The doors of the Lar-cupboard had been sealed with a strong invocation, and what was within was after all only one three-hundredth part of the whole. In after years it might bring power to its possessor, but it was not strong enough to break out against the command of a learned Rasenna.

He could rest until the meeting of the Senate later in the morning. He went into his private room at the back of the house, calling for cakes and wine. His wife herself brought them, and sat down to join him.

"Has anything been settled?" asked the lady Vibenna. "Can we leave this horrible place and go back to our own side of the river?"

"It has been settled that Rome will continue, and that we and our children shall live in it," answered her husband.

"I had hoped for a fresh start. I suppose you can't face it, if it means leaving your wealth behind you."

"There is that, of course," Perperna agreed with a smile. "You have had a hard time, my dear, I know it; going first to a strange husband of your father's choice and then, on the day you were widowed, being forced to take up with another stranger. But though you have to look after a foreign household and cook for a foreigner there is always food for you to cook. I have gone hungry and ragged and cold, and in great fear of my life. Now that I have wealth and safety I don't want to desert them, even to go back to Etruria."

"Safety? Are we safe here? Are we safe in any city in which we are foreigners?"

"Wherever I live I shall be a foreigner. My native city was conquered, and I must make do with the second best. Here is the second best. Rome is strong. After we have chosen a good King

Rome will be peaceful and prosperous. We shall stay here to see our children prosper in their turn."

"I hate these Latins. They're not canny. They are cruel and mean and grasping, and they don't know how to win the favour of the gods."

"The trueborn Rasenna are just as cruel and grasping, and among them we should never be accepted as equal citizens. All Romans are not Latins. If you tried you could find congenial friends among the women of the Luceres. In any case, we stay. Now leave me alone. The Senate meets in an hour, and probably I shall be called on to speak. I must have my thoughts in order."

The lady Vibenna withdrew with a formal curtsy, as though to emphasize that she was obeying the command of the head of the household, not taking the advice of her husband and partner. Perperna reclined for a few minutes, trying to rough out a speech on friendship and concord. He was aroused by someone battering on the door of this private room in which he should never be disturbed by messengers.

The intruder was his trusted client, Macro the Greek. He tried to smile in welcome, for he knew that such a sensible man would not disturb him without good reason. Macro blurted out:

"It's bad news, patron, and you must keep your wits about you. We may have to conceal it from the rest of the city. I was keeping an eye on that Lar-cupboard of yours when the lady Vibenna came out and stood before it. Suddenly she stabbed herself in the stomach as she stood praying. When I picked her up she was still alive, but it's not a wound that will heal. I put her in an empty room at the back of the hall. Now what shall we do? Mourn her sudden end, or give out that she is missing? If we are open about it people may say you yourself killed her."

"That doesn't worry me. People will say anything, and no one would dare to make a formal accusation. Poor woman, she hated Rome. I had just told her she would never leave it. Before the Lar, you say? That's a curious place to choose."

"In front of the Lar-cupboard, I said, patron. Yesterday you added some other holy object."

"And blood called for blood, you think? He has been swift to take vengeance. Let us hope that now he is satisfied."

"But what shall we do? Shall I take the body back to where she killed herself, and leave it for the steward to discover?"

"Presently, but not just now. I want to be at this meeting of the Senate, and the Fathers might be angry if I went knowing I was polluted by violent death in my household. Let her be discovered after the Senate has met."

As Macro turned away Perperna spoke to him quietly. "Your discretion deserves a reward, and it shall be rewarded. But we will talk of that later. I do not buy your silence, and I would not like to appear to buy it."

By evening every citizen within a day's march had crowded into the place of assembly. The Senate had been consulting since morning, and business could not begin until the Fathers came to open the meeting. Marcus Aemilius, sitting on a little stool in the front row reserved for veterans of the original foundation, saw with disquiet that all the young men were gathered by tribes, Sabines on the left, Latins on the right, with the heterogenous Luceres in the middle. It seemed more likely than not that his beloved city of Rome would continue, for unless they were making plans for the future the Senators would not have remained so long in private session; but it looked as though Rome would continue as the city of one tribal community, not as the international settlement which the genius of Romulus had called into being. Marcus was one of the few citizens who genuinely mourned for his departed leader; he remembered him as the great warleader and the wise lawgiver, not as the arbitrary tyrant of his later years. As for the murder of Remus, that was so far in the past that it did not enter his recollection.

Among the young men there was no grief, only excitement and pleased expectation. Here they were, by a strange freak of fortune sovereign voters in a free community; and all the wide lands of Rome were the prize for which they would strive, at first by voting in the assembly and then if need be with the sword. The glorious past, the stability of nearly forty victorious years, had vanished with the vanished founder of the city.

At last, as the sun was setting, the Senators approached in procession. They did not take their usual places at the front of the assembly; instead they remained in a close group behind the turf platform from which the King used to address his subjects, and they kept their heads veiled as though they were taking part in a religious rite.

Julius Proculus came forward. He carried a long bundle, which he set down carefully on the mound of turf. Then he lit a torch, as though to offer sacrifice to the gods below; by its light all the assembly could see that on the turf, which was very like any other temporary altar, lay the sacred things of Samothrace and Troy, the sacred things which grandfather Aeneas had brought to Italy, the sacred things which embodied the divine favour of Rome. For many years these objects had been touched by no mortal hand, save those of Romulus the son of Mars or of Prima the daughter of Romulus. Now Proculus laid his fingers on them.

The citizens veiled their heads and murmured an invocation, as though at the beginning of a sacrifice.

Proculus spoke: "My hand is on the sacred things of Samothrace. Here I fix in the ground the very spear of Mars himself, which the son of Mars kept by his hearthstone. If I lie to you may they blast me, but if I speak truth may they be a protection. I speak to all the gods, and to all the Romans. This is what I am commanded to say:

"Early this morning I was by the Goats' Mere. There I saw Romulus, taller and more splendid than he had been in life, glittering in the armour of his father Mars. He told me that it had been decided in the council of the gods that after a certain time on earth he should return to heaven. Then he said to me, and I repeat his very words: 'Tell the Romans that by courage and self-control they will attain to the highest peak of human power. To them I shall be for ever the protecting god Quirinus.' Now I have told you. Let us worship Quirinus in his emblem of the divine spear."

Every citizen bowed his veiled head, murmuring a formula

of devotion. A ram was brought out to be killed before the up-right spear. Then the lady Prima and her female attendants came forward to remove the sacred things. Proculus stepped back to join the group of Senators, and after a fumbling pause the citizens uncovered their heads and prepared to attend to the business of this world.

The next Senator to speak was a youthful Sabine named Velesius. Marcus was sorry to see him, for he thought of all Sabines as hostile to Latins, and knew that this particular Sabine had been restive under the rule of King Romulus; besides, he was an undignified young man, who liked to make mock of sacred things. But evidently the order of speakers had been arranged in advance, so that all parties should be represented; Proculus the veteran Latin should be balanced by a popular young Sabine. Anyway, it was better to endure in polite silence the speech of an unsympathetic young man than to bring strife and contention into this crucial meeting of the assembly. Marcus sat quiet to hear what was to be said.

Velesius began on a deliberately jarring note. "Well, spear-men," he said, with a play on the meaning of the word, "you know now that the speargod in heaven is looking after us. All my life I have worshipped Quirinus, like every other Sabine, and in future I shall worship him with even greater devotion. It's odd, isn't it? Quirinus has been there always, and yesterday King Romulus was a man like other men. Was he Quirinus come down to earth for a spell, or has his spirit now merged with that of Quirinus the god, or has he perhaps displaced the old god as once he displaced his brother? Odd indeed; but not perhaps important. Quirinus will look after us in heaven, and King Romulus will never return to this assembly. That's really what matters. King Romulus has gone, we know where he has gone, and you may as well stop speculating about what decided him to go when he did. There has been some talk on that subject, I'm well aware. There will be no further talk about it."

He paused, and continued. "I have spoken as Pompeius Velesius the Sabine. Those were my sentiments, and I don't expect all of you to share them. But what I tell you now is the considered judgment of the Senate. We have been all day deciding it, but now we are agreed. You must agree with us, or defy the Fathers of Rome. Here it is. We must choose another King. That has been settled. Rome needs a King, to lead us in war. If we try to live under a council of elders, like the savages to the south, the city will split asunder. So far the whole Senate is of one mind. But we can't agree on the choice of the next King. So just for the present we shall appoint a committee of Senators to rule the city. Or rather, the committee has already been appointed. There are three hundred Senators. We have made up thirty groups of ten each. One decury will govern Rome for ten days, and each member will sacrifice as King for one day. On the eleventh day another decury takes over. Simple, isn't it? All these decuries have been chosen by lot in the first place, so the members are not confederates who will help one another to tyranny. If in a single day the daily King can make himself a tyrant you deserve to be ruled by tyrants. That takes care of the government for the next ten months. But in less than ten months we ought to have found a new King. The Senate will choose him, but of course our choice must be ratified by the assembly. Now are you all agreed on that? If not we must put it to the vote. But before we set up the voting enclosures I must tell you that there are no more celeres. Will the celeres please hand in their rods of office immediately? You can lay them on this holy turf altar, dedicated to Quirinus your old leader. In future the voting will be supervised by elders chosen from the three tribes. As for summoning culprits to stand trial before the assembly, that will be the obligation of all free citizens."

This brought such a roar of delight that Velesius stepped back taking it as popular consent for all he had said.

It was nearly dark when Marcus stumbled up the hill to his cabin, for the assembly had not begun until sunset. He was not completely satisfied with what had been decided, but at least it was a good deal better than it might have been. The Sabines, the most dangerous element in the population, seemed content that Rome should continue on the old lines. The temporary form of government devised by the Senate was fair enough, and would certainly preserve freedom. It would be dangerously inefficient if they were engaged in a serious war; but luckily there was no war at the moment, and anyway Marcus was too old for military service. He would die of old age in the city he had founded, instead of going back to start a new life in his native village after forty years of exile.

Next morning at sunrise Perperna found Macro waiting in the porch, and was a little annoyed that his client should come so soon to remind him of the promised reward.

"The lady Vibenna was found dead in her bed this morning," he said sternly. "Until she has been laid on the pyre I cannot discuss business. This is a house of mourning."

"I have not come to discuss business, patron," answered Macro. "This is a religious matter, in which I seek your advice as a Rasenna and an augur. Last night I saw my brother, as I do whenever I dream. But this time he was not lying dead, he stood and menaced me with his sword. You told me I was safe so long as King Romulus ruled in Rome. Now that the King has become the god Quirinus will he continue to protect me?"

"I know, and you have guessed, in what manner King Romulus became the god Quirinus. All the same, it's just possible that he really is a god. Yet in the face of the underworld he will have no greater authority now, wherever he is, than he had on earth. What he had on earth was luck, and that he has bequeathed to his city of Rome. I think you will be safe enough in the city, provided you don't go outside it. Perhaps our next King will be able to cleanse you."

"But the place of assembly is outside the city."

"It's a templum, and sanctified by King Romulus. He will still protect you in every part of Rome; outside Rome you will be in danger. You deserve some discomfort. After all, you did murder your brother."

"I see, patron. . . . Who now looks after the King's storehouse of sacred things?"

"The lady Prima keeps it clean. No one performs the rites. We must wait for another King."

"Then I shall ask if I may help her, until the next King comes."

The house of Publius Tatius on the Quirinal was a prosperous rambling establishment, very unlike the artistic and luxurious mansion of Perperna. Room had been added to half-timbered room as the family increased and adjoining cabins were bought from the neighbours. It so happened that the nursery was larger than the reception hall, which had been built in the early days to celebrate the appointment of Publius to the Senate. Within, the plaster was washed a plain red; there were no life-size gods and heroes, no scenes of hunting and feasting. Most of the roof was plain thatch, very thick and gleaming with fresh golden rushes. Only one square of baked tile covered the inner end of the hall, where the Lar and the ancestors dwelt in the usual cupboard; that was because a lamp burned always before them, whose sparks ascended occasionally to the rafters.

There were very few slaves in the house, but it was always crowded. The daughters-in-law did most of the work, and they had plenty of visitors; their children ran about everywhere, and young men loitered in corners to catch a glimpse of the unmarried girls. Anyone who had nothing better to do was expected to join in the cooking and cleaning, and anyone who felt hungry was welcome to a share in the unpunctual meal when at long last it reached the table.

But this evening Publius had cleared a small room at the back, which happened to be a spare bedroom. Outside the closed door sat a young grandson, whittling shavings of kindling-wood and ready to use his knife to repel intruders. Within the bedroom Publius squatted on the floor with half a dozen eminent Sabine Senators and an enormous bowl of wine.

"We haven't a really first-class candidate," he said mournfully, "so we must make do with Pompeius Velesius, who is at least a good Sabine. He is not of the royal line, I grant you; but there are Kings among his ancestors if you go back far enough.

INTERREGNUM

The great thing in his favour is that he's the right age. The
Senate don't want an elderly King; after a few years they would
have to make another choice. This second reign is crucial. The
new King can't be expected to have the luck of Romulus; we
must keep the city together without special help from Mars.
Above all, we can't afford one election after another, each
leaving bad blood among the disappointed Senators and divi-
sions among the spearmen. So there you are. We need a young
man. Of course he must be a young Sabine. Pompeius Velesius
is the best we can do."

"They tell me he fights well in the ranks," put in another
Senator, "but he has never commanded men in battle. As far
as I know he has never done anything out of the ordinary. He
is not of the royal kin. Why should Latins and Luceres accept
the rule of such an undistinguished young man?"

"Because he is the Sabine candidate. I admit there is no
stronger reason," answered Publius. "But just occasionally we
Sabines ought to get our own way in the affairs of the city. We
came here led by a King of our own. After Tatius was murdered we ought to have chosen another King, but Romulus
overpersuaded us. There was some talk that Rome would be
ruled by Latin and Sabine Kings in turn, though as far as I
know it was never laid down in a formal agreement. All the
same, it seems fair enough. Romulus was a Latin; now it's our
turn. Some of my friends have suggested that I should be the
Sabine candidate, but I don't want the honour. I am too old.
We want a good long Sabine reign, to balance the thirty-seven
years of King Romulus."

"The Latins are putting forward Proculus, who is even older
than you," another Senator pointed out.

"Yes, but he has something no Sabine can offer. He fought
for Romulus in the old days at Alba, and saw the foundation
of the city."

"I still wish we could find a more eminent candidate," someone muttered.

"We can't, if we are all to support him. In the ordinary
affairs of life we don't remember all the time that we are

Sabines who must stick together against these Latins. Every one of us who matters has made enemies among his own people; perhaps enemies is too strong a word, but we have had our disagreements. Velesius hasn't an enemy in the world. If the Latins vote against him it will be solely because they refuse to be ruled by a Sabine."

"Why not let them make Proculus King, and get them to promise that when he has died of old age Velesius will succeed him unopposed?"

"I thought of that, but it won't do. If Proculus succeeds that means two Latin Kings in a row. After that it will be taken for granted that the third King must be a Latin."

"Then it's Velesius against Proculus, and we must keep our ranks united," said the oldest Senator. "Is there any danger that a third candidate will come forward?"

"No, or at least it's very unlikely. I was a little afraid that Perperna might try to collect support from the superstitious. He might claim that only a trueborn Rasenna can win the favour of the gods. But the death of his wife has spoiled his chance; he is now regarded as unlucky. It will be Sabines against Latins, with the Luceres holding the balance. I don't think those mongrels will vote as a unit. They have no candidate of their own, and they will divide between us. In the Senate Velesius may get a small majority on the very first vote."

"And that will be no good at all," said another Senator firmly. "I want Rome to continue as a great city, and if the King represents only half the citizens it won't. We can't expect Proculus and his kin to vote for a Sabine at the outset; but unless the Senate gives us a very big majority, at least two to one, it would be a waste of time to ask the assembly to ratify the decision. Furthermore, if we let the people see that the Senate is bitterly divided, that will be the end of our authority. I want to keep my authority as a Senator even more than I want to be ruled by a Sabine King."

"Very well," answered Publius. "In that case we must not be hurried. We shall go to the meeting of the Senate united in support of Velesius. The Latins will at any rate begin by putting forward Proculus. Then we keep on meeting again and again until the Latins begin to weaken. In the interval Rome will be adequately governed by each Senator in turn. Is that agreed?"

No one had put into words the chief strength of the Sabine case: that every Senator knew the truth about the disappearance of King Romulus, and knew therefore that Proculus was a time-server and a liar. Quirinus the god, indeed—his divinity the outcome of an unpremeditated but brutal murder! A man who said that and stuck to it on oath, with his hand on the sacred things of Samothrace, must be quite unscrupulous. . . . Unless indeed he was telling the truth after all, for no man understands the queer ways of heaven. Certainly Romulus had been mur-dered; it was just possible that all the same he was now a god. That possibility must have occurred also to the Latin Senators, or they would not now support the shifty old nonentity who proclaimed it.

The scrimmage for the head of the October Horse had been a half-hearted and slack affair, so closely supervised by anxious Senators that even the most ardent young spearman dared not let himself go. This was the second time that the festival had been held under the presidency of the daily King of the Sacri-fices; month slipped into month before you could notice it, but this annual ceremony brought home to all the citizens that it was now a year and a half since they had been ruled by a genuine King. Old Marcus Aemilius was grumbling about it to his friend Macro the Greek. Whenever there was an interesting religious ceremony he always called at the storehouse of sacred things to pick up young Macro. The poor fellow was so afraid of the gods that he could be enticed out of that lucky place only to attend a religious function. But when he got there he would study the ritual, and make the most interesting comparisons with similar rites he had seen in the course of his travels.

"That was supposed to be a wrestling match between two teams of strong young men," said Marcus with a sigh. "In the old days there would have been black eyes in plenty, and perhaps a few broken heads. Today they were so afraid of hurting one another that the contest was more like a sacred dance. The Senators won't let them do anything that might start a blood-feud. I suppose that is prudent, with public affairs as they are. But you don't please Mars just by running and leaping. He wants hard knocks."

"They struggle for the luck of the harvest, I suppose?" said Macro. "In Cumae it was the last sheaf of barley, as it is in most places; but then of course you can't hold it in October. Why do you use the head of a horse, here in Rome?"

"It's not harvest. In October, how could it be? Perhaps it's just luck in general, perhaps it's luck in war. There's a long story behind it, about chariots and the Sabine Women." He told the long story at full length.

"I see," Macro agreed at last. "But either they should give it up or else do it properly. A slipshod rite only angers the gods. Do you yourself think that if a Sabine blacked a Latin eye Rome would dissolve into civil war?"

"It's possible. Those stupid Sabines are being incredibly obstinate. No one wants that absurd puppy Velesius, who has never done anything to make his name famous; but they won't vote for our Julius Proculus, who has everything in his favour. Perhaps you don't know that all the Julii are descended from grandfather Aeneas, and so from the goddess Venus? Proculus has also been honoured by a vision of our new god, the only time he has appeared to a mortal man. Then, if you disregard the supernatural, Proculus has been here since the foundation of the city. As one of the oldest Senators he was deep in the counsels of King Romulus."

"But do you really fear civil war? I ask because my patron thinks highly of your opinion, and if you think the city is in danger I shall pass on your warning."

"Not perhaps civil war. We are all too bored for that, bored by a silly dispute that has lasted for more than a year and may last for a generation. But if we don't fight we may go away. The Sabines are always threatening to go back to their dismal mountains if they don't get their own way in everything. Of course they won't go, now that they are accustomed to civilized living. But the Latins might return to Alba, which has been a fine city for centuries and would be glad to have them. You can tell Perperna as much. We will go away rather than be ruled by an uncouth Sabine hillman."

"On the other hand, why not leave things as they are? The Senator of the day cannot bully us, and we enjoy greater freedom than if we were ruled by the best King in the world."

"King Romulus made these men Senators, and so we defer to them. But soon we must find another King, if only to fill vacancies in the Senate. More than a score of Senators have died in the last year. Where shall we find their successors? Someone suggested that the Senate itself might choose new members to fill its ranks; but that would be the end of our freedom. You can tell Perperna that the Latins will give up and leave Rome if it seems that the Senate intends to rule for ever."

The days were beginning to lengthen, and at the equinox they would celebrate the fortieth birthday of Rome. That is, if Rome were still inhabited, for the unlucky city remained without a King. Once or twice the spearmen had mustered at the frontier, to prove to greedy foreigners that they were still a mighty army; but as yet no foe had attacked them, for it seemed safer to wait until this gathering of land-pirates had fallen apart by its own discord. At home, each tribe judged disputes between its own members, so that there was not much work to occupy the ruling Senator during his single day of office. No one bothered to plan for the future, no one repaired the defences. The city was in a very bad way.

One evening Perperna sought out his client Macro at the storehouse of sacred things. He found the Greek sitting below the door, watching the sunset with a cheerful smile on his face.

"I'm glad to see you happy," he began. "Evidently the Old Women are not chasing you. Can you sleep at night?"

"I've got it worked out, patron. In daylight I am safe anywhere in the city, and at night I am safe in this storehouse. I don't dream any more. The lady Prima is glad to let me sleep here. She has to look after the fire in the King's hut, and there is no one else to perform the rites. The Senator of the day only sacrifices. There are no priests in Rome, unless I am a priest."

"Why not? If the Old Women are after you that makes you as sacred as any man in Rome. There has never been a true priest here. You will do as well as the next man. But now I want you to run errands, and I shall name the reward I offer for your services."

"Thank you, my lord, but there's nothing I want at present," said Macro cheekily. As caretaker of the storehouse of sacred things he lived an independent life, watching the world from the outside. No one else wanted his uncanny job, and he had forgotten his earlier ambitions.

"At least there is something you lack," Perperna went on, refusing to notice the snub. "You lack a wife. Next year my youngest daughter will be marriageable, and the young man who was betrothed to her died yesterday. Will you make a match of it?"

"You offer me the most precious thing in this city, patron. Who do you want me to murder? Of course I will do anything you ask of me. But can I marry while I lie under a curse?"

"When we have a King he will free you from the curse. These things grow weaker with time, and the work you do here every day should help you. When the next King has been chosen he will cleanse all your guilt, you will marry my daughter, and I shall teach you to be a true priest, a builder of bridges between human earth and the underworld. So now I want you to help me in the choice of a King. You must go first to the Sabine leaders. Tell them you come from me, and explain my plan."

"It's the only way out," said Publius Tatius to the leaders of the Sabine Senators. "We have to begin by making a very great concession; but the Latins do the same. We abandon Velesius, they abandon Proculus."

"So far we have the better of the deal," a colleague observed. "We chose Velesius because we wanted a Sabine; but the Latins really want Proculus, for himself."

"Perhaps they feel that they ought to be ruled by a liar, a toady so given to flattery that he flatters even the dead," said Publius with a sneer. "If they had been quicker to give up their absurd candidate we could have settled the question long ago. Now this is what Perperna advises, and he promises that if we back him we shall have the votes of all the Luceres. What we want really is a Sabine King, isn't it? Not King Pompeius Velesius in particular? Very well then. We go to the Latin leaders and ask them to take an oath. We promise that we shall agree to be ruled by the King of their choice, provided they choose a Sabine. How will that do?"

"Suppose they agree, and then choose someone on his death-bed? Old Horatius, for example, who won't last a month?"

"Then we do the same to them when the second King dies. I'm glad you made the point. I shall see that they are aware of it. But in actual fact it isn't likely. Even Latins have more sense than to do a thing like that when the whole future of our city is at stake. No, don't you see? If they must choose a Sabine they will naturally choose one of the leading Senators. That's the very thing we can't do by ourselves, because frankly we are too jealous of one another. If we leave the choice to the Latins we get a Sabine King, which is what we must have; in addition we get a capable Sabine King, whom we cannot choose by ourselves. Probably it will be one of us, here in this room. Now do you all agree?"

"I've just had a splendid idea," said young Aemilius, bubbling with enthusiasm. "If you follow my plan we shall dish those pompous Sabines."

Aemilius, by birth one of the leading Latin Senators, could not be left out of any important discussion. But he was known to be a scatterbrained young man, and as a rule his ingenious plans were disregarded.

"Look," he went on, "do you all remember the exact words of our promise? We swore that we would choose a Sabine for King of Rome, and Publius Tatius made us see that the deal would be off unless we chose a reputable and healthy Sabine. But we never said anything about choosing a Sabine who is now a Roman citizen. We can send explorers into the Sabine hills, and pick out the hairiest, roughest, most uncouth of the Sabine chieftains; someone who has never seen a wheel or a roof-tile. There is nothing in the oath against it, and it will be a splendid score over those worthy Sabine Senators."

Everyone was listening to him. This was wonderful; he was really taking part in the government of his city, as was the due of the chief of the Aemilian clan. But now the elderly and prosy Proculus had risen to his feet with a menacing cough, obviously prepared to address his colleagues at great length.

"Our young friend has made a valuable contribution," he said ponderously. "I had been hoping that someone would point out the loophole in the oath we swore, for it makes my proposal sound less extraordinary. I have in mind a Sabine who would make an excellent King of Rome, though he has never set foot in our city. I confess that this is not my idea. Perperna the Etruscan heard of the man and suggested his name to me. But when I mention it you will remember him. Do you recall the country Sabine who married the daughter of King Tatius?"

There was a gasp of excitement. Some of the younger men could not remember the wedding, which had taken place all of twenty years ago; but it was known to all that the daughter of King Tatius, to Latin ideas his heiress, had married a Sabine chieftain somewhere in the backwoods.

Proculus continued slowly: "The man is of good Sabine family. He will never be chief of his clan, because he has three brothers older than himself. In any case his father is still alive, though too old to lead his men in battle and more or less in retirement. The father is called Pompilius, because he is chief of the Pompilian clan; I don't know his first name. This younger son of his is known as Numa."

"But if he married the daughter of King Tatius why have the Sabines ignored his claim to the kingship of Rome?" asked an elderly Latin.

"Because they don't feel as strongly as we do about the rights of a daughter's husband. With them descent counts only in the male line. Anyway it so happens that Tatia is dead, and she left no sons; though I believe there is a daughter."

"Well, it's a good idea in itself, and a splendid snub for our Sabine Senators," said young Aemilius. "But does anyone know anything about this Numa as a man?"

"I know only what Perperna has told me. Of course we must check that before we go any farther," answered Proculus. "I gather that he's not much of a warrior. His hobby is serving the gods, and finding out how to appease them. I suppose that's why Perperna favours him. You know how Perperna always complains that in Rome we don't pay enough attention to religious affairs."

"Perperna is not a lucky man," Aemilius objected. "I can remind you in the privacy of this conference that it was chiefly by his urging that the reign of King Romulus was ended so abruptly. That should have brought him bad luck, and it did. There was something very fishy about that sudden death of his wife. No one had heard she was ill. It's just possible her husband murdered her."

"There was something fishy all right, but don't go about suggesting that he murdered her, young Aemilius," said an elderly and short-tempered Senator. "In the first place I think it can't be true; if Perperna were defiled by bloodguilt a man of such superstition would show it. In the second place, we depend on the Luceres. If we quarrel with them they may join the Sabines. Then there will be no room in Rome for Latins."

"That's quite right," Proculus announced gravely. "We must keep Perperna on our side. Of course he's not a lucky man. If he were lucky he would not have been driven to come to Rome. We, the founders, were lucky, for we shared in the luck of King Romulus. The later settlers came, not because they wanted to live in Rome, but because they could not find a better refuge."

"That's enough about Perperna, a dull man anyway," Aemilius said firmly. "Are we all agreed on how to trick the Sabines? Shall we begin by sending an embassy to this Numa, provided of course that he turns out to be as Perperna describes him?"

Chapter 15

ROME LIVES

★

The embassy was small, but distinguished. Velesius represented the Sabines and Proculus the Latins; Perperna held a watching brief for the miscellaneous Luceres who could not hope to provide a King from their own ranks. Then there were counsellors, and a few slaves to carry presents. It had not been easy to strike the right balance. This was a public mission, which represented the mighty city of Rome; but it had been despatched to a private spearman, not to another sovereign state.

The little backwoods settlement of Cures was no better than any other Sabine village; though because it was the headquarters of an ancient clan strangers sometimes referred to it as a city. Like other Sabine villages it was moved whenever the clan moved to new ploughlands; no building on the present site was more than thirty years old.

There was a big stockade for cattle; beside it a smaller enclosure defended a dozen houses. Facing the only gate was a small open space, and beyond it stood the biggest house in the village, the home of Pompilius the clan-chief.

Everything was made of wood, left grey and unpainted. But among the weathered timbers a few posts glowed a deep crimson, marking out a little templum before the house of Pompilius. In the house itself the doorpost on the right, the lucky side, was not only painted; at the top it was carved into the conventional owl-face of a divinity. The envoys stared at this holy thing in disquiet; even Romulus the son of Mars had never employed a

276

god to hold up his roof. The men who lived in this house must be on very good terms with the unseen.

About a hundred Sabine warriors stood round the templum; probably the full strength of clan Pompilia, which was more ancient than powerful. Though the Romans had been admitted within the stockade it could be seen that their hosts were taking no chances. After the embassy had formed up on the consecrated ground nothing whatever happened for a full hour. But that was standard tactics at the reception of unwelcome embassies, and the Romans were not dismayed.

At length Pompilius came out to his porch, his four sons and a few cousins at his back. He was a very old man, clad simply in a grey woollen gown; but for dignity he carried an ancient bronze sword hanging from a crimson baldric. He stood to survey the visitors; then tottered, supported by a son at each arm, down to the templum.

"Latins," he exclaimed with a snort, "Latins and renegades from anywhere. Men who live mixed up with one another's middens, because they are not brave enough to sleep alone in the greenwood. I suppose you have come to beg wives from clan Pompilia. You are always begging for women, except when you steal them by treachery. You can go away again. We have husbands for all our maidens, and if we had not we would not seek them among Latins."

"We have not come to seek women, or indeed to seek anything," Velesius said angrily. "On the contrary, we have come to confer a great favour. But our mission is with your son, Numa. May we speak with him alone?"

A middle-aged man came forward with a pleasant smile. He wore a white linen tunic down to his feet, and instead of weapons he carried an augur's staff. "My father does not like Romans, for he remembers the evil deeds of King Romulus. But that was a long time ago, and we younger men do not hold it against you. I am Numa Pompilius. What do you want of me? My wife came from Rome, and I would like to be your friend."

Proculus was surprised. Somehow he had taken it for granted that the fourth son of a reigning clan-chief would be a young man, though he should have remembered that Tatia had been given in marriage a full twenty years ago. "How old are you?" he blurted out, and then blushed at his discourtesy.

Numa answered as though the question were the most natural thing in the world. "On my next birthday, which is the 21st of March, I shall be forty years old."

"How extraordinary," exclaimed Proculus. "You must have been born on the day when King Romulus founded Rome!"

"The same day, and at the same hour, so they tell me. The soothsayers were interested. They seemed to think that it linked my fate with Rome's. That was one reason why I took a Roman wife."

"We want you to come to Rome. We want you as our King," said Velesius in sudden excitement.

"What a curious whim! But come inside and talk it over."

When he had received the formal proposal Numa answered without hesitation. He was smiling pleasantly, and obviously anxious not to give offence; but he did not try to soften his refusal.

"At my age I have found the way of life that suits me. Why should I change it? I like to live in peace, and I pass my leisure inquiring into the nature of the gods and discovering how to placate them. The King of Rome, a city always at war, would have no time for such a hobby. Of course, if I were a King I should be richer than I am now. But already I have enough to eat and a roof over my head. I don't want more. The other obvious drawback is the danger. King Romulus was the son of Mars, and his infancy was guarded by a divine wolf; the gods were on his side from the beginning. Yet at one time he was in danger from his colleague, my father-in-law, King Tatius; and his strange disappearance has given rise to all sorts of rumours, though now you tell me it was all for the best—in fact that your late King has been promoted to a high post in heaven. . . .

"But I am a mortal man, with no gods in my pedigree; and I have no reason to suppose that the gods will afford me special protection when I run into danger. You can't offer me anything

I want, and so far you have not claimed that I am under any obligation to help you. I prefer to stay here."

"But it has taken us two years to reach this compromise," wailed Proculus in dismay. "After all those long arguments, after coming to the very brink of civil war, the whole Senate was unanimous that you should be our King. If now we have to start looking for another candidate it's likely that Rome will fall to pieces before we find him."

"Consider that calmly and you will see that it's not such a dreadful prospect," answered Numa. "We have all heard of the luck of King Romulus, more luck than has ever been granted to any other mortal man. His luck was so tremendous that it did not even end with his death, and now he is happy in heaven. A man endowed with such luck did right to found a city, so that his followers might share his advantages. You shared his luck, and it has made you prosperous. But no one can maintain that your city was a good thing in itself. The world in general has not gained by it. Your city was founded on luck. That luck has now been withdrawn. Be sensible about it. Rome stood for forty years, and so that it should stand tens of thousands of spearmen died in the prime of their youth. Now it's all over. Go back in peace to your villages, richer and wiser for your experience of city life. Don't hazard more and more bloody battlefields until the luck turns against you and your widows are enslaved. Without Rome the world will live easier."

Proculus answered at once, speaking with a fiery energy that surprised his companions. "You hold yourself out to be a servant of the gods, Numa Pompilius. But if Rome falls the gods will be ill served. Five hundred years ago grandfather Aeneas brought to Italy the sacred things of Samothrace and Troy; he brought even the Palladium, the image of the Maiden. Her shrine must be in the heart of a great city; that is her due. For five hundred years we Latins tilled the soil and lived in villages, preparing to found a city worthy of her. We are not such evil people as our neighbours suppose. We can talk things over and abide by the decision of the assembly. We make good laws, and enforce them. Our wives are treated with honour, and our children reverence their parents. In war each man takes his place in the shield-wall, knowing that his comrade will guard his side. Thus after five hundred years we have our city. Omens sent by the gods tell us that one day it will rule the world. Remember those omens, the vultures in the noon sky and the bleeding head of the Capitol. It must be the wish of the gods that Rome should endure. But Rome cannot endure without you. Will you thwart the designs of the gods, and so become one of the most unlucky men alive —just because ruling a great city seems to you a burden?"

"That's a good point," said Numa. "I don't want to thwart the will of the gods. But I don't see how their will can be thwarted by any mortal man. If Rome disappears it will prove that after all the gods do not desire her to continue. Can anyone give me another reason, besides the supposed will of the gods, why Rome should continue?"

"I can," answered young Velesius. "I am a Sabine like yourself, and I don't see why the gods should want Latins in particular to live in a fine city. But Rome *is* a fine city, and worth preserving. In my father's time my clan fought against the Romans; we had good cause for our enmity. Then King Tatius led us to settle in the city, and the Latins dealt fairly by us. Is that the usual end of a bitter war? In Rome we make peace honestly, and our treaties endure. I was born in Rome, it is my home, and if everyone else goes away I shall never leave it. We have learned the art of living together, which is most difficult. Do you know of another city where two nations share in the government? I suppose there isn't another town like it in the world; a place where any stranger can find his own level, and no one inquires into his ancestry. There were men who said that Sabines could never learn to live in a crowded city. We have proved them wrong. But no other city has Sabine citizens. If Rome disappears you will have destroyed one of the glories of the Sabine race."

"That's even better," said Numa. "But you must not suppose that I owe a duty to the Sabine race. Besides, it may be our destiny to live as simple villagers. No. Rome began as a city of brigands. I don't like brigands. I don't see why it should continue."

"Then perhaps I can give another reason," said Perperna, "for in my youth I myself was a brigand. Rome cured me of brigandage. For the last few years we have lived without war, and if you come to rule us we shall remain peaceful. But that isn't really what I want to say. Rome is something unique, something that ought not to disappear from the world. The city is not yet forty years old, but the citizens are counted in tens of thousands; and every man of them is a Roman because he wants to be a Roman. We are a great community, inhabited only by willing settlers. And we are not exclusive. Besides Latins and Sabines we have a third tribe, open to foreigners of every kind. I myself am an Etruscan, a Rasenna of pure blood. I, and all my tribe of the Luceres, came to Rome because it was the city of our choice. We are equal to those who were born there. Only one thing is lacking in Rome. Though King Romulus gave us his own astounding luck, we do not know how best to serve the gods. You, if you become our King, will instruct us in that heavy task. So there it is. Rome the lucky, Rome the hospitable, Rome where law reigns, where men live in peace with strangers, Rome that is mighty in conquest and merciful to the conquered—all this will end unless you come to rule us."

"You have spoken of mercy. You need say no more. I consent to rule you."

The wedding feast of Macro and Domitia, daughter of Perperna, was a very splendid affair. At the high table couches were provided, in the Etruscan manner, and the King, the guest of honour, reclined graciously as though reclining at meals were also a Sabine custom. Of course the bride sat upright on a stool; and Macro sat beside her for a few minutes, while they shared the cake of old-fashioned lucky grain which was more pleasing to the gods than modern barley. The sacramental meal was an Italian custom, as novel to an Etruscan as to Macro the Greek; but in Rome they were twining together the rites of every race, for a man needs all the luck he can find.

The bride and the other ladies withdrew before the drinking began. Domitia would wait in the nuptial bed until her new husband was ready to come to her. She hoped he would not be helplessly drunk, though she must not blame him for anything. But Macro had promised to drink as little as politeness would allow, since he really wanted to please this frightened young girl who had come to him as a stranger.

Perperna, the host, made it as easy for him as he could, mixing plenty of water with the wine and seeing that the bridegroom had the smallest cup in his store. But Macro could not refuse when friends wandered up to sit on the edge of his couch and drink with him.

The first to come up was old Marcus Aemilius, who wanted to fulfil the obligations of courtesy and get home as early as he could. At his age all-night drinking had lost its appeal. He sat on the end of the couch, staring owlishly at the bridegroom; he had taken as much as he could carry, for at home he seldom tasted wine. With the solemnity of the half-tipsy he spoke his mind.

"Are you quite sure that you are free to marry? It would be terrible if you find that the Old Women still pursue you."

"I am really free at last," Macro answered without hesitation. "Our new King has power over the underworld, and he has freed me. Do you think my patron would have permitted the marriage if he had felt any doubt? Perperna knows the ways of the gods, and he can recognize the authority of King Numa. The blood of my brother no longer cries for vengeance. I may live in peace."

"I'm glad of that. What will you do now? Go home to Cumae?"

"Never. I am at home, here in Rome. You don't know the extent of my good fortune. The King has appointed me to be a priest, a builder of bridges between the worlds of the living and the dead. I am fitted for that, since my guilt made me sacred to the gods below. With my priesthood I shall be rich enough to become a horseman of Rome. When I have a horse in my keeping I shall never wish to leave the city."

"I am delighted to hear you speak so," said Perperna, who had strolled up to add his good wishes. "It's funny when you come to think of it. Most of us came to Rome because no other city was open to us. We came to the second best, meaning to go back when our troubles were over. But there is something about this city, its good luck or its favour with the gods or perhaps just its fertile fields, that makes everyone want to stay."

"It's none of those things," said Macro happily. "It's the other Romans. It's all of us. This is the home of justice. We live in friendship together, men from all over the world; and our descendants will rule the world."

"For so long as they do justice," added King Numa, from his place of honour.